Autumn Term

Antonia Forest was born in North London, the only child of part Russian-Jewish and Irish parents. She studied at South Hampstead High School and University College, London and went on to work in a government clerical job and in a library. She is best known for her series about the Marlow family, but she has also written historical novels including *The Player's Boy* and *The Players and the Rebels*. Her first book *Autumn Term* was published in 1948.

by the same author

THE READY-MADE FAMILY
THE MARLOWS AND THE TRAITOR
THE THURSDAY KIDNAPPING
END OF TERM
FALCONER'S LURE
THE PLAYERS BOY
THE PLAYERS AND THE REBELS
THE CRICKET TERM

ANTONIA FOREST

Autumn Term

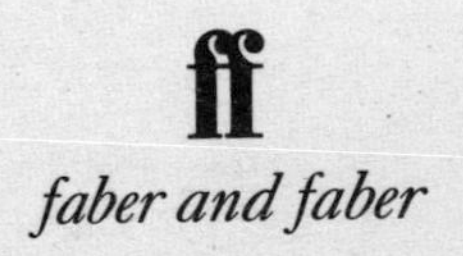

faber and faber

First published in 1948
Reset and published in this paperback edition in 2000
by Faber and Faber Limited
Bloomsbury House, 74–77 Great Russell Street,
London WC1B 3DA

Photoset by Avon DataSet Ltd, Bidford on Avon
Printed in England by CPI Bookmarque, Croydon

A CIP record for this book
is available from the British Library

ISBN 978–0–571–20640–7

2 4 6 8 10 9 7 5 3

Contents

Acknowledgement

The author and publishers wish to thank the Estate of the late Mark Twain for permission to include in this book quotations from *The Prince and the Pauper*.

No dramatisation of *The Prince and the Pauper* may be made without the permission of Messrs. A. P. Watt and Son, as literary agents to the Estate.

1 A Knife with Sixteen Blades

Train journeys, Nicola decided, were awfully dull. After the first half-hour no one seemed to want to talk any more, so that unless you had something to read you sat and looked at Karen and Lawrie and Rowan opposite or right and left at Ann and Ginty. Actually, Nicola had a book on her lap (Karen had seen to that before they left Victoria) but she wasn't in the mood for reading. She seldom was. Nicola's world had to be very calm and settled before she could sit down quietly with a book, a remedy frequently suggested by her weary relations as an antidote to Nicola's general air of being all agog.

It had been suggested very often in the last week or so; for even the excitement of going into town almost daily with her mother and Lawrie to be measured for their new uniforms and buy the startling number of new underclothes necessary for school, and (crowning glory) eat lunch and tea in a restaurant and order exactly what they liked (which meant that Lawrie stuck to chicken and ice-cream and Nicola dodged all over the menu to make sure she was missing nothing), had not, as Rowan so hopefully prophesied, tired her out. She still came back and stood on one leg near Karen or Rowan or Ann (Ginty was too unreliable) and went on asking questions:

'Will Miss Keith see us when we get there? Where do we go first? Do new girls have to sing on First Night like they do in books? Who will be games captain this term? Mother says I can wear Ginty's old blazer. Can I? Do people? Wouldn't it be better if Lawrie wore her hair a different way so that we don't look so much like twins? Will people be funny about it? Shall we share a sisters' room with the rest of you?'

'I hope not,' said Rowan emphatically. 'The first thing I do when I get back is look at the dormitory lists; and if we are in the same room I'm going straight to Matron to protest.'

'Oh, Rowan. Why?'

'Because I like my nights quiet, peaceful and undisturbed. I can't honestly feel that they'd be that with you around. And do go away, Nick. I'm supposed to have read this wretched book by the time I get back.'

Nicola went away and found Giles, who was the eldest, and was doing nothing at all but lie peacefully on his back in the sun.

'They won't tell me things,' she complained, sitting down cross-legged beside him. 'And I want to know so as to be prepared.'

'Prepared for what?' asked Giles sleepily.

'Just prepared. So that I don't do anything awfully silly and have people laughing at me like they do. And so that I know what it's going to be like.'

'No good worrying about being laughed at. There are sure to be thousands of new brats all making the same mistakes at the same time. And as for telling you what it's like – no one can do that.'

'Why not?'

'Because, my idiot sister, the same thing looks quite different to different people. Karen can't possibly tell you what the kindergarten—'

'IIIA,' said Nicola indignantly.

'Kindergarten,' said Giles firmly, 'looks like from the Sixth. Father tried to tell me what the Navy was like before I got there, but it wasn't like that at all. Not to me, anyway.'

'Oh,' said Nicola.

So she had, to the relief of her family, almost stopped asking questions. Not entirely, of course. But they only came out now when she had to ask or burst.

The train journey continued dull. Nicola swung her legs and looked crossly round the carriage, piecing together from her own and her sisters' uniforms the things she knew about Kingscote. The three black felt hats in the rack with the blue and scarlet hat-bands meant that Rowan and Ann and Ginty were seniors. The fourth hat, with the plain scarlet band was Karen's and meant she was a prefect. Head girl actually, thought Nicola accurately, and she has a special badge to pin her tie. The two scarlet berets with the bright blue crest belonged to Nicola and Lawrie and showed they were juniors. What else was there? There was Rowan's plain blue tie because she was in the netball team, and Ginty's striped girdle for second eleven hockey. Ann wore a Guide badge on her coat – but that wasn't particularly a school thing. Nicola yawned and kicked Ginty accidentally-on-purpose.

'Couldn't Lawrie and I go and stand in the corridor for a bit?' suggested Nicola hopefully, when the commotion had died down a little.

'For heaven's sake, let them,' said Rowan. 'If Nick's starting to fidget no one'll have any peace.'

'Well – all right,' said Karen. 'But *don't* go and fall out of a window. Miss Keith wouldn't be a bit pleased if the train were late because one of the school was careless about a little thing like that.'

She spoke in her head girl's voice which had returned to her a day or two before term began, making Giles salute and say: 'Yes, *ma'am*,' in a way Karen found particularly aggravating. But Nicola was only concerned with what Karen said, not how she said it. She sprang to her feet, knocking Ann's book from her hand, trod on Rowan's foot and tumbled out into the corridor followed by Lawrie. Rowan closed the carriage door firmly behind them.

'Good,' said Nicola. 'Now we can talk.'

Lawrie nodded. Like Nicola she was thin and blue-eyed with straight sun-bleached hair and an expression of alert enquiry. But she talked less than Nicola, and although she was just as interested, she was inclined to leave it to Nicola to find out and tell her all about it when she had done so.

'What time is it?' asked Nicola.

Lawrie looked at her watch, a parting present from her parents. Nicola could have had a watch too, but when she had been told to choose her present she had plumped for the knife with sixteen blades which had dazzled her for months every time she passed the ironmonger's window where it was the centre-piece. Her father had warned her that if she had the knife she would have to do without a watch till she was twenty-one. Nicola thought this no drawback. There were always clocks. And bells. Especially in school. One wouldn't need a watch. Whereas a knife with sixteen blades . . . she took it out of her pocket and stroked it affectionately.

'It's ten to three,' said Lawrie.

'Another hour,' said Nicola despairingly. 'I do think trains are dull, even in the corridor.'

'I wonder if we'll like it,' said Lawrie nervously. She meant, as Nicola promptly realized, since Lawrie had been saying the same thing every night for weeks, school, not the train.

'I don't see why not. The others do.'

'They're used to it,' said Lawrie.

'So will we be used to it,' said Nicola firmly. 'In two weeks, Giles said.'

'I hope Giles knows,' said Lawrie. She sighed deeply.

A few compartments down, a door slid back and a girl came out. Like Lawrie and Nicola she wore the scarlet beret of the juniors. She looked at them and then pretended not to look, leaning against the partition and staring at the scenery.

Nicola nudged Lawrie. 'Is she new too, d'you think?'

'I don't know,' whispered Lawrie.

'I think she may be or she'd be inside talking to people,' decided Nicola. She edged down the corridor and said:

'Are you new like us?'

The other girl turned and grinned. She had short, rough dark hair, and her face was tanned the colour of a brown egg. Her eyes were a lighter brown, with greenish flecks in them. Nicola, whose favourite looks just then were sleek black hair and grey eyes, could not decide whether she thought her pretty or not. Lawrie, who had already decided, thought she wasn't.

'New as paint,' said the other girl.

'Good,' said Nicola. 'How old are you?'

'Twelve and a half; how old are you?'

'We're twelve. That's Lawrence and I'm Nicola. Nicola Marlow.'

'Well,' said the other girl, 'I'm glad other people have odd names too. It makes me feel better.' She had a dry, amused voice.

'They're not odd at all,' said Nicola affronted.

'Not odd,' conceded the other girl, 'but not ordinary. Not like Joan and Peggy and Betty.'

'Well – no,' admitted Nicola, 'I suppose not.'

'Now mine is definitely odd,' said the other girl. 'And you

may as well know it at once and that will be two less people to tell. It's Thalia. Thalia Keith.'

'*Failure?*' said Lawrie startled. She was farther away than Nicola and the train had blurred the sound of Thalia's voice. 'Why did they call you that? Because you weren't a boy? That's why they called me Lawrence, 'cos they'd got it all saved up.'

'Not Failure.' She said it patiently as though she had said it many times before. '*Thalia*. It's the name of the Comic Muse. Mother would have it, though Father did his best.'

'It's quite all right,', said Nicola politely. Privately, she thought it very odd indeed.

'It's terrible,' said Thalia calmly. 'But people call me Tim. And if you don't mind, I'd rather you began at once.'

'All right. They call us Nick and Lawrie, actually. At least, they do at home.'

'Tim, Nick and Lawrie,' said Thalia thoughtfully. 'Tom, Dick and Harry. No, I think our way's better. Did you say your name was Marlow?'

'Yes.'

'Head girl's family?'

'How did you know?' asked Nicola, surprised. 'Or have you got sisters here too?'

'Not sisters,' said Tim impressively. 'An aunt.'

'An aunt?' said Nicola horrified. 'What kind of aunt?'

'The ordinary kind,' said Tim. 'Or perhaps not so ordinary. Actually it's – well, I call her Aunt Edith. You call her the Head.'

'The headmistress?' said Lawrie unbelievingly. 'Good gracious. She can't be.'

'She is, though.'

'How awful for you,' said Nicola, deeply sympathetic. 'It's bad enough being the head girl's sister. At least, I think it may be. But think of being related to Miss Keith.'

'I don't. Not more often than I can help,' said Tim. 'I told Father that it was simply silly and that I'd much better go to another school – if I must go to school—'

'Haven't you been to school before?' Lawrie interrupted.

'Not properly. At least, not for long at a time. We were always shifting because Father wanted something new to paint. I've been to school in America and Spain and France and Italy and Holland – all over the place. So, of course, I don't know a thing except languages. I do know those.'

'Gosh,' said Nicola, uncertain whether she was impressed or merely astonished. 'We haven't been to school either, much. Every time we started we always caught something. But we haven't caught anything now for six months—'

'Touch wood,' said Lawrie hurriedly.

'Touch wood,' agreed Nicola. 'So Father said we'd better get to Kingscote while the going was good.'

'It was Aunt Edith got at Father about me,' said Tim gloomily. 'He decided to come home for a bit and paint here, and of course Aunt Edith was asked to stay. And then she began finding out, in a nasty sort of way, all the things I didn't know – What were the Wars of the Roses, Thalia dear? – Don't know, Aunt Edith, and care less – you know the kind of thing – and then she sat down and had a long talk with Father and said the dear child simply must start her education, which hiking round Europe and America was *not*. And *I* said (when they mentioned it to me, which was pretty late in the day), If I must go to school I must, but not to Aunt Edith's seminary. And Aunt Edith said, Why? And I said, Because it's bound to be awkward. And Aunt Edith said, Nonsense, Thalia dear, of course you will be treated exactly like the others. And I said, That's just the point. If I go to an ordinary school – all right. But if I go to my aunt's school, I don't see why I *can't* be treated like the headmistress's niece. *Why* can't I have special privileges and sit in your garden and that kind of thing? She didn't see it, though,' said Tim bitterly, 'but I still don't see why not.'

Nicola and Lawrence listened, fascinated. It had been impressed on them also, by both Karen and Rowan, that they were on no account to give themselves airs simply because they happened to be the head girl's sisters. They had accepted this dictum meekly, protesting: 'Of course not, Kay. We wouldn't dream of it.' But there did seem to be something in what Tim said, although Nicola, at least, was aware that if she tried anything like that, Karen would certainly snub her, hard.

'Aunt Edith – I suppose I shall have to remember to call her Miss Keith –' continued Tim, 'she was full of helpful hints about lying low and showing the other girls that there was no difference between us. But lying low sounds so *dull*. I don't see why I should have to pretend to be a nonentity just because I'm her niece, and she doesn't want to be accused of – of nepotism—'

'What's that?' asked Lawrie, horrified. 'It sounds dreadful.'

'It only means favouring your nephews. Or nieces too, I suppose. But I don't see why I should be expected to come to Kingscote and be quiet and dreary and – and *crushed*, when I could go somewhere else and be perfectly ordinary. I told Aunt Edith all that, and she laughed in that idiotic way grown-ups have, and said: "Never mind, Thalia. You'll soon settle down in the Third Remove and find your own level—" '

'Third Remove?' cried Lawrie. 'Oh. What a pity!'

'Why?' asked Tim.

'Well, because we'll be in IIIA and I don't suppose we'll see much of you once we're there—'

'Do you know your form?' asked Tim, surprised. 'I thought no one did until they'd taken the form exam. Aunt Edith said I'd be in the Third Remove because of only knowing languages. But I didn't know anyone else was told.'

Nicola had gone rather red. She frowned at Lawrie.

'We don't know, really,' she said awkwardly. 'But all our family always have started in an A form and – well – you know – we've got to, too.'

'None of the others have ever been in a B form,' supplemented Lawrie. 'Not even Ginty and no one thinks she's a bit clever. And IIIA is the one for our age.'

'Aunt Edith talked quite a lot about your family,' said Tim, digging her hands into the pockets of her coat. 'Karen, of course – she's the head girl, isn't she? – she thinks an awful lot of her. And what's the next one – Rowena—?'

'No. Rowan.'

'Yes, of course. Sorry. Rowan. She's the one who's good at games, isn't she? She said – what was it? – something about her being an excellent person to have in a team because she always played best on a losing side.'

Nicola and Lawrie blushed with pleasure. 'Except for Giles, Rowan *is* the nicest,' said Nicola. 'Kay's all right, but she can be pretty snooty when she likes.'

'And then there's – Ann, is it? – the Guide one, anyway. Aunt Edith said she was kind and competent – very good with juniors – and the other one – Virginia, I think she called her—'

'She is Virginia, really,' said Lawrie, 'but she's always called Ginty.'

'Oh. Well, she said she was rather wild but that she had a lot of good stuff in her.'

'She didn't say that on her report,' commented Nicola. 'She put, "Virginia's conduct leaves much to be desired and she must make a real effort to improve".'

'There you are,' said Tim impishly. 'It just shows what hypocrites headmistresses really are.'

'It does, doesn't it?' agreed Lawrie, deeply moved.

There was silence for a moment. Then Nicola sighed. 'It's an awful lot to live up to,' she said sadly.

'How d'you mean?' asked Tim.

'Well, you can see for yourself the kind of reputations they've got. Kay's awfully clever, and Rowan can play anything, and Ann's a Patrol Leader and she's got her First Class, and Ginty – well, even Ginty's pretty good at games and people like her a lot—'

'And have you got to do all that too?'

'We must,' said Lawrie earnestly. 'We've simply got to be credits to the family. Specially as we're starting so late. All the others came to Kingscote when they were *nine*. We decided in the holidays,' said Lawrie confidentially, ignoring Nicola's warning frown, 'that first we've got to get into the junior netball team, so that next year Nick can be captain and me vice. And then – we've been Brownies at home, you know – so we're going to pass our Tenderfoot and fly up and get our Second Class badges all in one term.'

'Do shut up, Lawrie,' said Nicola gruffly, interrupting her at last. 'It sounds so mad when you say it like that. It probably doesn't matter with Tim, but you can't go round *saying* things like that to people.'

' "Vaulting ambition," ' said Tim solemnly, shaking her head at Lawrie, ' "which o'er leaps itself, and falls on the other." '

'Gosh,' said Lawrie abashed. 'Whatever's that?'

'That's Macbeth,' said Tim, 'and look what happened to him.' Nicola and Lawrie were vague on this point, but they looked as intelligent as possible.

'But you won't say anything to people about what Lawrie said,' urged Nicola. 'They might – well – you know – they might think we were conceited – and we're not. We just – it's only because—' she floundered unhappily.

'I won't tell,' said Tim. ' "Crorse me 'eart an' 'ope to die." ' It sounded trustworthy.

'Thank you,' said Nicola. 'Lawrie does talk an awful lot.'

'I don't,' said Lawrie indignantly. 'Nothing *like* as much as you. You know perfectly well, Nicola, that only last week Father said—'

'All right,' said Nicola hurriedly. 'I don't suppose Tim's a bit interested.'

'Where are your family?' asked Tim tactfully. 'I'd like to look at them from a discreet distance.'

'Second compartment up. Kay and Ann are by the windows and Rowan and Gin this end. Kay and Rowan have their backs to the engine 'cos they don't get sick in trains.'

'I don't expect head girls do,' said Tim, amused. She strolled off to look.

It was obviously the same family. They all had the same fair hair and blue eyes, although the others, except Karen, had curly hair, which Ann wore in plaits and Rowan and Ginty in short crops. Tim strolled nonchalantly past the compartment and back again.

'And very nice too,' she remarked. 'I'm glad to have seen the famous Marlows at last.'

They looked at her doubtfully.

'You're teasing,' said Lawrie at last.

'A little,' agreed Tim candidly. 'I think it's just a scrap funny to be so frightfully much esteemed. You don't mind, do you? Are there any more at home?'

'Not at home,' said Nicola a little stiffly. 'There's Giles and Peter. But they're away now.'

'Where do they come in? And what do they do?'

'Giles is the eldest. He's in the Navy. And Peter comes between us and Ginty. He's at Dartmouth,' said Nicola briefly. She still felt rather sore.

'I like the Navy,' said Tim. She grinned at Nicola with her friendliest expression. 'I like the Navy better than anything.'

Thawing, Nicola grinned back. 'So do I. Do you know—'

'*No*,' interrupted Lawrie. '*Please* don't talk Navy now. *Please*, Tim. If you lived in our family you'd want a rest from it too, sometimes. When Giles comes home, Nick always wants to know what he's done every single minute he's been away. And then she wants to tell me all about it. It isn't that I don't quite like the Navy; but I do get tired of having it all the time.'

'All right,' said Tim sadly. 'Only it's rather hard on me if I'm going to be in the Third Remove and probably never speak to you again because you're in IIIA. Never mind. Have some chocolate.'

She tugged a large bag out of her coat pocket and offered it. 'We may as well finish all we can,' she added with her mouth full, 'because I don't suppose we're allowed to keep sweets. Unless I can persuade anyone that as I'm Aunt Edith's niece I ought to be allowed to keep them. I shall try, anyway.' She looked into the bag and added: 'But I expect it would be *safer* to eat them now.'

They munched steadily, occasionally flattening themselves against the partition as other and unknown members of Kingscote passed up and down the train, looking for their friends. One tall dark girl smiled and gave them a lordly: 'Hullo, twins,' before disappearing into the Marlow compartment.

Lawrie choked and blushed.

'Who's that?' asked Tim.

'That's Margaret Jessop. She's the games captain. She stayed with Kay one holiday,' said Lawrie, blushing more deeply still.

'Lawrie's awfully keen on her,' explained Nicola unnecessarily. 'She's all right, you know. Quite matey.'

'She won't be matey at school,' protested Lawrie hurriedly, 'and you can't expect it, Nicola.'

'I don't,' said Nicola calmly. 'Is that the last piece, Tim? Because if so, you'd better have it as it's your bag.'

'All right,' said Tim. She put the square of chocolate into her mouth, squashed the bag into a ball and lowered the window to throw it out.

'Let's leave it down,' said Nicola. 'It's awfully stuffy.'

'Mother said—' began Lawrie.

'We're not leaning out,' Nicola forestalled her. 'Mother didn't mean we were to suffocate. What time is it now?'

'Twenty to four,' said Lawrie. 'Look, Tim. This was my parting present.'

'Super,' said Tim. 'Haven't you got one, Nick?'

'No,' said Nicola proudly. 'I've got a knife. Look. Sixteen blades *and* a corkscrew *and* a file *and* a thing for taking things out of horses' hooves—'

She handed the knife to Lawrie to pass to Tim. As she did so, the train rounded a curve, swinging them all against the farther side of the corridor.

'Ow!' cried Lawrie in anguish, as she knocked her knee. 'That hurt.'

'My knife!' cried Nicola in sudden horror. 'You dropped it! I saw you!' She pushed Lawrie out of the way and leaned out of the carriage window, her hair blowing wildly in the wind. 'It's on the step,' she gasped. 'Look!'

Leaning over her shoulders, the other two looked down.

There was the knife, jigging a little with the motion of the train, and quite out of reach.

Tim said hopefully: 'P'rhaps it'll stay there till the train stops and we can get it. . . .'

They watched in silence. The knife jigged a little this way and that; sometimes nearly over the edge, then back against the train. It seemed as though Tim might be right.

'Look out,' cried Lawrie suddenly. 'There's a tunnel! Nick!'

They pulled in their heads sharply.

'Oh, quick,' groaned Nicola to the express. 'Do hurry, you beast. Quick, quick, quick.'

There had never been so long a tunnel. The choking smoky darkness came into the corridor. Tim wrinkled her nose, but did not care to suggest that they should close the window. Nicola stamped angrily. 'Oh, do *hurry*, you – you *goods* train!'

The drift of smoke lightened a little. In another moment they were out of the tunnel and rushing through the last of the smoke. Nicola's head went through the window.

'It's gone,' she said after a moment in a too-calm voice. 'It's fallen off.'

2 'A Fine of Five Pounds . . .'

'In an emergency,' Commander Marlow was given to telling his family, 'act at once.' On occasion he amplified this, saying that it was also necessary to think clearly and sensibly and not act upon impulse. Nicola, however, had absorbed only the dictum that she was to act immediately. Before Tim or Lawrie realized what she was about she had ducked back into the corridor and pulled the communication cord.

A bell began to jangle. The train slowed. Nicola tugged at the door-handle, jerked it down, and leapt out on to the permanent way. A moment later she was racing back into the tunnel.

In the unexpected silence the sound of voices began to rise all along the train. Compartment doors were pushed back, and people looked out, asking one another what had happened. With the automatic reaction of authority to anything unusual, Karen and Margaret Jessop emerged from the Marlow compartment with Rowan, curious but unconcerned, at their heels. The queries promptly flowed in Karen's direction.

'What's happened, Karen?'

'Is there a breakdown?'

'Who pulled the communication cord?'

'Is someone ill?'

'I haven't the least idea,' said Karen calmly. 'I don't suppose it's anything at all, and you may just as well go back and sit down and stop fussing.'

'Ooo! Karen! There's a door open! Look! Someone's fallen out! They must have! *Look*, Karen!'

Karen turned sharply and saw her young sister Lawrie and another child she had never seen before clinging on to the jamb of an open door while they stared down the line with startled and slightly open-mouthed expressions. Nicola was nowhere to be seen.

Karen's usual air of calm authority over all events vanished. She strode across to Lawrie and said in a sharp, shaken voice:

'Lawrie! What's happened? Where's Nick?'

Lawrie, confused by the rapidity of Nicola's actions and Karen's frightened voice, became speechless. Karen shook her arm.

'What's *happened*, Lawrie?'

The guard, striding down the train, came to a stop by the open door.

'What's happened, miss? Has there been an accident? Who pulled that cord?'

'We don't know,' said Margaret Jessop, since Karen was clearly incapable of answering. 'Lawrie, can't you—'

'*Lawrie*,' cried Karen despairingly. 'Did you pull it? Has Nicola—? For goodness' sake—!'

'I *didn't*,' panted Lawrie. 'Don't *pinch*, Kay.'

The rest of the carriage looked on, amused, puzzled or apprehensive. Someone began to giggle nervously.

'There's Nick,' said Tim's cool voice. She pointed up the line. No one had asked her any questions and she saw no reason to volunteer information. Probably Nicola would prefer to tell her own story. But there was no reason why she should not call attention to a perfectly obvious fact.

Nicola, looking grimy but cheerful, emerged from the tunnel. The guard strode off to meet her. The colour returned to Karen's face. She was so angry with Nicola that had she been within reach she would have slapped her. She watched in silence, standing on the step, as Nicola and the guard met. Nicola beamed at him, talking earnestly. His back, thought Karen, did not look as though he were mollified by her explanation. The voices of the deeply interested school, hanging out of the windows, came to her quite clearly.

'Who is it?'

'New, isn't she?'

'She looks like Kay Marlow.'

'There can't be *more* of them.'

'Yes, there are. Look, there's another little one by Karen.'

'They must be twins.'

'Did she fall out?'

'Was it a dare?'

And then behind her came Ginty's clear voice from the compartment. 'Has Nick fallen out? Well, I can't *see*, Ann. What *has* she done, then?'

'Oh, you shut up, for goodness' sake,' muttered Karen to herself.

A lean, tweed-clad lady hurried past.

'That would happen,' said Margaret softly. 'Never a disaster, but Ironsides is on the spot.'

Karen said nothing, digging her hands down into the pockets of her blazer. Nicola, standing between the guard and Miss Cromwell, looked small and slightly alarmed.

The guard strode back past the open door, looking stiff and annoyed. Nicola, in Miss Cromwell's keeping, was brought up a moment later. Still in silence, Karen reached down a hand and pulled her into the corridor; together, and with more ceremony, Karen and Margaret helped Miss Cromwell up on to the step. Miss Cromwell climbed into the corridor and slammed the carriage door. The train began to move.

On principle, Miss Cromwell did not approve of prefects. She gave as her reasons that their duties interfered with scholarship work, and that their so-called responsibilities made them conceited and altogether above themselves. Where another mistress would have allowed the episode to rest until they reached school and a certain amount of privacy, Miss Cromwell attacked immediately, being of the opinion that bubbles of conceit required pricking hard and often.

'Well, Karen. What one might, I think, call a most unfortunate beginning to the term.'

The crowd in the corridor, who liked Karen, but were never averse to seeing authority in trouble, stayed to listen.

Karen said nothing.

'I should have thought that any senior with sense, let alone a senior who is, supposedly, entrusted with some responsibility, would have seen to it that a silly little girl was not allowed to roam at will, amusing herself by inconveniencing us all.'

'I didn't know—' began Karen, low-voiced.

'My dear Karen,' said Miss Cromwell, 'it's your business to know. If you are unable to control your own family, I fail to see how you can expect to have any authority over the rest of the school.'

Karen, scarlet-faced, said nothing. Rowan and Margaret exchanged a quick, angry glance.

'If Nicola is so childish and undisciplined, she should not have been allowed to play alone in the corridor. Stopping a train for no good reason is a very serious matter. I feel sure that Miss Keith will take a very grave view of the whole affair. As to the fine—'

'Father will pay the fine, naturally,' said Rowan in a gentle, courteous voice. Unlike Karen, she did not find sarcasm particularly disconcerting. So she spoke politely and smiled pleasantly at Miss Cromwell, as though they shared a joke.

'I'll pay it,' cried Nicola. 'Well, I will, Rowan. I've saved—'

Rowan trod quietly, but heavily, on her foot. Nicola relapsed into silence.

'Who will and who will not pay will be a matter for Miss Keith to decide. I shall report the whole affair to her as soon as we return and I trust that you, Karen, will hold yourself in readiness to see her whenever she sends for you.'

'Yes, Miss Cromwell,' said Karen. Her voice shook slightly.

'Everyone will return to her compartment,' said Miss Cromwell, satisfied that Karen had had enough. The crowd began to melt, casting sympathetic glances at Karen and amused smiles at Nicola. 'Karen – can you manage this child for the remainder of the journey, or must I sit with your family for you?'

Karen gasped.

'We can manage, thank you, Miss Cromwell,' said Rowan in the same composed voice. She took Nicola by the shoulder and pushed her gently in the direction of their compartment. Margaret Jessop had vanished unobtrusively and the Marlow family was left alone to sort itself out.

There was a long silence.

'I say, Karen,' began Nicola nervously.

'Oh, be quiet,' said Karen, an odd tremor in her voice. 'You make me tired. Always rushing round in a state of wild excitement and never stopping to think.' She hunched her shoulders and looked out of the window. The others looked at her apprehensively. They knew from long experience that Karen, who seemed as a rule calm and matter-of-fact, could be thrown off-balance as easily as Lawrie by sudden and unexpected disaster. Karen knew it too; and she was uncertain, this time, how well she had managed to conceal those moments of panic when she thought Nicola had been hurt, possibly killed. Not very well, she thought miserably; and it had been Rowan who had stood up to Ironsides, while she herself blushed and stammered like any junior—

'I must tell Peter,' burst out Ginty irrepressibly. 'He's always been absolutely wild to pull a communication cord or smash one of those things that stop escalators—'

'Be *quiet*, Ginty,' snapped Karen, without looking round.

'You needn't bite my head off,' retorted Ginty. 'For once I haven't done a thing.'

'Oh, Gin, for heaven's sake,' said Rowan. 'Don't talk as though you were the tomboy of the Remove. All through the holidays you kept trying to give the impression that a mild case of bounds-breaking had brought you to the edge of expulsion. I could have throttled you.'

'There was a row,' said Ginty indignantly. 'An awful row. Miss Keith said—'

'I know you went round weeping for days after whatever Miss Keith said,' said Rowan pitilessly, 'but that still doesn't make you the naughtiest girl in the Fourth.'

Ginty turned scarlet. 'I *didn't* cry.'

'All right,' said Rowan. 'You didn't cry. It was an extraordinary coincidence that just that week you had such a very bad cold. Now dry up, do.'

'Actually,' said Lawrie to Ginty, ignoring Rowan because it was so extremely mean to let people know that you knew when they'd been crying, 'actually Miss Keith doesn't think anything like that at all. She thinks – what was it, Nick? – that you're rather wild but that you've got a lot of good stuff in you.'

Ginty gaped.

'What on earth are you talking about?' demanded Rowan. 'How do you know what Miss Keith thinks?'

'I do,' said Lawrie loftily. 'I do. That's all.'

'I suppose,' said Karen acidly, 'she just happened to stroll past and give you her impressions of the family?'

'No,' said Lawrie nonchalantly. 'But we do know what she thinks. Don't we, Nick? We have it on – on the very best authority.'

Nicola smiled faintly. 'Yes.'

'How?' demanded Rowan curtly.

'Shall we tell them?' asked Lawrie of Nicola.

But Nicola was feeling too apprehensive of disgrace to play the game of tantalizing properly.

'We were talking to her niece,' she said flatly. 'She told us.'

'Oh, Nick!' cried Lawrie, disappointed.

'Her niece?' said Rowan, with much the same incredulity with which Nicola had remarked 'An aunt?'

'She's twelve and a half and she's going to be in the Third Remove,' elaborated Nicola. 'And her name's Tim. At least, it's Thalia actually. Thalia Keith.'

'Why Tim because her name's Failure?' puzzled Ann.

'That's what Lawrie thought it was. But it isn't Failure. It's Thalia. A muse or something.'

'Was she the child standing with Lawrie by the door?' asked Karen curtly.

Nicola subsided. 'I – I expect so, Kay.'

A gloomy silence fell on the compartment. For the moment, they had all, except Karen, forgotten that Nicola had stopped the train.

'Ironsides is always a beast,' murmured Ann hesitantly at length. 'And people do *know* she always likes to bite the prefects. It's one of her things.'

'But she doesn't always have the opportunity to do it so publicly,' snapped Karen, exasperated, 'and not usually with such good reason. And I've still got to see Keith and she'll think, naturally, that I'm a perfect imbecile.'

'Why?' breathed Nicola.

'Because if it's your family, the staff always think you ought to be able to see out of the back of your head. If it had been any other junior it would have been *her* fault, unless I'd been actually standing beside her. As it's you – well, naturally, I should have known by instinct.'

Nicola and Lawrie looked at one another guiltily from beneath dropped lashes.

'You look a perfect sight,' added Karen crossly, and turned again to stare out of the window.

'You do rather,' said Ann more gently. 'Turn round and let me tidy you up a bit. How on earth did you get so filthy?'

'I expect it was the tunnel,' said Nicola, licking Ann's handkerchief meekly.

'But what – why were you *in* the tunnel? Why did you pull the cord?'

'My knife,' said Nicola reluctantly, her eyes on Karen's averted head. 'It fell out. I couldn't help it, Ann.'

'I dropped it,' murmured Lawrie. 'It was an accident, honestly.'

'That knife,' said Karen viciously. 'I've a good mind to take it away altogether.'

'You can't,' cried Nicola. 'It's my parting present. You can't!' And they sat gazing furiously at one another, their expressions oddly alike.

The train slowed: slowed and stopped. They had arrived.

Karen sprang up and pulled her suitcase down from the rack.

'I'm going up by taxi,' she said abruptly, abandoning the

careful arrangements of the previous night, when they had decided that the four youngest should ride, since Ann was perfectly capable of ushering the twins into Miss Keith's room before they unpacked. 'If I can see Keith before Ironsides does, I will. But I'm not having Nicola along. She can walk up with you, Rowan, and arrive when things have cooled down. And besides,' added Karen honestly, 'I'm not owning her in that blouse. Everyone we pass will say: *That*'s the child who stopped the train. They must be related.'

'All right,' agreed Rowan calmly. She lifted the suitcase down from the rack and saw Lawrie and Nicola safely on to the platform.

'Rowan,' whispered Nicola.

'What?'

'*Will* they know from my blouse?'

'Not if you put your blazer on,' said Rowan coolly, handing it to her. 'Don't bother Kay just now. She's in one of her flaps.'

Nicola struggled thankfully into her blazer. Even so, she felt unhappily conspicuous as she followed Rowan meekly to the taxi and handed her suitcase to be stowed on the roof. People turned to look at her and say:

'She *is* a Marlow – Must be, she's with Rowan – Why did she? – Was she ill? – Perhaps she was trying to run away – Wasn't Ironsides in a bate?'

The taxi containing the rest of the family moved off. Rowan, who seemed unmoved by either glances or voices, spoke over her shoulder and said: 'Come on, infant.'

They turned out of the station with its beds of asters and nasturtiums and went up the High Street, Nicola running a few steps every now and then in order to keep level with Rowan. They had passed the grey bulk of the cathedral which reared up in the centre of the city, making the new shops which faced it across the spread of grass look small and flimsy, before Nicola ventured a careful:

'Rowan?'

''M?'

'Is it a very awful thing to have done?'

'It's not the most sensible thing the family's ever pulled out of the hat.'

'They couldn't – Miss Keith wouldn't expel me, would she?'

'Send you back by return of post and say you weren't what she was expecting? No, I shouldn't think so.'

Nicola looked relieved. 'You know, Rowan, I don't honestly see what else I could have done.'

'Don't you, now?'

'No, Rowan, honestly.'

'Well, I don't see what else you could have done to get the knife back. The only other thing you could have done would have been to say: Well, bless my soul. It's gone.'

'Just lose it?'

'Yes.'

'*Rowan!*'

'I suppose it never struck you, did it, my pretty, that another train might run into us from behind if we pulled up unexpectedly? I don't say it would. I say *might*, not knowing how railways arrange these things. Or, of course, that while you were skipping footloose in the tunnel, a train might have come the other way and squashed you flat?'

'Do you mean I might have been *killed*?' said Nicola incredulously.

'It does come within the bounds of possibility.' Rowan looked down at Nicola sardonically. 'Not, of course, that any of us would mind much. What's one more or less in a family our size?'

'Well!' said Nicola, flabbergasted. She was silent for quite five minutes; then, as they turned into a teashop, she found tongue to ask where they were going and why.

'So that you can get a little cleaner than is possible with handkerchief and lick. You don't need to arrive at school looking more conspicuous than necessary.'

Nicola found herself in the cloakroom at the back of the shop. Looking in the mirror she found that there was a good deal of dirt which Ann had only managed to move from the centre of her face to the outside rim. Rowan, leaning easily against the row of basins, directed operations.

'That's better,' she said at last, flicking at the tail of Nicola's skirt which had become unaccountably covered with whitewash. 'You look quite human now. Put on a clean blouse before you see Keith and she'll probably think the whole thing was a product of Ironsides' imagination. And if she should refer to it, just lie low and say, Yes, Miss Keith, and No, Miss Keith, at the appropriate moments.'

'Yes, Rowan,' said Nicola meekly.

'I'll stand you a drink if you like,' added Rowan handsomely as they went back into the shop. 'Orange, Lemon, or Raspberry?'

Since she had never tried it before, Nicola chose Raspberry. Her legs dangling from the high stool, sucking Raspberryade through a straw, she began to feel less uneasy.

'You'd better have a sundae too,' said Rowan thoughtfully. 'You can't be taken out more than once in a term by a senior, so we may as well make the most of it now we're here.'

Nicola agreed enthusiastically.

'I had chocolate on the train,' she said, studying the card with concentration, 'and I'm drinking Raspberry now, so I think I'll have a peach sundae, please, Rowan.'

'I suppose you can follow your own reasoning,' said Rowan idly. 'Was it the niece who provided the chocolate? Tim or Failure or whatever her name is?'

'Thalia,' protested Nicola. 'Yes, it was.'

'Which reminds me. Did she really tell you what Miss Keith had said about us, or was Lawrie being funny?'

Nicola grinned.

'No, she really did. D'you want to know what she said about you?'

Rowan considered.

'On the whole, not, I think. My relationship with Miss Keith is what you might call delicately balanced on a razor edge of mutual toleration. I wouldn't like to do anything to upset it.'

'But it was perfectly all right, Rowan. It's quite a thing you'd like said.'

'Then definitely not. I should blush every time I met her. And I think it might be as well – we did warn you and Lawrie, didn't we, not to go round spouting things Kay and I might have said about people?'

'Yes, you did. Lots of times.'

'Well, tell Keith's niece from me that it would be just as well if she didn't run round school saying: Aunty says – in a loud, clear voice.'

Nicola murmured noncommittally through a mouthful of peach and ice-cream. Probably Rowan was right. But for some reason, she didn't see herself telling Tim any such thing. She swallowed the lump of peach and asked Rowan politely about the state of the netball team.

Presently, replete and amicable, they strolled through the remainder of the town and out along the wood-fringed road to the school. It was all more or less familiar to Nicola, who had come down quite often with her parents and Lawrie to

Speech Days and end of term plays, and had strolled, shy but proud, about the pleasant flowery garden, watching the quick, admiring glances flung at Karen and Rowan when the juniors thought they weren't looking. But it was a new and different feeling to be wearing the school uniform herself; and though she was still pleased and excited to be coming to Kingscote at last, she did wish, uneasily, that she had not started her school career by stopping a train; and when at last they turned in at the school gates and walked up the drive to the big white stucco-fronted building, her heart bumped so hard that she thought Rowan would probably notice and tell her to sit down until it stopped.

Hall and stairs and landing were crowded with people passing to and fro, or standing in small gossipy groups, as Rowan and Nicola went in. Nicola, feeling very new and shy, kept closely behind Rowan and wished Lawrie were with her to share the feeling. She was glad that when people hailed Rowan, as they seemed to do continuously, Rowan only waved and did not stop. They had nearly reached the top of the stairs before a thin, brown-haired girl said in a voice which Nicola recognized with a shock as not friendly at all:

'Well, if it isn't our Rowan come back.'

'So it is,' said Rowan. 'How observant of you.' Her voice was not friendly either.

'And you've brought two more back with you, they tell me. Two more of your illustrious family to bring honour to the dear old school.'

Rowan looked cool and pleasant.

'Somebody has to,' she observed politely. 'If you will insist on leaving it to us, we have to do our best.'

'And one of them stopped the train, I hear. Such a clever and original way of making the Marlows conspicuous the very first day.'

'What a shame you didn't think of it first,' countered Rowan swiftly and ran on up the stairs.

'Who was that?' gasped Nicola when they were out of earshot.

'Lois Sanger,' said Rowan briefly.

'The one you had the row with?'

'I've told you before, Nicola, that you're to forget the things we told you before we knew you were coming here.'

'I'm only saying it to you,' said Nicola, injured. 'I don't even know what the row was.'

'Then forget it. That's Miss Keith's door. I won't go in with you. It looks so elderly. Just knock and await developments.'

She smiled briefly before she walked away, but she still sounded curt and angry. Nicola sighed and looked sadly at Miss Keith's door. It was a pity Rowan was cross. She would have preferred to have had someone with her to say, This is Nicola. But she supposed the longer she waited the worse she would feel. She knocked carefully and was told to come in.

Miss Keith had not been particularly pleased by Karen's story, but she had not said a great deal. Like Miss Cromwell, she had suggested that it had been unwise to allow Nicola and Lawrence to stand unattended in the corridor; and, after a pause had remarked that she would have to consider making a rule forbidding any junior to run about the train corridors unless travelling with her parents.

Karen murmured: 'Yes, Miss Keith,' and looked fixedly at an upturned corner of leather on Miss Keith's blotter.

'And I think, perhaps, that as Nicola is new this term, it would be better if you were to write to your father about the fine. I should be sorry to have to make an official school matter of something which has happened almost before Nicola is a member of the school.'

'Yes, Miss Keith.'

'Of course, had Nicola been here longer, I should have had to take a very different attitude. That type of impulsive action can have the most serious consequences, and not only for the person directly concerned. In this particular case, no actual harm did result. But at the same time, any members of the public who were travelling on the train will carry away a very bad impression of the way our girls behave.'

'Yes.'

'Your family has had a very good record here, Karen; and I should be sorry if that record were to be spoiled, particularly sorry if it were to be spoiled while you are head girl. But I'm sure it isn't necessary for me to remind you that Nicola and Lawrence must be treated exactly like any other juniors and if such a thing were to occur again I should have to consider very seriously whether I could allow Nicola to remain here.'

'Yes.'

'Very well, Karen. I will have a word with Nicola when she arrives. After that, unless she continues to be troublesome, we had better all forget the whole unfortunate business.'

That was that, and Karen removed herself, feeling depressed and humiliated. Had Miss Keith called her back to say that she had decided that Val Longstreet should be head girl, she would have felt dejected but not surprised. She wondered, as she ran up the stairs to her own room, whether her father, also, would think she should have foreseen that Nicola would drop her knife and hold up the Southern Region in consequence.

To Nicola, Miss Keith repeated much of what she had said to Karen, adding that she hoped Nicola would do nothing so foolish again, but settle down to be a good, useful member of society. Nicola said: 'Yes, Miss Keith,' for the last time, and whisked thankfully out of the study, shutting the door very gently behind her. The prefect who stood at the end of the passage with a list in her hand, ticked off her name and told her that she would be in Dormitory Six, first on the right at the top of the stairs.

'You're lucky to be so many,' she added with a friendly smile. 'It's much the nicest of the sisters' rooms. And did you really stop the train, or is that a rumour?'

Nicola said No, she really had, and fled upstairs to find the white door with the black six on it. Rowan, Ann, Ginty and Lawrie were there already, Ginty stuffing the clothes from her trunk into a drawer and Ann unpacking in a calm, tidy way for Lawrie. As Nicola came in Rowan was remarking lazily:

'You'll have to put all that tidy before you go down, Gin, so you might as well do it first as last.'

'I don't see why,' protested Ginty. 'We're a sisters' room, so we can't do anything for the Dorm Prize, so I don't see that it matters.'

'Shocking outlook,' said Rowan calmly. 'The point is, my dear Virginia, that Matron will inspect your drawers just the same as anyone else's, and if they're not tidy she'll come to me about it. And I can't be bothered with little idiocies of that kind.'

Ginty sat back on her heels, and pushed the hair out of her eyes.

'You are a bossy beast, Rowan. I do think Kay's lucky to have a room to herself.'

'When you're head girl, you'll have a room to yourself too,' said Rowan, unmoved. 'In the meantime, you can at least *start* with your drawers tidy, whatever happens to them in a week's time.'

'Hullo, Nicky,' said Ann. 'That's your cubicle. I'll unpack for you as soon as I've finished Lawrie's.'

'I can do it myself, thank you,' said Nicola quickly; she was sometimes irritated by Ann's unfailing good-nature. 'I s'pose I can't be by the window, can I, Rowan?'

'No, you can't,' said Rowan, who seemed to have recovered her temper. 'That's reserved for your respected seniors, meaning me and Ann. How did you get on?'

'All right,' said Nicola, kneeling down to tug at the straps of her trunk. 'No, don't *bother*, Ann. I can do it myself.'

She plunged into her unpacking, stowing her things away in frantic haste to be finished before Ann could come to her assistance. When everything was in place, she sat back on her heels and carefully unwrapped the two photographs allowed by regulation and put them tenderly on top of her dressing-chest. One was of the ship in which Giles was serving, the other a reproduction of Abbot's portrait of Nelson which Giles had bought for her at the National Portrait Gallery.

'It would show nicer feeling, Nicky dear,' commented Rowan, 'if you had Giles instead of his ship and possibly an expensively framed cabinet portrait of Father and Mother instead of Nelson. Don't you think so, Ann?'

Nicola grinned, but said nothing. She was far too used to being teased about Nelson and the Navy to trouble to argue. She sauntered over to the window and stood beside Rowan, looking out.

'We can see the cathedral from here,' she remarked.

'You can see it from everywhere,' said Ann. 'You can't get lost round here. You only have to look for the spire and make for that.'

'And the sea!' cried Nicola unheeding. 'Oh, look, Rowan. There's the sea!'

'It always is there,' said Rowan unmoved. 'Has been for years.'

'That girl was right about it being the nicest dorm,' said Nicola contentedly, hanging out of the window. 'I wish we didn't have this silly stuff with roses on it, though,' she added, flicking the window curtains.

'I suppose you'd like a nice grey chintz printed with battleships,' retorted Ginty, slamming the last drawer of a surprisingly tidy chest tight shut. 'Well, I'm going to see if Monica's back. So long.'

She went out, banging the door behind her. Someone shouted from the gravel path below. Nicola waved back.

'There's Tim,' she said. 'Come on, Lawrie. You must be ready by now. Let's go down.'

Lawrie looked doubtfully at Ann.

'That's all right,' said Ann, who was still filling Lawrie's drawers in a slow, methodical fashion. 'You run along. I'll finish this.'

The twins collided in the doorway, glared at one another impatiently and then rushed downstairs to the garden.

'Quite at home already,' said Lois Sanger dryly as Lawrie passed her at full speed with an inch to spare. 'I always feel it must be so gratifying to be a Marlow.'

3 A Form Examination

I

'Have a pear,' said Tim negligently as they met. She herself was munching a large, juicy specimen. 'They should be all right. They're Aunt Edith's.'

'Did she give them to you?' asked Nicola, accepting, but unable to reconcile the tall, fair, formidable Miss Keith of her experience with a cosy picture of Aunt Edith, donor of fruit.

'Certainly not,' said Tim calmly. She looked from one to the other and added: 'They grow on the wall in that nice little walled garden round the other side.'

Lawrie stared round-eyed, her teeth fastened in her pear. In trying to bite and protest at the same time, she choked and had to be hit, hard and repeatedly, on the back.

'Don't, Nick,' she protested, recovering. 'You hurt. You always do things so hard.'

'Sorry,' said Nicola. 'Next time I'll leave you to die. Much I care.'

'Good,' said Tim, chewing methodically, 'aren't they?' She tossed her finished pear core into the shrubbery and began another.

'But Tim—'

' 'M?'

'That's Miss Keith's garden.'

'Her private garden,' emphasized Nicola.

'Even prefects and parents can only go in if they're invited,' continued Lawrie impressively. 'You simply mustn't, Tim. Once there was an absolutely frantic row because the prefects thought they had a privilege to be there—'

'And they just went in,' continued Nicola, 'and Keith simply flamed because of discourtesy and taking for granted. Oh, goodness!'

'What?' asked Tim, unmoved.

'That's the kind of thing we're not supposed to mention. I mean, Kay says the school isn't supposed to know if the Sixth get into rows. You won't tell anyone else, will you, Tim?'

'I expect not,' said Tim placidly. 'I wish I'd taken some more.'

'But that's what we're telling you,' insisted Lawrie. 'You mustn't go into Keith's garden. No one may.'

'But I'm her niece,' said Tim. She grinned cheerfully. 'Bless me, if I can't take one of my own aunty's pears—'

'Four,' corrected Nicola.

'Five,' said Tim. 'I had one before you came down. As I was saying: if I can't—' she broke off.

'What's the matter?' asked Nicola. She was uncertain whether Tim's expression denoted remorse or sudden apprehension that she had swallowed a worm.

'Wait a minute,' said Tim, staring at the car which was turning in at the entrance gates. 'I may be wrong. I sometimes am. It happens to everyone now and then. I bet it is, though. And I was so sure they wouldn't.'

Nicola and Lawrie looked helplessly at the large black car which was causing Tim such pain. There seemed nothing wrong or unusual about it; large black cars (generally containing new girls and their parents) had been fairly frequent all the afternoon. This one drew up at the steps in the usual way and the expected child, mother and father got out.

The father was perfectly ordinary in a tweedy fashion, rather like Commander Marlow in mufti. The mother, who was not ordinary at all, was long and dark and dressed in a long greenish-brown garment, with sandals on her feet and long ear-rings which dangled to her shoulders; the child, who was fair and stout, wore sandals also and a loose green silk tunic. Her straight hair hung down her back unplaited and she tossed it to and fro as she looked about her. Tim groaned as one in agony.

'Don't, Tim,' protested Nicola. 'What is it?'

'That on the steps. It's enough to make anyone ill. Even your sister Karen is stricken with dismay.'

It was true that Karen and Margaret Jessop, who had come out on to the steps, had hesitated noticeably before asking courteously if there was anything they could do; and all of school within eyeshot were trying to look without seeming to stare. 'Come away,' said Tim brokenly. 'I can't bear it.'

'I wish you'd explain,' said Lawrie as they branched off towards the playing fields which were beginning to haze over in the September dusk. 'Is it someone you know?'

'My nearest, dearest neighbour,' said Tim in a lighter tone. 'My darling little pal, Pomona. Such a dear nice gentle little girl. Such a sweet little face. Such quiet pretty manners. Always answers so nicely and never makes a fuss if you ask her to sing. Such a pretty dear. *Everyone* loves Pomona.'

'Do they?' said Nicola doubtfully.

'Grown-ups do. She's awfully good with them. Clings prettily to their hands and says Oo! don't they like to think of tulips being beds for fairies? 'Course, she knows there aren't fairies *really*, but wouldn't it be lovely to peep into a tulip one day and find a wee wee fairy all cosy inside . . . Beastly brat,' said Tim with conviction.

'And do you have to know her?' asked Lawrie sympathetically. The Marlows, too, had a cousin who practised her pretty wiles on the unsuspecting grown-ups.

'My father and hers were at school together,' said Tim sadly. 'One fagged for the other, or they blacked each other's eyes or something equally touching. And Mrs. Todd – Pomona's mother – she dashes off little *objets* in tempera and rushes them round to Father with a tremendously pleased expression. Father isn't at all bad,' said Tim, carefully nonchalant, 'but Mrs. Todd is ghastly. She's frightfully artistic, you know, dabbles in practically everything—'

'But isn't your father artistic?' asked Lawrie, puzzled by the savagery with which Tim uttered the word.

'Father's not at all artistic,' said Tim austerely. 'Father paints.'

Lawrie gave it up.

'Mrs. Todd,' continued Tim, 'is also something of a poet. She also does little things in poker-work. And she acts. And she produces—' Tim sat down on a handy bench and laughed suddenly. 'She produced a pageant in the village last year. Pomona was a Bacchante in a leopard skin.'

The twins were not perfectly certain what a Bacchante was, but they thought it well to laugh also.

'I never thought her mother would let her come,' said Tim sadly. 'Never. I knew Aunt Edith got at her father the same time as mine, but I *never* thought anything would come of it. And she's sure to be in the Third Remove because she's delicate and highly-strung and backward.'

She brooded under the concerned eyes of the twins.

'Now if you two were going to be in Third Remove we could have an Anti-Pomona League and teach her not to have such winning ways. As it is—' she sighed sadly.

'It is a pity,' agreed Nicola politely. Because in many

ways it was a pity that they would not be in the same form as Tim; but of course, Marlows always did go into an A form. You couldn't alter that.

A bell began to ring in school.

'Tea!' said Tim enthusiastically springing up. She called over her shoulder: 'Race you to the house.'

Nicola ran. She could always beat Lawrie and it was suddenly tremendously important that she should beat Tim. Tim had had an unfair start, but it would be no satisfaction to point that out if she were beaten. She ran her hardest, feeling the gravel path sharply through her thin house shoes, seeing Tim's dark jerking hair come nearer and nearer until there was nothing but the wide white steps in front of her and the sound of Tim's thudding feet behind. She flung herself at the balustrade and clung to it, her chest heaving, perfectly speechless. Tim flung an arm across her shoulders, acting exaggerated exhaustion, and they staggered up the steps with Lawrie clinging to their girdles, and went in to tea in perfect amity.

II

Until the results of the Form Examination were known, new girls at Kingscote moved in a herd, all ages and sizes, using the Division Room beside the staff Common Room as a form room and eating at a table of their own. For the day and a half, therefore, before they sat for the Form Exam., the Marlow twins and Thalia moved about together, feeling progressively more regretful that they were going to be separated. Pomona also appeared in the Division Room, her hair still flying loosely about her shoulders, and wearing a pale blue sleeveless jibbah and the inevitable sandals. The other new girls, many of whom were also wearing home clothes until their uniforms arrived, stared a little, but felt too new for amused or hostile comment. A thin, dark, long-legged individual called Sally Burnett, who seemed obviously destined for IIIA, made a few shy advances to Nicola, saying that it looked as though they might be in the same form and it was nicer to know someone before you got there; Nicola agreed, liking Sally, though not so well as Tim. But since Tim was going to be in Third Remove, it would be silly not to make friends with IIIA probables as soon as possible.

The afternoon of the exam was warm as September days can be. A bee buzzed angrily against the window and on the tennis courts outside four of the Sixth were playing a belated game. To Nicola, reading the examination paper headed *Junior School*, first carelessly and then with a rising apprehension, the incessant buzzing of the bee and the irregular 'thud' of the tennis ball were an intolerable distraction. Her mouth rather dry and her heart beginning to thump, she read the paper over again. She was terribly afraid that she couldn't answer one single question. She glanced across to the next row but one, and looked at Tim who was smiling to herself and writing her name slowly in a large, careful round hand. Lawrie, sitting behind Tim, had not started either. She looked a little as though she might cry. Hastily, because she felt rather like that herself, Nicola returned to her terrified contemplation of the examination paper.

It became a trifle clearer as the afternoon went on. There were, Nicola discovered, bits of questions she could do. She wrote down the answers in a large, dashing hand, trying to spread her writing so that the meagreness of her knowledge was not too painfully obvious. In the last ten minutes a furious scribbling sound came from Tim who had been sitting dreamily contemplating the landscape for the past hour and a half; and then Miss Cartwright, the young mistress who was invigilating, put down her pen and said pleasantly:

'You must stop writing now. Clip your answers together and bring them up to my desk. The results will be put up in the Division Room just before supper.'

Gloomily, Nicola clipped the two pages of large sprawling handwriting together and watched sadly as they disappeared into Miss Cartwright's file. Sally Burnett gave her a quick little smile and seemed inclined to wait, but Nicola pretended not to see, gazing dismally at Lawrie who hadn't even used her paper-clip because she had only filled one sheet. All round her rose the nervous aftermath of the examination:

'Wasn't it awful?'

'Could you do number two?'

'Their standard's awfully high, isn't it? At my last school—'

'Let's go and get some tea,' said Tim at her elbow.

They went down to the big airy dining hall where tea and bread and butter and plain cake were spread on a long trestle table at the end of the room. You helped yourself and took your laden wooden tray over to the form table, laid cup and plate on the table and put the tray at the table's end to be collected by the scurrying tea-monitresses who had their own meal when everyone else had finished. Occasionally there were accidents, when over-careful juniors collided with clumsy middle-schools, but Miss Keith, for some obscure reason of her own, appeared to think it valuable social training.

'Wasn't it ghastly?' burst out Lawrie when they were all safely seated. 'Could you do any of it, Nick? I couldn't do a *thing*.'

'You did some of it,' muttered Nicola crossly. She was

trying hard to keep herself from knowing just how badly she had done.

'Only bits of things. I remembered amo amas amat from hearing Peter, but I didn't know any more. Did you?'

'No,' snapped Nicola. She took a long drink of tea and went off to get another cup.

'I only knew the French and German,' said Tim serenely, 'and I knew Aunt Edith didn't expect me to know any more so I didn't bother. It was a nice restful afternoon.'

'Golly,' said Lawrie. 'It wasn't restful to me. I kept staring at the beastly thing and wondering if it would look better upside down. Nick,' as her twin returned, 'd'you think we've done *well* enough for IIIA?'

'Shut up,' muttered Nicola, 'how should I know?'

'Pomona, the pet, looks frightfully pleased with herself,' said Tim, sliding the conversation out of Nicola's danger area. 'I expect she thinks she's passed straight into the Sixth. Look at her, munching cake with that smooth expression.'

Lawrie giggled.

'She has got a smooth face, hasn't she?' she chuckled. 'Smooth like one of those bladders of lard you see in farms sometimes.'

Tim grinned. 'She would be pleased with you. Bladder of lard, forsooth! You don't appreciate our dear little Pomona. Maybe we're just the weeniest bit sturdy, but there's no need to be coarse. None whatever.'

'I do wish we could be an Anti-Pomona League,' sighed Lawrie. 'It is a pity—'

And then she stopped, her small freckled face suddenly and deeply pink. She looked quickly at Nicola who looked quickly and furiously back; it might, Lawrie decided silently, be as well to say nothing more at all about IIIA until they knew for certain.

They spent the interval between tea and supper throwing a netball aimlessly about with some of the other new girls. The first three days at the beginning of the school year were generally slack and easy-going except for the Sixth and some of the Upper Fifth who returned and plunged into their work immediately. Margaret Jessop strolling past, her hands deep in her blazer pockets, stopped to watch them for a few moments, and Lawrie, who had been passing and catching with commendable accuracy, promptly turned scarlet and became completely disorganized, dropping the ball and kicking it towards Nicola in her wild efforts to retrieve it.

'Idiot,' muttered Nicola, throwing it back hard. Margaret had passed on by then, and Lawrie, her colour subsiding, caught the ball negligently on one hand and tossed it back.

The sun began to dip. Miss Cartwright came out on to the garden steps and waved. Nicola, who had the ball, flung it anywhere and ran, ran as hard as she had done to beat Tim the previous evening. With Tim and Lawrie and the rest close behind her, she dodged and ducked through the crowd on the stairs and struggled panting with the suddenly recalcitrant handle of the Division Room door. It gave abruptly and they all poured in, some of the rest of the school, who were always mildly interested in a list of any kind, crowding in behind them. With eyes which refused to focus properly, Nicola stared at the list.

Lower VB. Upper IVA. Upper IVB. Her glance skipped downwards, and her heart thumped in her throat. IIIA.

She stared, holding her eyes to it.

'S. Burnett.
R. Durrant.
M. Hopkins.
P. Jones.
B. Wateridge.'

That was all. IIIB was longer. Grimly Nicola read:

'S. Afford.
M. Rumsby.
R. Cowling.
E. Rose.
D. Kench.
J. Ross.
E. Jenson.
E. Shelland.
B. Newberry.
T. Upson.
L. Young.'

'They've forgotten to put us in,' thought Nicola, holding to a last hope. But she read on:

'*Third Remove.*
E. Collins.
T. Keith.
L. Marlow.
N. Marlow.
P. Todd.'

She stared at her name feeling quite sick. It wasn't true, perhaps. (But she knew it was.) Perhaps if Kay or Rowan were to make enquiries – or if she and Lawrie were to ask Miss Cartwright – and then someone would say: 'How absurd. What a ridiculous mistake. Of course Nicola and Lawrie are in IIIA. There must have been a slip in copying—'

Someone from the back of the crowd did say something; she said it loudly and clearly; Nicola recognized Ginty's voice even before she realized what she was saying.

Ginty said, in astonishment and unbelief: 'Kay, come here. Kay do you know what they've done? They've stuck Nick and Lawrie in with the Dimwits. It's an insult to the family. They *can't* be that stupid.'

Somehow that made it true, without any possibility of error. The crowd laughed a little, knowing and liking its Ginty. Nicola, misunderstanding, thought the laughter directed against herself and Lawrie. A lump rose perilously in her throat and she glanced hurriedly at her twin: but

Lawrie's expression was one of dazed bewilderment rather than dismay; it sometimes took time for disaster to penetrate her fully; in an hour or so she might burst into tears; until then she would probably assert violently that it was a mistake and that Miss Cartwright would tell them so in the morning.

Nicola swallowed secretly. One could not, of course, cry here, in front of all the crowd. Probably it would be better not to cry at all if it could be managed. And certainly one must not plunge for the door head down; one must wait until the crowd began to break up and then stroll nonchalantly away in company with anyone who cared to come. Nicola stuck her hands through her girdle, whistled softly between her teeth, and turned her head to give Tim a quick little smile. Tim smiled back quickly too, but as though she were embarrassed. She thinks I mind, thought Nicola crossly and correctly; and said rather loudly: 'It's pretty good, I think. We can have the A. P. L. anyway.'

4 Tim Bags a Desk—

Somewhat to her surprise, Nicola found that she cared a good deal less by the morning. Rowan had assured her that this would be so, and Nicola, feeling grateful for Rowan's casual sympathy, had pretended to believe her. But it was a fine, sunny day and even Lawrie, who had wept loudly and violently the night before, was eating her bread and marmalade and porridge with reasonable cheerfulness. It didn't show that she'd been crying, thought Nicola critically, drinking tea in measured gulps and wondering what the staff talked about up there on their platform. Not ordinary things, she supposed; most likely about examinations and prefects and frightfully difficult Greek and Maths.

Tim was eating another pear. She must, thought Nicola, have been out very early to get it; one day she would be caught, either by Miss Keith herself, or by Robertson, the silent old gardener whom some people thought even more terrifying than Miss Keith herself. With her thought, Nicola glanced up towards Miss Keith and saw that she too was eating a pear, just like Tim. A quick little twinge of laughter shook her and she nudged Tim, showing her the joke; Tim giggled too.

'Sit up, Tim and Nicola, and don't be silly,' said Miss Cartwright cheerfully. 'Where did that pear come from, Tim?'

Nicola jumped and blushed. Tim said:

'I brought it with me.'

'From home?'

Now it would come, thought Nicola miserably. And Tim

would probably feel frightfully silly saying she'd taken it from Aunt Edith's garden. Nicola ducked her head, cutting her bread and marmalade into babyish squares.

'Yes, Miss Cartwright,' said Tim's voice easily.

Nicola gasped, a small choked sound, unheard in the steady clamour of the dining hall.

'Extras from home are supposed to be kept for tea-time,' said Miss Cartwright in the kind impersonal voice the staff were using just now to explain breaches of rules. 'Remember another time, won't you?'

'But I like pears for breakfast,' protested Tim gently.

'Perhaps you do. But that's the rule.'

'Perhaps I'd better ask Aunt Edith about it,' suggested Tim.

'Is that your guardian? Because if so, and she particularly wants you to have fruit for breakfast, I should ask her to write to Miss Keith.'

'It *is* Miss Keith,' said Tim carefully.

Miss Cartwright frowned. '*Who* is Miss Keith?'

'My Aunt Edith. But she's not my guardian. I have two quite normal parents.'

Miss Cartwright gave Tim a quick, wary look, as though, thought Nicola, to decide whether she was being ragged and if so, how much. But Tim stared candidly back as though there had been no silly evasion over where the pears came from.

'If Miss Keith is your aunt,' said Miss Cartwright, still friendly, 'I think – don't you? – that you need to be rather specially careful not to ask for any special favours, even very small ones. I'm sure you'd rather, really, that Miss Keith didn't treat you differently from anyone else. Wouldn't you?'

'No,' said Tim tranquilly. 'I want a lot of special privileges, actually. All I can get.'

The friendliness went out of Miss Cartwright, leaving her brisk and impersonal.

'I think you're being rather silly, Thalia. Finish your breakfast quickly, please. You're keeping us all waiting.'

Nicola stared at her plate and waited for what Tim might say next. But surprisingly, Tim said nothing at all. She gulped her tea and ate the rest of her pear quickly, swallowing the last of it as Miss Keith said grace in a clear final voice which assured everyone that they had had quite enough to eat. After that, the school marched out to the Assembly Hall to sit cross-legged while Miss Keith read the form lists, beginning with the First and working up to the Sixth, accompanied by the inevitable small flurries of congratulation or dismay as someone achieved a move of which she had been uncertain or found that for some reason she had been separated from her friends. Nicola felt glad she knew all there was to know about her form; it would have been rather dreadful to have heard the news suddenly, this morning, at Assembly. She grinned at Lawrie, listened respectfully to Miss Keith's beginning-of-term speech, and scrambled quite cheerfully to her feet to march back to the Division Room for the last time with the rest of the new girls to collect pencil box and ruler and all the oddments before they separated and went off to their form rooms.

'If you give me your book-list,' said Nicola to Lawrie, 'I'll go down to the book-cupboard for our books and you can go and bag desks for us.'

'Get my books too?' said Tim disarmingly, holding out her book-list.

'All right,' said Nicola briefly, remembering about the pear. 'You can take my junk, then.' She planted her pencil box and atlas in Tim's arms and went off down the stairs and corridors to the basement where the book-cupboard was.

It didn't matter so fearfully, thought Nicola, arguing with herself all down the flights of stairs. Sometimes if you were asked unexpectedly you couldn't be absolutely truthful; and over a thing like this it would sound so silly to say, Oh, I forgot, actually I picked them in Aunt Edith's garden. Besides, it wasn't as though someone were being Falsely Accused. It didn't really matter, in a practical way, whether Miss Cartwright thought Tim had brought that pear from home or picked it in the garden. At least, thought Nicola, beginning to feel muddled, if Miss Cartwright hadn't asked it wouldn't have mattered if she'd thought Tim had brought the pear with her; but since she had asked – Nicola shook herself, remembering that that wasn't the conclusion she wanted to arrive at. Because of course, if it should become important to know who had picked the pears – standing in the dark turn of the stairs, Nicola's imagination began to spin: Old Robertson had been accused of stealing the pears and had denied it; and Miss Keith had called a special Assembly and made a speech about it: 'If anyone knows anything of this unhappy matter, will she please come forward now.' And then, of course, thought Nicola in relief, then, *of course*, Tim would get up and say: 'I did it.' Of course she would. Feeling positively light-hearted, Nicola skipped down the rest of the stairs to the basement and presented herself at the book-cupboard.

The Lower Fifth girl in charge, a serious, conscientious individual, was unexpectedly understanding over Nicola's desire to have as many Marlow-used books as possible. They sorted through the piles together, Nicola setting aside the cleanest-looking copies for Tim. When the lists were complete, Nicola signed for them and staggered off to Third Remove. She hoped Lawrie had bagged good desks and had not allowed herself to be pushed out of them by some forceful latecomer.

Third Remove was always a small class and so was given the smallest form room. It was a small square room, with french windows opening on to the balcony above the front porch, on which successive Third Removes were forbidden to stand under threat of direst penalties. The walls were painted dull green and white, and there were one or two pictures on them at which no one ever looked unless they were searching for a word. The twelve desks were arranged in four rows three deep and Tim and Lawrie were seated firmly on the lids of two in the front row, arguing the point with an indignant trio on the floor in front of them. Tim looked amused, Lawrie alarmed; as Nicola staggered forward with her load, she thought it as well that Tim had been there to fight.

'Which is mine?' she demanded.

Tim jerked her head at the one at the end of the row. Nicola slackened her aching arms and let the books pour over lid and seat; then she prepared to fight too.

'It isn't fair,' said the most aggressive of the opposing trio, a pale bony individual, with lank brown hair bobbed in a fringe which parted in limp strands on her forehead. 'It isn't fair. We got here first.'

'But that's what I'm trying to point out,' said Tim easily. 'You *didn't. I* did. Who got up at five in the morning and pasted labels on the desks? Me. You never thought of it. You were snoring in your beds.'

'So she did get up early,' thought Nicola uncomfortably.

'But that doesn't count,' persisted the bony individual. 'It only counts after Miss Keith's read the lists. You can't bag before that.'

'But I have,' said Tim. 'Who made that rule, anyway?'

The three looked at her, nonplussed.

'No one ever does, honestly,' ventured a dark, startled-looking child. 'It really isn't fair, you know.'

'*Fair*,' said Tim contemptuously. 'Besides,' said Tim in an injured voice, 'it's our privilege to sit in the front row. You can't go against that.'

'What privilege?' asked the bony child uneasily.

'Goodness, didn't you know? Oh, well, if you didn't *know*—' She paused tantalizingly.

'Didn't know what?' muttered her opponent.

'About me being Miss Keith's niece and Nick and Lawrie the head girl's sisters. I mean to say, obviously we sit in front.'

There was a slight quiver in Tim's voice as though she badly wanted to laugh, though Nicola couldn't see why. And she wasn't absolutely certain that she wanted to be drawn into the privilege affair; she would have preferred to fight it out on the basis of *I bagged first*. But Tim's method seemed effective; the other three looked at one another, and then retreated, grumbling, to the back of the room. Lawrie climbed down from her desk with a relieved expression and came round to help Nicola pick up and sort the books.

'It is all right, d'you think?' she asked softly.

'I suppose so,' said Nicola doubtfully.

'I wanted to sit next to you,' added Lawrie, 'but Tim said she wanted to be in the middle, and she'd bagged them, so I couldn't say anything. And she said you were to have the new desk. Don't you think she's a bit bossy?'

'Yes,' said Nicola. But she was pleased about the new desk, which stood out, shinning with clean golden varnish, from all the others with their scrubbed rough lids. Even the inkwell looked especially smooth and white and there was a bright brass cap to cover it when it wasn't in use.

'You aren't far from me,' said Nicola encouragingly. 'We can easily talk if we want to, and if we can't in lessons I expect that's just as well.'

' 'M,' said Lawrie. 'Of course, I *like* Tim. It isn't that.'

She scrambled up, her pile of books in her arms, and went off to put them in her desk. Nicola gave Tim her share and began to put her own books away, quietly and neatly, as befitted the desk's immaculate condition.

A muttered argument at the back of the room began to grow in volume. Nicola, her cheeks hot, tried to ignore it and failed.

'Yes, but it isn't fair when you're new to rush in and bag everything.'

'But, Marie, I said we ought to come up early and you said—'

'You didn't say anything about five o'clock. No one's ever thought of getting up at five o'clock before.'

There was a pause.

'Anyway, even if they're going to sit in front, I don't see why that one should have the new desk.'

'No, it isn't fair. Hazel's been here two years. Hazel, you have it.'

'Let's tell them.'

Another pause. A low earnest whispering, too low to be heard. Then:

'Yes, but you *ought* to have it, Hazel. Go and tell her.'

'You tell her. I don't want it specially.'

Nicola concentrated on the arrangement of her pencil box. Suddenly Marie Dobson – the bony one – leaned heavily on her desk lid. In a nervous burst Marie said:

'I say. Hazel wants to change desks with you.'

'No, I don't,' insisted Hazel from the rear. She was pale and dark and serious. 'No, I *don't*, Marie. It's you who's making all the fuss.'

'Well, anyway,' said Marie, shooting a look of fury at Hazel, who seemed relatively unmoved, 'anyway, you can't keep it. You'll have to wait till the others come and draw lots or vote for it or something.'

Nicola's face crimsoned. She wasn't absolutely sure of the ethics of getting up at five in the morning to label desks, but she was perfectly certain she wasn't going to give up her desk because Marie Dobson wanted to make a fuss.

'I'm not going to move my things now. You should have thought of all that ages ago.'

'That's the spirit,', agreed Tim. Her dark crest struck up aggressively. Nicola felt relieved; she was not too sure yet of Tim's reliability as an ally. She had a feeling that Tim might switch to the other side, unexpectedly, for the fun of it.

'I was form prefect last year,' said Marie, pushing at her spectacles, 'and if I say so, you've got to.'

'Last year doesn't count,' retorted Nicola.

'We'll just see,' said Marie ominously. She retreated to her own desk and began to lump her books into it in silence. Nicola, with a great show of nonchalance, began to rearrange her books all over again.

The door opened and the rest came in, the day girls amongst them. They did not contest the tenancy of the front row, but flowed over the rest of the desks, choosing them (so they said) for their distance from the staff desk and the view they commanded of the drive. The other new girl, E. Collins, sat down tentatively and shyly in the vacant desk by Lawrie and began to put her books into it as softly and unobtrusively as possible.

Third Remove settled down with a good deal of noise and a fair show of amiability. For form's sake there were a few who said:

'Oh, you are mean. I bagged sit next Audrey (or Jean or Elaine). Didn't I, Audrey? Didn't I bag first?' But in so small a room, where everyone could lean across to shout to everyone else, such disturbances were few. In the general atmosphere of beginning-of-term goodwill no one was prepared to take Marie's earnest grumbles about the new desk very seriously. Marie Dobson had bossed the Second the year before and they were all rather tired of her. So they said, good-temperedly enough: 'Oh, dry up, Marie. Who wants to vote about an old desk? Go away, Marie; I want to talk to Jean. Well, if you want the desk, go and tell the new girl so. I say, is she the Marlow one who stopped the train?'

They slewed round to talk to Nicola about the train and what Karen was like at home. By the time Pomona Todd came in, carrying her load of books with a disgruntled and injured air, Third Remove (with the exception of Marie, who had retreated behind her desk lid with the smug air of the offended) were well on the road to forgetting who were new girls and who were old and were giggling over a chart Tim was drawing up under the headings: *Backward, Delicate, Plain Stupid*, saying that it would be just as well to know the reason why each had been dumped in Third Remove.

'You never know when it might come in useful,' said Tim, ruling a thick black line under her three headings. 'I'm going to be Backward. What are you, Nick?'

'Plain Stupid,' said Nicola quickly in case anyone else said it first. 'And so's Lawrie, aren't you, Lawrie?'

''M,' said Lawrie. She had been sharpening pencils for the past half-hour and it required all her concentration. Pencils were Lawrie's delight; and Giles had given her a dozen before she came to school and all required sharpening.

'I'll be Delicate,' said Daphne with a giggle. 'What'll you be, Hazel?'

'I'll be Delicate too,' said Hazel.

'And me,' said Audrey. 'What are you going to do with that list, Tim?'

'Pin it inside my desk till it's needed. Who else wants to be Delicate?'

'I'm delicate,' said Pomona Todd. 'I told Matron so and that Mother wouldn't like me to carry all these books, and she told me to make two journeys of it.'

Third Remove, most of whom were leaning over Tim or one another to watch the progress of the chart, turned to look at Pomona, as she hugged her books to her chest, expectant of sympathy. But Third Remove merely stared in silent hostility, wondering why Matron had not hustled her into stockings and tunic and plaits, instead of allowing her to disgrace them with that frightful silk jibbah thing and messy hair.

'Where am I going to sit, anyway?' asked Pomona in a tone of increased injury, into the hostile silence.

Third Remove looked unhelpful. Tim said impishly:

'There's no room for you. You're too late.'

Third Remove took her up joyfully.

'Poor old Pomona.'

'Not one desk left.'

'You'll have to ask IIIA to take you in.'

'Oo, yes! There's lots of room there, 'cos they're so clever.'

'You ask IIIA, Pomona. They won't mind.'

'You can't stay here. There isn't any room.'

Pomona's chest heaved and the end of her nose grew pink. Jean Baker, a kind-hearted child, observed these symptoms with alarm. She said:

'There's a desk by Elaine. Over there, in the corner.'

Pomona ceased to look as though she were on the verge of tears and looked sulky instead. She said sullenly:

'I'm not going to sit in the dark like that. Mother wouldn't want me to. She's most particular about my eyes.'

'Why, Pippin?' asked Tim. 'Are they your one beauty?'

'You're not to call me that,' cried Pomona, and, to the shocked surprise of Third Remove, who had, on the whole, outgrown such manifestations, stamped her foot. 'You're to call me by my proper name. Mother says if you've got a beautiful name it's stupid to cover it up with a silly nickname like you do.'

'What *is* her name?' asked someone who had not encountered Pomona before.

Tim told her. 'It's the name of the Roman goddess who presided over the fruit trees,' she added with a coy simper. 'You remember, dear, the French lessons you had last year? La Pomme – the apple: la Pomme-de-terre – the potato? That's our Pippin.'

'Apple blossom,' said someone hopefully.

'Winter russets.'

'Cox's orange.'

'Blenheims.'

'Cider,' shouted someone on a burst of inspiration.

'One a day will be enough,' decided Tim. 'To-day it will be Pippin. To-morrow Audrey can think of something. Write it up on the blackboard before prayers, Audrey dear, so that we all know Pippin's name for to-morrow.'

Third Remove laughed heartlessly, pleased with its victim. It was, perhaps, as well that Miss Cartwright should come in at that moment, remark what a nice day it was and add that someone might really have opened a window. Miss Cartwright's fetish for fresh air was unusual among the staff; she was apt to eye the windows regretfully, even when the ledges were rimmed with snow. Hazel and Jean leapt to the french windows.

'And don't go out on the balcony, you two. Remember, all of you, never walk on the balcony. Not even if the school's on fire.'

Lawrie, looking alarmed, wondered if Miss Cartwright meant by that that a fire was a likely occurrence.

'Pomona, haven't you found a desk yet?' added Miss Cartwright briskly.

'Only in that corner,' said Pomona plaintively.

'Right. Go and sit down, then; and put your books away. I'm sorry I'm late,' added Miss Cartwright, strolling over to the french windows and looking as though she might wander out through sheer absent-mindedness, 'but I think we've just time before the bell goes to elect the form officers. Twelve of you, aren't there? Suppose we elect the two form prefects and put the rest of the jobs into a hat and draw for them? How will that suit you? Right. Let's have your nominations.'

'Jean,' said Elaine.

'Hazel,' said Audrey.

There was a pause. Marie Dobson turned a dull red and looked down at her desk.

'Tim,' said Lawrie suddenly, blushing hotly.

'I don't think we'll have a new girl,' said Miss Cartwright cheerfully. 'Anyone else, besides Jean and Hazel? No? Well, that makes it all very pleasant and straightforward. Right. Then I'll write down the rest of the jobs on these slips of paper – give me that wooden box, Jean – right – and they can go in there – and Jean can pass it round.'

Tim and Lawrie drew the Flower Monitress slips and were reasonably pleased about it. Pomona became Thermometer Monitress and Marie Dobson drew Stationery. Nicola drew Tidiness, to her infinite disgust, although she listened with her most polite expression while Miss Cartwright explained that it was up to her to see that the desks were in line, morning and afternoon, that the racks were tidy, and that all the waste paper was inside the waste-paper basket.

'If we win the Tidiness Picture it will probably be mostly your doing, though everyone should help you by keeping their bit of the room straight,' said Miss Cartwright encouragingly.

Nicola said obediently: 'Yes, Miss Cartwright,' and Tim said under her breath: 'See you make us all shipshape and Bristol fashion, mate,' at which Nicola giggled.

'Just one thing,' said Miss Cartwright, looking at her watch. 'I know the school is apt to be rather silly about the Third Remove, and Miss Keith is particularly anxious that no one should feel it's a disgrace to be here. Most of you know why it is that you're behind with your work – Hazel was away nearly all last term with whooping cough, Elaine missed a lot last year through her brothers getting mumps – and all the rest of you have equally good reasons. Tim, for instance, has done so much travelling that she hasn't had time for school, have you, Tim?'

Tim grinned.

'So don't feel, any of you, that you've been put in Third Remove because you're outstandingly brainless. Just tell IIIB from me that there are far more *really* stupid people amongst them than there are here.'

'Hear, hear,' said Third Remove.

'This is really a coaching form for people we think are worth it, so in its way, it's really rather a compliment to be here for a while. Some of you may not even spend a full term here. It wouldn't surprise me if one or two of you were moved into one of the other Thirds at half-term. So don't feel discouraged; just make up your minds to get on with your work and don't take any notice of the people who try to be funny.'

'There's only one snag in that,' said Tim, as Miss Cartwright left the room.

'What?' asked Lawrie, disappointed.

'Our Pippin. I can't truly feel anyone would class her among the most promising girls in the school.'

5 —And Nicola Loses It

In the general confused excitement of settling-in, Nicola forgot that there had been any argument about her possession of that particular desk. Marie Dobson did not forget, however. Marie remembered her defeats, sucking persistently at the memory as though it were a particularly hard, particularly unpleasant-tasting toffee. Out of favour with her contemporaries for no better reason than that she was herself and they no longer liked her, she became Pomona Todd's best friend in the peculiarly obvious manner in which Marie became best friends with anyone. Marie, leaning over Pomona's desk between lessons, talking privately with Pomona in a corner of the gym, or walking round the playing fields with her arm round Pomona's waist, made their status sufficiently plain to everyone. When the rest of Third Remove referred to Pomona as Apple Peel, Marie rushed to her friend's defence, saying, in the monotonous delivery which made Nicola tingle with irritation, that it was awfully unkind to be so beastly to a new girl; and by way of retaliation, would whisper rapidly to Pomona, look quickly at any member of Third Remove within eyeshot and then burst into loud snorts of suppressed laughter.

Pomona submitted passively to these favours, eating steadily through the parcels of food which came to her from home (Mrs. Todd, said the Third Remove enviously, seemed to think her Pippin got nothing to eat between one meal and the next) and occasionally offering Marie one of the less interesting biscuits. Her outward appearance was now (following a short sharp engagement with Matron on the subject of uniform which had ended in complete victory for Matron) perfectly normal; but no one could quite forget their first sight of her. She appeared to listen to Marie's earnest complaints about the cheek and rudeness of new girls who bagged the front row and the newest desks, and now and again held the floor herself with long rambling statements about her headaches and the meanness of Miss Cartwright in letting her sit at the back of the room. After a few days, Marie began to see that they might, with advantage, put their grievances together.

She tried constitutional means first. With Pomona waiting hopefully at a distance, she accosted Miss Cartwright outside the Staff Room and put the case to her. Pomona, said Marie in effect, was subject to headaches; Pomona was, through a mere accident of faulty timing, sitting in the back row; now that these facts had been brought to Miss Cartwright's notice, surely nothing could be easier than for Miss Cartwright to rectify the position. Preferably by letting Pomona change places with Nicola Marlow.

Miss Cartwright was unsympathetic. Why, with a glance at the distant Pomona, had Pomona not come herself? Did Pomona wear glasses? Because if Pomona could not see across the very short distance of Third Remove classroom, then Miss Cartwright felt she should see an oculist. Marie, said Miss Cartwright briskly, but not unkindly, must not become a busybody. If Pomona or anyone else wanted to complain about something, they must come to her themselves; not send messages by Marie.

Marie withdrew, hurt and baffled, but by no means defeated, being possessed of a dull obstinacy which could carry her successfully through any number of snubs. Pomona, her interest aroused, suggested that they should ask Nicola to change; or, since it didn't very much matter where she sat, so long as it was in the front row, that Lawrie or Elizabeth Collins might be easier.

Marie considered this. She suffered from the conviction, common in junior forms, that one face was much the same as another to the form mistress, and that Miss Cartwright would, therefore, be unlikely to notice the substitution of a P. Todd for a Marlow twin or an E. Collins. Elizabeth would be the most easily tackled; much more easily than Nicola, for instance; but then there was the question of the desk. To Marie it was of supreme importance that Nicola should lose that new and glossy desk, which had been obtained by such extremely questionable methods. They *could* ask Nicola; on the other hand, if Nicola refused there was little more they could do; better, thought Marie with sudden inspiration, *much* better if they were to change the books over themselves and present Nicola with a *fait accompli*. There would be nothing for Nicola to do then, thought Marie triumphantly, with the narrow vision of the set purpose, but go grumbling to the back of the room and sit down in the desk assigned to her.

They changed the books over during the half-hour break following midday dinner. In the usual way they would have had time and to spare, but it was a wet day and the only amusement offered was games with bean-bags in the gym, taken by Val Longstreet, who was one of the duller prefects. After a while Tim jerked her head and she and Nicola and Lawrie slipped unobtrusively out of the gym, and made their way upstairs, stopping now and then by the various notice boards to read the notices out of pure boredom.

'Let's go up to Third Remove and rearrange the flowers,' suggested Tim at last. 'I didn't really care for this morning's effect, did you? A trifle – what shall I say? – *sans intérêt*.'

'Swank,' said Lawrie automatically. 'All right. Let's. Nick can watch and tell us what it looks like.'

'Thanks awfully,' said Nicola. 'It's most trimmensely good of you.' But even watching Tim and Lawrie do flowers was more amusing than bean bags with Val Longstreet who was constantly blowing her whistle for silence, and never starting the race at all.

Marie and Pomona had just finished. They had arranged that when Nicola and the rest came up at half-past two, Pomona would be sitting in the seat of the desk and Marie on the lid, chatting easily to one another. There would be hardly any time for argument before Miss Cromwell arrived for maths, and by the end of the afternoon Pomona's claim to the front desk would be established. In the event, however, Nicola, Tim and Lawrie opened the door at two-fifteen to find Marie and Pomona standing giggling by Nicola's open desk.

'What are you doing?' said Nicola sharply.

The conspirators looked taken aback; then Marie, making the best of a bad job, said ingratiatingly:

'You don't mind, do you, Nick? Poor old Pomona can't see a thing from the back row and I was sure you wouldn't mind changing.'

'Were you, by gad?' said Nicola. 'Well, I do mind. I'm not changing for anyone.'

She slid quickly into her desk seat and sat stubbornly, looking as much like a fixture as she could manage. Then she became aware of the different arrangement of the books. She looked more closely.

'Have you had the unspeakable nerve to shift my stuff?' cried Nicola furiously.

'It's awfully selfish of you to behave like this,' said Marie reproachfully. 'I never thought you would, you know.

I mean, honestly, when a person can't see—'

'Rotten,' said Tim, wagging her head. 'After all, Nick ought to be jolly grateful to you for taking the trouble to change the books over and pointing out what a meanie she is to want the desk our Worcester Permain happens to have set her heart on. Thank the kind lady, Nicola dear; thank her nicely and say you're sorry.'

'She jolly well ought to take the books back again,' cried Lawrie indignantly. 'Marie, I mean.'

'I shouldn't dream of it,' said Marie quickly. 'And nor will Pomona. She's got just as much right to that desk as Nicola has.'

'Then I've as much right to it as she has,' retorted Nicola. 'That makes us even.'

'Good,' said Tim approvingly.

'Well, I'm not going to move them,' said Marie righteously. 'So if you're going to be so absolutely mean, you'll have to do it yourself.'

'Right,' said Nicola. She plunged both hands into the desk and began to fling the books over her shoulders in the easy fashion of one throwing salt.

The others watched fascinated for a moment; so did the rest of Third Remove who had begun to collect in the form room with the over-promptitude common to wet days; then, as a *Hall & Knight* crashed to the floor with a perceptibly loosened cover, Pomona broke into loud outcry.

'Stop it, Nicola! Leave my things alone! You're breaking them! Nicola! Stop it!'

'Shift them yourself, then,' said Nicola unmoved. 'I don't mind. This is my way of moving them. If you know a better—' She continued to toss books over her shoulder.

Scuffling clumsily, Pomona gathered up all she could reach and tried to stuff them into the new desk again. Tim giggled. Nicola slammed the lid shut, just missing Pomona's hurriedly withdrawn fingers. Pomona stamped hysterically.

'I want this desk! I won't sit at the back!'

'Don't be so silly,' retorted Nicola.

Marie, who had also been picking up the books within reach, dropped her pile with a sudden thud on the lid of the desk. A blob of ink jumped out on to the shining varnish. Nicola looked with rage, first at the little circle of ink, then at Marie's dumb, red, angry face above her.

'Take those beastly books off my desk!'

'I won't. Pomona's going to sit here.'

'She – is – *not.*'

'She *is.*'

With a quick, furious movement, Nicola pushed at the slowly sliding books; they fell to the ground in a series of small thunderclaps. Third Remove looked on with interest.

'You go away,' said Nicola, leaning protective arms over her desk lid.

'I won't,' said Pomona tearfully, groping once more on the floor. 'I *want* to sit here. I think you're beastly.' She picked up the unfortunate *Hall & Knight* whose cover now hung by a thread; grabbed at it as the pages swung loose, and only succeeded in tearing the first leaves. Her voice rose. 'And now look what you've made me do. You've made me tear it. Look! *Look* at it! I shall tell Miss Cartwright! I shall tell her you—'

'I shouldn't bother,' said Tim negligently. 'You won't understand *Hall & Knight*, anyway.'

'She's crying,' said someone from the back of the room in an impersonal voice which suggested that whoever might be responsible for that calamity it was not the speaker.

Pomona was. Not quietly and unobtrusively as people did if it were forced on them, but loudly and without restraint.

She climbed to her feet and began to try to pull Nicola out of her seat.

'I'm *going* to sit here,' wept Pomona.

Nicola fought back happily, pitting her small wiry strength against Pomona's greater height and weight. The Third Remove cheered them on, drunk with the joy of battle, and with no notion of the noise they were making. Inch by inch, Nicola prised Pomona's fingers from her person and the desk. She had almost freed herself, when Pomona made a last desperate plunge at her. They swayed for a moment, locked together; then desk and combatants fell sideways in one final, glorious crash.

The room went quiet. Nicola, who was underneath, fought urgently to get her mouth free of Pomona's hair. Then Pomona was jerked suddenly away from her and her sister Karen's voice said icily:

'Get up at once, Nicola. What on earth d'you think you're doing?'

Rather shakily, Nicola got to her feet. The desk – her beautiful desk – lay on its side, a stream of ink running down the lid. 'Blue blood,' thought Nicola, but said nothing aloud.

It was Pomona who plunged into loud and incoherent explanation. Marie, her face crimson, had gone back to sit in her own desk, so ostentatiously dissociated from all commotion that her very detachment was conspicuous. Karen's attention, however, was focused on the chief combatants and Pomona's tearful outcry. From it, Karen gathered that both had bagged the same desk at the same time on First Day and had done battle for it ever since. Third Remove protested.

'Oo! They *didn't*, Karen!'

'Nicky's had it *ages*.'

'Pomona never said a *thing* about it before.'

'Be quiet, all of you,' snapped Karen. If any of the staff came in and saw the room as it was now – desk overturned, ink flowing across the boards, books lying all over the place – there would be the most appalling row. And afterwards: 'Where were you when the trouble began, Karen? In the prefects' study? But surely you must have heard—? Then why—?' And her reason, if she were so foolish as to give it, that she had been trying to finish a history essay for Miss Ferguson before half-past two, would sound even more feeble than her angry and futile hope that the noise was merely Third Remove's normal method of settling down for the afternoon.

'Pick up that desk,' said Karen curtly, '*and* those books. How on earth did they get there?'

'I threw them,' said Nicola with equal curtness. She sounded cross and scornful and she refused to look at Karen, twisting round to brush the back of her short pleated skirt.

'Then you'd better pick them up again,' returned Karen sharply. She wished that some other junior could have been involved or else that some other prefect could have heard that frightful culminating thump; it was, she recognized, equally embarrassing for both Nicola and herself. She said quickly: 'It's a particularly idiotic way to behave, whatever the reason. If you weren't both so new, I'd report you to Miss Cartwright and let you see what she thought of such nonsense.'

Nicola said nothing; she had split the knee of her stocking and the sleeve of her blouse was torn; also her shoulder felt sore where she had bumped it. Pomona sniffed pathetically.

'You mustn't be so incredibly childish,' continued Karen. 'I don't know why you both want this particular desk and place and I'm not interested. But since you are so set on it,

Nicola can have the place and Pomona the desk—'

'Just like Solomon,' said someone, inspired.

Karen glanced up sharply. A desk lid opened and the speaker hid her confusion behind it.

'You'd better change desks now,' said Karen stonily. 'Quickly, please.'

Nicola opened her mouth and shut it again. Karen, her hands in her pockets, stood and watched, thinking optimistically that she was being both fair and impartial. Third Remove knew she wasn't. But no one protested. In silence the desk was set the right way up again, in silence the desks were changed, in silence Nicola gathered up Pomona's books from the floor and placed them with exaggerated care on the new desk lid. Pomona rubbed her knee and continued to sniff, sitting, with an injured expression, on the staff dais. Karen ignored her, watching Lawrie, who, in evident, but suppressed, fury was using the week's supply of form blotting-paper to mop the spilt ink off the floor. Nicola sat down in her desk and stared nonchalantly out of the window, whistling a little. Karen eyed her. If she were sent to change blouse and stockings now she would be late for the afternoon's lesson and then there would be more fuss. Better to leave it alone and trust to luck that whoever took the Third Remove should suppose that her appearance was caused by over-enthusiasm for bean bags.

'There are only two minutes before the bell goes,' said Karen. 'D'you suppose you can behave yourselves without supervision for that long?'

Sulkily, Third Remove agreed that they could. They continued to sit in quite unnatural silence when she had gone. No one, remembering that Karen was the twins' sister, cared to remark that she was a silly ass and that it wasn't fair.

6 A New Patrol

I

Out of pure perversity, Lawrie said, it rained regularly the first two weeks every Tuesday and Thursday, simply, said Lawrie, because those were the afternoons on which the Thirds played games. It also rained, as Rowan pointed out, an occasional Wednesday and Friday when the school teams were supposed to practise. But Lawrie was not concerned; it was far worse, she contended, for the Thirds to miss their games because the school teams knew they were good; the Thirds didn't.

'Nice for us,' said Rowan laconically. 'Anyway, it looks fine today. You ought to get your run in the park this afternoon.'

'We're not dogs,' said Nicola with dignity.

'N-no,' said Rowan doubtfully. 'Though when you haven't combed your hair there's a distinct resemblance.'

Nicola, looking proud, refused to continue the conversation. She hung out of the window, sniffing the smoky autumn air and watching the soft haze which hid the sea.

'Put on your dressing-gown,' said Ann, 'if you must lean out of the window at this hour of the morning. You don't want bronchitis again.'

Nicola took no notice.

'Or better still, get dressed,' said Rowan indolently. 'It's getting on for breakfast.'

Nicola dropped back into the room, eyeing the lump and scrumple of hair which indicated Ginty in bed, grabbed dressing-gown, sponge, toothbrush and towel, and announced as she shot through the door:

'*I* bags the bath this morning.'

'Blast the child,' said Ginty, sitting up. 'She knows it's my turn.'

'Your own fault,' said Rowan with a grin. 'It's after quarterpast seven. Anyone can grab now.'

'Wish I was in an ordinary dorm,' said Ginty, lying down again. 'They're much more civilized there. Monica never gets up till a quarter-to and no one ever dreams of grabbing.'

'Probably they're just more grubby,' said Lawrie. 'Why are you so early, Rowan?'

'Going to early practice. The first cup match is next week.'

'Oh. With anyone? I mean,' Lawrie sought for words of ineffable tact, 'we couldn't sort of drift along and – and be coached a little so as to be ready for this afternoon? Could we?'

Rowan looked silent discouragement. Ginty said: 'Shrieks of silent mirth,' and Ann said: 'But you won't be playing netball this term.'

'Nor you will,' said Rowan mildly, and began to knot her tie.

'Wh-what d'you mean?' said Lawrie. Her inside felt as though the strings holding it had suddenly slackened. 'Of *course* we shall play. We told you in the holidays that we were going to be in the team this term because of the tradition and be absolutely the youngest Marlows who ever played—'

'Wait, wait, wait,' said Rowan patiently. They all knew Lawrie's wild spate of words when confronted with disaster. Lawrie stammered and subsided into uneasy silence.

'All *that*,' said Rowan, 'was before your intellectual débâcle.'

'You do swank, Rowan. Before our *what*?'

'Before you were stuck in the Third Remove.'

'But that's absolutely nothing to do with netball, Rowan. Nothing at all. You can't pretend it is. It's simply silly—'

'Listen, my poor goop. Third Removes, according to Miss Keith, are delicate, gentle little souls who aren't strong enough to romp in rough games like netball. But exercise being good for them they *are* allowed to go into Upper Field and play rounders.'

'But, Rowan,' said Lawrie gently, as one who informs the ignorant, 'the other Thirds play netball. IIIA and IIIB do, I mean.'

'Of course they do. I didn't say anything about IIIA or IIIB. I said Third Remove.'

'I don't believe it,' said Lawrie at last. 'I don't believe it, Rowan. You're teasing like you do, and I don't think it's specially funny. It'd be much better for you to take it back now before we find out. Because this afternoon we shall find out, you know—'

'Don't be an ass,' said Rowan kindly. 'I'm not teasing in the least. Ask Cartwright. Ask anyone. Ann told you before I did, as a matter of fact. Gosh, I'm going to be late.' She dragged her pullover over her head and dashed out of the room.

'I don't believe it,' said Lawrie defiantly, to Ginty and Ann.

Ginty yawned and rolled out of bed. Ann, splashing at the washbasin, dried her face and said: 'It's quite true, Lawrie, honestly. I'd no idea you didn't know.'

'You might as well believe it,' added Ginty, 'because you're obviously going to cry about it and you may as well do it now as at breakfast.'

Lawrie's chin quivered. ''M not,' she said in a shaken voice.

'All right. You're not. Then you'd better get dressed.'

'You've not even started,' said Lawrie crossly. 'And I *don't* believe it.'

'I'll be ready before you are,' retorted Ginty, which was true, because Ginty's dressing average was four and a half minutes. 'And you know you do believe it, so you may just as well stop saying that.'

Lawrie stamped into her cubicle and dragged the curtains shut with a rattle. Ginty and Ann looked at one another, shrugged resignedly and went on dressing. Ginty pulled a comb through her hair and went out, looking clean, neat and unruffled. Ann tied the ribbons at the end of her plaits and asked doubtfully:

'Are you all right, Lawrie?'

'*Yes.*'

'Are you getting dressed?'

'*Yes.*'

'I've got to go and do the form flowers. Are you *sure* you're all right?'

'*Yes*, I tell you.'

The door closed on Ann.

Lawrie, savagely untidy, her tie knotted so that one end hung below her waist and the other poked out just below the knot, sat on the edge of her rumpled bed, the tears sliding down her cheeks so fast that her face was wet where she had wiped the tears aside with the back of her hand.

Because this was absolutely the very worst thing that had ever happened. Lawrie, looking back through memory as through the wrong end of a telescope, saw an occasional minor disaster seeming amazingly flat, tame and babyish in comparison with no netball for Third Remove: there was, for instance, the time she had torn up some of her father's most important papers in a sudden, inexplicable fit of tidiness; and there was the time Nicola had put the entire family in quarantine for mumps the morning of the day they were going to the circus. And on both occasions, Lawrie supposed distantly, she had cried a bit. If only she had known what was coming, she wouldn't have bothered to cry for the other things. She would have saved it all up for this.

Because it had been going to be so glorious, the way she and Nicola had planned it. Going into IIIA and immediately capturing the first and second places in the form; and then being picked out, after the very first practice, to be coached for the junior team, so that everyone said: 'Goodness, the two newest Marlows are better than all the rest put together.' 'If only we hadn't *told* anyone,' thought Lawrie, who always and inevitably told what she planned to do, because to Lawrie the planning itself meant accomplishment, 'if we hadn't told anyone they wouldn't know we hadn't done it.'

She continued to cry, her hands squeezed tightly together between her knees, the tears sliding down her cheeks and splashing like thunder drops on her serge skirt.

Nicola, returning from her bath and seeing Lawrie's drawn curtains, was instantly certain something dreadful had happened. It might, of course, be something dreadful to Lawrie only, like breaking her tooth glass or losing her plimsolls. Without wishing to be at all unkind or heartless, Nicola rather hoped it was something of that sort.

'It's nearly breakfast time,' she said, ducking through Lawrie's curtains. 'What's happened?'

In a desperate, tear-flawed voice, Lawrie told her.

II

'So we'll have to join Guides,' said Nicola to Tim. 'There's really nothing else we *can* do.'

'Isn't there really?' said Tim lazily. She and Lawrie were sitting on their desk lids, consuming eleven-o'clock buns and milk and watching Nicola tidy the form room. Nicola, who was apt to become fiercely involved in the odd jobs which came her way, had taken the office of Tidiness Monitress seriously. No one ever knew when Miss Craven, the gym mistress, who marked the form rooms throughout the term, would appear with her note-book and pencil; it might be two days running, or there might be an interval of a fortnight. Other people forgot about form tidiness, but Nicola remembered. Grimly, but with a certain enjoyment, she bullied the rest of Third Remove into keeping the room reasonably tidy, and stayed behind, when necessary, to put the finishing touches to it herself.

Tim watched placidly while Nicola shoved Pomona's desk into line with a vicious little jerk. She still coveted the new desk, although its pristine freshness had vanished after its fall, and the trail of ink and long splinter of wood which had broken away from the lid had ruined its beauty for ever. Nevertheless, Nicola still felt annoyed that Pomona should have won it, and still more annoyed that she should not appreciate what she had won. No one who really enjoyed a new desk, thought Nicola crossly, would leave crumbs and stickiness all over it for other people to put their fingers into. She muttered crossly and rubbed hers resentfully on the top of her stocking.

It had been necessary to tell Tim what had happened that morning because she was so persistent. Unlike the rest of Third Remove, she had refused to accept politely the normal fiction that Lawrie had a cold. 'It's perfectly obvious,' Tim had remarked calmly and without malice, 'that Lawrie's been howling her head off. And I'd like to know why, if it's not asking too much.'

'Do you *want* to be Guides?' pursued Tim, nibbling the sugar off the top of her bun.

'Y-yes,' said Nicola doubtfully. 'Not as awfully as all that – not as much as being in the team, I mean – but quite. And anyway, that's not the point. It's that we've got to be good at *something*.'

'You oughtn't to put it like that,' said Lawrie reproachfully, eyeing Nicola over the rim of her glass. 'Being Guides was always one of the things we said we'd do. You know it was.'

Tim looked impish. 'I remember. "We're going to pass our Tenderfoot and fly up and get our Second Class badges all in one term." That was the Guide bit, wasn't it?'

Lawrie turned pink.

'Yes, it was,' she said defiantly. 'And I don't see why we shouldn't. We were extremely good Brownies. Nicola was a Sixer.'

'Look out! We're the jolly Pixies,
Helping others when in fixes.'

quoted Nicola dreamily. She picked up a ball of paper and dropped it into the waste-paper basket.

'We're the Fairies glad and gay,
Helping others every day.'

countered Lawrie instantly.

Tim looked faintly sick.

'Did you really say things like that?'

'Yes,' said Lawrie, surprised. 'Those were our Sixes' calls. Why?'

'I suppose it does sound a bit mad at our age,' agreed

Nicola, blushing, 'but that was years ago. When we were quite young.'

'H'm,' said Tim. 'And what do Guides say?'

'Oh, they're perfectly reasonable. They only have a Law and a Promise.'

'And how do they go?' asked Tim innocently.

'I haven't the least idea,' said Nicola swiftly.

Tim grinned at her and desisted.

'What I don't see,' she said, swallowing the last of her bun, 'is why you go on wanting to be so amazingly outstanding at everything.'

'Because all the others are,' said Lawrie simply.

'Yes, but if it doesn't come natural—'

'We told you on the train,' said Nicola, pink with the effort of explanation. 'It's that – well, that there's Giles being brilliant in the Navy, and Kay doing an Oxford Schol, and Rowan in all the teams she can be and Ann always winning the form prize and absolute yards of Guide badges, and Ginty in second eleven hockey and Peter doing awfully well at Dartmouth and what do we do? Catch measles.'

'And they all say – perfectly kindly, mind you – oh, well, the twins can't help it and the twins are delicate and naturally the twins are all behind and of course everyone understands why and we aren't to worry about it in the least,' added Lawrie breathlessly.

'Very trying,' said Tim. She looked at Nicola who was gazing over the immaculate form room with a satisfied air and added: 'Are you eating that bun, Nick, or just holding it?'

'Eating it,' said Nicola, biting hastily. 'How hungry you always are. Couldn't you be a Guide too, Tim?'

'No, I shouldn't think so. Why?'

'Because then it won't be so bad,' said Nicola frankly. 'For us, I mean.'

'If it's going to be so awful—'

'Oh, not Guides themselves. They'll be all right; one goes on hikes and things and there are Rallies,' said Nicola vaguely. 'No, it's having Ann. She's awfully kind and all that and on all her reports they say how good she is with the younger ones, but she is most horribly helpful. If she thinks she can do something for you, you never get within an inch of it. I bet you anything you like she asks to have us in her Patrol.'

The bell began to ring for the end of recreation. Tim shook her head.

'I feel for you deeply,' she said kindly, 'but nothing on earth could make me wade into something with Laws and Promises and Hikes and Rallies – not to mention your sister Ann's Patrol. Besides, my poppets, our Apfelstrudel is going to be a Guide. I heard her and Marie talking about it yesterday.'

III

Ann was tremendously pleased when Lawrie, squatting on her haunches beside her in the empty gym while Ann tied morse and semaphore flags into separate bundles, asked whether Ann thought Miss Redmond would have them. Ann, who took Guiding seriously, was apt to be periodically distressed that none of the rest of the family would be Guides also. Kay and Rowan said, with truth and reason, that one way and another they simply hadn't the time; Ginty said regretfully that though she would adore camp, she'd never be able to summon up energy enough to work for badges all the time as Ann did, what with hockey in the winter and spring, and swimming in the summer, and school work on top of that. That left the twins. And for months now the family had listened with a certain amusement to what Rowan called Ann's propaganda service, urging Nicola and Lawrie not to be taken in when Ann said persuasively: 'Shall I tell Captain you want to join as soon as we get back?' or 'It's a shame there isn't a company near enough for you to join here. It'll be fun when you get to Kingscote, won't it?'

So now Ann sat back on her heels and said:

'Of course. Why not?'

'Well, we haven't been exactly brilliant this term, so far,' said Lawrie sadly, 'and she can't possibly know whether we'll turn out to be credits to the Company or not, but we thought—'

'We thought as there wasn't anything else we could be good at this term, we'd better have a shot at Guides,' said Nicola abruptly.

It wasn't quite what Lawrie had been going to say, nor at all what Ann had hoped for, but she immediately became reassuring.

'No one will expect you to be outstanding,' she said. 'Only to do your best and join in things and have a good time. Don't worry so about being good at things. You'll get on all right as soon as you've settled in. I'll see if I can't have you in my Patrol, at any rate while you're recruits.'

'You don't have to bother about us,' said Nicola gruffly, leaning against the wall-ribs. 'We don't want to be a nuisance. We just wanted to know how we got hold of Miss Redmond and told her and all that.'

'That's perfectly all right,' said Ann at once. 'People who join nearly always ask someone in the Company and she asks Captain . . . I'll look after you, Nicky; don't worry about it.'

'I'm not,' said Nicola. 'Look, Ann, you don't have to bother having us in your Patrol. I mean, you needn't, you know. It's awfully kind and all that, but—'

'But I'd like to,' said Ann briskly, getting up with the bundles of flags in her arms. 'I've got to take these to Captain now, anyway. I'll ask her at once and let you know.'

IV

Miss Redmond, who, besides teaching domestic science, was also the Guide Captain, looked nicer, Lawrie thought, in her navy uniform, cocked hat and light blue tie than in her everyday clothes. All that afternoon Lawrie had been regretting bitterly that their Brownie uniforms were so unmistakably too small for them; Ann had polished their Brownie badges for them and it was certainly something that they had those to wear, but it wasn't the same as having the right clothes for the part . . . Lawrie, who secretly saw her Guide self as someone quite different from her school self – taller, for instance and very much more dashing – was deeply disappointed that she could not wear her uniform and give Captain the full salute.

Captain, however, did not seem to notice any deficiencies. She seemed very friendly, and not at all as though she had, only that morning, told Lawrie that she would never catch a husband if she couldn't remember to put salt in her greens. She shook hands with them left-handedly and said how nice it was to have two more Marlows in the Guides and that she hoped they would be very happy in the 3rd Wade Company.

'I think Ann would like to have you in her Patrol, at least until you pass your Tenderfoot,' said Captain, smiling over their heads at Ann who stood behind them. 'Have you got anyone among the Cornflowers, Ann, who needs to teach a recruit for her First Class?'

'Rita and Pamela both need one,' said Ann confidently. She and Captain liked and trusted one another, and Ann was never nervous of being snubbed by her as she occasionally was by other members of the staff who, like Nicola, were apt to find her helpfulness a trifle exasperating.

'Run along to the Cornflowers, then,' said Captain cheerfully, 'and when you've passed your Tenderfoot we'll see about a permanent home for you. Just a moment, Ann. There are one or two things—'

Nicola remembered her half salute before she turned away; Lawrie, to her annoyance, forgot. Glad of one another's company they went over to the Cornflower Patrol corner and announced themselves, shyly, to Denise Fenton, the Patrol Second.

To their relief, however, no one seemed to think it a tiresome thing to be saddled with Ann Marlow's young sisters who were in the Third Remove and condemned to play rounders. On the contrary, the Cornflowers seemed to feel they were being specially favoured: and rather to her surprise, Nicola discovered that this was because they liked and admired Ann. She had taken it for granted that though Ann was a Patrol Leader and had passed all sorts of badge tests, people would be apt to feel for her the same vague, constant irritation that Nicola herself felt. But this apparently was not so. 'Ann's *heaps* the best Patrol Leader,' she was informed by Rita Calthrop, as she helped the latter unpack the Patrol cupboard and arrange the various items in their proper places. 'You're awfully lucky not to have been dumped in the Daisies with Jen Wallace. She's frightfully wet.'

'Is she?' said Nicola politely, sitting back on her heels to admire the Patrol log-book with its canvas cover worked in squares of bright blue wool. She opened it and grinned at the sight of the matchstick men who rioted across the pages as illustrations to the manuscript. 'Did Ann do these?'

asked Nicola. 'She can draw a bit, they tell me.'

'No, we all do them,' said Rita, looking over her shoulder. 'That's what's so reasonable about Ann. She doesn't bag all the best things for herself like some of them do. She hands out the jobs and lets one get on with them.'

'*Does* she?' said the astonished Nicola. 'Well, I'm blessed!'

'Why?' said Rita severely. 'What are you being so surprised about?'

'Nothing,' said Nicola hastily, 'nothing at all.' It was not, she felt, for Ann's sister to tell Ann's Patrol what Ann was like at home. Definitely not. Then, to her relief, Ann herself came running back and Captain blew her whistle for inspection.

Being recruits, they stood, as Ann had told them that afternoon, at the end of the Patrol line and did not count for or against their Patrol's score. None of the Cornflowers, to Lawrie's passionate relief, lost a mark, although, when she looked down the line after Ann had stood them at ease, she noticed that no one else looked specially exultant. Probably, thought Lawrie proudly, none of the Cornflowers ever lost a mark at inspection; and Ann, when questioned that evening, admitted that on the whole this was so. Because they had won the Patrol Shield the year before, the Cornflowers stood in front of the others and so could not see how the rest of the Company fared; but they could hear all that went on, and although they kept their faces severely expressionless, not one of them missed the fact that the Daisies and Snowdrops both lost a mark apiece; they refrained from comment, however, when the parade was dismissed, returning to their Patrol corner, and falling immediately into talk of Patrol matters. And then Nicola and Lawrie were handed over to Rita and Pamela to begin learning their Tenderfoot test, while the others settled down to practice signalling or watch

Ann demonstrate the proper way to fix a splint.

'We're all going in for our Ambulance badges so that we can put it on the Patrol flag,' explained Pamela, seeing that Lawrie's attention was wandering from the Law and Promise which were being explained to her. 'We've all got Book Lover's – that's frightfully easy – and Child Nurse and Cook because you need them for First Class. If you and your sister stay in the Cornflowers, you'll have to get them jolly quickly once you've passed Second Class, or we'll have to take them down again.'

Lawrie nodded, not at all alarmed. Certainly she and Nicola would win those and any other necessary badges – heaps of badges, more than anyone else, except Ann. Her attention, however, was not really on what Pamela was saying, but on the Guide meeting hall, a long, low hut, hidden from the school by a belt of trees. There was a platform at one end, with the King's Colour on one side and the Company Colour on the other; and each Patrol had its own permanent alcove with shelves and a small cupboard and any other equipment they cared to add. At the other end of the room were two big cupboards, where signalling flags and buzzers and bandages and birds' eggs and an orderly jumble of other things, which Lawrie could not identify, were kept. On all the plain spaces of wall someone – or perhaps lots of people – had painted big bold panels of Guide scenes: Guides in camp, chiefly, and one which Lawrie particularly liked of Guides round a camp fire; there was the fire, and a moon and an owl and a dark blue sky and the glow of the flames which silhouetted the figures round the fire. Directly below it, to Lawrie's resentful disgust, sat Pomona and Marie, ostentatiously busy and absorbed by Pomona's Tenderfoot test. Or rather, Marie was absorbed and Pomona's attention was wandering as badly as Lawrie's.

Lawrie looked away quickly before their eyes could meet, and tried to listen properly to Pamela's quick, explanatory voice. But though she fixed her eyes on Pamela's face and made as though she were listening with every nerve, Pamela's voice came only in snatches through her cloudy imaginings of the time when she would be a Patrol Leader, carrying the Colours with an escort on either side, and absolute masses of badges down her right arm.

'Here,' said Rita, handing over the box of specimen knots, tied in string of two colours (the Cornflowers did these things properly); 'mine knows all its knots and then some. You'd better try yours.'

Nicola blushed faintly, twisting a piece of string in a competent and sailorly fashion between her fingers. Lawrie eyed her enviously. People always said how *well* Nick did things; and she sighed, looking at those bits of string. No one had ever been able to teach Lawrie how to tie knots; and very likely no one ever would.

V

Fortunately, this proved to be one of Lawrie's exaggerations, and at the third meeting, they sailed through their Tenderfoot test in style. Pomona, who was tested with them, was told that she must practise drawing her Union Jack and come to Miss Redmond for retesting before prayers on Wednesday. Pomona said uninterestedly: 'Yes, Captain,' and went off to tell Marie, who declared passionately that it wasn't fair, until Jen Wallace, her Patrol Leader, remarked shortly that one shouldn't say that kind of thing, and anyway, she should have taught Pomona her test properly. Marie coloured violently and went off to sob in a convulsive fashion in the small lobby where their outdoor coats were hung.

Lawrie, who had gone to fetch a handkerchief, saw, and in acute embarrassment, ignored her, supposing, wrongly, that this was what Marie would prefer.

'Thank goodness *we're* through, anyway,' said Nicola, flopping on to her bed and beginning to take off her shoes and stockings preparatory to changing for supper.

'Of course we are,' said Lawrie buoyantly. 'Why not?'

'Oh, I don't know. Just that everything else we've tried this term has come to pieces. Captain says we can be enrolled next week, Ann. She's writing for our uniforms at once.'

'Good,' said Ann.

'Ann.'

''M?'

'Does it take long? Being enrolled, I mean.'

'You're not flying up, are you?'

'No. Captain said would we mind not, because of keeping Pomona company.'

'About five minutes then, I should think. Why?'

Nicola turned pink. 'Oh, nothing.'

Lawrie looked observant. 'You won't have much to say,' she said comfortingly. 'Only the Promise when Captain does.'

'I don't mind saying things,' protested Nicola, blushing more deeply. 'But supposing I salute at the wrong time or something awful. I shall feel such an ass.'

'You only salute four times,' said Lawrie. She ticked them off on her fingers. 'Half salute when you say the Promise, full salute when Captain pins on the badge and shakes hands, full salute to the Colours and full salute to the Company. Easy.'

'Good gracious,' said Nicola startled. 'How on earth d'you know all that?'

'Read it in Ann's book. 'S easy,' said Lawrie again. She

pranced across to the basin in her vest and knickers and began to wash.

'Oh well,' said Nicola, comforting herself, 'this time next week it'll be over. And then we can start Second Class. What Patrol are we going to be in, Ann? D'you know?'

Ann hesitated. 'It isn't really a secret,' she said at last. 'We're going to have a fourth Patrol because the others are beginning to burst. It's quite likely you'll be in that. I think Captain was only waiting till the recruits were enrolled.'

'Waiting for *us*,' triumphed Lawrie.

'Waiting for Pomona, too,' Nicola reminded her.

'Waiting for Old Pip-and-core!' crowed Lawrie exultantly.

'You *are* pleased with yourself,' said Nicola flatteringly. 'Hullo, Rowan.'

'Hullo,' said Rowan. Her outdoor coat swung from her shoulders and showed the plain blue girdle of the First Senior netball team.

'We passed,' Nicola told her. 'We're going to be enrolled next week.'

'Clever,' said Rowan. She strolled over to the mirror, dropped her coat on the end of her bed, frowned at herself in the glass and began to comb her hair. Her right sleeve was stained with mud as though she had fallen. Guiltily, Nicola remembered that the second round of the cup matches had been played that afternoon: only Kingscote had held the County Shield for so long now – at least four years – that no one thought it worthwhile to get excited until the semi-finals.

'How much did you win by?' asked Nicola in the proper take-it-for-granted tone, as she pulled her tunic over her head.

'We lost,' said Rowan briefly and lightly.

Nicola and Lawrie froze, aghast, Nicola dangling her tunic

from her hand, Lawrie jerking her half-dried face from the towel. Even Ann, whose main interests did not include games, looked startled.

'*Lost!*' they said incredulously.

'That's right,' said Rowan. She peered at her reflection. 'I can't say that my beauty's improved when one cheek's veiled in mud.'

'Were they *so* good?' asked Nicola desperately.

'No,' said Rowan. 'Just average.'

'Was *Margaret* playing?' asked Lawrie.

'Everyone was playing.'

'Then what happened?'

'Nothing. We lost. Just one of those things.'

'By a *lot*?' asked Nicola, seeking comfort. Because if it were just one goal—

'Sixteen to twenty-three.'

Lawrie whistled in sheer shocked surprise, unable to stop herself. Rowan gave her a quick, tight smile.

''M. I know.' She looked at Ann and said: 'Little Lois Sanger'll have lots more time to devote to the Snowdrops now. Having no cup matches'll reduce our fixture list quite a bit. Well, you're welcome.'

Ann coloured and said nothing. Rowan, as though the little outburst had relieved her, said: 'Well, I'm going to have a bath,' and disappeared.

Nicola and Lawrie looked at one another and then at Ann. There seemed nothing to say, only saying nothing seemed almost more miserable than not talking about it. So Nicola said savagely: 'How absolutely awful,' and waited, only half-listening, for Lawrie's reply, while she thought disconsolately of the big fluted cup downstairs, which was now no longer theirs, and would be a reminder of defeat every time they passed it.

''M,' said Lawrie, her attention elsewhere. 'I say, Ann, what did Rowan mean about Lois Sanger? Is she in Guides? I've never seen her.'

'She's the Snowdrop Patrol Second. She only hasn't been to meetings because there are always extra practices at the beginning of term.'

'What's she like?'

'Very good, really. She's awfully keen. People like her a lot.'

'Rowan doesn't,' said Nicola gloomily.

'No-o. I don't know why. They always seem to be having a flaming row about something. It must be a nuisance when you're in the same teams.'

They finished dressing rather silently and went down to supper. Tim received the news of the Tenderfoot test with polite reserve and said she supposed they knew about the match. And did they also know there was a rumour that their sister Rowan and Lois Sanger had fallen on one another foaming with fury and had had to be parted by the umpires?

'Tim!'

'Fact,' said Tim solemnly.

'Truth and honour?'

'Truth and honour,' said Tim instantly. Then, as Nicola and Lawrie looked at her in scared dismay, she added: 'I mean, truth and honour there's a rumour. I don't suppose it's true.'

'Oh,' said Lawrie, relieved. 'Well, no. It couldn't be, could it?'

'There seems to be something up, though,' said Tim hopefully. 'Everyone seems to be seething over with stories about some sort of row in the team. And some say they bit one another and others simply say they tore each other's hair out by the roots. No one says what it was *about*, though.'

Nicola said nothing. She supposed it didn't matter if Tim didn't really care that they had lost the match. Probably it was rather foolish in herself to feel this chilled, despondent emptiness in her chest almost as badly as when she had first read in one of her mother's library books of the sinking of the *Prince of Wales* and the *Repulse*. Defeat was the most beastly feeling, thought Nicola crossly; and she looked across to Rowan's table, where Rowan sat eating her supper calmly and unemotionally. Farther down sat Lois Sanger, rather flushed under the eyes, laughing over-excitedly, the centre of a group which, at a junior table, would have been called silly and told to sit up and behave. Nicola watched, her lip curling a little with dislike.

Lawrie nipped her little finger.

'Don't stare so, Nick. D'you know what I feel like? I feel like a Scot after Killiecrankie.'

'No, you don't,' said Nicola, feeling better. 'You feel like a Scot after Culloden. Killiecrankie was the one they won.'

VI

Her heart banging fast and evenly, Nicola stood at attention in her place in the horseshoe and watched Pomona being enrolled. Pomona was first, because the Daisies were an older Patrol than the Cornflowers; then Nicola, because she was the elder twin; then Lawrie. Nicola was glad she was not Lawrie; she wanted to have her enrolment over quickly and not to have made any stupid mistakes; nor to have to be shoved into position like Pomona, nor to have Captain needing to stop and whisper the things she should do next. Pomona was nearly finished. Nicola took a deep silent breath and tried to rearrange her breathing.

Then she was marching up beside Ann. It wasn't really

difficult; one bit followed from another until the moment when she was twisted round to face the Company and they saluted one another. But she felt queerly disappointed as she marched back beside Ann, and took her place, hot-cheeked, in the horseshoe. It had all gone by so swiftly, slipping away from her like sand through her clenched hand. She hadn't made any mistakes, but neither had it been the splendid, different-feeling thing it should have been. She sighed and watched Lawrie.

And, oddly enough, Lawrie seemed to be doing it as Nicola had wanted it done. In her new, crisp uniform she looked light and triumphant, as though at any moment she might fly. Her small, distinct voice saying the Promise made it sound like something real, not just a mumble of words to be hurried through because it was a formula which had to be said. Very erect, she saluted Captain, saluted the Colours, and then swung round to salute the Company as though – Nicola stumbled on to her smile – as though she had just been given the V.C. and were saluting her regiment: a *cheering* regiment, thought Nicola, tucking her chin down to hide a wholly admiring grin. Then Lawrie and Ann marched back, Captain stood the Company at ease, and then, dropping formalities, told them they could sit down.

'Well,' said Miss Redmond when everyone was comfortably settled, 'I think most of you know what's coming. As you must have realized, the three Patrols we've got have grown much too big. The Snowdrops are the worst off – there are twelve of them – but the others are nearly as bad; and as you know, six or eight is the proper number. So there's nothing for it. We've put it off and off and now there's got to be another Patrol. I've tried to arrange it so that the existing Patrols aren't too badly broken up, and I know you'll all be sensible about it, and not grumble even if your best friend has been snatched away from you.'

The Company grinned uneasily.

'All right. Well, here it comes. Snowdrops: you lose Lois Sanger. She's going to be the new Patrol Leader and I know we all wish her the very best of luck.' (The Company murmured its congratulations; Lois coloured, looking down at her hands.) 'Lois has asked if she may take Jill Ballam with her to be her Second – yes, sorry, Muriel – and I'm sorry again, Muriel, but you're losing Juliet and Penelope as well. All right, Snowdrops, that's all. You can breathe again now. Daisies: you lose Marie Dobson and Terry Hunt. Cornflowers: I know you'll be sorry to lose them, but I told Ann how it would be from the beginning; you lose Nicola and Lawrie. Well, that's all. How d'you feel about it?'

'It's not fair,' said the Company cheerfully.

'Not fair a bit. I'll give you a quarter of an hour to say how awful it all is and then I'll expect all the Patrols to be divided up in their new order. Company: '*shun*. Company: dis-*miss*.'

Everyone pulled off her hat and fled to her Patrol corner.

'Ann,' said Nicola urgently, catching her by the sleeve, 'can't you do something about it?'

'No. Why?' said Ann, surprised. 'You knew you weren't going to stop in the Cornflowers once you'd done your Tenderfoot.'

'It isn't that,' said Nicola impatiently, looking at Lawrie. 'It isn't that we want to hang on to you specially; I mean we'd gladly go to the Daisies or even the Snowdrops, though I'm not keen on their badge, but Lois Sanger—'

'You know she's having a row with Rowan,' said Lawrie reproachfully, sticking her hands through her belt. 'Everyone says it's simply murderous. And she won't want her arch-enemy's sisters in her Patrol; I'm sure she won't.'

'Besides, she hates all the family. She was beastly about us on First Day,' said Nicola, kicking at a knot in the boards. She had never mentioned that encounter before, and would have kept it to herself now, only Ann looked so aggravatingly sure of herself.

'Don't be silly, Nick. Besides, she can't possibly have a row with you, simply because she's having one with Rowan,' said Ann in a sensible, grown-up voice, which Nicola found highly exasperating. 'And anyway, Captain hates school quarrels being brought into Guides. Besides, it's so *feeble* to ask if you can't have things altered specially. Look at Marie Dobson.'

Because they were near the platform, they could hear as well as see Marie. She was protesting against being separated from Pomona, and suggesting an entirely new arrangement: that she and Pomona should be in the new Patrol and one of the Marlow twins take Pomona's place in the Daisies: '*Couldn't* we, Captain?'

Captain, engaged in marking the Company Roll book, had not looked up; but she obviously wasn't pleased. Nicola and Lawrie looked at one another. Then Lawrie clapped her hat on her head, slapped her belt and said grimly: 'Our blood be on your heads. Come, Nicola,' and marched off to the empty corner.

''S long, Ann. 'S long, Rita. Thanks for teaching us,' said Nicola rather shyly, moving after Lawrie. Terry Hunt, a light-haired, freckled individual, waved good-bye to the Daisies, and came across to join them.

'Hullo,' she said. 'What's our name going to be?'

'Don't know,' said Nicola. 'Has it been decided yet?'

'I don't know,' said Terry. 'I thought you might know from Ann.'

'Nobody knows yet,' said Lois Sanger from behind them.

'Not even me. Captain left it for us to choose. As soon as the others come over we'll make it the first thing we do. Till then – let's see. I may as well get the Roll Book made out. Sit down, infants – we *must* try to have cushions by next week – now then: there's me, Jill – which is the senior of Pen and Juliet? Juliet, I think; then Pen, then you, Terry, then the Dobson child, and last but not least, our two Marlows.'

She said it quite nicely, thought Nicola warily.

'And Nick was enrolled first, so Lawrie comes last.' She smiled at them. 'Nice to have two tenderfoots. We'll have you through Second Class in practically no time at all.'

So perhaps Ann was right and the row with Rowan didn't count. Without looking at one another, Nicola and Lawrie gave Lois an identical shy smile.

The rest of the Patrol came running over, Marie an ostentatious last, clutching Pomona's hand convulsively before she left her.

'What are we missing?' asked Penelope.

'Not a thing. We haven't started yet. Captain's given us the rest of the meeting to get going in, so we've lots of time. And the first thing's a name. I've got Captain's book here, so if you people can make yourselves comfortable, I'll just go straight down the list and you can stop me when I hit one you like.' She waited while they settled themselves and then began to gabble:

'Bluebellbuttercupbuttercup'n'daisyclovercornflowerdaffodil—'

'Stop,' said Juliet; and Lois made a mark with her pencil and went on full speed:

' – daisydandelionforget-me-notfuchsiaheatherholly—'

'Stop,' said Penelope.

' – honestyirisivylilylilyofthevalley—'

'I like that,' said Marie loudly.

' – margueritemistletoeorchidpansypoppyprimrose—'

'Both those,' said Terry.

' – redrosescarletpimpernel—'

'Oh, *yes*,' said Lawrie, hugging her knees.

' – shamrocksnowdropspeedwellsunflowerthistle—'

'Stop,' said Nicola.

' – violetwhiteheatherwhiterose,' finished Lois in a final burst and grinned at them, panting a little. 'That's the lot. You would all choose different ones, wouldn't you? We've got Daffodil, Holly, Lily of the Valley, Primrose, Poppy, Pimpernel and Thistle. How are we going to choose? Draw lots?'

'No, wait,' said Terry. 'You can take out Primrose if no one else wants it. And Lily's *awful*. Who said Lily?'

Marie blushed crimson.

'Marie's perfectly entitled to choose Lily of the Valley if she likes it,' said Lois quickly. 'Jill, what d'you think? Which d'you like?'

'Well – not Lily, for choice. It is a bit maidenly. And not Thistle, perhaps. After all, we're not a Scotch Patrol.'

Nicola, who had chosen Thistle because she was reading *The Flight of the Heron* and was temporarily devoted to Ewen Cameron, nodded quickly and said: 'All right.'

'That's got us down a bit. Daffodil, Holly, Poppy, Scarlet Pimpernel—'

'Oh, please have Scarlet Pimpernel,' begged Lawrie. '*Please* do. Because of Sir Percy, you know. None of the other Patrols have anyone like that.'

' "They seek him here, they seek him there",' said Lois automatically. 'It's a thought. Shall we be demmed elusive Pimpernels?'

'I'd rather be a Lily,' said Marie obstinately.

Nicola choked and apologized. 'I'm sorry,' she said. 'It was just the way you said it.'

Marie said nothing. But the rest of the Patrol were inclined to be pleased and amused over Sir Percy.

'It's a nice shoulder knot, too,' said Terry, leaning over Lois's shoulder. 'Plain scarlet. I always liked the Cornflowers' blue one better than our green and white thing.'

'Which is one reason for not having Lily of the Valley,' said Lois kindly and casually in Marie's direction. 'The shoulder knots are too alike. Good. That's one thing settled. Log-book next. Is there anyone besides Juliet who can draw? No, I thought not. There never is. You again, then, Jay. Do us something dashing in the way of a cover and a title page, and – wait a minute – we'll all sign on the second page in case the plague strikes us before next week. And when anyone leaves the Patrol we'll record the reason and the rest will sign again.'

The book went round the circle in order of seniority; Lawrie, looking at Nicola's careful round hand, would have liked to attempt a flourishing signature, but just managed to restrain herself.

The discussion went on. Patrol cushions, signalling flags, a notice board, perhaps a screen later, a patrol box for oddments—

'What oddments?' asked Jill.

'Oddments,' said Lois firmly. 'All self-respecting Patrols have oddments. A First Aid kit, a bean bag, nature specimens, string—'

'Can we have knots in two colours like Ann does?' burst in Lawrie. 'It's an awfully easy way of learning them.'

There was a queer little silence. Then Lois said:

'I don't think we need bag ideas from other Patrols. I don't doubt we can think up plenty of our own.'

Lawrie subsided, tingling as though someone had slammed a door unexpectedly. She knew she had been snubbed, but she wasn't at all certain why.

'Well,' said Miss Redmond, kneeling down beside Juliet. 'And how are you getting on? Have you chosen your name yet?'

They told her that and various other things. She listened and nodded and seemed pleased. 'It all sounds very satisfactory. I was wondering – Lois, isn't your hike the last test you have to pass for First Class?'

'That's all,' said Lois. She wrinkled her nose and she and Miss Redmond laughed at one another.

'I thought it might be fun if you were to take it this Saturday. And – how would you like to take the whole Patrol? I know the rules say only two Guides, but we shan't be able to have many more hikes this year and it does seem an excellent opportunity for you people to really get to know one another.'

The Pimpernels looked hopefully at Lois. Lois made a laughing grimace and said:

'All right, Captain. If you say so.'

'Good. Miss Leslie, the new District Commissioner, will come along to pass you, and I expect I shall be there to keep her company. You know what you have to do, don't you? Follow a map to the place where you're actually going to have the hike, cook your dinner, amuse your guests and bring the Patrol home intact.'

The Pimpernels giggled.

'Right,' said Miss Redmond, getting up. 'Well, I'll leave you to make your plans. Come to me on Saturday morning, Lois, and I'll give you the food you're to take with you.'

She went back to the platform to talk to Lieutenant, and the Pimpernels grinned joyfully at one another.

'It'll be marvellous when you pass,' said Lawrie in a clear, pleased voice, anxious to atone for whatever it was she had said that was wrong. 'Next meeting you'll be the only Patrol Leader with First Class except Ann.'

Nicola caught her breath. For an instant she thought Lois was going to say something sarcastic about the illustrious Marlows, but she didn't. Instead she laughed and said: 'Don't count your chickens, young Lawrie. I may not pass, you know.'

'Oh, Lois, of course you will,' protested Jill.

'Can but try,' said Lois. 'Now, let's make plans. We can't do anything about the map, because we shan't see it until the time comes, but you can all practise reading a compass. And we'd better decide what each person is going to bring. Jill, you'd better bring the matches; Juliet, you bring string and a knife; Pen . . .'

It took up the rest of the meeting.

7 A First Class Hike

I

'And where are you off to now?' asked Tim indulgently.

'To pass our fire-lighting,' said Lawrie, gulping the last of her mid-morning bun, and brushing down her tunic. 'Captain said she'd do us now if we hurried.'

'Keen,' said Tim sadly. 'Keen is what you are. To think that I should have taken up with a couple of pot-hunters.'

'We're not!' said Lawrie, appalled.

'You are,' said Tim firmly. She ticked off the items on her fingers. 'You were enrolled on Tuesday. Yesterday after prayers you were haring round to get someone to pass your bed-making; in dinner rec. you went romping round Upper Field running a mile in twelve seconds or some such; every time there's a lull in a lesson I can hear Lawrie tapping on her desk and hissing "dot, dot, dash"; and now you're both rushing off to light a fire with no matches.'

'If we do,' said Lawrie uneasily, trying to carry it off, for Tim might be teasing and then again she mightn't, 'that'll be three Second Class tests in two days. Good going, that; and all for the honour and glory of the Patrol.'

''M,' said Tim. 'Honour and glory of the Marlows more like.'

Nicola raised her eyebrows. 'That'll be quite enough from you,' she said in Giles's voice. 'What we pass and what we don't pass are very much our affair.'

Their eyes met, Nicola's combative, Tim's faintly startled.

All right, said Nicola's glance, if you were being funny, so was I: if not, not.

'But of course,' said Tim with old world courtesy. 'Only don't overdo it, will you?'

Nicola spun round and went off towards the wood. Lawrie followed. Left by herself, Tim produced another bun from her pocket, and strolled towards a sunny uninhabited spot on the bank which bordered the playing field. She sat down, nibbling her bun, not much minding being alone, but a little astonished that she should be. Without being consciously complacent, Tim felt in her bones that the occasional person on whom she bestowed her friendship should not ask anything more of life. Often they didn't, and were proportionately hurt and dismayed when Tim, tiring of their single-mindedness, showed plainly that she had had enough. But Nicola, although most friendly with Tim, was also friendly, in a casual, unemotional fashion with everyone else in Third Remove except Pomona and Marie Dobson; and moreover, she liked to be doing things.

'The contemplative life,' thought Tim, chewing grass since she had finished her bun, 'is not for Nicola.'

She grinned, feeling better; and then, as suddenly, felt solitary and perverse. The rest of Third Remove were all with someone, doing something; even Pomona, despicable ass, was wandering round with Marie Dobson. Tim frowned, chewing her grass stem. She supposed she could go down and join Jean and Hazel in the form garden – go down brandishing a trowel and saying: 'Bring out your worms' – but she didn't much want to. She wasn't particularly interested in gardening, and although she didn't mind Jean and Hazel, two neat, careful, unexciting individuals, who were thrilled to bits if their preparation were marked Beta plus and given to giggling insanely if anyone said anything even mildly funny, she didn't like them particularly. Come to that, she didn't much care for any of the Third Remove except Nicola – Nicola and Lawrie. You couldn't have one without the other.

The smell of wood smoke drifted on the breeze. Tim sniffed it testily. Their blessed fires, she supposed. They should never have joined Guides, thought Tim irritably, knowing she was being unreasonable, and none the less cross for that; they should certainly never have joined Guides after she had made it plain that she thought the idea a poor one. Tim scowled faintly to herself. She supposed she could join Guides too; but there wouldn't be much point in it now when she would be so far behind the twins in everything; and besides, Guides weren't a thing she wanted to join. Quite suddenly, Tim felt intolerably homesick. She frowned the harder, staring with intent and unknowing fury at a group of IIIA who had begged the loan of a netball and were practising shooting with the enthusiasm and orderliness for which they were noted.

A twin sat itself down on either side of her.

'We passed,' said Lawrie joyfully. 'We did. Mine almost didn't light, but I blew like – like—'

'Boreas,' suggested Tim morosely.

'Is he a good blower? Well, Boreas, then. And suddenly it caught and blazed like anything,' said Lawrie lying back in the recaptured glory of that moment.

'Good,' said Tim, without enthusiasm.

'Aren't you pleased?' asked Lawrie, puzzled and a little hurt.

'She doesn't have to be,' said Nicola quickly. 'It isn't her thing.'

Tim pulled herself together. 'Of course I'm pleased. Delighted – *enchanté* – *contentone*—' she leaned over Lawrie, tickling her nose with a seeding grass. 'D'you know you have the most impressive smudge to the left centre of your chin?'

They were not deceived by her change of tone, but they realized that she was doing her best. As a family, the Marlows were not given to enquiring deeply into one another's moods, acting on the principle that it was best to let people alone until they felt better. So Nicola said: 'If you can call it a chin,' and Lawrie retorted complacently that it was no good Nicola's being rude about her chin since it was too like Nicola's own.

'Are you people sitting on cushions?' asked Karen, stopping in front of them. Margaret Jessop, who was with her, smiled faintly at Lawrie, who promptly blushed to the hairline.

Nicola looked resigned. Authority, which had a curious prejudice against the young sitting on damp grass, had issued mackintosh cushions to each form with the injunction that no one was to sit anywhere out-of-doors unless she had her cushion with her. The Upper Fifth and Sixth generally remembered; so did a few of the Lower Fifth; below that, the rule was carefully forgotten, the juniors protesting that it looked so frightfully silly to go carrying cushions around with you wherever you went; and the Thirds in particular were apt to leave their cushions swinging quietly from the hook provided on each desk, that they might collect dust at leisure.

'No, Karen,' said Nicola politely, getting to her feet. With any other prefect she would have argued, insisting innocently that the ground was as dry as a bone and that it was nearly the end of rec. anyway; but it had been pointed out before they came to Kingscote that it would be most unfair to be anything but instantly obedient to Karen's lightest word. Next holidays, Nicola resolved, as Karen passed on, she and

Lawrie would point out that Karen ought not, in fairness, speak to them in her capacity of head girl, unless there were no other prefect within a range of fifty miles.

The interlude served, however, to break the faint tension between Tim and themselves. When the bell rang for the end of recreation they sauntered amiably into school together; and when Juliet Beesley dashed in between lessons to show the twins and Marie the linen cover she had stencilled for the Log-book – a shadowy, eighteenth-century figure in the background and a vivid formal Scarlet Pimpernel flower in the centre – Tim tilted her chair to get a better view of the cover as it lay on Nicola's desk, and remarked on its beauties quite as though she were properly interested. It was scarcely noticeable that when the rest of Third Remove began to crowd round enthusiastically and make admiring comments, Tim unobtrusively tilted her chair back to normal, and, sticking her head inside her desk, began to hunt feverishly for a missing protractor until Miss Cromwell, standing in the doorway with eyebrows raised, melted the group into individual and apologetic scufflings.

II

Since it was Thursday, the afternoon was spent playing rounders. Quite often, when the Third Remove came down from the rounders pitch, the school teams would be practising on the asphalt netball court, and no one minded if they stopped to watch for a little. Third Remove stopped accordingly, pleasantly conscious that the weather was too fine and warm – a St. Martin's summer had set in since the rain of the first two weeks – for them to be told to run along and not be so foolish as to stand about in the wind. They stood and watched their seniors, commenting profoundly on the finer points of the game, while one or two spoke loudly of Rowan's prowess in the hope that Nicola or Lawrie might hear and report it back to her.

'I say,' said Lawrie suddenly, 'Lois Sanger's playing for the Second.'

'Of course she is,' said Marie Dobson scornfully. 'Everyone knows that.'

'Well, I didn't,' retorted Nicola. 'So everyone can't have done. Why is she?'

'It's since the row,' said Jean Baker eagerly, for her sister Pauline was in the Second and might possibly profit by Lois's displacement. 'You know – the cup match row. Lois has been playing for the Second in practices ever since. Didn't Rowan tell you anything about what happened?'

'No. I keep telling people that and they never believe it. Rowan hasn't said a thing.'

'Rowan doesn't gossip,' said Lawrie loftily.

'Aren't we noble?' remarked Marie.

Lawrie coloured and said nothing. Third Remove, remembering that tea time was approaching, began to drift away in twos and threes, leaving Nicola and Lawrie, Tim and Jean Baker. Tim, who was not particularly interested in the teams, was merely waiting for the twins.

'As a matter of fact,' said Lawrie, her voice carefully indifferent, her eyes on the game, 'as a matter of fact, I think Lois is better than Rowan.'

'But not as steady,' said Jean importantly. 'Pauline says' (she glanced sideways at the twins to see whether this would be condemned as gossip, but the twins looked mildly interested and she went on) 'Pauline says Rowan's very good always, but that Lois has off-days sometimes; and that's why Rowan got her colours last year and not Lois, though they did both play in all the matches.'

'Oh,' said Nicola. She swung her rounders stick and said casually: 'Is Lois much better than Rowan when she's feeling like it?'

'Better than anyone, Paul says. Only you can't tell when she's going to feel like it. She played frightfully badly the other week in the cup match.'

'Was that why we lost?'

'Rowan said so, Paul says. That's why they had their awful row. Rowan was rather wild about it – losing the match, I mean.'

Nicola and Lawrie said nothing. Hazel turned, waved and shouted, and Jean ran on to join her. In silence the twins contemplated the teams. Lois, who was playing Centre against Margaret Jessop, was obviously playing her hardest; as though, thought Lawrie, tingling with sympathy, to show Craven what an ass she was to drop her from the First.

'I say, Nick,' said Lawrie softly, drawing closer to Nicola, 'do you think Rowan may have been rather beastly to Lois?'

Tim tucked her chin into the neck of her blouse and yawned gently to herself. Teams and teams and more teams; and who was in and who was not in; all vastly important, Tim supposed, enjoying her assumption of superiority, if that was what interested you. For herself, she wouldn't care if she never saw another ball again. She clasped her hands behind her back and strolled negligently away, hoping that the twins would see and come after her. But the twins did not notice.

'Oh no,' said Nicola hurriedly. 'But she may have lost her temper a little. Like she does at home, you know.'

'But if she was beastly,' persisted Lawrie, 'you can understand why she – Lois, I mean – feels about Marlows like you say she does. Specially now she's been chucked into the Second.'

'It isn't our fault if she has,' said Nicola sturdily. 'And anyway, she felt hot under the collar about the family long before that happened.'

'Yes,' said Lawrie, 'but—'

Miss Craven, suddenly realizing that two of the Third Remove were still hanging about, called to them to go in and wash for tea at once. They ran obediently, Nicola streaking ahead, Lawrie trotting behind at less than her usual pace; if asked, she would have said that thinking always slowed her up.

She continued preoccupied underneath all the normal business of tea and preparation, Free Hour and supper, prayers and bed. Nicola had handed on *The Flight of the Heron* and all Lawrie's sympathy was, for the time being at least, with the disgraced and disinherited; it must be terrible, thought Lawrie, half-pitiful, half-thrilled, to be thrown out of the team because you had lost a match for the school; much worse than if you had never been in at all. Eating her bread and butter and stewed fruit, which, with a glass of milk, constituted the juniors' supper, Lawrie, very round-eyed, watched Lois Sanger eat her macaroni cheese, endowing her with the romantic haze which had previously belonged to Margaret Jessop; and she pondered the position, devising fantasies in the course of which Lois was reinstated in the team owing entirely to Lawrie's courage, ingenuity and self-sacrifice.

She waited until they were in bed and sitting up with their torches, ready to practise signalling, before she broached the subject to Nicola. They both knew morse (Nicola because it was used by the Navy, Lawrie because Nicola did) and, as Ann said, with a little practice in reading and sending, would be ready to pass their Second Class test. It had not occurred to Ann that this practice would take place with torches after 'lights out', but Nicola and Lawrie thought it an excellent, time-saving idea. Usually Nicola began, but tonight Lawrie's torch began to flicker the 'ready' signal almost before the prefect on dormitory duty had closed the door.

'A-b-o-u-t L-o-i-s S-a-n-g-e-r,' clicked Lawrie.

'W-h-a-t a-b-o-u-t h-e-r?' replied Nicola.

'I-t i-s s-o r-o-t-t-e-n a-b-o-u-t t-h-e t-e-a-m,' flashed Lawrie in the laborious phrasing forced on her by having to spell every word, 'c-o-u-l-d n-o-t w-e d-o s-o-m-e-t-h-i-n-g t-o m-a-k-e u-p?'

'W-h-a-t?' replied Nicola's torch. 'A-n-d w-h-y?'

'B-e-c-a-u-s-e o-f R-o-w-a-n.'

'Rowan hasn't done anything,' said Nicola's voice indignantly.

'Sh,' said Lawrie. 'Signal it. E-v-e-r-y-o-n-e s-a-y-s s-h-e h-a-s.'

'Y-o-u c-a-n-n-o-t b-e-l-e-e-v-e a-l-l-l y-o-u h-e-r-e,' clicked Nicola wildly and inaccurately.

'A-l-l t-h-e s-a-m-e w-e c-o-u-l-d d-o s-o-m-e-t-h-i-n-g t-o h-e-l-p L-o-i-s a-t G-u-i-d-e-s.'

There was a pause. Then Nicola's torch flashed again.

'H-a-v-e y-o-u g-o-n-e c-r-a-k-e-d o-n L-o-i-s?' It enquired pertinently.

In the covering dark Lawrie felt her cheeks grow hot. She replied crossly:

'I s-u-p-o-s-e s-o.'

'Y-o-u a-r-e a-n a-s-s. W-h-a-t a-b-o-u-t M-a-r-g-a-r-e-t?'

'I c-a-n l-i-k-e M-a-r-g-a-r-e-t t-o-o.'

Nicola snorted. 'You never like the same person for two minutes together,' she said scornfully.

'I do,' said Lawrie furiously. 'That simply isn't true, Nicola. You know it isn't.'

'It is true,' said Nicola unmoved. 'I've watched you for years.'

'Just because you go on for years and years wallowing in Nelson—'

'I don't wallow in Nelson,' said Nicola distantly.

'Well, it's much more sensible to like real people. Anyone'll tell you that.'

'Nelson was perfectly real. Much more real than Lois Sanger.'

'He's dead now. So how can he be?'

Nicola said nothing, gazing sadly into the dark. She was silent for so long that Lawrie leaned forward as though by so doing she could pierce the darkness and said tentatively: 'Are you crying, Nick?'

'No,' said Nicola truthfully; but her voice sounded chastened. 'What do you want to do about Lois?'

'Well – I don't know exactly—'

'Be good and inconspicuous at Guides and not lose any marks for the Patrol?'

'Not inconspicuous,' protested Lawrie, quickening to Nicola's more responsive mood. 'We've got to be a credit to the Pimpernels and make them top Patrol. Even better than the Cornflowers. Because it does sound to me, Nick, whatever you say, as though Rowan had been very mouldy.'

'Well, we're doing what we can about Second Class. Only nine more things to do, counting morse and knots.'

'Yes, I know,' said Lawrie, dissatisfied. 'But I mean something special, like it being all through us she gets her First Class.'

'Well, we're going on the hike and that's all she's got to do. I suppose we can look frightfully keen, if that'll help.'

'I thought perhaps,' said Lawrie, hugging her knees, 'that we could bring everything that all the others are supposed to bring so that if anyone forgets anything Lois won't be in a hole.'

Nicola thought this over. It seemed a harmless enough idea; and if Lawrie really wanted to—

'All right,' said Nicola, 'Only don't tell anyone beforehand or they'll think it's swank. 'Cos probably no one will forget.'

'Just in case,' said Lawrie firmly. 'I'm being prepared like I'm supposed to be. 'Cos it would be awful if anything went wrong. And we must keep our eyes open on the hike and if there's anything that wants doing quickly—'

The door opened and Karen stood in the long shaft of light from the passage.

'Are you two still talking?' she demanded. 'It's been "lights out" for hours.'

'Sorry,' said Nicola.

'Have you been talking ever since or is something the matter?'

'Talking ever since,' said Nicola.

'An order mark each, then. Unless there was a reason.'

'No reason,' said Nicola.

'All right. Good night.'

'G'night,' said the twins politely.

'You would think,' murmured Lawrie as Karen's footsteps died away, 'you would think she could turn her deaf ear to the telescope sometimes, wouldn't you?'

''M,' said Nicola. 'G'night.'

'Oh, all right. G'night,' said Lawrie regretfully.

III

They both woke early on the morning of the hike, pleased to see that it was a fine day. Nicola, having ascertained that it was a fine morning like other mornings, turned over and went to sleep again. But Lawrie got out of bed and stayed by the window for some time, before she convinced herself, first, that there were no clouds and second, that it wasn't so bright that it would rain punctually at ten o'clock. Then she went back to her cubicle, opened the bottom drawer of her chest-of-drawers and began to divide all the necessities of the hike into two piles, with a box of matches on top of each. Matches were much the best thing to take, so it seemed easiest to have a box each than to argue about who was to carry them. Sitting cross-legged on her bed to polish belt and badge and shoes, Lawrie considered fire-making. Of course, for one's test, one had to do it properly with dry leaves and bark and only two matches. But how much more fun to scatter matches all over the fire as you built it, or build them into a little pyramid in the centre, and see them flame suddenly with their fierce small roar. Lawrie sighed. She supposed Lois would light today's fire . . . she hoped everything would go all right . . . She was surprised to find that she felt unhappy and sickish, almost as though she were going to the dentist.

The feeling persisted through breakfast and bed-making and changing into uniform. But she felt better when she and Nicola were actually walking down the drive to meet the rest of the Pimpernels at the school gates; it was a lovely morning, far too hot even to think of overcoats; and though they were much too early, it was fun to lean nonchalantly against the gates and feel exclusive and privileged above those who were going off on the ordinary Saturday morning occupations of walks and gardening.

'Our haversacks do bulge,' said Nicola with some misgiving.

No one remarked on them, however, as the Pimpernels

collected, first one and two and then the rest in a bunch; there were spasmodic crackles of conversation as people wondered abruptly if they had forgotten something and then found it again; Lois, very spruce and rather white, came flying down the drive, her haversack swinging from one hand; and immediately afterwards Miss Redmond and the District Commissioner came out and down the drive, laughing and talking as though nothing of the least importance were happening. The hike had begun.

Miss Redmond handed Lois a map.

'Miss Leslie has decided that she'll give you ten minutes' start. You'll follow the map and make the ordinary tracking signs to show us which road you're taken. No difficulty about that, is there?'

'No, Captain,' said Lois. Her voice was husky and apprehensive. Lawrie shut her eyes in sympathy.

'Just have a look at the map,' said Miss Leslie pleasantly, 'and see if there's anything you want to query.'

Lois fumbled the square of paper, clutched at it and missed. Without a pause Nicola shot forward, picked it up, unfolded it, handed it to Lois, and leapt back into place. Lawrie looked at her with marked dislike. Miss Leslie's mouth twitched.

'You'd better all look,' she added as Lois regarded the map in silence and thc Pimpernels remained standing back in respectful silence, evidently of the opinion that it was for Lois to say.

Nicola saw at once what was missing. It seemed so obvious that she supposed Lois must be hesitating out of politeness as one sometimes did with the staff when they asked foolish questions. But when, without looking up, Lois said: 'No, there's nothing, thank you,' she turned pink with embarrassment. She wasn't sure whether it would be conceited and Marlow-like to say what was wrong, or worse if she said nothing.

'I think the little fair one knows,' said Miss Leslie's voice above her. 'Not the quiet one. The jumping bean.'

The Pimpernels laughed, relieved by the sudden slackening of tension. Lawrie looked thoroughly affronted. Nicola said hurriedly: 'You've forgotten the compass directions,' and then hoped she hadn't sounded as though she was accusing the District Commissioner of carelessness.

'Good child,' said Miss Leslie approvingly and Lois laughed nicely enough and said: 'Thank you, Nicola. That was idiotic of me.'

'Right,' said Miss Leslie, taking the map from Lois, filling in the compass directions and handing it back. 'Now, run along, and don't try so hard that you can't manage to enjoy yourselves.'

The Pimpernels saluted and set off.

'How did you spot that, Nicola?' asked Lois, dropping back after they had gone a little way.

'Father's in the Navy,' said Nicola uneasily, 'and he often shows us maps. He says compass directions are the first things to look for.'

'Yes, of course,' said Lois. 'It was so obvious I simply didn't see it. It was a bit unfair, I think.'

Nicola agreed politely and Lois moved forward again. Always ready to over-emphasize the importance of events in which she took part, life for Lois was apt to jerk between triumph and catastrophe. When things went right for her she was gay and arrogant; when they went wrong, she minded desperately, supposing (needlessly) that her contemporaries gloated over her ruin. Because things had gone badly for her that term, the hike and her First Class badge had assumed a monstrous importance. But the day had begun badly; she had slept heavily and woken late, too late to finish, as she had intended, the inevitable odd jobs before breakfast. Then Matron had come in while she was changing and commented that her cubicle was a disgrace for a senior and was to be put straight before she went out. Because she was late already, Lois had left her cubicle as it was, gambling on the hundred to one chance that Matron might forget; at the time it had seemed worth it; now, looking back, thunderclouds of disgrace seemed likely to be piling up behind her; perhaps even a report to Miss Keith. And then that business over the map; and of course there must be a Marlow at her elbow, ready and willing to put her right. Lois frowned, thinking of Nicola, then of Rowan – Rowan, so calm, so certain of herself, apparently without ambition, but achieving success with such effortless inevitability.

'Which way now?' asked Jill.

Impatiently, Lois came back to the job in hand.

The map was not a difficult one and she and Jill were able to follow it easily enough; Penelope, Juliet and Terry had been detailed to lay the trail. This left the twins and Marie at a loose end and after a time they became faintly bored. Of course, a hike was fun, but getting there was dullish, particularly when the route took you over ground you knew so well. Marie, not deigning to walk with the twins, stalked ahead, dashing at the hedge every now and then to collect, in heavy secrecy, a nature specimen of, so her manner conveyed, extreme rarity.

'Dandelions, probably,' said Nicola to Lawrie, who showed signs of being taken in by this performance.

Lawrie giggled, and, taking the box of matches out of Nicola's haversack, began playing the match trick. 'Just like you,' she commented, as the horizontal match sprang away from the uprights. 'Just like you leaping forward to snatch the map from under the feet of the District Commish.'

Nicola giggled too, and Marie turned round to see what they were doing. Instantly and loudly she began to remonstrate with them; Lois too swung round to see what the trouble was.

'Put those matches away at once,' she said crossly. 'Who brought them?'

'I did,' said Nicola, closing the box hastily.

'I don't see why. I told Jill to bring the matches. Put them at the bottom of your haversack and don't bring them out again unless I say you may.'

'Sorry,' murmured Nicola, doing as she was told; and she and Lawrie trudged on down the lane in silence.

It became clear at last that the map was leading them to the little sheltered cove where the school bathed in summer. Lois stopped, frowning, waiting for the younger members of the Patrol to catch up.

'What a pest! The map takes us all the way round by the cliff and we lost a lot of time that time you would turn right, Jill. They can't help knowing we didn't read the map properly.'

Lawrie coloured violently. 'I say, Lois—' she said hesitantly.

'Well?'

'Couldn't Nick and I take the short cut through the farm? Then we could collect the driftwood and stuff and have the place all ready for the fire when you arrived.'

Lois looked back along the lane. There were no Guiders' hats in sight. Nevertheless—

'I don't know,' said Lois doubtfully. 'It would help, I suppose, but I don't expect you ought to go wandering off alone.'

'We'd be all right,' protested Nicola resignedly, since one

must support Lawrie if she wanted to be useful. 'And we couldn't possibly get lost.'

'Well—' said Lois, wavering.

Lawrie waited for no more; she swung herself over the gate and ran. Nicola followed.

'No! Come back,' shouted Lois, suddenly panicking, too late. The twins grinned over their shoulders, waved, and disappeared round an outhouse.

'Shall I fetch them back?' asked Jill.

'No,' said Lois worriedly. 'No. I'll need you on the beach. Marie – I shan't need you. Go after those kids and tell them to come back. And for heaven's sake don't let Probyn catch you. The rest of us had better get down to the beach before Captain sees we're not all together.'

She set off, walking quickly, the others close at her heels. Marie, twisting her hands together, opened her mouth and took a step forward, then stopped helplessly. Nervously, she retreated to the gate, climbed it cautiously, stood in the straw of the rick-yard for a moment, her face crimson with fright, and then made a tiptoeing dash to the straw-covered space between the rick and the flint wall. She crouched motionless, the blood drumming in her ears. Lois had said: 'Go after those kids and tell them to come back'. But even as she had heard the order, Marie had known she could never obey it; to Marie, a timid child, who still fled panic-stricken from dark landing to lighted hall, all animals were monsters who would rend and tear one, given the opportunity; as for farms, where huge dogs leapt baying at the end of chains and bulls bellowed menacingly in their stalls, they were places of real terror. Even turkeys were a source of panic to Marie, with their cold dead eyes and loose dewlaps. Whenever she saw them, she went softly by, glancing constantly over her shoulder lest they should band together behind her back to hunt her down.

It had never occurred to Marie that for the sake of her own self-respect she should confront her personal hobgoblin, however much her teeth chattered and her knees shook. She was the kind of child who evades most trials on the score of minor infirmities: turning somersaults in the gym made her dizzy; she could not play cricket (the hard ball hurt) because she was liable to sunstroke. When illness could not serve, she was swift to invent a plausible story. Now, crouching in the straw, counting a hundred slowly, her heart leaping in her throat every time the hens clucked or the straw rattled faintly in the breeze, the necessary story took shape easily enough: She hadn't been able to catch the twins because she had twisted her ankle a little – a very little – it was all right now – getting over the gate; but she had run and called and she thought the twins had heard her, only perhaps they hadn't quite known what she was saying; so then she hadn't liked to go on because of what Lois had said about Mr. Probyn, and so she'd come back. She was awfully sorry, Lois.

'. . . ninety-nine . . . a hundred.'

Marie straightened herself cautiously. Captain and the Commissioner were still not in sight. She sprang to the gate, scrambled wildly over as the farm dog barked in the distance, and ran heavily down the dusty lane and along the cliff to the comforting blue uniforms ahead of her. Panting at Lois's elbow as they reached the sands, she told her story. But Lois, seeing the twins in a well-chosen spot with a trickle of blue smoke rising from a small pyramid before them, was not particularly attentive. She said: 'Oh, well, it doesn't matter. All's well that ends well.'

She and Jill took charge of the fire, while Penelope and Juliet unpacked the dinner. The other four went off to find warm, flat, grey stones to serve as seats: 'For the grown-ups,' Lawrie had said, meaning the Guiders and Lois and Jill. But Terry thought they might all have stones: 'And we can build sand armchairs for the grown-ups,' she said cheerfully. 'Goodness, I haven't played bucket-and spade for years.'

'I like making sand-puddings to go along the battlements of forts,' said Lawrie, who was devoid of proper pride. 'Rowan and Gin make terrific forts and we've kept the sea out for hours, sometimes. Don't scowl at me, Nick. You like forts yourself. You know you do.'

Terry laughed and said that she liked being marooned best.

'And it gets smaller and smaller and bits crumble off,' agreed Nicola, tugging at a stone several sizes too large for her, 'and at last there's only enough for one foot at a time. And if you jump into a wave getting back, you drown.'

'I say,' muttered Marie at her elbow as they staggered, stone-laden, back to the fire, 'why didn't you come back when I called?'

'Did you?' said Nicola indifferently. 'I thought I heard someone shout, but I wasn't sure so I didn't bother.'

She dumped her stone and went back for another. Marie, satisfied that her story was established and accepted, began to build an armchair round the stone designated as the District Commissioner's.

The Guiders, watching the preparations from the cliff-top, thought they seemed to be getting on well and that a friendly atmosphere prevailed.

'Though I'm not sure that I approve of those small ones being allowed to lug those great stones up the beach,' said the Commissioner doubtfully, her pencil hovering over her note-book. 'Excess of zeal, I suppose. I think I'll mention it at the end, even if I don't actually deduct any marks. Shall we go down now? I think we've given them plenty of time to get over the first snags.'

Lois greeted them gaily. The hike was going well enough now for her to have forgotten the morning's frets. Bacon and sausages were spluttering in one billy, slices of potato in another; and Jill was preparing 'campers dreams', which, filled with jam and butter, would serve as a sweet. It was going to be all right, thought Lois thankfully, as nothing burned and nothing spilled and nothing seemed to be overcooked; it would be all right and she would have her First Class and be a Patrol Leader and the team would be forgotten.

They boiled sea-water for washing-up and scoured the plates with sand. A piece of driftwood, reserved for the rest-hour, not because it was chilly, but because it seemed a pity to waste the fire, sparked and spluttered, long imbrued with pitch and saltpetre. When they were all comfortable, Lois explained to the District Commissioner the origin of the Patrol's name. 'It was Lawrie's idea,' she said, smiling quickly at Lawrie, who blushed until her cheeks were as scarlet as the dark Juliet's; 'and I thought, as this was our first thing as a Patrol, we ought to have a ceremonial reading as – as a mark of respect and appreciation.' She held up a copy of *The Scarlet Pimpernel*, laughing a little.

The Pimpernels laughed too, and settled themselves comfortably. Lawrie, a rather set expression on her face, rolled over on to her front, making as though what really interested her was the line of shells she was placing across the smoothed sand in front of her. Being read to was one of the things she particularly disliked, unless the person who was doing it was really good at it; if she wasn't, something inside Lawrie seemed to go stiff with a feeling that was neither all crossness nor all unhappiness, but was compounded of a large slice of both. As Lois began, she pushed her hands into the warm, weightless sand, which clung to her wrists in obstinate patches even after she had pulled them out again, and pretended preoccupation as an antidote to the flinching apprehension that Lois, who ought to do everything a little more than perfectly, was about to make rather a fool of herself. It would be dreadful if she read like Miller, the wire-haired, round-faced, junior English mistress, who, every Friday, second period, persevered with the formal intricacies of *The Fairie Queen*. Lawrie dug her hands deeply into the sand and made an expression on her face as though she wasn't really listening.

For a moment or two her apprehensions deafened her to the actual sound of Lois' voice; and then, as she dug with concentration, one arm elbow-deep and the fingers beginning to scrabble on the larger, damper grains, she realized abruptly that Lois was very far indeed from making a fool of herself. Carefully, as though afraid she might disturb something, Lawrie withdrew her arms from the silent, trickling sand and laid them gently crossed in front of her so that she could rest her chin on them. And when Lois came to the end of the first chapter and made as though to hand the book on to Jill, Lawrie had to curl her toes hard inside her plimsolls to prevent herself from protesting aloud that no one else should even think of reading while Lois was there – but it was all right, for Jill declined, saying, as though in reference to some private joke: 'Bless me, no. Not me. Not after what Kempe said last *Hamlet* lesson.' And the elder members of the Patrol also murmured their protests, saying, as though it were something they all knew, that of course Lois must go on with it; she read much the best.

They were all sorry when rest-hour ended, but jumped up at once at Lois's suggestion of tracking games, remembering that Lois's passing depended a good deal on their enjoying themselves. Jill and Terry went off to lay a trail through the caves and the rest followed, Marie with her heart in her mouth, Nicola and Lawrie racing ahead and calling to one another in order to start the long rolling echoes.

'I suppose we couldn't count this as our Second Class track?' suggested Lawrie hopefully, and Lois laughed and said she didn't think so, but that she'd ask Captain to arrange a proper track for them soon.

They all came out blinking into the sunny afternoon, surprised that the shadows were already lengthening.

'One game of tip-and-run,' said Lois, 'and then I expect we'll have to pack up. And for goodness' sake don't anyone groan when I suggest it.'

They assured her that they wouldn't think of it, and Lois handed the bat to Lawrie. As she did so, there was a shout from the top of the cliff; Miss Redmond began to hurry up the cliff path and the man who had shouted came down to meet her.

'It's Probyn,' said Lois flatly. She did not start the game, but stood watching silently. Miss Redmond was shaking her head emphatically; Mr. Probyn was as emphatically insistent. Miss Redmond, with a gesture which seemed to indicate: 'Wait a minute', came running back down the cliff path.

'Children,' she called as she came across the sands, 'none of you went through Mr. Probyn's farm this morning, did you?'

Lawrie heard Lois catch her breath.

'Because Mr. Probyn says that one of his labourers saw two small girls in blue run through the rick-yard—'

'We did,' said Nicola hurriedly, with much the same feeling as the first time she had jumped into the deep end of the baths. 'Lawrie and me, I mean, Captain.'

'But – how was that?' asked Miss Redmond sharply. 'The map showed the path down the cliff quite clearly and your tracking signs – do you mean you went alone?'

'Yes, Captain,' said Nicola. She kept her eyes on Miss Redmond's face, thinking how alarming even perfectly nice people could look when they were angry.

Miss Redmond looked at Lois.

'They just ran off,' said Lois in a quick stammer. 'I called them back, but they simply ran on.'

'But *Lois* –' said Lawrie.

'What's the trouble?' asked Miss Leslie at the same time. 'Have they been trespassing?'

Miss Redmond turned to her with a quick grimace.

'Trespassing, of course. But worse than that, I'm afraid. A fire started in the rick-yard this morning and the damage is rather serious. Mr. Probyn thinks that we may have been responsible.'

'Well, but wait a minute,' said the Commissioner. 'It's a great pity that it should be just this morning that these two should have taken it into their heads to be tiresome. But could they have started a fire? Had they anything to start it with?'

Miss Redmond looked relieved.

'No, I don't suppose they had. Lois, who brought the matches? Yourself?'

'No, me,' said Jill.

'But Nicola had some,' said Marie Dobson. 'She and Lawrie were playing with them as we came along.'

Nicola reddened angrily. For the moment she felt so stiff with rage that she couldn't speak.

'Oh, Nicola,' said Miss Redmond despairingly.

'But I didn't light them in the rick-yard,' said Nicola

contemptuously. 'Besides, they're at the bottom of my haversack. They couldn't start a fire there.'

Miss Redmond flushed. 'There's no need to be rude, Nicola. Let's make sure, at least, that they are still in your haversack.'

'I had some too,' said Lawrie defiantly.

'What on earth—? Well, get them out,' then, Lawrence, and let's see them.'

Nicola, her face burning, thrust her hand into her haversack. To her incredulous relief it closed instantly on the box of matches. Wordlessly, she brought it out and displayed it.

'That's something,' said Miss Redmond. 'Well, Lawrie?'

Lawrie said nothing. She went on groping in her haversack, her heart thumping with fright. At last, in desperation, she took her haversack by the bottom corners, held it upside down and shook it. An assortment of string, dry twigs, notebooks, pencils, and white chalk fell on the sand. They all stared hopefully at the little pile. But it was useless. The matches had gone.

IV

They found them, twenty minutes later, by the gate leading out of the rick-yard. The box had opened and the matches were scattered broadcast among the straw and on the cobbles. Lawrie, fighting tears of fright, reiterated desperately that they must have fallen out when she was climbing the gate. She hadn't dreamt of taking them out in the rick-yard. She wouldn't be such an ass.

Mr. Probyn, standing by with a certain grim satisfaction, said, Well, there it was. There were the matches. There was the fire – or the remains of it. (They all turned and stared despondently at the charred and blackened half rick from which smoke still rose in a depressing and malignant trickle.) There was nothing for him to do but write to their head teacher about it – no, he didn't doubt but that Miss Redmond would tell her what had happened, but he'd as soon get his say-so in as well. And now he'd be obliged if they'd kindly step off his land. And he wished them a very good afternoon.

They caught a bus back. There was no longer any pretence that they were on a hike. Nicola and Lawrie sat together on the front seat, unspeaking, Lawrie staring out of the window and trying to pretend that the tears which rolled so persistently and infuriatingly down her cheeks belonged to someone else. No one talked much, except the Guiders on the back seat, who kept up a low-voiced and worried conversation, until the bus stopped at the school gates and they all got out.

'It's no use crying, Lawrie,' said Miss Redmond, not unkindly. 'Whatever's done is done now. Try to pull yourself together before we go into school.'

Lawrie gave a sudden choking sob. She put her head down and fled past them, scudding up the drive and into the comparative safety of school. Nicola looked uneasily after her, but did not move. No one else said anything. They all went up the drive, thankful that few people were about to see them come home.

In the entrance hall, Miss Redmond turned to them again.

'Miss Leslie and I are going up now to see Miss Keith about – well, about what's happened. But of course we shall have to hold a very much fuller enquiry into all the whys and wherefores. I shall try to arrange for a Court of Honour sometime Monday afternoon. That will mean Lois, Jill, Nicola, Lawrie – no one else, I think. At least, no one else went into the rick-yard, did they? Or knows anything useful?'

'No, Captain,' murmured the Pimpernels in subdued voices.

'Marie did,' said Nicola bitterly. She felt she owed Marie one for piping up so readily with the information about the matches. 'At least, she said she called us, so I suppose she was there.'

Marie crimsoned.

'Lois told me to go,' she gasped quickly.

'I see,' said Miss Redmond. Her voice was flat and chilly. 'Then you'd better be prepared to attend as well.' She glanced at the forlorn group before her and said: 'I'm sorry the day should have ended so badly. It all started off so well.'

The group broke up in silence. Miss Redmond and Miss Leslie went off in the direction of Miss Keith's study; the others went sadly away to change; Lois hesitated; she desperately wanted to ask if this would mean that she must fail her test, and yet, because she knew the answer, did not dare to ask and so destroy the last possibility of hope. She glanced across the vestibule and saw that Nicola was still there, making as though she were reading the fixture list. As she looked, Nicola swung round with an air of scared determination and came towards her.

'I'm sorry about it, Lois,' she said stiffly. 'We only meant to be helpful.'

'Then it was a pity,' said Lois savagely, 'that you piped up so glibly about chasing off across the rick-yard. Why didn't you keep quiet about it, you little ass?'

'But the whole Patrol knew,' said Nicola. 'There wouldn't have been any point. Even if I'd thought of it.'

'And the Marlows are as honest as the day,' said Lois. '*I* know.'

Nicola coloured, but she stood her ground.

'I wanted to know,' she said with an effort at nonchalance, 'are you going to go on pretending that we just ran off and you don't know why?'

They stared at one another, silent and furious.

'Yes, I am,' said Lois at last, her heart thudding. 'And it isn't particularly pretence. Lawrie gabbled something about a fire, but—'

'All right,' said Nicola. 'I only wanted to know.' She swung her haversack across her shoulder like a Dick Whittington bundle and went off up the stairs.

8 A Court of Honour

It was a long Sunday. In the normal way, Sundays were long, but pleasant; this one was merely long. Even the fact that it was Third Remove's turn to go to the cathedral failed to cheer the twins. It was, as Nicola pointed out, a pity it had to be that particular Sunday, because they had both been quite keen to see the cathedral from the inside; and Lawrie in particular had wanted to see the tomb Rowan liked – the one of the crusader who had taken off his gauntlet so that he might still hold his lady's hand – and now it was wasted. Lawrie saw the tomb, nodded dispiritedly, and walked silently home beside Nicola. Nicola talked to Tim who was walking in front with Elizabeth Collins. But it was hard work, covering Lawrie's silence.

Third Remove knew by then that there was a terrific row on; but Lawrie had disappeared after lunch and Nicola said flatly that it was nothing to do with anyone outside Guides; Marie, while hinting darkly, told the curious that she couldn't possibly say anything till after the Court of Honour.

'And you won't be able to then,' snarled Nicola. 'Courts of Honour are secret. So there.'

'I don't need to have you tell me about Guide things,' said Marie haughtily.

Nicola lunged at her. Only physical violence seemed likely to take that smug expression off Marie's face, and physical violence seemed an immensely satisfying thing at that moment. Marie got up slowly, holding the back of her head and whimpering that very likely she would have concussion.

Nicola retorted that that would be a very good thing and went out, slamming the door gloriously behind her. Tim, following her out, remarked that with luck Marie had a fractured skull and what was the row anyway?

'Oh, don't you start,' growled Nicola. 'I could tell you if I liked, I suppose, but I don't want to a bit.'

'Oh,' said Tim. She said hopefully: 'I thought, you see, that you might be being Falsely Accused and that I, as the Headmistress's Niece, could Exert my Influence to Clear Your Name.'

Despite herself, Nicola grinned.

'Well, I'm not and you can't and I don't want to talk about it. Let's go and play table tennis in the gym.'

'All right,' said Tim. 'Where's Lawrie?'

'Goodness knows,' said Nicola, who had given up wondering where Lawrie was, but suspected the map-cupboard in the attic. 'Let's go before the seniors bag all the tables.'

They played table tennis for the rest of the afternoon. Lawrie put in no appearance at tea; but when Nicola went up to change for supper, she found Lawrie already there, sponging her face wildly with cold water. She looked dusty and woebegone. Nicola scowled at her.

'You might have come down this afternoon. Everyone's in a frightful flap to know what it's all about.'

'Did you tell them?' asked Lawrie. Her voice sounded rough and shaken.

'No.'

Lawrie looked dubiously at her reflection.

'Do I look frightfully cried on?'

'Yes,' said Nicola crossly. 'You do.' She began to wrench off her Sunday house frock.

'Don't you be livid, please,' said Lawrie piteously.

Nicola, muffled by the folds of her frock, said nothing.

Then the rest came in and there was no need to say anything.

'Hullo,' said Ginty. 'Good heavens, what's the matter with Lawrie?'

'What on earth have you been doing with yourself?' enquired Rowan. 'Nick, what's the matter with Lawrie?'

'She feels sick,' said Nicola, tugging off her stockings. 'She's got a headache. She wants to go to bed.'

'I'll see to her,' said Ann. 'I'll see Matron about her and get an aspirin and some hot milk. Would you like my hot-water bottle, Lawrie?'

'She's got her own,' snarled Nicola over her shoulder. 'There's no need to slop.'

'This sounds quite like home,' observed Rowan. 'If you're in a bate, Nick, wouldn't you like to get dressed and clear off?'

'Yes, I would,' retorted Nicola. 'And if Ann will be so good as to move so that I can wash my face, I'll be out of here before you can say—'

'Horatio Nelson,' suggested Ginty.

Nicola glowered. Ann, looking hurt and slightly bewildered, went into Lawrie's cubicle and drew the curtains. Nicola splashed briefly, pulled her velvet supper dress over her head and went off, tugging at the zip-fastener. She slammed that door too.

Some of her fury ebbed, however, during supper; and she went up to bed intending to be calm and swaggering and resourceful and to remind Lawrie that by this time tomorrow everything would be over and probably nothing would have happened anyway. But Lawrie was asleep – truly asleep, thought Nicola, who knew all Lawrie's devices for seeming so. She undressed cautiously by the smothered light of her torch and got into bed to cuddle the hot-water bottle left there by the kindly Ann. Probably Lawrie had told her about the row, thought Nicola, and felt cross again. She didn't want to be petted by Ann; and, taking care to do it quietly, she dumped her hot-water bottle on the floor beside her bed. Then it occurred to her that the Court of Honour would probably not be much fun for Ann either, and, groping resignedly, pulled the hot-water bottle into bed again.

She woke early, contended for a moment with a sensation of nameless apprehension, and then remembered. She sat up, shaking back her hair, and saw that Lawrie, too, was awake, lying on her back with her hands clasped behind her head and staring forlornly out of the window. Nicola caught her eye and in dumb show suggested that they might as well dress and go out. Lawrie nodded. Quietly they got out of bed, quietly gathered up their clothes, quietly tiptoed down the dormitory; quietly they stole into the corridor and along to the bathroom.

'And we may be breaking a rule for all I know,' said Nicola, 'but it's better than lying in bed and thinking about it.'

Lawrie nodded. She seemed, to Nicola's relief, more composed this morning. She noted enviously, however, as they ran gently downstairs and out through a side door, that Lawrie had, overnight as it were, exercised her gift for losing substance. When trouble impended, Lawrie could always contrive to look orphaned and pathetic; her face became thin and wan, dark shadows appeared under her eyes and she lost weight visibly. No one – not even a Court of Honour – could be very furious with Lawrie when she looked like that. Remembering her own normal reflection, Nicola sighed despondently.

It was a soft, smoky-scented autumn morning. Large cobwebs, shimmering with small drops of water, were slung across the bushes, and the grass was white with dew. Lawrie looked interestedly over her shoulder at her black foot-prints.

'I wish we could run away to sea,' said Nicola mournfully, slashing at the bushes with a stick she had picked up.

''M,' said Lawrie. 'What's going to happen, d'you think? I mean, what exactly have we done?'

Nicola knitted her brows. 'Well – we trespassed; and we disobeyed our Patrol Leader; and p'rhaps we were responsible for the fire.'

'We didn't disobey our Patrol Leader. She said she didn't know and then she said Well. You can't call that saying we weren't to.'

'No,' said Nicola grimly. 'But Lois can. At least, she says she can. Or rather, she's going to forget all that and say we bolted and she called us back and we didn't come.'

'But she can't,' said Lawrie, standing still. 'She *can't* say that. It isn't true.'

'I don't think that's going to worry her much, if you ask me. At least – I don't quite know. She sounded as though she'd got it all pulled round her way so that it *was* true. D'you remember how Peter used to be when he was little – when he broke my ship and said it was my fault 'cos I hadn't fixed the mast properly? Like that.'

Lawrie considered this in silence.

'And what are we going to do?'

'I don't know,' said Nicola frankly. 'P'rhaps when it comes to the point, she'll be decent about it. If she isn't – well, she's a Patrol Leader, and I expect Captain'll believe her most.'

Lawrie shivered, looking scared.

'Will you do all the talking, Nick?' she besought her. 'You know I never can.'

''M,' said Nicola. 'Yes. All right. Don't let's talk about it any more now, anyway. Let's go down to the stream and see if there are frogs. Twelve hours from now it'll be all over one way or the other.'

'That's what you always say,' said Lawrie. 'And I don't think it's very helpful. You've got to get through the twelve hours first.'

The frogs and the stream were comforting, however, and they went into breakfast damp but comparatively cheerful. Then routine caught up with them and it was only as sudden patches of darkness that they remembered the inexorable coming of the afternoon. It was at one o'clock, as they were putting their books away, that Muriel Pollick, the Company Leader, came in to tell them that the Court of Honour would be held at half-past three.

'But we've got Maths,' said Nicola, dismayed.

'Yes, I know. Miss Redmond's arranged all that. Ironsides is letting you two and Marie go early. You'll wear uniform, of course. You'd better change after dinner.'

'All right,' said Nicola. Her legs felt queer – stiff and shaky at the same time.

The afternoon dragged itself away. History – the last barrier – ended and gave place to Maths. Nicola wondered what they should do – ought they to ask Ironsides when the time came or hope Ironsides would remember? She glanced at Lawrie who had pulled her cuff unobtrusively above her watch. Perhaps Marie would ask – Marie was their senior in lots of things.

But Miss Cromwell was unexpectedly kind about it. At twenty-five past three she remarked: 'Nicola, Lawrence – and who's the other one? You, Marie? You'd better run along now. Put your books away before you go. And don't forget to get the preparation from one of the others.'

They said dutifully: 'No, Miss Cromwell. G' afternoon,

Miss Cromwell,' and went out, watched covertly by the rest of Third Remove. Now that it was so nearly upon them, even Lawrie felt too numb for panic. In silence they went out of school and down the long path to the wood.

Denise Fenton was waiting by the door of the hut.

'You're all right,' she said. 'You're not late. We're still waiting for Captain. I expect someone's pastry burned at the critical moment.'

Marie giggled. Nicola and Lawrie tried to smile in acknowledgement of Denise's friendliness, but found it impossible. Then Captain came down the path and passed them with a quick salute. Denise followed her in, and the twins and Marie looked at one another, wondering what happened next. Then Denise came out again.

'You're all to come in,' she said.

Lawrie drew a deep silent breath and closed her eyes. She was not perfectly certain what she expected to see in the hut; had rack and thumbscrews been displayed she would have been fearful but not astonished; all she could see, however, were the Patrol Leaders and their Seconds seated on three sides of a big bare table just below the platform. And that was bad enough, thought Lawrie, as they went down the long room towards them, Marie's heavy shoes sounding loudly on the bare boards; it was awful that they all had to look so frightfully clean and tidy and official.

Rita Calthrop, the Company Scribe, gave her a quick, friendly smile; Ann, looking rather white, made an attempt at a reassuring nod. Lawrie stared solemnly at them both, her mouth refusing to smile, and then glanced quickly at Lois. But Lois was absorbed by the pattern she was drawing on her blotting-paper. Lawrie dropped her eyes until they rested on the edge of the table in front of her.

'We shan't want you for the moment, Marie,' Captain was saying. 'I'd like you to go and wait in the Guiders' cloakroom until I send someone for you. I don't suppose we shall keep you very long.'

Marie went off to the small room at the back of the platform where Captain and Lieutenant washed their hands and hung their coats. The twins waited.

'Now,' said Captain; and with the knowledge that the enquiry had really started, a small sigh and rustle went over the Court.

'Now,' said Captain. 'I think, perhaps, it would be simplest if you two were to tell us in your own words exactly what happened.'

Lawrie stared fixedly at the table. Nicola felt the colour rise in her cheeks.

'I—' she said. 'We—. We were—.' She stopped helplessly.

'Captain,' said Ann hurriedly. 'I think they'd probably find it easier to answer questions.'

Captain looked at her pencil for a moment. 'Very well,' she said.

'Now – you were carrying matches with you, weren't you – both of you?'

'Yes, Captain.'

'And you took them out and played with them while you were going down to the beach?'

'Yes, Captain.'

'When you say "playing with them", what exactly do you mean by that?'

Nicola took a breath. 'You fix two matches into the top of the box, and wedge another between them, and then you light the – the two heads that are together and the one that's wedged jumps out.'

'I see. And did you notice whether the matches went

out or not when they'd "jumped" as you put it?'

'I didn't notice specially,' said Nicola, her heart thumping. 'But it was all on stones.'

'But you didn't take any care to see that they were out – you didn't stamp on them, for instance?'

'No, Captain.'

There was a slight pause.

'Now. Why were you carrying matches at all? Did your Patrol Leader tell you to bring them?'

'No. I told Jill to bring them,' said Lois swiftly, scoring a deep line on her blotting-paper. 'The twins were there when I said it.'

'Yes. But I want Nicola's story. Did you think you were supposed to bring matches, Nicola?'

'No, Captain.'

'Then why did you?'

Nicola reddened again. 'Because we – well, because—' because Lawrie went cracked on Lois and wanted to be so beastly helpful, was all that occurred to her. And obviously you couldn't say that.

'New Guides always do bring things, specially on their first hike,' said Ann's voice. 'They always carry heaps of extra things.'

Captain smiled at her quite pleasantly.

'I realize that this isn't very comfortable for you, Ann. And I think perhaps Nicola and Lawrence would find it easier if you were not here. In the ordinary way – if it were only a matter of Company discipline – I would ignore that. But I'm sure you'll see, Ann, that this business is too serious to be considered by anyone who isn't strictly impartial. So will you leave us, please?'

Ann's face flamed. She got up wordlessly and went out, passing the twins without a glance.

Miss Redmond waited until the door of the hut had closed behind her.

'Now. How long were you playing with your matches?'

'Not long,' said Nicola. 'Lois saw us and told me to put the box away.'

'And did you?'

'Yes, Captain.'

'It was your box, not Lawrie's, that you were playing with?'

'Yes, Captain.'

'And you didn't take it out again?'

'No,' said Nicola definitely, 'Lois said we weren't to.' And then she remembered. Her face flamed as Ann's had done. 'I mean – but it was only on the beach—' she said incoherently.

'I don't mean when I asked you to see if you still had them,' said Captain impatiently. 'I mean at any other time?'

'Yes,' said Nicola, crimson from chin to brow. 'We were on the beach first—'

'Well?'

'So we lit the fire,' said Nicola, her heart banging. It seemed to her as she said it that now Captain must see why they had gone through the farm, and Lois wouldn't be able to wriggle out of it. For a confused instant she didn't know whether she were pleased or sorry. She stared at the floor, not much wanting to see the moment of discovery. But nothing happened. Captain, neatening her papers, said levelly: 'Is that so, Lois?' And Lois, after an instant's silence, said: 'Yes. Yes, it is.'

'I see.' There was a pause. 'Now. Why did you suddenly break away and run across through the farm?'

'For a joke, I should think,' said Lois, with an attempt at a laugh. Nicola looked at her. Lois went on shading her monogram, her fingers very white where they held the pencil.

'Perhaps we'd better have your version first, Lois. What happened, exactly? No, wait a moment, Nicola.'

'Well. It may have been my fault in a way,' said Lois unevenly. 'I said – I'm afraid I said something about it being a pest that the map took us the long way round by the cliff. And one of them – Lawrie, I think – said: "Oh, we'll take the short cut." I said they couldn't go wandering off alone – it didn't occur to me that they meant it – and Nicola said something about that they couldn't possibly get lost. And then they legged it over the gate.'

'And you called them back?'

'Yes.'

'Well, Nicola?'

Nicola said nothing. It was so nearly what had happened that her own vision of what had taken place was blurred. Perhaps Lois was right. Perhaps she hadn't thought they were going—

'Well, Nicola?'

'I – I don't know,' said Nicola helplessly.

'What do you mean, you don't know? You heard Lois call you back?'

'Yes,' said Nicola. 'Yes, I suppose so. But I didn't think she meant it.'

'That's a silly excuse,' said Miss Redmond acidly. 'No one gives an order unless they mean it.'

Nicola said nothing. Her father was apt to say the same thing.

'So then you sent Marie Dobson after them?' said Miss Redmond, turning back to Lois.

'Yes.'

'This, I think, is where we'd better have Marie in. Denise, will you call her?'

Since the Saturday afternoon, Marie had had plenty of time to consider her story. She had the facility, common to the fearful, of remembering exactly what story she had told first, of knowing how it could be improved upon and of coming, eventually, to believe that that was, in fact, how it had happened. She followed Denise down from the platform and stood by the table, a flushed, unattractive child, but apparently stolid and honest.

'Now, Marie,' said Miss Redmond, 'tell us what you did. Lois sent you after the twins and—?'

'And I climbed the gate,' said Marie, 'and as I came down off it I twisted my ankle a bit. So I ran after Nicola and Lawrie only I couldn't run very fast because my ankle hurt and I saw them in front and I called and one of them looked round and waved and then they went on. So I called again and then they were so far in front it didn't seem as if I could do anything so I ran back to Lois.'

'You think they definitely heard and saw you?'

'We *didn't*,' said Nicola indignantly. She wasn't sure about the Lois part, but she knew that wasn't true.

'But you did,' said Marie. 'When I asked you on the beach why you hadn't stopped, you said you'd heard me but you didn't bother.'

'No, I didn't,' said Nicola. 'I said I heard someone shout, but I didn't know who it was. And we didn't wave to anyone.'

Marie looked at Miss Redmond – a puzzled, honest glance.

'Well, I thought they did. Truly,' she said.

'All right, Marie. Is there anything anyone would like to ask her? Right. Then we needn't keep you any longer. Run along to preparation and explain to the mistress on duty that I kept you.'

Marie's shoes went back across the floor; the door opened and closed behind her.

'Now, Nicola, are you quite certain that neither you nor Lawrie saw Marie come after you? After all – wait a moment, Nicola – there's no reason why she should say you did if you didn't, is there?'

'P'rhaps she thought we did,' said Nicola uncertainly. 'P'rhaps she doesn't see very well.'

'But you heard her shout? Surely, since Lois herself had told you to come back, it must have occurred to you that someone else might have been sent after you?'

'No,' said Nicola. 'It didn't sound like that kind of shout.'

'Oh, Nicola—' said Miss Redmond, exasperated. 'I think you're being rather silly. Don't you?'

There was nothing to be said to that. Nicola stared at the floor, flushed and furious.

'Now, there's one last thing,' said Miss Redmond after a moment. 'When you were going through the rick-yard, did you, either of you, take out your matches to play with?'

'No,' said Nicola. She felt her feet were on solid ground again.

'I see. Well now, how was it then, that Lawrie's box came to be in the rick-yard? No, Nicola, not you. I think Lawrie must try to explain this.'

Lawrie jumped and turned scarlet. She stared at the floor desperately, hoping that if she stayed perfectly quiet and still, Captain would let Nick go on talking. Nicola rushed into the silence.

'They were on top when we packed the haversacks. They must have jolted out.'

'*Nicola*. Well, Lawrie?'

Lawrie clenched her hands behind her back.

'I–I expect they did,' she whispered.

'Lawrie, you must speak up and answer for yourself. Nicola has taken the whole weight of this enquiry so far. Where was your box of matches? Do you remember?'

There was no answer.

'Did you play with them as you went across the yard?'

Lawrie, the blood humming in her ears, said nothing.

'We're all waiting, Lawrence.'

She looked up. The faces at the table blurred together and she burst into tears; Miss Redmond looked down at her blotting pad; the other members of the Court of Honour glanced at one another uncomfortably.

'I think you two had better wait in my cloakroom while we discuss the whole matter,' said Miss Redmond after a moment. 'That will give Lawrie time to pull herself together. Run along.'

It seemed a long way round the table, up the steps and across the platform, and the handle turned awkwardly, slipping from Nicola's hand, but they got inside at last. Nicola closed the door and sat down in the broken-springed armchair, staring at her toes. Lawrie went on sobbing, standing awkwardly with her back to Nicola.

'I can't help it,' she sobbed. 'I didn't mean to. It just b-burst out.'

'I know,' said Nicola, not caring overmuch. 'Only do shut up now, or they'll hear you in there.'

Lawrie buried her head in a coat that was hanging from the wall, and went on sobbing in a muffled fashion.

'We've got to go back soon,' said Nicola, 'so you'll have to stop. And I don't see what's the matter anyway. Nothing's happened. There's a glass there; have some water.'

She filled the glass and pushed it into Lawrie's hand. Lawrie, the tears still rolling down her cheeks, detached herself from the coat and sat down on a hard chair. Her teeth chattered on the glass.

'What d'you think'll happen, Nick?'

'Nothing, probably. I expect they'll tick us off for this and that and tell us we've got to be good in future or else.'

'Or else what?'

'How should I know?'

'You aren't going to tell Captain about Lois?'

'I don't know what *to* tell her. What Lois said was almost what did happen. And if I did, I expect Captain'd tell me not to be silly again like when I said it didn't sound like that kind of shout.'

They relapsed into silence. Beyond the door the hum of voices rose and fell interminably. But at length they ceased, a chair was pushed back, and footsteps crossed the platform. Lawrie set the tumbler down with a thud.

'You can come in now,' said Denise. It sounded like a parlour game. They went round to the front of the table again and waited.

'Nicola and Lawrie,' said Miss Redmond at last. 'We have talked the whole thing over very carefully and we have come to certain decisions. The question of your responsibility for the rick fire is something we can't decide here. I am perfectly willing to believe that if it was due to either of you in any way, it was unintentional; but it will be up to the insurance company to decide what was the actual cause of the fire and whether either of you were in any way responsible. That doesn't affect the other matters with which this Court is more directly concerned.' She paused for a moment, straightened her pad and went on: 'It seems quite evident that you gave Lois a great deal of trouble all day. First, there was that irresponsible episode of playing with the matches; it is quite obvious, from what Nicola said, that it never occurred to you to take the most elementary precautions against starting a fire, although you knew how dry the weather had been: secondly, you disobeyed Lois in the most flagrant fashion when you ran away across the farm and then ignored the person she sent after you: and thirdly, you disobeyed her again when you lit the fire on the beach although she had told you that your matches were not to be used again without permission.' She paused again. No one moved. 'It isn't enough to look on Guides as a form of glorified picnic; I know you have been very anxious to pass your tests and to look smart and all those things; but Guides are also supposed to have a sense of responsibility, to be able to think sensibly on their own account, and to keep their promises. When you were enrolled you promised to "obey the Guide Law". Last Saturday you broke the seventh law in the most disgraceful fashion possible; and I don't think you came very near to keeping the spirit of many of the rest.'

She paused. Nicola stared stubbornly past Captain's shoulder. She wondered whether Lawrie was going to cry again.

'So we have decided that, although you would no doubt be useful members of your Patrol and of the Company in many ways, you are not really ready to be Guides yet; we have decided that it will be best if you are suspended from the Company until this time next year, and then, if you have really thought about what Guiding means – not merely winning badges and scoring points against other Patrols – and you decide that you would like to try again, we shall be very glad to have you. In the meantime, I must ask you to hand back your badges.'

Lawrie gasped. No one looked at them. Nicola undid hers at once and laid it on the table; Lawrie struggled momentarily with hers, then jerked it so that a small piece of tie tore, and laid it beside Nicola's. Miss Redmond nodded. 'That's all, children.'

They saluted uncertainly and went away down the hut. Outside it was nearly twilight.

The Court of Honour packed itself up in silence; in ones and twos they murmured something about grabbing some tea before it was all gone and left the hut.

'Oh, Lord,' said Muriel Pollick, grabbing at a rolling pencil. 'I always hoped I'd live to see a full dress Court of Honour about something that mattered. Why on earth did I think I'd enjoy it?'

'It wasn't a lot of fun,' agreed Lois. She felt so relieved that it was all over and that Nicola had said nothing awkward that she sounded almost gay. 'Coming in to tea, Jill?'

'No,' said Jill confusedly. 'No, I don't think so. I've got to practise and things. So long.'

'See you at supper, then,' Lois called after her. There was no answer. Perhaps she hadn't heard. Lois stirred uneasily.

'Oh, well,' she said. 'I'd better be getting along myself. Coming, Muriel?'

'Don't go for a moment, Lois,' said Miss Redmond, glancing up. 'I'd like a word with you before you go.'

Lois's heart began to thump. She watched Muriel hurriedly gathering her possessions together and hastening away. The only light was that which hung above the table; it cast a greenish-white glare. The rest of the room lay in darkness, a darkness which seemed to Lois to come flowing in until she could see only the white sheet of paper in front of her. She put her hands between her knees to warm them.

'There are just one or two things I want to say to you, Lois. I agree that Nicola and Lawrie behaved badly, and I agree, too, that they are quite old enough to know better. But at the same time, I can't feel that you displayed much common sense or initiative. That business about the match tricks, for instance; I'm quite sure that if those two had been given a definite job to do, they wouldn't have resorted to that kind of childishness. And I fancy what happened was that it was the older members of the Patrol who were given the map to follow and the trail to lay, and the juniors who were left to tag on behind. Isn't that so?'

'Yes,' said Lois after a pause. She went on staring at the piece of paper in front of her.

'Quite. And then, when they ran away from you, instead of going after them yourself or sending Jill – or even Juliet or Penelope – you sent another junior. It might have occurred to you, Lois, that if they were in that kind of harum-scarum mood, a child from their own form would be the last person they would be likely to obey.'

'But—'

'Well?'

'I wanted to get down to the beach. I needed Jill—'

'In fact, my dear Lois, you behaved as though nothing mattered but your badge test. And I don't suppose, when you got down to the beach and saw them there, with their fire all nicely lighted, that you took them to task either for running away or for lighting the fire with matches you had forbidden them to use.'

Lois said nothing.

'Did you?'

'No. No, I suppose I didn't.'

'Exactly. Well, that's all, Lois; but think it over. I'm not perfectly certain that I'm doing wisely in allowing you to remain a Patrol Leader, but at the same time I feel I should make allowances for lack of experience and even for excess of zeal. Anyway, we'll go on as we are for the rest of this term. But try to remember, as I said to Lawrie and Nicola, that Guides should mean a good deal more than simply passing all the tests you can manage in the shortest possible time.'

Lois clenched her hands between her knees. It was idiotic to ask – and tactless into the bargain.

'I suppose – I suppose I have failed my hike?'

'Naturally,' said Miss Redmond, surprised. 'Did you think there was any question about it?'

'No-o,' said Lois, 'only in some ways it went quite well – and they did enjoy themselves, I think. It's only – only the rick part—' She couldn't imagine why she was arguing about it.

Miss Redmond, her face expressionless, began to stack her papers into her attaché case. She said nothing.

'I'm sorry,' said Lois at length.

'Yes, Lois. All right. You'd better run along and see if there's any tea left.'

But Lois, her heart beginning to thud again, did not move. Perhaps it would be better to say what really had happened. There wasn't a lot to lose, anyway – she'd failed her hike – Captain didn't think much of her as a Patrol Leader – it might be easier, almost, to say: Look, they didn't exactly run away. They wanted to get the fire lit and I didn't stop them in time. I did almost say they could go.

Biting her lower lip she rehearsed the sentences in her mind. When Captain closed her attaché case—

Miss Redmond snapped the locks shut.

'Well, Lois? Don't you want your tea?'

'I suppose I do,' said Lois.

She got up and they went down the hut and out into the playing fields. Miss Redmond nodded to her and turned off down the path which led to the staff entrance.

So that was that. The moment was over and she hadn't

said it. It would have been an awful thing to have to say; she'd been an ass to think she could. And anyway, what she'd said at the Court of Honour had been quite fairly true . . .

She kicked a pebble and sent it spinning in front of her into the shadowy dusk. The thing was over now. People would forget. She'd work like mad and make the Pimpernels infinitely better than the loathsome Cornflowers; and Captain would probably say something like: You've done very well since that unfortunate hike, Lois; we're all very proud of you. Lois kicked another pebble. Perhaps she'd say that; perhaps not. If not, there was always Matric. in the summer. She could always make that an excuse to chuck Guides. Lois sighed disconsolately. She supposed she ought to be feeling relieved that she had got off so lightly; but she didn't; she felt depressed and apprehensive and queerly humiliated. Of course, Captain had been pretty venomous – rather unfair in some ways—

'*Unfair*,' thought Lois derisively. 'Don't be such a clod.'

9 Half-Term

I

Half-term came at the end of that week. The whole family was going home immediately after midday dinner on Friday and would not return until Monday evening. That, said Nicola, banging at her hair, as they were getting ready for bed on the evening after the Court of Honour, would be absolutely marvellous.

'Do you wish you could go home for good and never come back?' enquired Lawrie, sprawling across the bed. 'I do, I think.'

'No, you don't,' said Nicola sternly. 'You don't want Marie Dobson to think you *mind*, do you?' She went on banging at her hair.

Lawrie watched her in silence. If Nicola had not been in that kind of mood, Lawrie would have retorted, truthfully, that she didn't much care what Marie thought. But Nicola had been like that – swift and furious – ever since the previous evening when she had whirled out of her own uniform and pulled Lawrie out of hers, and made two neat piles – tunic, tie, belt, knife and hat – on Ann's bed.

'What's Ann going to do with them?' Lawrie had asked, feeling tired and stupid. And Nicola had retorted:

'*I* don't know. Anything she likes. Make dusters of them for all I care.'

Then she had wriggled into the red and blue caterpillar-striped jersey which all the juniors wore, and rushed off to play ping-pong in the gym.

Lawrie heaved a sigh. 'I suppose she'll know all about it by now,' she observed. 'Marie, I mean.'

'Probably.'

'Do you think they'll put us in the Log-book?'

'Probably. On the second page. "L. and N. Marlow. Kicked out. Monday, October 27th." '

'It sounds like an epitaph,' said Lawrie sadly.

'It probably is,' said Nicola.

Lawrie, too depressed to query this, rolled into bed and lay on her back, her knees humping the blankets.

'I shall make a chart,' she said at last, 'of all the hours between tomorrow morning and Friday dinner and black them out as we get through them.'

'Do, if you want to,' said Nicola. She dropped her hair-brush with a clatter and leapt into bed.

'Nick,' said Lawrie after a time. There was no reply. Lawrie propped herself on one elbow and gazed through the darkness. It didn't sound as though Nicola were asleep, but if she wouldn't talk, she wouldn't. Lawrie lay down again and romanced gently and pleasantly about the possibilities of pulling Lois Sanger out of the river just as she was being whirled towards the weir . . . and afterwards, in the San., a feverish and conscience-stricken Lois would demand to see Miss Redmond and confess everything, despite Lawrie's valiant protests . . . and then they would be reinstated, and Lawrie would be decorated with the Bronze Cross . . .

'And very nice too,' thought Lawrie, grinning to herself in the dark. 'Only I wouldn't save her. I'd jolly well let her drown. And I'd let her see I was letting her drown, what's more.' And feeling a good deal better, she humped her pillow and went to sleep.

II

'Half-term reports,' said Ginty, rather as though she had come unexpectedly on a long-forgotten but once favourite doll; 'well, well. Thank goodness I've grown out of those. I never realized before how Middle School I was.'

It was Saturday morning and they were sitting at their own breakfast table, so neither Nicola nor Lawrie cared much.

'There can't be anything in them,' said Nicola, 'because we haven't done anything. Are you going to read them, Father?'

'Tell us what they say,' begged Lawrie. 'Do. It's the first time we've ever had a Kingscote report.'

'The event of a lifetime,' remarked Rowan. 'What do they say, Father? "Fair, fair, very fair, could do well if she tried"?'

'Why should they?' said Lawrie indignantly. 'None of the rest of you get that kind.'

'That's why we probably have,' said Nicola with bravado. 'Pass the butter, Peter.'

Peter, who had week-end leave from Dartmouth, spun the butter-dish across the table.

'Not bad,' commented their father, skimming the forms. 'They mostly confine themselves to remarking that you've made a good start; and one good lady bursts into pæans of joy and says that Nicola "mimes with enthusiasm". Lawrie, on the other hand, "mimes convincingly". I wonder what the subtle difference is? And what, if one may ask, *is* miming?'

'I know,' said Peter, his mouth full of toast. 'Some girl gets up and recites the most frightful bilge about being where Helen lies, night and day on him she cries, and another ass does the dying and what-not. One of our chaps' sisters had a

Speech Day and he wangled me in because of the tea. They did a lot of that. Miming, I mean.'

'Pig,' said Nicola. 'Fool.' But she had to admit, when pressed, that miming was something like that.

'And,' said Commander Marlow casually, 'you seem to have been suspended from the Guide Company. What was all that?'

'We had a chap suspended too,' said Peter serenely, before Nicola could answer. 'Don't know what he did. Stole something, they *said*.'

'We didn't steal,' said Nicola hotly.

'Never said you did,' retorted Peter. 'Anyway, girls' schools don't. I suppose you smacked another brat and you both howled and the teacher said: Naughty girls, don't do it again.'

'*Staff*,' groaned Ginty. 'Not teachers, you dope.'

'It was nothing like that,' said Lawrie loftily. 'We burned a rick-yard.'

'*What!*' said her father.

'Don't be an ass,' said Nicola hurriedly. 'We didn't burn it. They only said we did. And it was only half a rick, anyway.'

'But, darling—' said her mother.

'Nicky,' said her father, 'do me the favour of telling me the story from the beginning. But before we go any further, just tell me this. Am I going to get a bill for the damage?'

'No,' said Karen quickly. 'I don't think so. Keith said that even if the insurance company proved it was Nick and Lawrie, she took the view that it was the school's responsibility because there'd been insufficient supervision. I think Keith was quite bitter to Redmond about it.'

'Was she?' said Lawrie, deeply and immediately interested. 'Was she, Kay? How d'you know?'

'Head girl's evening,' said Karen, who spent from six till eight every other Thursday drinking milky coffee and discussing school politics with Miss Keith. 'And of course you don't know anything about it.'

'Of course not,' said Lawrie impatiently. 'Was there a fearful row?'

'It sounded rather like it,' said Karen cautiously. 'But then Keith's always been a bit dubious about Guides. She always felt something like this would happen and now it has, if you see what I mean.'

'You must hear the most interesting things,' said Lawrie rapturously. 'Go on, Kay. Tell some more.'

'Never mind the inter-departmental rows for the moment,' said her father. 'The great thing is that I'm not getting the bill. And now, Nicky, give us the details; and you too, Lawrie, if you can be sensible.'

Put like that, Nicola found it perfectly easy to tell her story, the Lois episode sliding neatly into place without any doubts at all.

'Just like a lot of females,' said Peter insultingly at the end of it. 'All getting into a panic over a twerpish little badge—'

'Just like you got over whether you'd be in your prep. school cricket team,' retorted Ginty.

'But Nicky,' said Karen, 'there doesn't seem to be any question of your having started a fire. You couldn't have done. Matches don't strike of themselves.'

'N-no,' said Nicola. 'But I suppose one *might* have struck itself when it fell on the cobbles. Could it, Father?'

'Once in a million times, perhaps.'

'Or,' added Nicola, her colour deepening, 'they may still think we were mucking about striking matches all over the place and – and don't like to say.'

'Tell me, Nicky,' said her father. 'Were you?'

'*No,*' said Nicola. 'We're not utter asses. I'd as soon strike a match in a powder magazine.'

'But didn't you tell them so at your Court of Honour?' asked her mother.

'Well, I think so,' said Nicola wearily. 'Sort of.'

'I know exactly what happened at the Court of Honour,' said Rowan. 'No, Mother, I wasn't there, but intuition tells me. Everything was filthily full dress, the twins were petrified, someone asked a leading question, Lawrie burst into tears and guilt was assumed forthwith. Why didn't you do something, Ann?'

Ann flushed. Nicola said hotly: 'We weren't petrified. And Ann did try. Captain sent her out because she wasn't im-something.'

'Impartial,' suggested Karen.

'Then actually,' said Commander Marlow patiently, 'all you really did was to run through the farm instead of going down with the others by the cliff?'

'Yes,' said Nicola, '*but,* you see, Lois said she told us not to.'

'And did she?'

'*No,*' said Lawrie vigorously. 'She didn't. Definitely not. First, when we suggested it, she said, Of course it'd help, and then she said, Well, and then when we went off she sort of yelped, No, but when we waved she didn't do any more. Honestly, Father, she was only saying No for show. Only Nick wouldn't say so.'

'Why didn't you?' asked her father dryly.

Lawrie blushed.

'I would have,' said Nicola hastily, 'only Lois told about it first and I got muddled. And besides, Captain practically said I wasn't telling the truth about Marie. So I didn't see there was much point.'

'But why,' said Ann in a queer, tight voice, 'why would it have been helpful, Lawrie?'

'We've told you,' said Lawrie impatiently. 'Because she'd gone wrong with the map and she thought she'd lost a lot of time. So I said – or Nick said – we'll go down the quick way and get the fire ready and the District Commish won't know.'

Ann said nothing at all.

'*That* Lois Sanger,' said Rowan wrathfully. 'That's typical. Completely typical. Of all the lowest forms of animal life in the Royal Navy—'

'Thank you,' said Peter with dignity. 'We don't take the scum of the earth.'

'No, honestly, Father, she's a poisonous female. Before every match, she jumps the last three steps and pretends to sprain her ankle. Then if she plays badly she can say she wasn't feeling up to it and we're all expected to say: Awfully sportin' of you, old girl, to make the effort.'

'And do you?' asked her father, amused.

'No,' said Rowan, subsiding. 'At least – well, we had rather a flaming row at the cup match. All very virulent and rather disgusting.'

'Go on,' said Nicola with a meaning glance at Lawrie. Lawrie made a long leg and kicked her on the ankle.

'It's not specially interesting,' said Rowan in a withdrawn voice.

'Tell all the same,' said Ginty. 'I never heard the whole of it. Did you grab her by the short hairs and try to kick her teeth in?'

'No,' said Rowan shortly.

'*Please*, Rowan,' said Nicola.

'So long as you don't gossip,' said Rowan severely. 'This is strictly off the record.' She straightened her knife and fork and said abruptly: 'Well, we lost the wretched match and Lois couldn't have played worse and she was confiding all round that her ankle hurt frightfully – or maybe her wrist was broken – I forget which – and I said if that was so she should have had the decency not to play at all. And Craven pounced and said: "What?" in a very icy voice because it seemed we weren't losing in at all a gentlemanly way and Compton were getting the full benefit. So Lois wriggled and muttered and said something weak about Rowan having pushed her, and Craven looked ferocious and some misguided ass piped up: "But please, Lois said she did it falling downstairs", so Craven said to Margaret: "I will see the whole team when we get back. Go in to tea quietly." So we did.'

'Go on,' urged Ginty. 'This isn't a bit the story we've got.'

'Naturally not. Well, we got back to school, Craven a bit scratchy over losing anyway, and up we all trooped to the gym. And then we had a perfectly filthy half-hour, with Lois jumping from one story to another, and Craven gradually pinning her down and it more or less coming out that even the falling downstairs tale was a phoney – only Craven didn't quite press that. Anyway, in the end, Craven said that Lois had acted very selfishly in playing when she wasn't fit and that until she'd learned more team spirit she'd play for the Second. Then Craven stalked out, and Lois accused me of engineering the whole thing to get her out of the team, and there were lots of tears and recriminations – and it was all very low and beastly,' said Rowan suddenly closing up with an air of ineffable distaste.

'You *see*?' said Nicola to Lawrie.

'All *right*,' said Lawrie. 'There's no need to gloat.'

'But,' said their mother, 'if they know she's that kind

of girl, why did they make her a Patrol Leader?'

'Character training,' said Karen and Rowan simultaneously; and Rowan continued laconically: 'Redmond and Craven are great on it. They're always getting together and saying: Now what about so-and-so? Lacks confidence in herself, doesn't she? Skips out of the way if she sees a ball within a mile of her? Good: let's stick her in the First Eleven.'

'She – she – Redmond, I mean – doesn't believe in bringing school things into Guides,' said Ann shakily, 'and Lois has always been all right—' she stopped abruptly. The family stared.

'What's up with you?' asked Ginty.

Ann dug her fork into the tablecloth. 'Don't you see? It never came out at all about Nick and Lawrie going through the farm so that Miss Leslie shouldn't know that Lois had muddled the map. And lots of the row was about their disobedience – I see now what Nick meant when she said she didn't think Lois meant them to come back – and if Captain knew that part of it, I'm sure she wouldn't let Lois go on being a Patrol Leader – she *couldn't*—'

'Honour of the school at stake, what?' said Peter with a grin.

'My dear Ann,' said her father decisively, 'there's nothing you can do about it now; the twins should have stood by their version at the Court of Honour. And in any case, it's just as well they're out of Guides; they've plenty of leeway to make up in the way of ordinary school work at the moment without going in for extras. Besides, you can't go back next week when the whole thing will be dead and buried and start raking amongst the skeletons. For one thing, the twins wouldn't want you to, would you, Nicky?'

Nicola and Lawrie looked at one another across the table. They thought on the whole they would rather like to be cleared in a blaze of glory and have their badges handed back and Lois Sanger's nose rubbed in the dust; but Father obviously thought it wasn't worth making a fuss about, so Lawrie sighed silently and Nicola said with fine nonchalance:

'Good gracious me, no. It doesn't matter at all,' and stared rather hard out of the window and down the drive to the gates. Then she yelped wildly, sent her chair flying, and whirled out of the room and down the hall.

'Drunk,' said Rowan, 'or sunstroke. She thinks she's seen Giles.'

'*Giles?*'

'That's what she said.'

'She said quite correctly,' said her elder brother, strolling in with Nicola behind him beaming from ear to ear. 'What a long time you sit over breakfast. Is there any left?'

He kissed his mother in passing, nodded cheerfully at his father, waved to the rest of the family, and sat down in Nicola's place, eyeing the last of the bacon and eggs hopefully.

'It's nearly cold,' said his mother dubiously.

'Doesn't matter. I've had breakfast – a sort of breakfast. I only want to eat. I'll eat out of the dish if you like. How considerate of the hens to be laying at the moment. Or are they pickled?'

His mother passed him the dish resignedly.

'I thought,' said Peter accusingly, 'that you were on your way to Malta?'

'So I was,' said Giles. 'You're right, Mother, it *is* nearly cold. It tastes very interesting.'

'Then why aren't you now?'

'Military secret.'

'Oh, Giles—'

'No. As a matter of fact – by the way, where's the chorus of welcome that ought to have greeted me as I stood framed in the doorway? *Aren't* you pleased to see your little brother?'

'Pleased but stunned,' said Rowan grinning at him. 'Kay and Father are obviously reckoning up all the crimes for which you've been wrongfully cashiered.'

'How untrusting of them,' said Giles going on to toast and marmalade. 'Actually, nothing to do with me at all.'

'What isn't?'

'The military secret.'

'Can't you tell us, Giles, or are you being aggravating?' asked his father, raising one eyebrow.

'Put like that, Commander – only, of course, officially you *don't* know – we had a collision in mid-Channel and were ordered back for repairs.'

'Oh, Giles!'

His father waited patiently.

'*Nothing* to do with me,' said Giles happily. 'There I was, just come off watch and sleeping the sleep of the brave and the just, when,' catching sight of Lawrie's round eyes and expression of breathless interest, 'there was a thunderous crash and the next moment I was lying in the scuppers and the scuppers were running blood.'

'Oo-oo. What happened then?' breathed Lawrie.

'Then there was a lot of that orderly chaos I'm always reading the service is so good at, and there seemed to be a lot of sea in places we usually try to keep it out of. So all hands to the pumps,' said Giles wagging his knife at Lawrie, 'and come the dawn we were still afloat.'

'What had you collisioned with?' asked Nicola.

'Another destroyer, fortunately. She felt like a battle-waggon. Well, anyway, as soon as it was light the admiral came and looked at us and said we were an '*orrible* sight. Couldn't possibly disgrace his squadron with two wrecks like that – so back we came. Our old man and theirs signalling the rudest messages to one another all the way to Pompey.'

'How rude?' asked Lawrie.

Giles and his father laughed.

'Ruder than I can tell you,' said Giles.

'And how long will you be at home?' asked his mother hopefully.

'Truthfully, I don't know. Depends on how long the repairs take and whether Their Lordships let us wait around or not. In the meantime, that was a very good secondary breakfast. Can I have some more coffee?'

'It is lucky we were all home,' said Nicola, leaning against the table beside him.

He looked at her. 'And how are you? What measle have you been catching lately?'

'Not one,' said Lawrie proudly. 'Not for ages. We're at Kingscote now.'

'So you are by – (what's a good salty oath?). And are you ornaments of IIIA or otherwise?'

Because they never took the twins over-seriously, and because it suddenly seemed incredibly funny, Karen and Rowan and Ginty combined to give Giles a résumé of the twins' thwarted ambitions. They didn't intend to be unkind or to hurt anyone's feelings, or do more than make a good story for Giles. But Nicola, leaning silently against the table, was gradually overwhelmed with misery. It had been beastly and not funny in the least: and it wasn't fair to laugh: 'I suppose this is how Lawrie always feels,' thought Nicola, trying unsuccessfully to ignore the lump in her throat and the rainbow flashes before her eyes—

'Do shut up,' said Ann suddenly. 'Nicky doesn't like it.'

Two large tears rolled down Nicola's cheeks and she bolted. From the stairs her suddenly stricken family heard a choked sob. Giles pushed back his chair and went after her. Since his legs were longer than hers, he was able to grab the tail of her skirt as she was whirling into the bathroom.

'That isn't necessary,' said Giles firmly. 'Here's my handkerchief. What's the matter?'

'It isn't funny,' sobbed Nicola who was doing her best not to cry, but found it difficult to stop.

'You're making me very damp,' said Giles reproachfully, 'and to be truthful, I've seen as much salt water at close quarters as I care about for the moment. Shut up, Nick, and don't be an ass.'

Obediently, Nicola mopped her eyes. ''M sorry,' she said.

'Then we'll say no more about it,' said Giles magnanimously.

'But honestly, Giles, it wasn't funny. It was absolutely beastly.'

'Do you want to talk about it?'

'N-no. Except that you – you ought to know how it was properly. And it isn't fair for Kay and Rowan to be so funny about it. We were only trying to be credits to them – and – and – not to be the only duds – and they don't care a bit.'

'That,' said Giles, 'is life. Never expect, young Nicola, to be sufficiently praised for your virtues, or sufficiently condoled with over flagrant injustice; but always remember – no, I can't imagine what it is you should always remember. I am now going to bed for the rest of the morning to sleep off my recent maritime adventures—'

'Might you have been drowned, Giles?' said Nicola, suddenly envisioning a green sea and an empty rocking boat.

'Certainly. Thank you for the thought. This afternoon, however, I shall have recovered. If you and Lawrie like to pick out a reasonable flick, we'll go and see it and have tea at Harper's afterwards. Then, if you like, over a quiet cup, you can tell me all the ghastly details.'

'Oh *yes*, Giles. That'll be simply marvellous.'

'But not a programme consisting entirely of Mickey Mouse if you can help it.'

'We grew out of him years ago,' said Nicola haughtily.

'Pity,' said Giles perversely, vanishing into his room. 'I haven't.'

III

It seemed a great waste, Nicola thought, not to go and see *In Which We Serve*, which was on at one of the cinemas which didn't mind showing old films. But one couldn't expect Giles really to enjoy seeing people hanging on to a raft and probably Lawrie's thriller was a better idea. Giles, when asked, agreed that this was something he too wanted to see, and they set off after lunch, Giles assuring his mother all the way down the drive that if Lawrie looked over-excited he would bring her out immediately.

'You *wouldn't*, Giles, would you? Not in the *middle*,' Lawrie besought him, when they were out of earshot.

'It all depends on your face,' said Giles solemnly. 'If you can keep that from looking over-excited, of course I shan't need to. Otherwise, I shall have to take you out and dump you all amongst the palms and red plush.'

'Oh, *Giles*,' said Lawrie, in tones of such dire apprehension that Nicola felt moved to assure her that he was only teasing. Giles laughed and asked if they still needed to hold someone's hand when the hero entered a dark and silent house in order to get shot?

'Definitely,' said Lawrie and Nicola together.

'Just so long as we know,' said Giles with calm – a calm which did not desert him until the film was over and they were having tea – a mixed tea of lemonade and sandwiches, ice-cream and more ice-cream, and cakes and coffee with cream in it to finish off with.

'I don't see how you can help being sick to-night,' he remarked gloomily, 'and Mother will say it's all my fault, which will be true.'

'I don't feel at all sick,' said Lawrie affronted, digging her fork into her fourth éclair. 'You know, I'd like to be a film star.'

'You don't say,' said Giles. 'The beautiful heroine, I suppose, who tags round after the hero and nearly dishes them both with her lunacy?'

'No,' said Lawrie scornfully. 'Not that kind at all. I mean like the girl this afternoon who stood at the top of the stairs and shot him as he came up.'

'Nice, gentle little soul, aren't you?' commented Giles.

'I don't *mean* that,' said Lawrie, waving her fork agitatedly. 'I don't mean because she shot him. I mean because—'

'Then you wouldn't be a star, you'd only be featured,' said Nicola helpfully.

'Some features,' added Giles candidly.

Lawrie opened her mouth, shut it despairingly, and speared another éclair.

Giles pushed the plate towards Nicola. 'You'd better have another, too. Just to keep level. Now then. Do you still want to tell me the tale of woe?'

She told him briefly, without overmuch detail, Lawrie listening in silence.

'But what I don't see,' said Giles at the end of it, 'is why you were so anxious to shine so brightly.'

Nicola sighed. She always seemed to be explaining that. She said patiently: 'Because the Marlows always are good at things. And the staff jolly well expected us to be. They were always saying things like: "A Marlow who can't do History! Well!" '

'So what?'

'How d'you mean?'

'Well – so what? I mean, what are you going to do for the rest of the term?'

Lawrie sighed deeply. 'That's what's so awful. There's nothing left to be good at.'

'You could enjoy yourselves,' suggested Giles.

'I suppose so,' said Nicola dubiously.

'Ginty said last night,' said Lawrie, 'that it was a pity we hadn't concentrated on being bad – wicked, she meant, not flops. She said we were obviously more cut out for that than for anything else.'

'What did she mean?' asked Nicola indignantly.

'When you stopped the train and when we got cashiered,' said Lawrie.

'It might be more amusing,' said Giles idly. 'Only if you're going to be wicked, do it on the larger scale.'

'How d'you mean?'

'Well – if you're going to have a midnight feast (that is what all the books have, isn't it?) don't put up with bath buns under the bed-clothes. Do it properly with sausages in a deserted house.'

'D'you mean it?' said Lawrie.

'Certainly. Why should you be credits to the family? Is the family grateful for your efforts? No. On the contrary, they roar with laughter whenever they think of it. Take my advice and try being bad. At least it'll be something new for Kay to think about.'

'Go on, Giles,' urged Nicola, 'what else can we do?'

Giles looked at her, his cheeks sucked in to hide his grin.

'We-ll,' said Giles, who was considered by his

commanding officer to have the makings of a brilliant and responsible officer, 'you might break bounds to go to the evening performance of the circus (if you get one)—'

'Won't a theatre do?' asked Lawrie solemnly.

'Hardly,' said Giles, equally solemnly, 'a theatre hasn't quite the verve – the élan – the oomph—'

'I can see that,' agreed Nicola. 'We must talk this over, Lawrie.'

Lawrie flushed. 'No,' she said. 'I'm not going to. I loathe rows. That Court of Honour will last me for years and years. And Giles is probably only having you on, anyway.'

'He's not,' cried Nicola. 'Are you, Giles?'

'Good heavens, no,' said Giles.

'Well, anyway, I won't,' said Lawrie. 'I'm going to be good and quiet and no trouble to anyone. I don't mind being anti-Pomona, but that's as far as I'll go.'

'Then I'll be bad by myself,' said Nicola crossly. 'And I think it's very low of you. Very low indeed.'

'O.K.,' said Giles soothingly. 'You be bad, then. And drop me a line every now and then. I'd like to know how you get on.'

10 Kitchen and Jumble

It was curious how remote half-term made the events of the previous six or seven weeks. Nicola, stalking into Third Remove, her chin in the air, ready to be swiftly and instantly aggressive if anyone so much as mentioned Guides, found that those who had stayed behind for half-term were discussing the bazaar the Thirds were to hold at Christmas in aid of the new wing for the library. In its way it was disconcerting to have churned up so much anger and find no use for it; for even Marie Dobson, who might have been expected to be more annoying than anyone else, was full of grandiose schemes for side-shows and magic caves and stalls crammed with perfect merchandise. Certainly no one had any interest in week-old rows involving Nicola Marlow; and equally certainly no one would want to listen to possible schemes for breaking bounds. Perhaps, thought Nicola, listening silently to Audrey Fudge's ideas for lampshades and Elizabeth Collins's shy disclosure of being awfully keen on patchwork, perhaps people always did forget things which didn't actually affect themselves. Perhaps that was something one should be pleased about.

'And what are you going to make?' asked Tim, giving her a little poke. Tim, who for five weeks had hoped that something would happen which would force Lawrie and Nicola to drop Guides, was affected by the queer, uncertain feeling of guilt which arises from seeing one's secret ill-wishing with regard to other people come true; and because she felt guilty and in an odd way responsible, she was a little afraid that

Nicola might think she was pleased the row had happened. All this lent her manner an unfamiliar heartiness when talking to Nicola, which irritated them both.

'Don't know,' said Nicola crossly. 'And don't *poke*.'

Tim swung round on her desk lid and talked to Lawrie. Lawrie, who had plunged into the new atmosphere with enthusiasm, wanted to have a furniture stall. She thought they could easily make a dining-room suite in Carpentry between now and the end of term. The Sixth were allowed to make chairs; so why not Third Remove? Third Remove, too, could see no reason why not. There was a lot of talk and laughter and Lawrie was the centre of it. Nicola prodded at her desk lid with the point of her compasses and tried to stop feeling cross and out of it.

All the forms from the Sixth to the Fourth had done something for the Library Fund; the previous summer the Sixth had produced *As You Like It*, contriving an open-air theatre in the part of the garden which sloped down to the little wood; the Fifths had held a swimming gala; the Fourths, who were keen on handcraft, had staged a puppet show. It was the great event in the form calendar; and even Nicola, in her present tight mood of crossness, felt moved to join in the instructions and admonitions given to Jean and Hazel when they went off during Free Afternoon to meet the prefects from IIIA and IIIB and make preliminary arrangements for sharing out the stalls.

In theory (and generally in practice) Free Afternoon was given over to the quiet pursuit of one's own bent. There was no supervision and people painted birthday cards, wrote letters, made laborious attempts in cross-stitch, labelled collections, or chatted quietly with their neighbours. But that afternoon they all talked, speculating as to what might be happening at the meeting and predicting the pleased astonishment of the other Thirds at the superior ideas produced by Third Remove. The only thing would be, as Daphne Morris sagely remarked, if Jean and Hazel took on too much; Third Remove couldn't, after all, be expected to do the whole thing.

'Well,' they said expectantly, on their prefects' return, 'what was it like? How did it go? What are we going to have?'

Jean and Hazel looked at one another.

'It was all right,' said Jean.

'I think it'll be quite good,' said Hazel nervously. 'There's going to be a flower stall and fancy work and people with trays—'

Third Remove gazed at them doubtfully.

'Are we going to have a furniture stall?' asked Lawrie.

'I don't think so—'

'Didn't you suggest it?' asked Lawrie indignantly.

'There was such a lot to talk about. There wasn't really time—'

'You sound about as enthusiastic as a dead cat,' said Tim suspiciously. 'What stalls *are* we having?'

'We've got two,' said Jean reluctantly.

'Well, tell us,' said Nicola impatiently.

'We've got Kitchen and Jumble.'

There was silence for a moment. Then Third Remove fell on its prefects in wrath and indignation.

'I suppose Miranda West did all the talking.'

'Did you *tell* them any of the things we said?'

'*Kitchen* and *Jumble*.'

'There's no fun in those.'

'You can't make anything for Jumble.'

'You can't make much for Kitchen.'

'You can make those doll things with wooden spoons and dusters,' said Hazel weakly, 'and we can knit floor-cloths—'

'*Knit floor-cloths*,' said Nicola scornfully. 'I can see myself. I s'pose Miranda West said that.'

'Why didn't you get us proper stalls?' cried Lawrie. 'What d'you think you went for?'

'How many are there going to be?' asked Elizabeth Collins, folding up her patchwork in a flat and disappointed way.

'Twelve,' said Jean.

'And you let them bag all the best ones?' flared Tim, above the rising clamour. 'You are feeble asses.'

'They said we could make things for theirs if we liked—'

'*Make things for theirs*,' said Nicola in tones of ineffable scorn. 'I wouldn't do a bookmarker for them.'

'They'd got it all worked out before we got there,' said Jean, very flushed. 'There wasn't anything we could do about it. They said – Miranda said – those two were quite good enough for – for Third Remove and there were only twelve of us, anyway.'

They looked at one another doubtfully and in silence.

'You – you could have said you wouldn't have those,' said Lawrie at length, uncertainly.

'No, we couldn't – don't be silly—'

'It isn't silly,' said Tim furiously, thumping her desk lid. 'We won't have a thing to do with it.'

Third Remove looked at her.

'We must be *in* it,' said someone doubtfully.

'Why?' demanded Tim.

'Well – if we're not, we'd be the only form who hadn't done anything for the Library Fund—'

'I'd rather be that than a Jumble stall,' retorted Tim. 'And anyway, why should we be out of it? Why can't we do something on our own?'

They thought this over.

'We couldn't on our own,' said Elaine Rees.

'Why on earth not?'

'Well – because we *couldn't*. No one has. Not for the Fund.'

'What could we do?' asked someone else sceptically.

'A play,' said Tim at random.

'A *play*?'

'We might.'

'What play, Tim?'

'Miming ballads do you mean?'

'No, a proper play,' cried Lawrie. 'With parts. Yes, let's Tim. We'll do it properly in the school theatre – after the bazaar – we can have posters up, saying: This way to – whatever it is – and we'll have proper programmes – not jellied—'

'But we can't,' insisted Jean. 'We've got to be in the bazaar. Everyone thinks we're going to be. There'd be the most awful row if we suddenly said we were doing something else. Cartwright'd say we must fit in – don't *push*, Tim! Where are you going?'

'To see my Aunt Edith,' said Tim over her shoulder as she whirled out of the room. 'Anyone ever tell you I was the Headmistress's Niece?'

'Tim, you can't,' shouted Hazel, alarmed. But Tim had gone.

She had been at school long enough by now to know that immaculate tidiness was a help in dealings with the staff; but not so long that she felt impelled to run down two flights of stairs to the Third Form cloakroom when the Sixth's was handy. She dodged in, smoothed her hair, turned down her collar, fastened a wrist button, wriggled her skirt round so that the side-fastening came at the side instead of in front and dodged out again, passing a potentially indignant Val Longstreet on the way out. She raced on down the passage, knocked on Miss Keith's door, was told to come in, and entered.

She found she had not the remotest idea what she was going to say.

'Well, Thalia,' said Miss Keith pleasantly. 'Come and sit down.'

Skirting a small table covered with patch-boxes and small Dresden figures, Tim remembered that on Free Afternoons one might go and see Miss Keith more or less informally. Since it was a privilege of which the Thirds and Fourths never dreamt of availing themselves, it was scarcely surprising that she had forgotten. In her sudden confusion and by way of breaking the ice she remarked on this.

'I'd forgotten this was Visiting Day. It was only I wanted to speak to you.'

Miss Keith looked faintly amused.

'That's what Visiting Day is for. Pull up that humpy, Thalia. You'll be swallowed in the armchair.'

'I mean,' said Tim with hot cheeks, sitting on the humpy and feeling extraordinarily ridiculous, 'it isn't about me – I'm not in any difficulties – or whatever it is the Lower Fifth come about. I only wanted – it's a form thing, really—'

'Miss Cartwright' said Miss Keith tranquilly, 'tells me that you are settling down quite well, and that your work is improving. I hope you find you quite like school after all?'

'Oh yes,' said Tim. 'Yes. Yes, thank you.'

'Good. And I suppose you are all starting to think about the Third Form effort for the Library Fund? I hope it's going to be a good one?'

'That's what I came about,' said Tim, plunging hurriedly.

'Oh?'

'Yes. Yes, you see – we – we were going to be in the bazaar with the others, but—'

'Well?'

'Well, we thought we'd rather do something on our own. A – a play.'

Miss Keith regarded Tim thoughtfully.

'What does Miss Cartwright say?'

'We haven't asked her,' said Tim uneasily.

'Why not?'

'Jean – the others – thought she'd say we must fit in—'

'Is there any particular reason why you shouldn't?'

Tim's heart sank.

'We'd rather do a play,' she muttered.

'Why?'

'Oh, I don't know. We just would.'

Miss Keith's hand moved towards the book she had been reading.

'I don't think it's really a question for me. If the other Thirds and your form-mistresses agree, I've no particular objection. But there seems no good reason why you shouldn't join in the bazaar with the others and help to make it a success. Was that all you wanted?'

Dumbly, Tim nodded.

'I see. Well – that's all then, Thalia.'

Tim found herself in the passage. She felt hot and foolish and extremely undignified. And she could not possibly go back to Third Remove and tell what had happened; she couldn't even bear to go back and say baldly that she had failed. They would probably be quite kind about it, but they would have a very 'I told you so' air about them. And they would have to put up with those two dreadful stalls – and any time anyone wanted to take her down a peg or two (Tim was not unaware that her contemporaries frequently found her conceited) they'd remind her that she was the Headmistress's Niece—

Tim looked about her. The passage was perfectly deserted. She set her teeth and plunged back into Miss Keith's study without even the formality of knocking.

'Look – Aunt Edith—'

Miss Keith looked at her.

'Look, it's like this,' said Tim hastily before her nerve deserted her. 'This is quite unofficial. We were going to do the bazaar, and we'd thought of loads of things for it, only today the form prefects had a meeting and they chucked us Kitchen and Jumble. And I said we'd do a play and I'd ask you b-because—'

'Because you're my niece,' said Miss Keith.

'Yes,' said Tim briefly.

There was a pause.

'Well, Thalia. That was very silly of you.'

'Yes,' agreed Tim.

There was another pause.

'Look, Aunt Edith, *please*,' said Tim. '*Please* say we may do a play. It'll be quite all right, honestly.'

Miss Keith said nothing.

'I shall look such an ass if I have to go back and say you wouldn't.'

Miss Keith raised an eyebrow.

'It isn't only that,' said Tim desperately, 'but everyone's so fed up. They've all been thinking up masses of things to do for the bazaar and one can't do anything with stalls like that.'

'But my dear Thalia, surely you can arrange with the other Thirds to change one, at least, of the stalls for a more exciting one?'

'No, we can't,' said Tim gloomily.

'Surely! Why not?'

'Because we're Third Remove. Anything's good enough for us.'

Miss Keith looked up sharply.

'You mean that these stalls have been given to you *because* you're Third Remove?'

Tim looked alarmed.

'Well – yes. But don't sound so fierce about it, Aunt Edith.'

There was silence for a moment. Miss Keith, looking reflective, rose to draw the curtains and shift the reading lamp nearer to her chair. Tim waited despondently.

'What play had you in mind?'

Tim caught her breath. To steady her voice she gripped her hands together behind her back.

'We hadn't quite decided,' she said carefully, 'but something perfectly respectable, of course.'

'Scenes from *Twelfth Night*, perhaps,' said Miss Keith absently, 'as you have the Marlow twins. It would be a pity to waste your assets—'

She tilted the lamp-shade a fraction. Tim held her breath.

'Very well, Thalia. But on the understanding that whatever you do doesn't last more than an hour.'

'No, Aunt Edith. Of course not.'

'And of course your play will have to be held the same day as the bazaar. To that extent it must be a part of it.'

'Yes, Aunt Edith. And may we—'

'Well?'

'May we use the theatre? Because if we do it after the bazaar the – the Hall'll be so full of things.'

'Yes. Yes, you'd better use the theatre. You may hold three rehearsals there, including the dress rehearsal. For the others you must use the Assembly Hall.'

'Thanks most awfully,' said Tim, relaxing at last into pleasure and relief, and beaming from ear to ear.

Miss Keith looked at her; a calm, rather disconcerting glance.

'Thanks awfully,' repeated Tim hastily, more than a little dashed. 'If you don't mind, could you – would you square Miss Cartwright for us?'

'I'll speak to Miss Cartwright,' agreed Miss Keith. She opened her book again.

Tim retreated hurriedly to the door. 'Thanks awfully,' she said for the third time, and went out quickly and quietly.

So that was all right. But it very nearly – far too nearly – hadn't been. 'Never again,' thought Tim, blowing a strand of hair off her forehead and feeling a weak desire to giggle, 'never again will I mention to anyone that I'm the Headmistress's Niece. Never. They can arrange their own plays. Or not. As the case may be.'

She shook herself impatiently. It didn't matter that she'd made a fool of herself. No one except Aunt Edith would ever know. And if the play were a success, even Aunt Edith would be pleased and forget that she had – that she had presumed on their relationship. All that Third Remove would know would be that she had got them permission to be out of the bazaar and do a play instead—

'Blood for breakfast,' said Tim aloud, standing at the head of the flight of stairs which led to Third Remove. 'What play are we doing, anyway?'

11 Tim Needs a Note-Book

It would be no use asking Third Remove. They wouldn't know. Probably they wouldn't have any ideas either, unless Pomona wanted to do a fairy play, or something with gods and goddesses – 'Orpheus and Eurydice', thought Tim, once more fighting a tendency to giggle weakly, 'and little Apfelstrudel picking lots of imaginary flowers while her nymphs skip round to unseen music. Well, she's not going to be in my play.'

She acknowledged a moment later that as a threat it would be more impressive if she knew what the play were going to be. She sighed and turned, wandering slowly back along the passage. *Twelfth Night*, Aunt Edith had said. Tim grimaced impatiently. People always did Shakespeare; there wouldn't be any fun in that. But Aunt Edith had been right about the twins: it would be a pity to waste their twinnishness. 'There must be other plays besides *Twelfth Night* with twins in them,' thought Tim stumping slowly down the main stairs: 'there's *The Prisoner of Zenda* . . . that's not a play: and *The Comedy of Errors* . . . that's no use . . . there are two too many twins in that . . . and we don't want to do a children's play . . . where am I going, anyway?'

Since she was now crossing the dimly lit Assembly Hall, it seemed probable that she was making for the library, which lay at the other end of the Hall up a short flight of stone steps. Tim paced on, taking long regular strides across the polished floor so as to tread on every eighth block. Twins. There was a play – or a book – or something – with young twins in it – 'and it isn't the Princes in the Tower,' said Tim crossly to herself, 'but it's something awfully like it.'

She pushed the swing doors of the library and went in. The only occupants were Karen Marlow and Margaret Jessop who were seated at opposite ends of one of the polished oblong tables with a Greek lexicon apiece. The Sixth and Upper Fifth customarily used the library to work in during the late afternoon and evening, but there was no rule against the juniors being there too, provided they moved softly and talked not at all. Walking on tiptoe, Tim turned on the light over the English literature section and began her quest.

She had no intention of disturbing anyone, and it did not occur to her that the steady rustle and thump of books as she took each volume out, looked through and returned it to the shelf, could be, and was, incredibly distracting. As she went methodically along the shelves, drawing a blank each time, the thumps grew progressively louder and more hopeless. Margaret Jessop (who held that even the Thirds should be allowed to live in peace, but to whom, unlike Karen, Greek prose was a burden) found herself waiting tensely for each next irregular thud. Val Longstreet, in similar circumstances, would have told Tim to stop that row and clear out; Margaret, being of a courteous disposition, asked Tim if she were looking for anything in particular.

'I was librarian last year,' she added as Tim, holding a collection of Galsworthy's plays, looked up, flushed and doubtful, 'so I do know, more or less, what we've got and where it's likely to be.'

'Well, I don't know if you'd know it,' said Tim rather hopelessly. 'I can't remember the title or who it's by – but it's about twins – boys – and I think it's historical—'

'*The Prince and the Pauper*,' said Karen instantly, without looking up. 'Mark Twain. Fiction. Other end of the room.'

'Oh, yes, of course,' said Tim gratefully. 'Thanks a lot.' She switched off the light over the Literature section and tiptoed down the room. Karen and Margaret grinned briefly at one another, and went back to work. *The Prince and the Pauper* sat quietly in its appointed place, low down on the fiction shelves. Kneeling on the floor, Tim took it out and began to read.

It seemed queerly different from the book as she remembered it. Her memory had retained only the bare story of the two boys who had changed places for a time – she had thought for fun. But it wasn't for fun, it was a mistake; and there were many more characters than she remembered. . . . 'But we could scrap some of them,' thought Tim, not quite realizing what her thought implied, 'and we needn't have all these side issues. It can just be about Tom and the Prince – we needn't have Sir Miles really – there's plenty of dialogue – I needn't alter much – except it needn't be quite so odds boddikin-y—'

She realized then just what she was proposing to do.

'Well, I don't see why I shouldn't write a play,' thought Tim fascinated, gazing unseeingly at the bookshelves in front of her. 'It isn't as if I'd got to make it up. It's mostly there. It only needs pulling together a bit. I don't see why that should be so awfully difficult.' She blinked, drew a long blissful sigh, and returned with renewed concentration to her reading.

Lawrie, putting her head cautiously round the door some time later, found her still kneeling on the floor, her arms clasped across her chest, still reading from the book on the floor in front of her. Holding her breath out of consideration for Karen and Margaret who were beginning to pack up, and treading softly because the library was so still, Lawrie crept across and sat down beside Tim.

'Matron's crying out for you,' she whispered hoarsely. 'Something about your laundry hasn't come back or you didn't give in enough. So I came to find you. Did Keith eat you?'

'No, it was all right,' said Tim abstractedly. 'I mean, we can do a play.'

'Well!' whispered Lawrie in astonishment. 'When you didn't come back we thought Keith had absolutely finished you. Was she decent about it?'

'All right,' said Tim without emotion. 'Look. I thought we'd do this.'

Margaret and Karen halted beside them, clasping books and writing blocks. The Sixth, rarely, if ever, used attaché cases.

'Are you two staying here much longer?' asked Margaret.

'Not very,' said Tim.

'Well, don't forget the lights. The windows are all closed. Good night.'

'G'night,' said Tim and Lawrie. The door swung shut behind the seniors and their feet clattered down the short stone flight.

'Now tell me all about it,' demanded Lawrie in her normal voice.

'Well, it's all right,' said Tim, sitting back on her heels. 'We're out of the bazaar. And we can do a play. And Keith said we ought to do a play with twins in it because of you and Nick. So I thought of this.'

'What's it about?' said Lawrie hugging herself, her eyes very blue with excitement.

'One of those things where people are so alike that no one can tell them apart. It's Edward VI—'

'The one who came after Henry and before Mary,' said Lawrie intelligently.

'Yes. And he swops clothes with a beggar boy who looks exactly like him, and then, before they can change back, Edward's pushed out and they all think Tom is the Prince.'

'And that's Nick and me? Super,' said Lawrie happily. 'Where are we going to do it?'

'In the theatre. After the bazaar.'

'Oh, Tim—! How heavenly.' She scrambled to her feet. 'Let's go and look at the theatre now.'

They remembered to switch off the lights before they dashed out and across the covered way to the theatre. The main doors were not locked, and they went softly in, the dark silent little building making them feel a little like trespassers. Tim switched on a light, and they sat down in the back row of seats, gazing reverently at the empty stage.

'It'll have to be in a lot of short scenes, like Shakespeare,' said Tim at last. 'And I think we'll probably have to have someone to read bits of it – a sort of story-teller, you know—'

'Did Shakespeare have those?'

'Well – sort of. He had a thing he called a Chorus – like in *Henry V* – you know – he keeps dashing on to tell the audience what's happened since the last scene and where they're going next—

> '*There is the playhouse now, there must you sit:*
> *And thence to France shall we convey you safe,*
> *And bring you back charming the narrow seas*
> *To give you gentle pass*—'

'I've never even heard it before,' said Lawrie, pink with admiration. 'What a lot you know, Tim. Is our Chorus in poetry?'

'Bless me, no,' said Tim. 'I can't write poetry at all. No, it'll have to be in prose and as much Mark Twain as possible.

All that early part, about Tom and his imaginary court – that'll have to be read, I think—' and she clasped her hands round one knee and rocked gently, her play progressing easily through her mind.

Lawrie possessed herself of the book.

'It's a *story,*' she said at length. 'Not a play at all yet. You mean you're going to *make* it a play?'

Tim looked at her quickly. 'Yes, I think so. Does it sound frightful cheek?'

'Oh, no,' said Lawrie. 'I'm sure you can. Kempe's always saying your essays are good as far as they go.'

'Perhaps it is cheek,' said Tim, suddenly dubious. 'Perhaps it would be better if we did something someone else has written.'

'Oh *no*, Tim,' protested Lawrie. 'There isn't anyone else – not unless we do Shakespeare. Or *Make-Believe*. There was a time when Ginty was always doing the boy in that. It'll be much more fun if we do something that's properly our own.'

'Well, I think so,' said Tim. 'But p'rhaps people will think it's swank. P'rhaps Third Remove would rather have Shakespeare.'

'They'll be so pleased you've got them out of that awful bazaar thing, that they'll do anything you say,' said Lawrie serenely. 'There was the most frightful row after you'd gone and Hazel cried and Marie wanted to depose them, only Nick never agrees with Marie so we didn't. Let's go and look at the stage properly.'

They ran down the centre aisle and up the short flight of steps on to the stage. Lawrie, disappearing into the wings, found the electric switch panel and spent some happy moments lighting the stage and darkening the auditorium.

'Isn't it wonderfully *black* down there?' she said rapturously.

'It's a bigger stage than I thought,' said Tim, prowling happily. 'That makes it lots easier. We can have the court scenes set right back and when we have the street scenes we can pull curtains over and use about half the stage. Of course, we shan't be able to have much scenery. The court scenes will have to make do with a throne—'

'—and curtains at the back,' interrupted Lawrie, 'with heraldry things on them—'

'Yes. And then the curtain that's drawn across ought to have a Tudor street on it – and we want a forest, too, sometimes – at least, I think we do. I say,' said Tim, suddenly descending to earth again, 'aren't we taking on rather much?'

'No,' said Lawrie sturdily. 'We must just arrange it properly, that's all. I tell you what. If we tell Jennings next time we have a drawing lesson that we've got scenery to do, I bet she'll show us how. You know she's mad to have frescoes all over the place only Keith won't let her except in the really new bits that don't matter.'

'I didn't know that,' said Tim. 'Where did you hear it?'

'Oh. Well, I suppose it was Kay, and I oughtn't to have told you, but I don't expect it really matters. But I'm sure she'd show us how to paint heraldry things if we asked.'

'The bazaar's on December the twenty-first,' said Tim abruptly. 'We've got about six weeks.'

'That's ages,' said Lawrie. 'You'll take about a fortnight to do the play, I s'pose. And that leaves a month for rehearsals. If we don't do anything else, that's loads of time.'

'It may take me more than a fortnight,' said Tim cautiously.

'Well, it can't,' said Lawrie. 'I'm sure we'll need a month. And while you're doing the play we'll be getting on with the costumes. I don't suppose it matters if they aren't sewn frightfully well, so long as they stay on. 'Sides, I expect there are some in the Acting Chest we can use, come to that.'

Tim gazed at her.

'You are feeling certain about this, aren't you?' she said at last, more in statement than question.

'Yes,' said Lawrie briefly. 'Aren't you?'

'I don't know,' said Tim uncertainly. 'Not as positively as all that.'

'Oh, well,' said Lawrie, 'you will. What are those lights up there called?'

'Battens, I think. And those stand ones are Floods. We'll have to see if there's a book in the library on stage production. I know a little about lighting and make-up, but not much. Father did some scenery for a theatre once when we were in America, and I used to look in sometimes. If I'd known this was going to happen I'd never have left the place while rehearsals were on.'

'It's lucky you know anything at all,' said Lawrie calmly.

Tim gave her a little shake.

'Don't be so *sure* about it, Lawrie. It's frightening. What's the matter with you, anyway? It's usually you who have to be calmed down over things.'

Lawrie blushed, more for her past than her present.

'Well, I do think this is going to be all right. Can I have the book to read to-night?'

'You won't have time.'

'Not to read it properly. But I can sort of skim it with my torch.'

'Don't get caught, then,' said Tim, handing her the book, 'and put everyone against us from the beginning.'

'I won't,' said Lawrie. 'I say. Who's going to tell Miranda we don't want her beastly stalls?'

'Oh, anyone,' said Tim, who did not care what happened to the other Thirds now she had her play. 'Let's write her a note: "Dear Madam. With reference to your esteemed offer of two stalls, viz. one Jumble and one Kitchen—" '

Lawrie giggled. ' "—we regret to inform you that we have received a better offer from the firm of Keith and Sons Ltd—" '

' "—and must therefore beg to decline your kind invitation. Yours truly, Third Remove Productions Inc." ' finished Tim rapidly. 'Let's go back and tell the others. What's the time, anyway?'

Lawrie looked at her watch, gasped and began to chuckle.

'It's half-past *six*, Tim. People'll think we've run away to sea.'

'I s'pose we ought to be changing,' said Tim, gazing round her stage. 'Let's not tell the others about the play to-night, then – not even Nick. There won't be really time to, properly.'

'Nick and I aren't talking much at the moment, anyway,' said Lawrie candidly. 'She's being so fierce and snarly that it isn't very encouraging, if you know what I mean. So she can just be told tomorrow with everybody else.'

Tim nodded. She switched off the foot-lights and put on the light by the far door. They caught hands, jumped the steps, and tore back up the centre aisle.

'Let's look at it just *once* more,' begged Lawrie; and they swung round and stared down over the empty rows of seats to the blank stage with its raised curtain swinging a little in a draught.

'Oh, Tim,' said Lawrie ecstatically, squeezing Tim's hand hard with the sudden upsurge of excitement.

'What you've got to do tomorrow when we order stationery,' said Tim with an attempt at great calm, 'is to get me a large brown history note-book. To write the play in, you know. *I* can't put down for one. I had one last week.'

12 Tim Loses Her Temper

Nicola heard about the play with mixed feelings. She was glad, of course, that they were out of the bazaar; and it was amazingly clever of Tim to have managed it; but it was rather low of Lawrie to have known about it before she did, and not particularly nice of Tim to have told her. Nicola went on putting her books away in her desk with immense care and said nothing. The rest of Third Remove were being tremendously enthusiastic, so it was unlikely that anyone would notice whether she said anything or not. After a while they all went off to look through the Acting Chest. No one asked her to come, so she stayed behind to tidy the form room. It was much better to be on one's own, thought Nicola proudly, than with a yelling mob who didn't care whether one were there or not. She pulled Tim's desk into place and thumped the atlas down into the rack – Tim's atlas always stuck up above the level of her desk – just as Miss Craven appeared with her note-book and pencil.

Nicola turned pink, put her hands behind her back, and tried to look as though tidying the form room were the last thing she were doing. But Miss Craven only remarked, scribbling a figure in her note-book and shutting it with a snap: 'So you're the Tidiness Monitress this term?'

'Yes,' Nicola admitted.

'H'm,' said Miss Craven and went away. It might mean anything, thought Nicola, surveying the room with a critical eye. H'm – very good; H'm – pretty fair; H'm – poor effort; one couldn't tell. She picked up a piece of string from the floor by Hazel's desk, opened a window to appease Miss Cartwright, who would like fresh air even though it was a cold, rain-sodden day, had a look at the bulb bowls at the bottom of the stationery cupboard and went off to buy a bun.

Stationery was given out at four o'clock and at five past, three large brown history note-books lay on Tim's desk. Nicola glanced at them enviously, liking, as they all did, the thickness and cleanness of them.

'I shall wake at half-past five to-morrow and start,' said Tim, stroking the cover of the topmost one affectionately.

'Bet you oversleep,' said Nicola. 'Besides, you can't have a light on in the dorm then.'

'Shan't try,' said Tim briefly. 'I'll dress and come down here.'

'Someone's sure to catch you.'

'There's no rule about getting up early,' Tim pointed out. 'It's late you mustn't be.'

Nicola said nothing.

Elizabeth Collins, sitting on the lid of her desk, was trying to make a list of the costumes they would need; since she had confessed, half-defiantly, that she liked sewing and had made nearly the whole of a cotton frock the previous summer, Tim had appointed her wardrobe mistress. There was no competition for the post. The rest of Third Remove were delighted with the prospect of acting and painting scenery, but they were not at all anxious to sew.

'There are the two boys,' hummed Elizabeth to herself; alone of Third Remove she had read the book at home; 'Henry, Elizabeth, Jane and nobles. Beggars. Tom's father, sisters, mother. Sir Miles Hendon—'

'I live at Hendon,' said Elaine Rees helpfully.

'I may leave him out,' said Tim.

Elizabeth chewed her pencil.

'Are we going to be able to have all those, Tim?' she asked at length. 'There are only twelve of us, counting you – are you going to be in it?'

'No. I'm going to do the reading,' said Tim.

'Eleven of us. And Nick and Lawrie are the boys. That's nine. It's not an awful lot to make crowds of – four beggars and five courtiers – or the other way round. And the people who are one person like Henry and can't be anyone else—'

'What d'you mean?' asked Tim. 'Can't be anyone else?'

'Well, you can't, can you? I mean, if you've got one part, you can't have another.'

'I should think everyone but Nick and Lawrie will have to have about four,' said Tim promptly. 'Soon as they've stopped being nobles they'll have to rush on again as beggars. You'd better allow for two costumes each, except Nick and Lawrie. And make the beggars awfully simple so that they can just pull them on over their noblemen's things. They won't have time to change.'

'Oh,' said Elizabeth. She chewed her pencil reflectively, and said: 'There are those monks' things in the Acting Chest from when the Lower Fifths did St. Francis, Lawrie says. Would those do for beggars' things?'

'So long as they don't look like monks. I expect you'll have to turn them up, or do something to them. Anyway, that's your worry,' said Tim, unable for the moment to visualize the exact change necessary to transform monks' robes into beggars' rags.

Elizabeth tore the page from her block, screwed it into a ball, shied it at the waste-paper basket, and began a new list.

'Rotten shot,' said Nicola. She strolled over, put the paper in the basket, and stared nonchalantly over the dripping playing fields.

'And what am I going to be?' asked Pomona, heavily. She had not been pleased to find that the two chief parts were already bespoken and she was determined that the second lead should not go by default.

'That,' said Tim, 'is one of the mysteries of the future.'

'I mean in the play,' said Pomona.

'So do I,' said Tim.

'Do you mean you haven't cast it yet?' asked Pomona. 'Good gracious. That's the very first thing Mummy does when she's getting up a pageant. You don't really know much about producing, do you?'

Tim, who was a good deal more conscious of this than Pomona, flushed to the eyes. She said quickly: 'I know enough not to give you the chief part, *meine kleine apfeltorte*.'

'You've cast the chief parts,' Pomona pointed out stolidly, 'so I want the next biggest. I don't mind being Elizabeth.'

'Anyone who does Elizabeth will have to be able to act,' snapped Tim, who would have liked to have been able to retort that Pomona would not even be walking on, but had come to realize that her possible actors were fewer than was comfortable.

'I can act,' stated Pomona. 'Next pageant I'm going to be Persephone.'

Third Remove laughed unkindly.

'There's nothing funny about that,' cried Marie, rushing to the rescue.

'With your hair flying loose on your shoulders and your bare feet tripping on the sward,' suggested Tim, unheeding. She sketched idly on the page in front of her. Lawrie squealed with delight.

'Nick, come and look! It's *exactly* like! Look, *isn't* it Pomona?'

Third Remove, crowding round, was loud in its

admiration. Tim regarded her sketch complacently.

'It's inherited talent,' she said calmly. 'Nothing to do with me really. Look, this is Marie chatting to a staff—'

'Oh, Tim, *yes*. Go on. Do some more!'

' – Audrey getting stuck on the horse,' said Tim, drawing rapidly, 'and Elaine not knowing what Ironsides is talking about.' Her victims giggled. Tim drew again. 'What's that?'

They looked at it.

'Nick being cross,' crowed Lawrie. 'Oh, Tim, it's *good*!'

Nicola, standing by the desk, felt as though someone had struck her hard in the chest. There was nothing she could do about it. She grinned briefly, and went on standing there, fidgeting with the broken corner of Tim's atlas.

'You still haven't said what I'm going to be,' said Pomona, with a stubbornness Third Remove felt to be overdone.

'You'll know when the others do,' retorted Tim, slamming the note-books into her desk. 'And when I've written the play I'll know what the parts are. See?'

It was surprising, Tim thought, that no one questioned her ability to write a play. She rather wished they would. In a way, their apparently unbounded faith in her capacities was more disconcerting than a little healthy opposition would have been. If someone else had wanted a hand in the writing they could have argued themselves over the difficulties and if they had failed they would at least have been two together. But Third Remove, though more than ready to enquire how it was going, to admire Tim for getting up so early, and to take on prep. for which she had no time, never expressed the slightest doubt but that she would finish it in the fortnight and that the result would be excellent. Tim, coming out of the first ecstatic headlong rush of the first few days, found herself sucking the top of her pen more than she wrote and wondering uneasily if she had made the most tremendous ass of herself. 'And if I can't do it,' she thought, staring miserably from the printed page to her agonized manuscript with its furious obliterations, 'I ought to say, so that we can get on with *Twelfth Night* or drop it altogether. I wish to goodness I'd never started this.'

The seven-thirty bell rang. It would be breakfast time in half an hour. There seemed no point in going on. Tim yawned, screwed the cap on her fountain-pen and pushed the note-book and her copy of *The Prince and the Pauper* into her desk. It was a dark, blowy morning, with rain spattering on the window panes. Tim stretched, got up, and wandered over to the blackboard, beginning to draw for the pure pleasure of using white chalk. 'I'll draw one of Pippin,' thought Tim; 'it's a long time since she's had a new name. I know. Where's that one I found in the library ages ago and never used?' She dived into her blazer pocket and fished out the small spiral-backed note-book which went with her everywhere. She flipped the pages. 'Here we are. "*Pomona: a small planet or asteroid between the orbits of Mars and Jupiter, discovered by Goldschmidt 26 Oct.*, 1857." I can make a picture of that – Mars and Jupiter and little Pippin-Asteroid between them.' She grinned impishly and began to draw rapidly, stepping back now and again to admire her work.

She had just finished the drawing and was writing the legend underneath when Nicola dashed in.

'Hullo,' said Tim companionably. 'Come and look at my pretty picture—'

'Wipe the thing off,' panted Nicola. 'Craven's coming.'

'Well, I don't mind. She can see it too, if she likes.'

'Don't be so stupid. She takes marks off if there are things left on the blackboard.'

'This hasn't been left,' said Tim aggravatingly. 'I've only just done it.'

A door closed farther along the passage. There was the sound of footsteps.

'Wipe it off,' urged Nicola frantically.

'No,' said Tim. 'I don't think I will.'

Nicola sprang forward, wiped the board clean, hung the duster on its hook, and leapt off the dais, beating her hands together to clear them of chalk. Miss Craven came in, nodded 'Good morning', scribbled in her note-book and went out.

There was a silence. Tim put the chalk back on its ledge as carefully as though a rough movement would shatter something valuable.

'Sorry,' began Nicola, 'but she takes off an awful lot of marks—'

'So you're after the Tidiness Picture now,' said Tim distantly.

Nicola stiffened.

'I'm *not*,' she said.

'No? Just an abstract desire for perfect order? How choice.'

'Don't be an ass.'

'Thank you,' said Tim elaborately. 'But one quite sees, you know. Wrong form, wrong games, kicked out of Guides, so you must win something. One sees, absolutely.'

Nicola turned white.

'It's a mistake,' continued Tim, who, on the infrequent occasions when she lost her temper, surprised herself unpleasantly by the things she found to say, 'it's a mistake to try to be distinguished when you haven't anything to be distinguished with. It makes you look foolish. People laugh.'

Nicola said nothing.

'Laugh like anything,' Tim amplified pleasantly. 'I daresay even your family find your efforts pretty funny. Unless, of course, they find you embarrassing. One must admit that even the superlative Rowan doesn't go around pot-hunting quite so obviously.'

She could not be allowed to go on like that.

'I'm not,' said Nicola incoherently, 'and if I was, that's better than stealing other people's pears and then saying I haven't.'

'What on earth d'you mean?'

'At the beginning of term. When you were swanking round being the Headmistress's Niece. That day at breakfast.'

'I can't think what you're talking about,' said Tim in the light, amused voice of one who is in perfect control of the situation.

Nicola clenched her hands.

'Yes, you can. When you wanted a special privilege of eating pears for breakfast. And Cartwright asked you and you said they came from home.'

'*That*—' said Tim. 'Well; so they did.'

'They didn't. You said yourself you'd' (Nicola sought for the most degrading word) 'you'd pinched them from Keith's garden.'

Tim laughed.

'You silly ass,' she said with indulgent contempt. 'You didn't really believe I'd taken them from there, did you? Bless my heart and soul.'

'Where did you get them from, then?'

'I brought them from home, of course. Where else?'

'I don't believe you,' said Nicola flatly.

'Don't you indeed? How interesting.'

'And if you didn't pinch them,' said Nicola with cold logic, 'then you were lying when you said you had. So I don't see it's any better.'

'I couldn't care less what you think,' said Tim furiously.

They stared at one another, suddenly alarmed by the dimensions of the quarrel.

'Hullo,' said Lawrie, strolling in. She looked at them, and added, faintly alarmed, 'is anything up?'

'No,' said Nicola. 'Nothing.' She spun round, sat down at her desk and began to sharpen a pencil, snapping the lead time and again.

Lawrie looked at Tim.

'Oh, nothing,' said Tim sulkily. 'I was drawing a portrait of dear Pippin on the board, and Nick wiped it off because it messed up her beautiful form room. So then we had a row.'

'Oh, Nick, you are a nuisance,' cried Lawrie. 'Do it again now, Tim.'

'May I?' said Tim to Nicola with elaborate courtesy.

'Do what you like,' snapped Nicola.

'I don't know what's the matter with you lately,' said Lawrie to Nicola in the tone only adopted by one sister to another, 'but you're as cross as – as two sticks. And we're sick of it. And you can just stop it.'

'For goodness' sake *you* be quiet,' retorted Nicola.

'I won't,' said Lawrie. 'You're being frightfully silly and you're an awful nuisance. And if anyone's going to be quiet, it's you. Go on, Tim, do your picture again.'

The breakfast bell rang. Nicola got up and walked off; the other two, talking gently to one another in the embarrassed aftermath of the quarrel, gave her time to get ahead before strolling nonchalantly out to join the main stream of school going down to breakfast. Nicola, standing behind her customary chair at the breakfast-table, pretended not to see them come in; when they walked casually to two seats at the other side of the table she pretended to be unaware of this also.

Miss Keith said grace.

So now, of course, everyone would know there had been a quarrel, thought Nicola, spooning porridge with furious resolution, lest anyone should think she cared. People ought to keep these things to themselves, very secret and private, so that outside people shouldn't be able to lean across and say: 'What's up with you and Lawrie?' in the silly, nudging kind of voices people used when something happened that mattered a good deal to one person and was only something to be gossiped over by the others. She went on eating porridge in a haughty, miserable silence. Quarrelling with Tim wasn't much fun, but it made it much worse that Lawrie should be on Tim's side; and Lawrie ought not to be; Lawrie ought to be with her whatever happened . . . she always had been before . . . 'I can't think what's come over her,' thought Nicola, 'except that it's being the most beastly kind of term, anyway.' And she dashed a quick glance at Lawrie who was chuckling over something Tim had said . . .

'Probably something about me,' thought Nicola, and looked quickly away. 'I'm not going to stand for this. I shall run away to sea.'

13 Operation Nelson

It was a pity that she couldn't mean that. Nicola, pretending to search for an elusive handkerchief, so that she need not appear to see Tim and Lawrie dashing out of the dining-hall to take their regulation ten minutes run in the garden, regretted bitterly that the days were past when almost anyone could run away to sea with a fair chance of ending up as a powder monkey on the *Victory* at the moment of Trafalgar. *School*, thought Nicola fiercely, dawdling over the rolling of her napkin so that no one should suppose she had any desire to catch up with Tim and Lawrie, and packing into her sternly contemptuous thought the implication that she had no use for school at all; a foolish place, on the whole, where one squabbled with silly little girls (Nicola relished this description of Tim) and where so-called Patrol Leaders landed one in the most appalling rows. Nicola got up and strolled away, her chin in the air, including in her contempt those members of the Lower Fifth who still sat on at their table in earnest conversation over the inner meaning of *Paradise Lost* and the possible reaction of Miss Kempe, the literature mistress, to the essays they were handing in that morning. Ridiculous, thought Nicola, squeezing past the end chair. The most any self-respecting person should say about prep. was: Wasn't it ghastly? I couldn't do any of it, could you? Nicola, jolting Fay Phillips rather more than she need in her efforts to pass, was caustically glad to see that Ann was not of their company.

No. The Navy was the thing. Nicola, climbing the stairs

to the dormitory, so as to make her bed and be out again when Lawrie came up, allowed herself to indulge a light pretence that she was planning to run away almost immediately. 'I should think the *Rodney* would be a good ship to join,' she thought grandly, striding the stairs three at a time. 'Plenty of room to stow away. And when she was one day out I could – I could *emerge* and mingle casually.' She walked into the dormitory. 'I don't suppose for a moment they'd notice that they hadn't seen me before. They'd think they'd overlooked me in the crowd.'

'Hullo,' said Rowan, glancing up from her study of that morning's post. From the comparative tranquillity of the Upper Fifth table she had noticed Nicola's isolation and had wondered mildly what the row was about; it was unusual for Lawrie and Nicola to quarrel to that extent. Since, however, she regarded it as no affair of hers unless Nicola chose to remark on it, she merely said: 'Finished your run already? There's a letter from Giles. Want to see it? He's got a new ship. She's commissioning at Port Wade.'

Nicola gazed at her. 'Port Wade?'

''M. Says he'll come over Saturday afternoon *if*. A whole string of *ifs*. But I shouldn't think it's over likely, so don't count on it with that blissful expression.'

'Oh, Rowan. Why not?'

'You know Giles. Can you honestly see him dragging round the countryside in the local puff-puff all of a Saturday afternoon to see his dear sisters at their nice school?'

Nicola eyed her doubtfully. 'I don't know. Mightn't he?'

'Frankly, I should say not. Besides, so far as I can make out,' Rowan wagged the letter in her hand, 'the continued existence of his ship *and* of the Royal Navy depend entirely on Giles being an efficient little officer. You know how solemn Giles gets about his ship.'

A little dashed and not entirely convinced, Nicola stooped to the tumbled bed-clothes on the floor at the foot of her bed, found a corner of sheet, tugged it free, and began to make her bed. She considered the matter.

'Couldn't we go and see him?' she suggested at length.

'Be your age,' said Rowan, engrossed in another letter. 'Port Wade's miles out of bounds.'

'It isn't so awfully far, is it?' asked Nicola casually, after a moment, so casually that the question seemed scarcely worth asking at all.

'Don't think so. It's about forty minutes by car. By train, I fancy, it takes about an hour and a half. You know. The engine goes for five minutes, stops for ten, and you change twice – once at Shawton and once at North Wood. Lovely run.'

'It can't,' said Nicola, thumping her pillow, 'cost much. The fare, I mean.'

'Be too expensive for Giles?' said Rowan indifferently, her interest at the moment on a letter from Carol Ingram who had left the previous term for a finishing school in Switzerland. 'Shouldn't think so. But I don't think he'll come.'

Nicola said no more. Lawrie came in, looking self-conscious, and strolled aloofly in the direction of her bed. As so often happened to Lawrie when she was feeling haughty, she caught her foot on a loose tag of linoleum and tripped ridiculously, blushing pinkly down the back of her neck. Nicola allowed a suppressed snort of mirth to escape her, smoothed her sheets with speed, pulled the butcher-blue bed-spread over all, and swung out of the room without further comment.

She dashed exultantly down the back stairs and out into the playing field. The rain had stopped, but there was a chill, sodden wind, faintly sticky as though still salted from its passage over the sea. Nicola shivered involuntarily, then stared with a superior eye at those (the majority) who were wearing coats; the Thirds made it a point of honour to go out in their blouses until the staff became too obviously annoyed. To show that it was unnecessary to run in order to keep warm, Nicola clasped her hands behind her back and sauntered down the broad centre path in the direction of the little stream, smiling blissfully into thin air.

Hadn't Giles himself said that it would be a good idea to be bad? And going to Port Wade, alone, by train, would be one of the worst things one could possibly do. It was sheer providence that this afternoon was Free Afternoon. That meant no mistress in charge, and little danger of her absence being discovered. Not, added Nicola, swaggering splendidly in her thoughts, that she cared if they did find out. There could only be a flaming row and probably some idiotic punishment. Nicola, in her present mood, thought she would rather enjoy that. Thousands of lines, perhaps, or being stopped games and having to go for walks with the invalids. It wouldn't matter. Against all that she would be able to set the lustre of a gay, friendly afternoon with Giles. Her thoughts racing rapturously ahead, she imagined the meeting with Giles, the enormous tea at some small dark-windowed inn which had once been a meeting place for smugglers . . . and just, just possibly seeing over his ship . . . at the very thought of so much glory her eyes clenched tightly shut for a moment.

And moreover, when Giles had sailed, she would be able to say casually: *I* saw him before he went. I just slipped over one afternoon. No, I didn't say anything before. I didn't think you'd be specially interested. And Lawrie would be furious and want to know why she hadn't been told so that she could come too. And Nicola would say:

Oh, I don't know. I expect it was that time you and Tim were being so snooty. I don't expect I wanted you along.

She dropped a twig into the rapid water and grinned impishly to herself. It would be sucks to the lot of them. And she would go directly after lunch.

It had been unbelievably simple. Nicola, scudding along the path across the fields, which was the short cut to the station, and on which, this afternoon, she skidded and slithered every now and then as though she ran on butter, was still amazed that she could be there without discovery. True, dormitories were always untenanted in the middle of the day, queer, empty, rather disconcerting places, with flat, unfriendly beds and the wind blowing gustily through the open windows. Nevertheless, it seemed amazingly fortunate that no mistress or prefect had felt impelled, by some seventh sense, to open the door as she snatched off her school tie or knelt before her chest of drawers, rummaging for her purse and the navy-blue beret which she wore at home when it rained and which had come back to school by mistake in her mackintosh pocket. Anyone, Nicola had thought, visualizing herself, could wear a navy gaberdine waterproof buttoned to the neck, black brogue shoes, black stockings and a beret. There was nothing in that to identify her as a Kingscote girl and make the station people wonder why she was there alone with a ticket to Port Wade.

As for getting out of school, the rain had helped enormously. During wet dinner-recs. the staff and seniors, with the exception of those who were supervising the juniors and middle school for bean bags in the gym or country dancing in the Assembly Hall, were shut away in their respective common rooms. There had been no one about as Nicola had gone softly down the stairs, clutching hard on the purse in her pocket, and dashing, her heart in her mouth, across the vestibule to the front door; she had had to lean against it from the outside to restrain it from closing too heavily and finally behind her, for the secretary's office overlooked the front steps and her attention might be attracted by a loud slam. But the door had swung gently closed with the smallest possible click. A moment later she had been flying down the drive, the wet gravel crushing underfoot. Then she was on the main road. No one had called; no one come running after. It had been as easy as that.

Still clutching her purse, Nicola ran on. The railway lines stood up on an embankment in the middle of the flat fields so that one would see for ages, Nicola thought, if one were going to miss one's train. But there was no sign of a train along the whole empty stretch . . . Nicola, feeling the shapes of the coins through the thin leather of her purse, hoped that two and tenpence ha'penny would be enough. It was a perfectly good amount for ordinary things, but not a great deal for travelling by train. It was a pity she hadn't been able to borrow from Lawrie; five shillings would have been a much better sum. But though she knew, of course, where Lawrie kept her purse, and, in the usual way, would have borrowed without compunction, you couldn't very well borrow from someone you were quarrelling with . . . Nicola ducked her head and ran on.

The last few hundred yards led through the town, and she could no longer see the track; but as she pelted into the station and up to the booking office she heard the long faint shrilling of an approaching train.

'What time's the next to Port Wade?' she panted to all she could see of the booking clerk.

He stared at the clock in leisurely fashion.

'That's it, coming in now. It's the through train.'

'Oh, good. Third return, please.'

He rose slowly, crossed to a pigeon hole and tossed the ticket down on the brass oval.

'Three shillings, please.'

'Oh—' said Nicola. The train was just chuffing into the station, hissing out clouds of steam. Oh, well, Giles would pay her fare back. 'I mean a – a single, please.'

The booking clerk sighed, muttered something, reached over to another pigeon hole and substituted another ticket.

'Two shillings and three pence. *If* you please.'

Nicola pushed five sixpences on to the brass oval, snatched up the ticket and the threepenny bit and dashed through the barrier on to the platform. The guard's flag was still furled under his arm, so there would be just time . . . Nicola swerved aside, bought a bar of chocolate and a packet of toffee from the station buffet and hurled herself at an empty compartment an instant before the guard slammed the carriage door. The train jolted hugely as she fell into a corner seat. She was off.

So that was all right. She pulled off her beret and tossed it on to the opposite seat. There was no corridor on the train and with any luck she would have the compartment to herself all the way. She felt gay and irresponsible, able to put her feet on the seat, whistle *Cock of the North* as loudly as she pleased, and suck the paper-wrapped butterscotch – all things that Nicola Marlow wearing a Kingscote beret could not do, but which were gloriously possible in an anonymous runagate. The rain had stopped and a sudden flood of white sunlight lit the compartment, making a pale shine of the dust which hung in the air. Nicola wriggled happily, liking her compartment for its smallness and its privacy; there was much, she felt at that moment, to be said for doing things alone sometimes.

The train chugged regularly along, leaving small drifts of smoke just above the surface of the fields. The cathedral was still in sight, an easy, familiar landmark, seeming to swing above the red and grey roofs of the houses, like a liner above its tugs. Odd, to think of school going on without her, of Third Remove tumbling into the form room and settling down for the afternoon, perhaps asking one another where Nicola was, giggling a little and asking Lawrie what the row had been that morning . . . Nicola, pleasantly detached, found that she couldn't care less. Perhaps it was being in a train that made everything seem so diminished and remote, almost as though school no longer concerned her. A lovely thought. Nicola, having finished her butterscotch, started on the chocolate and began to imagine the meeting with Giles; his quick, amused look and his admiring: That's the spirit. Never let a little thing like bounds worry you.'

It was not far from the station to the docks, so the ticket collector told her, jerking his head towards the sea. Nicola thanked him and went out of the station, striding light-heartedly over the cobbles and sniffing happily at the cold air which stung damply against her cheeks. She stared observantly at the passers-by in case one might be Giles, although in her private image she would meet him, not in the street, but on the quay-side by the gangway of his destroyer. She walked on down the street and suddenly, turning a corner, saw masts sticking up into the air beyond the last of the houses.

She sighed happily, tilting her head to watch the gulls which cried overhead, gliding rapidly down wind, their hard little bodies dark against the white sky, their heads turning from side to side. Ports were quite the best places . . . although she would be glad to be out of this street whose houses rose immediately from the cobbled pavements, tight-shut against rain and cold, with thick lace curtains and ferns screening the windows, and sometimes a couple of large spiked shells on either side of the glazed china fern pot. Nicola dug her hands into her pockets and walked on, wondering if hostile eyes really watched her progress or if it only seemed as if they did. She would not run, but she would be tremendously glad to get into the open of the quay-side and find Giles . . .

The quay was less crowded than she had imagined, but she could not see Giles. Nor, at the moment, could she see his destroyer. Nicola, glancing over the piles of lobster pots and spread nets, decided that this must be one of the smaller quays, meant only for fishing vessels. The high shapes of cranes and derricks lay a long way to her left. Probably the naval part of the docks would be over there. Well, it didn't matter. There was lots of time. She wouldn't mind if she had to traverse the whole length of the quays.

She strolled easily, her hands in her pockets, pausing every now and then to stare fascinated at some small cargo ship alongside, her hold and decks crammed with coal or timber. She loitered past, grinning shyly at the fair, friendly sailors who smiled back and shouted to one another in tongues she could not begin to understand. Tim might have known . . . Nicola dismissed Tim impatiently, avoiding the sprawled legs of some boys about her own age who hung over the quay-side fishing for dabs, but seemingly catching only small crabs whose legs moved agonizedly as they were drawn up, to be detached from the hook and dropped into the sea again.

She passed another, higher-decked ship, which might be Norwegian, since the name contained an 'O' with a line through it. Leaning to the curve of the prow was the figure-head of a woman, painted gaudily in blue and gold, her arms crossed on her breast, her hair streaming back in stiff, carved lines. 'We'll have a figure-head too,' thought Nicola, who, on the rare occasions when she was alone, liked to plan the ship she and Lawrie might share, as other people planned their houses. 'I hope there'll be some clippers left . . . or else we'll have a very small ship . . . with red sails . . . unless that's a bit childish . . . perhaps red sails are rather young . . . brown would be all right . . . or blue? No, *definitely* not blue . . . party frocks are always blue . . . when I'm in my ship I shall wear jerseys that are as darned as possible . . . and very holey plimsolls . . .'

A church clock chimed tunably from the town – a three-quarter chime, not specially helpful until the hour struck. Nicola, jerked back into time once more, began to hurry, and bumped into a sailor carrying a kit-bag. The air had begun to smell heavily of oil, and she recollected, with a sense of shock, that she was supposed to be looking for Giles. She hoped, with a faint touch of uneasiness, that she hadn't already passed him.

She glanced over her shoulder. She seemed to have come a very long way. Almost without realizing it, she had come into the midst of the crane and derrick area she had seen from the first quay. The quays were very crowded here; she would have to go pretty carefully so as not to miss Giles . . .

Suddenly she was out of the crowded quarter and at the end of the docks. The quay-side stretched before her, quiet, almost deserted, with damp paper blowing over the cement blocks and dark flat water slapping against the wall. She walked on mechanically and stood at the very end, gazing over the long stretch of water which lay between the quay-side and the dark, cloudtopped downs beyond. Nearer to the downs than to the quay, the three destroyers lay momentarily in a patch of pale sunshine which struck them from between the hurrying clouds and then raced on across the water.

So that was that. Giles was undoubtedly on board and she wouldn't see him. She felt flat and disappointed, the pictured pleasures of the afternoon thinning into nothingness like smoke in a high wind. There seemed nothing more to do except walk back along the quays, return to the station and wait for the next train. She hadn't even enough with her to give herself tea . . . Nicola, peering into her purse to make certain that she really did possess only threepence ha'penny, gasped suddenly as though a cold wave had drenched her and fumbled in her pocket in wild agitation. But it was true. Of course it was true. She had only bought a single ticket. And now she would never be able to return. Never.

14 A Part For Pomona

There was no use pretending it had been a good afternoon, because it hadn't. Nicola, staring forlornly out of the carriage window at the steadily darkening fields, could only hope that Giles would forget the whole thing and not hold it against her. Except for that one moment of ecstatic relief, as she trudged up the High Street, her heart thudding with panic, planning desperately what she might pawn – her purse, her beret, her handkerchief – if only she could find a pawnshop – and even then they probably wouldn't fetch much, only a few more pence to get her that much nearer to Kingscote before she had to get out and walk – and she couldn't possibly pawn her knife, though probably people would say it was idiotic to risk being expelled when a knife might save you – except for that one moment of ecstatic relief as she saw the two officers approaching and realized that one was Giles, the whole thing had been the most appalling fiasco. It had been idiotic of her to forget that Giles would loathe having his family around unless he had invited them specially; particularly loathe to have them turn up when he was engaged on official business. Certainly he had seen that she was in a mess; and certainly he had arranged instantly to stop what he was doing and meet the other lieutenant somewhere as soon as he had seen her on to the train. But he had been coldly, furiously aloof – as who wouldn't be, thought Nicola, fiercely and instantly taking Giles' part against herself, if they were in the Navy and were suddenly clutched by a sister looking disgustingly grubby and practically *yowling* – from the moment they turned up the narrow alleyway, which was a short cut to the station (Giles striding ahead, his long coat curling from his legs, as though nothing would please him better than to abandon her among the dust-bins with which the alley was cluttered), to the instant when he had seen her into an empty compartment, said: 'You'll be all right now, I suppose?' and gone off without even waiting for the train to start.

The rain slanted coldly on the glass. It had been a mistake (she saw that now) to suggest to Giles that she had come partly because he had said she ought to try being bad. Naturally, he had told her not to be such an ass, and had added a few curt comments about so-called dare-devilry in what Rowan, disrespectfully, was apt to call his 'quarter-deck' voice. She had kept her eyes on her plate after that, gulping the bitterish tea and determinedly chewing the dry railway sandwich, overwhelmed by the impossibility of crying in a crowded station buffet, even when you had made a fool of Giles as well as yourself. Now, of course, when she had a carriage to herself and could have howled as loudly and openly as a baby, had she been so minded, she no longer wanted to.

It was the slow train, and, as Rowan had said, you changed twice. The platforms were cold and windy, almost deserted, with greenish-yellow patches of light where the lamps were. And the train, when it came, chugged doggedly along, halting for useless minutes by empty platforms, then jolting on again. She had long since ceased to wonder what the time was and whether she would be back in time not to be missed. She was only anxious to be back at school, have her supper and go to bed. And if people expelled her while all that happened – well, there was nothing she could do about it now.

The train stopped at West Wade. Stiff with cold, Nicola climbed down on to the platform, gave up her precious ticket and went out of the station. The clock above the booking office showed twenty to six. She might, she thought, just do it. It would probably be better if she did. She remembered Rowan saying that Ginty (who was not at all the crying sort) had wept for a week after what Keith had said to her for breaking bounds. And that, as Nicola now knew, had been a very small break indeed – only round a corner and into a stationer's to get a special kind of rubber band which was the fashion in the Lower Fourth that term. There was nothing for it then, but to take the short cut across the fields again. Hating it, she plunged from the irregularly lit road into the windy darkness of the fields and ran and slithered heart-shakingly along the path, trying to pretend she did not see the unexplained movements in the darkness nor hear the odd creaking noises which reminded her with a horrid insistence of Curdie's goblins. In her agitation she scarcely turned her head to watch the train go by, although in the ordinary way she and Lawrie loved trains at night, when the fire pulsed under the smoke, and the little lighted carriages rocked past, looking gay and secure and homely.

She was over the stile and on the main road again. She thought as she ran that perhaps the garden door would be open. If it were, and if she were lucky, she could dash upstairs and into the dormitory and perhaps no one would ever know that she had been to see Giles and that it had been one of the beastliest things that had ever happened.

She tiptoed up the drive, her heart thudding, and turned aside to walk on grass. The moon was rising – but perhaps it was only in books that people leaned out of the window as you passed and saw you as clearly as though it were day. The garden door – oh, blessed, blessed miracle – opened easily to let her in. There was no one about. Nicola whipped off her beret and leapt up the stairs. If anyone saw her now they might think perhaps that she had been in the garden, and think her mad, but not villainous.

The dormitory door was closed. Holding her breath, Nicola turned the handle and walked in. It was dark and empty. It was all right. She was safe.

She switched on the light and sat down limply on the nearest bed. Wearily she pulled off her mackintosh and contemplated her muddy shoes. She thought she would just sit there until the others came up – though perhaps she should put her mackintosh away so as not to arouse comment . . .

She yawned hugely, too tired to move.

The door opened with the utmost caution and Lawrie put her head round. 'Hullo,' she whispered, with a hoarseness calculated to arouse the deepest suspicions if she were overheard by authority. 'Did you get back all right?'

Nicola gazed at her. Lawrie shut the door and tiptoed across to sit on the bed facing Nicola.

'Did you see Giles?' whispered Lawrie. 'How was he?'

'How did you know?' said Nicola helplessly.

'When you seemed to be gone I thought you must have,' said Lawrie, still whispering. 'Rowan said he was at Port Wade. Only you might have told me.'

'Did anyone ask about me?'

''Course.'

'What did you tell them?'

'I said you must have gone down to the Carpentry Shed. You wanted to finish your bookshelves. It wasn't anyone who *mattered* who asked – only Daphne and people.'

'Did you tell Tim?'

'Of course not. You can't let outside people in on things

like that. They always think it doesn't matter if they talk.'

'Thanks awfully,' said Nicola humbly.

'Did you see Giles?'

'Yes.'

'Was it fun?'

'Yes,' said Nicola. Sometime she might tell Lawrie – who had really been very masterly about it all that afternoon – just what had happened. But not now. Not yet. P'rhaps never.

'Well, you were jolly lucky,' said Lawrie in her normal voice. 'We've been having the most flaming row.'

'Who have?' asked Nicola, alarmed.

'Us and Cartwright. About our Pippin. Tim was drawing things on the board – you know, the one she did this morning that you wiped off – and Cartwright came in and saw and said "*What*—?" the way she does – you know—'

Nicola knew: prepared to see a joke if there was one, but ready to be grandly crushing if one were merely being silly. 'Go on. What happened?'

'Marie happened,' said Lawrie gloomily. 'She started on how *horrid* we all were to little Pippin, and how Tim was worst, and then everyone got awfully worked up and said No they were in it too, and Marie said it was Tim who was keeping her – Pippin, I mean – out of the play and Pippin was one of the best people we'd got 'cos of all her experience at home – I *ask* you,' said Lawrie in parenthesis, 'being a Bacchante *experience* – and then Cartwright flamed and said we were all miserable cads and low-down bullies—'

'*Cartwright* did?'

'Well – not exactly in those words, but she did say we were bullies. And it isn't even *true*,' said Lawrie, bouncing on the bed, wrathful and indignant. 'Bullying's twisting people's arms and roasting them and things, isn't it? And we've never laid a finger on the little beast, have we?'

'N-no,' said Nicola doubtfully. 'At least, I did fight her that time, but she fought back. Did Cartwright mean that?'

'*No.* She just meant teasing her and calling her Blenheim and Apfelstrudel and things.'

'Oh. Well, what happened?'

'Well, she's got to have a proper part in the play. Tim's thinking one up now. She's simply livid. And Cartwright said we could either have a form order mark, or go on a day's silence. So we said we'd do the silence, because of the Form Shield and losing such masses of points for form order marks. Tomorrow, that's happening. And we're not to talk at all – not even in rec. – except for something absolutely necessary.'

'Oh,' said Nicola. She supposed she ought to feel punished. But, on the whole, she thought a day's silence might be rather pleasant than otherwise. Sometime, Lawrie was going to ask: 'What did you and Giles do all the afternoon?' and it would be better, perhaps, to have as thick a cushion of time as possible between the reality and the telling.

The door opened a crack and swung gently on its hinges. 'Oh, good,' said Tim. 'I was afraid the whole family might be here. Hullo, Nick. Has Lawrie told you?'

'About the Pippin row? Yes.'

'You chose a good afternoon to go carpentering.' ('So I gather,' said Nicola.) 'I've never *heard* such a shindig about nothing.'

'You'd better let her do Tom,' said Nicola more easily. If the quarrel were over, swallowed up in the greater stresses of the moment, she hadn't the least intention of reviving it.

'*Funny* joke,' said Tim. Then she giggled. 'As a matter of fact, I've found the perfect part for her – dear, round, little soul. She can do Henry. She lies on a sofa and looks fat and she dies practically when we start. Couldn't be better.'

'Will Cartwright think that's all right?' said Nicola doubtfully.

'I don't suppose Cartwright knows. If I say "Henry the Eighth" she's sure to think it's a whacking great part. Besides, in the book it is quite large. It's only in the play that there isn't so much of it.'

'Cunning,' said Lawrie appreciatively.

'Well, we can't mess the whole thing up, finding star parts for Pippin. Oh, dear. I suppose we'll have to start casting it properly soon.'

'Haven't you nearly finished it?' asked Lawrie sternly.

''M. 'Bout half-way through,' said Tim gruffly.

'Well, you've got another week, just on. And if you haven't finished it by then, we'll have to start rehearsing what there is.'

'You are a bossy one,' said Tim sadly.

'Are you stuck?' asked Nicola sympathetically.

'A bit,' admitted Tim reluctantly. 'There's an awful lot to leave out and then it's a bit difficult linking on again.'

'It's no good me saying I'll help,' said Nicola candidly, ''cos I don't know anything about plays. But I'll do your maths prep all next week if you like.' To everyone's surprise and her own pleased astonishment, Nicola had suddenly emerged as quick and clear-headed over figures.

'Thanks. Only mind you make plenty of mistakes or there'll be dark suspicions that it isn't me. I usually get one quite right and the others I make slips in working. If you could just remember that I usually call four and three: six, and twice nine: nineteen, it ought to be all right.'

Nicola chuckled.

'Oh, well, I'd better rush off before your family come up

and tell me visiting's against the rules,' said Tim, moving off. 'What a little misery Marie Dobson is. You should have heard her, Nick.'

'I wish I had,' said Nicola sincerely.

Tim went off.

'I think I'll have a bath,' said Nicola contemplatively after a pause. 'There isn't a rule that Thirds mustn't at night, is there?'

'Don't think so,' said Lawrie abstractedly. 'I wish Tim would hurry up and finish the play, don't you?'

''M,' said Nicola, collecting towels and soap. She really had been rather an ass to go off that afternoon. It might have meant the most tremendous row. She was extraordinarily lucky that it was so safely over. The quarrel was over too; another good thing. And there was a large form row that they were all in together, so no one need feel specially disgraced. And there would be the play . . . Nicola swung her towel across her shoulder, half-listening to the beginning of the evening noise in corridors and dormitories. Nice, safe school. Much better than being lost in ports and bolting over dark fields – very, very much better than having Giles thinking one an insane nuisance. But he'd be too busy to remember for long – and anyway, he *had* said it would be a good idea to be bad. 'He couldn't have been wronger,' thought Nicola, watching Lawrie divest herself of blouse, skirt and stockings, and drop them negligently on the floor to be picked up by Ann as she always did; then she grinned to herself, yawned, and went to have her bath.

And yet, thought Nicola, sitting on the side of the bath, enveloped in clouds of steam, while the water ran in, now that it was safely over, there had been nice bits. She wouldn't really, for instance, have wanted to miss that moment when the masts suddenly reared themselves at the end of the street, nor the first sight of that figure-head gazing eternally out to sea. Life, thought Nicola solemnly, was a very funny mixture. And there seemed to be practically nothing to be done about it.

15 A Form Meeting

I

'Well, I think we ought to start now,' said Lawrie definitely, slapping closed the note-book which held the completed half of the play of *The Prince and the Pauper*. 'There's lots there for us to rehearse. And you must just finish it off as we go along.'

Tim, pale and inky, looked at her crossly. Because she found it difficult to admit that she might not be as clever as she thought, she did not want to suggest that she might be unable to finish the play. Tim liked doing things which could be finished in a swift, concentrated rush; and she had found, with some dismay, that a play demanded sustained effort. All the same, she did not want to fall back on *Twelfth Night*; but she would have liked to leave the play for a little and then finish it off in another grand rush . . . only Lawrie was so insistent.

'We'll have to start copying parts, too,' said Lawrie reflectively. 'I should think people like Elaine and Hazel might do that. They won't be doing anything else much. Or else everyone can do their own.'

Tim supposed gloomily that she was right. It wasn't much use pretending that there was a lot of time left or that you could rehearse a play properly in less than a month. She said, carefully nonchalant:

'What d'you think of it, so far?'

'Oh, I like it,' said Lawrie with genuine pleasure, hugging

the note-book against her chest. 'I think it's awfully good – not a bit as though you'd done it.'

Tim, appreciating Lawrie's meaning rather than her words, was pleased. 'I suppose we ought to have a form meeting and read them bits and tell them what happens. They're awfully good about it, aren't they? They rush off and do scenery and costumes and things and they haven't an idea, really, what it's all about.'

Nicola came in, looking hot, with a smudge of purple paint on one cheek. She hoisted herself on to the lid of her desk and said: 'We've finished the forest curtain. How're you doing?'

'Could be worse,' said Tim.

'It's very good,' said Lawrie. 'I've been reading it.'

Nicola hugged her knees and accepted this without injury. She had discovered that although she and Tim and Lawrie were the prime movers in the play, it meant much more to Tim and Lawrie than to herself. Except her part. She minded a good deal about that and wished Tim would hurry up and cast it and put her out of her apprehension. But about the play as a whole she did not mind so deeply; and she had been energetic about the scenery, mostly because she liked sloshing paint and size about, partly because Jennings had been extremely helpful, drawing outlines on the canvas backcloths in charcoal and writing in the colours they were to use on each bit. Nicola had been surprised about the colours. She had supposed one used green and brown for trees, but Jennings had said, No, that blues and yellows and purples would be better and that she would see that this was so when the backcloth was finished and she came to look at it from a distance. This afternoon Nicola had found this to be true and interesting; and in any event it was a pleasant pastime on wet afternoons, even when the others gave up, saying they'd had enough and that the smell made them feel sick.

'By the way,' said Tim suddenly, as though Nicola's thought had touched off an answering note in her own mind, 'what parts do you two want? I mean, I don't care a scrap which does Tom and which does Edward, so you may just as well say if you've any feelings one way or the other.'

Nicola hugged her knees more tightly and hoped the others wouldn't notice.

'I don't mind,' she said.

'That's helpful,' said Tim. 'Lawrie?'

Nicola stared down at the pleats in her skirt. Lawrie did mind more about the play than she did, so it was only fair that she should have first pick. Only she wished she'd hurry up and choose so that Nicola herself could start saying all the proper things about it being all right and of course she didn't care which she was . . .

'Oh, I'm going to be Tom,' said Lawrie as though that had been known and settled from the beginning.

Nicola gasped. Tim looked mildly surprised.

'You needn't on my account, honestly,' said Nicola hastily. 'I mean, truly, I don't mind as much as all that.'

Lawrie looked blank. 'I don't see what you mean. Don't you want to do Tom, too?'

'*No*,' said Nicola, her cheeks pink with relief and astonishment. 'Of course I want to do Edward. Edward has all the best bits. You do know what you're saying, don't you? I mean, you do know that Tom's the beggar one?'

'Yes,' said Lawrie politely. 'Of course I know.'

'Well, then—' said Nicola helplessly. Because surely anyone would want to do Edward and have all the fun of being wrongfully dispossessed and coming gloriously into your kingdom at the end.

'Tom's miles more fun,' said Lawrie, amazed as Nicola,

though for the conflicting reason, that anyone should question this. 'Miles more fun to act. I mean.'

'Why?' asked Tim, interested, tilting her chair.

'Well, because – well – because – oh, just *because*,' she said at length impatiently, and was silent, flicking over the leaves of the note-book as though the sight of the play itself might help her. She could not find words to express her instinct that Edward's part was too straightforward to be interesting, whereas with Tom you must make the audience see that he was pretending all the time and at the last coming almost to believe his own pretence. She thought Tim and Nicola very foolish not to see this as clearly as she did without saying 'Why?' and looking at her as though she were a freak; and she said crossly:

'I don't see why you have to gape at me. Nick *wants* to be Edward and I *want* to be Tom, so it's all right.'

'All right,' said Nicola, still dubious. 'If you're *sure* that's what you want.'

'I suppose we'll have to have readings before we cast the rest,' said Tim scribbling idly. 'To-morrow's Saturday, isn't it? We could have a meeting in the morning and then I can tell everyone what it's about at the same time.'

Lawrie chuckled suddenly.

'You ought to have Marie as John Canty. Great bony thing. She'd simply love cuffing Nick around. It'd be the best time she'd had in years.'

II

Tim was not often nervous, but she felt unwontedly self-conscious the following morning as she marched up to the staff desk and slammed her note-book and the library copy of *The Prince and the Pauper* on to the lid.

'Sh,' said a wit. 'Quiet, everyone. Miss Keith's here.'

'Funny bunny,' growled Tim, half-kneeling on the chair, because the desk was otherwise too tall for her. She would have preferred to have sat on the lid of her own desk, but, as Nicola had pointed out, it was much easier to talk to people if you were properly in front of them.

'Oo, Miss *Keith*. You mustn't say things like that. Must she?'

'Oh, dry up,' said Tim. 'Be funny some other time. D'you want to hear about the play or not?'

'We-ll . . .' said Third Remove, giving the matter their earnest consideration. They were quite prepared to settle down in time, but they couldn't have Tim taking herself over-seriously. 'Do we want to?'

'Let's vote on it.'

'Let's have a secret ballot.'

'We'll think it over, Tim, and let you know.'

Nicola thumped her desk.

'Do stop waffling. The whole morning'll be gone if you don't shut up.'

'All right. Go ahead, Tim,' said Third Remove kindly. 'Nick can wake us when you've finished.'

Tim, rightly interpreting this as an intimation that they were prepared to listen, plunged into her exposition.

'Well – it's about Edward VI. Partly when he's Prince of Wales and partly when he's King.'

'Is it history?' interrupted someone dubiously.

'Not real history, no. It's a – it's a sort of legend.' Tim had an inspiration. 'There was a film of it ages ago, only it was before our time. At least, I never saw it.'

'Oh, well. If it's a *film*,' said Third Remove, reassured. 'Go on.'

'Well,' said Tim hurrying on while they were in the mood.

'There's another boy – Tom Canty – born in the slums on the same day – the same day as Edward's born, I mean. He lives in a frightful hovel and goes out begging, but a priest who lives in the same house tries to educate him, and after a bit – the priest reads him legends about kings and princes, you see – Tom starts to pretend privately that he *is* a prince and has a pretend court and all that. That won't come into the play. That'll be read as a sort of prologue.'

She paused nervously for a moment, but no one interrupted and the silence was an interested one, so she went on more confidently.

'Well then, one day, while he's out begging, Tom loses himself and wanders about until he comes to the Palace of Westminster. That's where the play starts properly. He comes to the palace gates – at least, in the play it won't be gates, he'll meet Edward in the street with his retinue because that'll be easier for scenery – and the guards shove him off, and Edward interferes and takes him into the Palace. Then they talk, and Edward has a meal brought for Tom and thinks Tom's kind of life sounds frightfully romantic and for a joke they change clothes. And then they see that they're exactly alike and that no one could tell that they'd changed at all. And then Edward gets frightfully worked up over the way the guards shoved Tom about and rushes off to tear them off a strip and of course they think Edward is Tom and throw him out of the Palace.'

Tim, who had been talking at top speed, stopped to take breath.

'Which of the twins is going to do which?' enquired Hazel.

'Nick's Edward and Lawrie's Tom.' (Third Remove, agreeing with Nicola that it was more fun to be the rightful heir, and, on the whole, liking Nicola the better of the two, nodded intelligently.) 'Well, then, the rest of the play is about the two of them being mistaken for one another. Everyone in the Palace thinks Tom is Edward and that he's suddenly gone mad when he can't remember all the things he should know by – by instinct; only, you see, Tom has always pretended to be a Prince and so he gradually gets into the way of it. And Edward falls in with a gang of beggars who all think he's a terrific joke because he will keep saying he's Prince of Wales and later on, when Henry dies—'

'Henry *who*?' asked Elaine Rees blankly.

'Henry VIII, you ass,' said Tim crushingly. 'I told you it was Edward VI. When Henry dies, Edward insists that he's King and they think that's even funnier. Well, then, at last – there are lots of things happen to Edward, but you'll see all that when we start rehearsing – Edward escapes and gets back to London on the day that Tom is going to be crowned in his place. So he creeps into the Abbey – *Westminster* Abbey' – with a glance at Elaine – 'and hides in one of the tombs. And just as Tom is going to be crowned, Edward leaps out and says that he's the rightful King. No one believes him, of course, though Tom says at once that he's speaking the truth, and then Tom remembers that only Edward knows where the Great Seal is, and Edward tells them and everything comes right and he's crowned. And that's the end,' said Tim, her nervousness returning, so that she dropped her note-book and had to climb down after it.

'It sounds an awful lot of Lawrie and Nicola, and not much of anyone else,' said Marie Dobson aggrievedly.

Fortunately, Marie, after the affair of Pomona and her nick-names, carried very little weight; and people promptly disagreed with her in voices designed to show how extremely little they thought of her.

'That's stupid. Tim said at the very beginning that there were masses of parts, didn't you, Tim?'

'Besides, you were only giving us an outline, weren't you, Tim? Any dope could see that.'

'I don't think,' said Tim, hastily seizing her opportunity while they were on her side, 'I don't think there are any other parts that run right through the play, like Tom and Edward. But there are lots of smaller parts and everyone'll have to do three or four, so it'll be practically the same thing in the end.'

'I'd rather have lots of little ones,' said Hazel with a giggle. 'Then if I'm frightfully bad or forget the words it won't matter, will it?'

Tim let this pass.

'Well, we ought to start rehearsing practically at once, so I thought we might try to get as much of the casting settled as we can. I haven't *quite* finished the whole thing,' said Tim glossily, avoiding Lawrie's eye, 'but we can cast all the first half and by the time the play's complete we'll know exactly what people can and can't do.'

'What are you going to do?' asked Audrey Fudge suspiciously.

'Oh, I'm going to do the reading,' said Tim, genuinely off-hand. 'It's not awfully interesting, but I can't produce and have a part too. And someone's got to read the linking bits.' She answered Audrey's unspoken question. 'We can't act the whole thing from beginning to end, 'cos we've only got an hour, and we couldn't do all the scenery and stuff, so bits that are just sort of explanation or that we can't work in any other way will have to be read as if it were a story. I've had to leave out masses that was in the book, anyway.'

'Oh—' said Audrey doubtfully.

'Now then,' said Tim briskly, ignoring Audrey ruthlessly, lest she should start one of her long, rambling, obstinate arguments. 'Jean, will you try Lady Jane Grey? And Daphne the Lady Elizabeth – well, she isn't Good Queen Bess yet, fathead – nothing like enough people have died – and Lawrie, you'd better come and read Tom's speeches. You'll have to share, I'm afraid—'

'When we've done the casting,' said Lawrie firmly, coming up to the dais to read Tom, 'everyone can have one night with the book to copy out their parts. But *only* one night. We haven't time for more. So if anyone wants any prep. done the night they're doing speeches they'd better say so early.'

III

'Well,' said Tim, yawning a little, as they went upstairs to wash for lunch, 'that didn't go badly, did it? Elizabeth'll be rather a nice Lady Jane Grey, I think. And Marie's frightfully bucked that there's so much of old Canty. She'll probably lay off her thing about it not being fair for you two to have such huge parts.'

'You know what,' stated Lawrie grimly, 'don't you?'

'No,' said Tim, mildly alarmed. 'What?'

'Pippin-Asteroid's going to be jolly good. You'd better shove back all those bits you cut out that time.'

'Oh, *Lawrie*—' protested Tim uneasily. But she knew Lawrie was right. Even on a first reading Pomona had been surprisingly in character as the old king. 'It's so enfuriating. She's such a fat ass.'

'She needs to be a fat ass,' Nicola pointed out with a grin, 'if she's doing Henry. I think Lawrie's right, Tim. And she'd better have a good hefty part in the second part, when Henry's dead, too.'

'No,' wailed Tim. 'Oh *no*, Nick. Why?'

'Because she's good, silly. And we haven't got *so* many people who're much good. Look at Daphne.'

'Isn't she awful?' agreed Lawrie. 'I don't see how anyone can be so silly over acting. She can't even say "The Prince approaches" without giggling like a sausage.'

They reached the door of the twins' dormitory and Tim went on alone, feeling unexpectedly cross and cantankerous. She knew that the twins were right and that Pomona would have to be given decent parts; but: 'I wish I'd never thought of a play,' said Tim to herself, walking moodily into her dormitory. 'I didn't want *Pomona* to make a name for herself. Her and her pageants and her pretty name! She'll be ten times worse after this.'

16 A Question of Elocution

It was a curious and rather unexpected sensation to see your own play take on form and substance. Tim, sitting grandly in Miss Keith's carved chair, placed for that purpose in the middle of the Assembly Hall, or walking towards the stage calling concise directions about entrances and movements, found that as soon as people began to speak her lines they were hers no longer. This was fortunate in its way, for once rehearsals began, she discovered that certain lines and speeches which had pleased her immensely on paper, needed drastic alteration before anyone could speak them with conviction. 'It's as well I don't mind,' thought Tim, scribbling vigorously, while the rehearsal waited, obedient and admiring, 'but perhaps it's because it was Mark Twain's first. If it had been mine from the beginning, I daresay I'd feel differently about it.'

Fortunately for Tim, Third Remove enjoyed rehearsing. Even Daphne Morris lost her tendency to giggle when she found that the others regarded her as a dreary nuisance and not at all funny; and Elaine Rees, who at her own request had been given the smallest parts available, was gradually achieving courage enough to speak above a whisper, having discovered that no one became specially convulsed with mirth because they could hear what she said. The rest, thought Tim cautiously, hoping she wasn't allowing herself to be unduly carried away, were at least average good. When she forgot to be cautious and allowed herself to think just how effective it might be on the night, when everyone knew their parts and had their proper clothes, and the stage was properly lit and all the scenery in place, she thought also how surprisingly well most of them managed their parts. It was still a pity, perhaps, that Pomona was so astonishingly good as Henry (but astonishingly, Tim comforted herself hastily, only if you knew her well off-stage; if you didn't, she probably didn't seem more remarkable than Elizabeth, for instance). And besides, thought Tim, as rehearsals proceeded and people began to say proudly: 'I say, Tim, I know all my parts now,' it was Lawrie, as any fool could see, who was really best. Nick was awfully good too, proud and fierce and plucky; but Lawrie could *act*. Tim, who had, quite early on, ceased to tell Lawrie what to do and how to do it, sat and watched fascinated, while Tom Canty, gradually losing his first terror of being exposed as an impostor, gathered confidence, and learned, never to be royal, but, by furtive glances to see whether he were acting correctly, to imitate, with obvious enjoyment, the show of royalty. '*Horrid* little beast,' thought Tim crossly, watching Tom Canty parading graciously to his throne, simulating princely condescension and conversing, all complacent affability, with the Lady Elizabeth and Lady Jane Grey; and then giggled, remembering that this was her own play (more or less) and that it was surely foolish to be annoyed by characters one had oneself created. (For it had become increasingly difficult, as time went on, for Tim to remember just exactly where Mark Twain left off and Thalia Keith began.)

It was, perhaps, a pity that once rehearsals began, there seemed to be little else that was important. Lessons became a tiresome interlude and preparation something to be raced through so that you could go on learning your part or sewing your costume. Each Friday, when Miss Cartwright had read the weekly marks, she commented ruefully that the play seemed to be taking up far too much of their time and energy and that they really must try to pull themselves together before the exams. If Nicola could work sensibly, surely it wasn't beyond the powers of the rest of them?

Third Remove looked reproachfully at the blushing Nicola, who protested uneasily that she wasn't really working, it was only that the work seemed easier now. To which Miss Cartwright replied that however simple she might find it, five-page history essays of reasonable intelligence could not be completed in ten minutes, as Thalia's had apparently been, despite the large clear handwriting which managed to cover so many sheets. Tim grinned and agreed without embarrassment that this was so.

'Well,' said Miss Cartwright, 'I'm not going to threaten you people with the cancellation of the play. It's been put into the official programme for the bazaar and people outside school will be coming. I can only warn you that if you continue like this, you'll certainly do badly in the exams and there'll be no one worth recommending for a move to one of the other Thirds next term.'

They listened sadly, promised amendment, and for half an hour radiated conscious virtue. But it was no use. There were rehearsals to be attended in every spare half-hour, props to be made, odd lengths of material from home to be criticized and worked into someone's costume; and occasional quarrels to be sorted out, even though, on the whole, they were all getting on rather well together. No one could do all that and work as well, except Nicola, who also spent such spare time as was left to her in the studio, painting the street backcloth, sometimes with one or two of the others, but, more often, as the first riotous enthusiasm declined, alone. She did not mind this, for scene painting was a job she enjoyed, and it was going to be rather pleasant to feel (though naturally not say, since that would be swank of the first order) that for all practical purposes the scenery for the play would be her own unaided work. Nicola smiled to herself, painting in the broad timbering of one of the houses, and then took the statement back with some haste. You couldn't possibly say that the scenery was yours alone when Jennings had drawn in all the outlines and said exactly which colours were to go where. Nicola knelt back on her heels, approving of Jennings, who had drawn their backcloths for them with a certain serious relish and then left them to it without further interference. There were still the throne room curtains to do and the exterior of the Palace of Westminster – and it was just as well, thought Nicola, glancing to where Jennings sat in her bright painting smock, marking, with a ruefully amused expression, the Lower Fourth's attempts at picturing a circus, that they'd had Jennings to turn to. As a form Third Remove were weak at Art, though Jennings frequently told them that their efforts, poor as they were, were too funny to be depressing.

The Westminster Abbey interior, fortunately, was ready and waiting for them. People would probably recognize it as the Rheims Cathedral set from the school's performance of *St. Joan*, but that couldn't be helped. It would be senseless to waste a perfectly good cathedral when there was so little time anyway, the Day Itself galloping nearer and nearer . . . Nicola shivered pleasurably and gripped her brush tightly.

'Have you decided yet what you want to call the tavern?' asked Miss Jennings abruptly, holding a Lower Fourth circus away from her as though she found it difficult to believe. She had remarked, when drawing in the outlines, that their Tudor Street must have its tavern or it would scarcely be in character.

Nicola wasn't sure. The Royal George, her first choice, would, Miss Jennings had informed her, be an anachronism; but she could have the Prince of Wales, or the Golden Lion or the White Stag—

'But of course,' added Jennings suddenly, stubbing out her cigarette on a small, brilliantly coloured saucer, 'I don't know whether you want it to be the same street all the time. Do you?'

Nicola thought not.

'Then you'd better make a separate wooden stand for your tavern sign and I'll draw you several different ones. I don't suppose many of the audience will notice, but it'll amuse those who do.'

Nicola thought this a brilliant idea, and, since she was then due for a rehearsal, rushed down to the Assembly Hall to tell Tim about it. The rehearsal had been in progress for about half an hour when she arrived and Tim was rehearsing one of what she called her 'mob scenes' and conducting a furious argument with Lawrie simultaneously.

'Oh good,' said Tim in relief as Nicola came up to them. 'Now we can start from the beginning and go straight through.'

'That's what I'm saying,' said Lawrie belligerently. 'Don't you think so too, Nick? Tim ought to rehearse her reading now, oughtn't she? We've only got another fortnight.'

'Yes, I should think so. Why not?'

'It doesn't need rehearsing,' snapped Tim. 'Why should it? It's a perfectly easy thing to do. Any fool can.'

'Then if it's so easy, I don't see why you should mind,' retorted Lawrie. 'And it *isn't* easy. Look what tripe *The Fairie Queen* sounds when Miller reads it and how different it sounded when she was ill and we had Kempe.'

'Oh, all *right*, if you're so set on it. But it sounds like sheer waste of time to me. Look here. I'll read the Prologue bit. And if your royal highness passes that, the rest'll be all right too.'

Lawrie nodded. 'If you can read that, you can read anything.'

Tim, looking as though she suspected an insult, but wasn't sure about it, put the prompt copy of the play – she had finished it that morning – under her arm, and leapt on to the platform, shooing off the mob.

'I'll read it to where Edward and Tom meet,' she called down to them, 'you know the bit: ". . . *his whole being was strung to one desire – to be close to the prince as the passed and to fix his image in his memory for ever.*" And then you be ready to come on.'

'All right,' said Lawrie, unmoved. 'Where are you going to be?'

'Centre stage in front of the curtain, to begin with,' said Tim briskly. 'And then go to the side with the curtain and stay there. That'll be a good strategic place for prompting.'

Lawrie nodded. Tim, standing at the front of the platform, began to read.

'I can't hear,' remarked Lawrie critically, after a bit. Tim lifted her eyes from the page in a glance of silent fury, but raised her voice obediently. Third Remove began to edge gently towards Lawrie.

'I say,' murmured Hazel tentatively, 'she's not awfully good, is she?'

Lawrie grunted.

'D'you think she's doing it properly?' suggested Elizabeth softly. 'Or is she just sort of running it over?'

Lawrie looked doubtful.

'If that's the best she can do,' remarked Marie, rather more loudly than the rest, 'it won't do at all.'

Nicola, sitting on the steps at the back of the Hall where the Sixth stood for Assembly, hugged her knees and said nothing. It was queer how reading aloud affected people's voices. Tim's went flat and strained and she stumbled over the easiest words. You'd scarcely know it *was* Tim unless you were actually watching her.

Tim, suddenly sensing criticism in the air, stopped dead and eyed the group at the back of the Hall with hostility.

'What's the matter?' she said.

They looked at Lawrie.

'It's no good,' said Lawrie clearly. 'You can't read a bit.'

'What on earth d'you mean?' asked Tim indignantly. She jumped down from the platform and they all met, an agitated group, in the centre of the Hall.

'Were you reading it properly?' asked Elizabeth eagerly. 'Or were you just sort of rushing through?'

'No,' said Tim offended. 'Of course I was reading it properly. What was wrong?'

The critics looked at one another doubtfully.

'Your voice goes so *funny*—' ventured someone.

'It's difficult to hear what you're saying.'

'It doesn't sound interesting a bit.'

'It's worse than Miller and *The Fairie Queen*, heaps,' said a character who believed in candour.

Tim looked bewildered. 'Well, if you say so – look here, I'll try it again. Perhaps I was rushing it too much.'

She went back to the platform and began to read again, nervous and faintly alarmed, but desperately anxious to get it right. The rest listened silently. At length Lawrie detached herself from the others and walked down the Hall.

'Do stop, Tim,' she said flatly. 'It's simply awful. You can't possibly do it like that.'

Tim flushed and was silent. She closed the book slowly

and sat down, her legs dangling over the edge of the platform. The rest came up to them and stood round in anxious silence.

'Well,' said Tim jerkily, at length, making the edge of the book whirr again and again under her thumb, 'what are we going to do now?'

'Couldn't one of us read?' suggested Heather Price tentatively.

'Not very well. We've only just managed to fit in all the parts as it is. And I couldn't possibly act *and* produce.'

'I suppose we couldn't act all the bits you were going to read?' said Daphne with an air of cleverness.

'No,' said Tim politely. 'It would take far too long, mean changes of scene every five minutes and lots more characters into the bargain.'

'What are we going to do, then?' demanded Lawrie in a hard little voice.

'Could we leave the reading out altogether?' murmured Audrey cautiously.

'No. If we did, no one'd know what was going on.'

'If *you* read it, no one'll know, anyway,' snapped Lawrie. She sounded, thought Nicola, perilously near tears.

'But I don't honestly see what's wrong,' said Tim sincerely. 'Can't you tell me, Lawrie? I don't see why I couldn't put it right.'

'Your voice is all wrong,' said Lawrie, too distressed on the play's account to consider Tim's feelings. 'I can't explain, but you don't make one *see* things. D'you remember how Lois read on the hike, Nick? That's the proper way. Yours is awful.'

'You needn't be beastly about it,' said Hazel. 'Tim can't help it.'

'It doesn't matter that she can't help it. It's that it's all wrong,' retorted Lawrie furiously. 'And now time's so short. If she'd rehearsed it ages ago, like I said—'

'Well,' said Tim with sudden energy, 'there are only two things we can do. We can drop the whole thing—'

'*Tim!*'

'—or you can let me get it as good as I can, and if it isn't awfully good it can't be helped.'

'We can't not do it,' said Third Remove horrified.

'No, we can't,' stated Nicola grimly. 'The other Thirds all think we won't be able to, anyway. When I was in the wash-room yesterday, Miranda West started talking like mad about how we were keeping what we were acting a deadly secret because we knew it was going to be a flop and at the last minute we'd have to mime *Young Waters*.'

'What did you say?' asked Tim.

'Nothing. I smiled at the soap and came away.'

'We can't possibly drop it after that,' said Marie loudly, looking smugly round for support. 'Not now everybody's learnt their parts and everything.'

'Oh, dry up,' muttered Tim.

'I'd rather drop it than it be all wrong,' said Lawrie abruptly, her voice uncertain, 'and if Tim—' She stopped, her chin quivered and she went out, the swing doors of the Assembly Hall clashing madly behind her.

The rest looked at one another, uneasy and silent.

'Well, it's no use rehearsing any more to-day,' said Tim at last. 'You may as well all run away and play and I'll try to think of something.'

Nicola stayed behind to help her carry Miss Keith's chair and table back on to the platform and replace the vase of flowers contributed by the Sixth.

'What did Lawrie mean about Lois on the hike?' said Tim out of a long silence.

Nicola coloured. 'Only that she read the beginning of *The Scarlet Pimpernel* to us in rest hour.'

'And was she specially good?'

Nicola considered the matter, endeavouring to be fair, even to Lois Sanger.

'Yes. I think she was. She made you feel as though – as though it were happening all round you.'

'I suppose you don't know *how* she did it?'

But that was beyond Nicola. She could only say, rather helplessly: 'It was just the way she read it.'

They parted after that, by tacit consent, Nicola returning to the studio to assuage her gloom by more scene painting. Tim found a vacant music room and, sitting hunched on the window-sill, read aloud to herself, wondering why it sounded so normal to herself and so dreadful to the others. But the mystery was insoluble, and at length she slammed the book shut and stared miserably at the bare, dusty floor, wondering what was to be done. 'Pity Lois Sanger isn't a bit younger,' she thought despondently. 'If she was even Upper Fourth I wouldn't mind asking—Well, bless me, I don't see why I've got to come over all school conventional now. Even the Upper Fifth have the elements of humanity in them, I suppose.'

She jumped up and flew downstairs to the senior common room, composing her face to what she hoped was a proper expression of junior deference, and knocked. Rowan came to the door.

'Please,' said Tim with the utmost propriety, 'is Lois Sanger here?'

'No,' said Rowan, equally courteous, 'I'm afraid not. But I think you'll find her in the library.'

'Thanks,' said Tim. She raced back across the Assembly Hall and entered the library panting and breathless. To her delight only Lois was there, frowning over a French prose. She crossed the floor decorously and stood waiting at Lois's elbow until Lois should look up and be ready to attend.

Lois, suddenly aware of an immobile presence at her side, looked up with a faintly distracted air.

'Did you want me?'

'Are you busy?' countered Tim.

'Yes,' said Lois, 'moderately. Why?'

'I'm afraid I shall take some time,' said Tim in her gentlest voice. 'So if you'd rather I came back another time—?'

Lois eyed her French prose with dislike and screwed the top on to her fountain pen. 'No, I don't mind a break. In fact, I'd go so far as to say I'd be glad of it. What's the excitement?'

Tim drew a deep breath and sat down on the edge of the table, facing Lois.

'Will you treat what I'm going to say as absolutely secret?'

'Now look,' said Lois, mildly alarmed. 'You haven't come to consult me over an Epidemic of Cribbing in your form and shall you go to Miss Keith and Sneak, have you? Because that's not my cup of tea at all. Try a prefect or—'

'Bless me, no,' said Tim, amused, recognizing something of herself. 'Nothing like that. I wouldn't bother if they were. No. It's about our form effort for the Fund. We haven't told anyone what we're doing, you see, and we want it to stay absolutely secret.'

Lois looked intrigued. 'I can promise to be secret about that, I should think. Go on.'

'*Well*,' said Tim. Talking fast, lest Lois should lose interest, she described the events which had led up to the play, the dramatizing of *The Prince and the Pauper*, and the afternoon's débâcle. 'And they say I'm hopeless,' finished Tim breathlessly, 'and Nick and Lawrie say you're absolutely super at reading, so I wondered if you'd mind frightfully listening to me and telling me what was wrong.'

To her surprise, Lois coloured hotly. 'Nick and Lawrie said so?'

'Yes. You read to them on a hike or something.'

'Yes,' said Lois embarrassed. 'So I did. Yes, all right. I'll hear you if you like, but I don't know that I can be very helpful about it.'

Snatching up the play, Tim began once more on the Prologue, reading it with as much care and expression as she could muster. Lois listened, her chin on her hand, her eyes fixed on the metal inkwell. 'Stop there,' she said abstractedly, at last. Tim closed the book softly and waited. 'I don't quite know *what* it is you do,' said Lois, groping for words. 'Your voice seems to go all knotted up in your throat and become so monotonous – I say, you do want me to be honest, don't you?'

Tim swallowed, her eyes on the brown cover of the notebook. 'Yes, of course.'

'I don't mean to be unkind,' said Lois uncertainly.

'No, I know,' said Tim gruffly. 'But what can I do about it?'

'Don't you feel yourself doing it?'

'No. It sounds all right to me.'

Lois considered.

'There's no one else in the form who could do the reading?'

Tim's heart sank. She shook her head.

'If it's just the Prologue,' suggested Lois after a moment, 'perhaps—'

'But it isn't,' Tim interrupted gloomily. 'There's heaps to read. Some quite important bits. That's why Lawrie's so upset. It's going to ruin the whole thing if the reading's bad, and honestly, all the rest of it's going so well. Even the mobs are much better than you'd think. You couldn't tell me how to do it properly?'

'I don't know enough about it,' said Lois candidly. 'If it were just a matter of putting in the right expression, I daresay I might. But I can't tell you how to loosen up your voice, for I don't know.'

'Could you read a bit?' said Tim. 'P'rhaps if I heard it done properly—'

Not unsusceptible to the implied compliment, Lois took the play, and began to read. Tim, nursing one knee, and listening to the low, flexible voice, appreciated instantly what the twins had meant. 'I couldn't read like that in a hundred years,' she thought. 'And I can't think what we're going to do. I couldn't possibly get up and read it now that everyone's said I'm so ghastly. *I* don't know. And if we chuck it, the other Thirds'll laugh themselves sick.'

She said nothing when Lois fell silent, but sat sadly on, becalmed by her heavy-footed thoughts.

'Look here—' said Lois abruptly.

Tim jumped. 'Sorry. Yes?'

'Look. I've been reading this. I think it's immensely good. If you can't think of any other way, would you like me to do the reading for you?'

Tim lurched and nearly over-balanced in her astonishment. 'Would you *really*?'

'Yes,' said Lois firmly, slightly over-emphatic because she had her qualms. The Sixth could, without undue comment, interest themselves in junior enterprise in a kindly and impersonal fashion if they were so minded; but it was not the function of the Upper Fifth. People might, probably would, say that she was doing a popularity hunt among the Thirds. But – but it was a surprisingly good play; not at all the sort of thing one expected from a junior form. And it would be fun to use her odd talent of reading to such shining advantage; for Lois could not act; without her book she was as stiff and ungainly as was Tim's reading. And it would, thought Lois reluctantly, for she did not wish to think this, be rather a relief to do something, even indirectly, for the Marlow brats. Very probably, if they were asked, thought Lois glibly, they would say that they would much rather she helped them with the play than bothered to do anything about Guides – as, of course, she might have done if she hadn't been chucking them herself at the end of term ... Nothing seemed to have gone quite right since that hike ... the Pimpernels hadn't become at all a good Patrol ... with the exception of that awful child, Marie Dobson, they were slack and tiresome and untidy, almost as though they were daring her to ask them why ... Jill must have said something ... Jill had been almost openly unfriendly since that Court of Honour ... 'Lawrie's so upset,' Tim had said. Lois shifted uneasily, remembering from experience just how upset Lawrie could be. With a small sigh of relief, Lois remembered that if she were openly criticized she could say that there were people who were, or had been, in her Patrol among the Third Remove; so *naturally* she had been the person they asked ...

'... that'll be absolutely marvellous,' Tim was saying joyously. 'And such a good way of soothing Cartwright, too. She's been getting a bit restive lately, wanting to know how things are going and whether we're sure there's nothing in it Keith will mind. I'd been thinking we'd have to let her in to a rehearsal soon – but if you're there, you're a senior and that'll make it perfectly harmless and guaranteed not to offend—'

'Will it?' said Lois.

Tim looked at her, slightly puzzled by her tone.

'I don't mean that we're going to alter anything because you're there. Only that they'll feel happier about it – won't they?'

'I daresay,' said Lois lightly. But she thought, with a faintly uneasy twitch of nerves that Tim's mental processes and her own were not unlike. And it was disconcerting and not too pleasant to hear it done aloud.

17 *The Prince and the Pauper*

I

The day itself. 'Dies ipse,' thought Tim, hoping it might sound less ominous in Latin, but finding that it only sounded uncomfortably like 'dies irae'; so: 'This time tomorrow—' thought Tim after Nicola's fashion, and like Lawrie, found it small comfort. There was all today to get through first.

The week of exams was over. Third Remove had consoled one another by remarking loudly that anyway they'd all done equally badly and that no one would mind in the least about the badness of their results after they'd seen the play. That, Third Remove had said, happily confident, was going to be absolutely marvellous; and wasn't Lois terrific?

They were all a trifle quenched this morning, however; Tim decided that once breakfast was over they must all get frightfully busy on odd jobs. Not that those needed much inventing; there were the costumes to be taken over to the theatre and arranged in neat piles with the owners' names on them; there was the Westminster Abbey set to be concealed once more behind the trappings of the Throne Room; there were the Peers and Peeresses to be stacked away until they were needed – Tim grinned to herself, thinking of her Peers. That had been Lois's idea, when Tim was remarking worriedly that though they seemed to have plenty of people for mobs in all the other scenes, there was practically no one left over to be a Peer at the Coronation. 'Couldn't you use dummies?' Lois had suggested then. 'You could put them well to the sides, in rising tiers – three'd probably be enough – and keep the lighting concentrated on the action in the centre – I don't think people would notice that they weren't real or that it'd matter much if they did—' They had had a good deal of amusement out of dressing the dummies, painting eyes and mouth on any white material they could muster (some people were running short of handkerchiefs and beginning to wonder how best to explain this to Matron), sewing on gilt cardboard crowns, and covering the bodies with such pieces of material as could be spared. They had thought at first that arms and legs could be dispensed with, but at the first dress-rehearsal Tim had thought the effect might be improved by an arm or two resting negligently on the edge of the pews. So they had made half a dozen and distributed them irregularly along the lines; and the effect now, as Lawrie said relishingly, was perfectly *beastly*. 'It looks like one of those nightmares,' she said with deep admiration, 'you know – where Things come after you. And when you push them you can't, because they don't feel anything.'

Hazel attracted Tim's attention from across the table. 'Miss Cartwright wants to know if everything's all set,' she said loudly, and Tim, returning to her surroundings with a jump, said Yes, she thought they were absolutely ready: 'Sealed, signed and delivered,' she added with a propitiatory smile, for she was uneasily conscious that perhaps she had been almost too successful in keeping Cartwright at a distance; and if, by any evil chance, the play should collapse dismally, she had no doubt but that Cartwright could, if she chose, be a formidable antagonist. The Pomona row would be nothing in comparison . . .

'What are you doing about posters?'

'We're putting them up this afternoon,' said Nicola calmly, ignoring Tim's momentarily agitated expression.

'When the others are getting the stalls ready, you know. And we've done enough proper programmes for the staff and the guest of honour to have one each, but everyone else'll have to have a jellied one, I'm afraid. We thought,' said Nicola, permitting herself a glance at Tim to see how she was taking it, 'that we wouldn't charge for programmes because there's really nothing on them. Just "Third Remove Presents" and then the title and the changes of scene. Is that,' said Nicola deferentially, 'all right, d'you think?'

'Quite all right, I should imagine,' said Miss Cartwright.

Tim heaved a deep, silent sigh of relief. Nicola was really an excellent person to have around. She herself had forgotten every word about posters and programmes and she wondered when Nicola had found time to do them.

'It'll save us having programme sellers,' added Nicola, 'and we haven't anyone to spare for that, anyway. We can just put one on each seat before we rush to change. Oh, *goodness*, how awful! Think of it being as near as that!'

Miss Cartwright laughed.

'And what are you charging for admission?'

'Well, the other Thirds are making it a threepenny and sixpenny thing, aren't they? So we thought we'd better too. Threepence for the school and sixpence for the grown-ups.'

'We're worth much more than that,' said Lawrie unexpectedly and with deep conviction.

'Ass,' said Nicola. 'You know grown-ups nearly always give more. Any time we've come with Father to things, he always says he doesn't want the change. Don't you think it's best not to charge much, Miss Cartwright? Because, anyway, we come right at the end of the afternoon when people will have spent an awful lot long before they come to us.'

'Very practical,' said Miss Cartwright. 'And are you people going to the bazaar?'

'We think we ought to,' said Hazel hastily, glancing at Tim, for Tim had thought it might be rather amusing to ignore the bazaar altogether. 'Not that we can afford to buy much—'

'—all our pocket money's gone buying gold paint for largesse,' said Lawrie grinning. 'But we thought we'd go and look friendly and p'rhaps buy a Christmas present or two for people we don't like much.'

'Let's see your posters,' said Tim to Nicola as they jostled out of the dining hall with the crowd. 'It was bright of you to remember them. When did you do them?'

'Yesterday morning. I asked Margaret J. if I could, instead of listening to whatever she was going to read us to keep us quiet. And she said Yes, anything I liked so long as it was legal. So I did. They're in the studio.'

She led the way across the polished studio floor with an oddly proprietary air to where the four posters lay side by side to dry. Tim, standing over them, gave her approval. 'Neat, not gaudy. I didn't know you could do lettering, Nick.'

'I can't,' said Nicola simply. 'Jennings lent me her stencil. And here are the programmes. They aren't frightfully exciting, but they'll do, I think. And anyway, I loathe junior things with beastly little pictures on them, don't you? They look so revoltingly young.'

II

Even Tim felt bound to admit that the bazaar was rather attractive, simple enough, but bright and gay. Third Remove circulated among the stalls according to plan, but they had fallen rather silent and were apt to grimace apprehensively when they encountered one another. Nicola and Lawrie saw their parents come in, and went to meet them with the air of distrait politeness which usually afflicts juniors meeting their parents in the presence of their contemporaries, relieved to see that their mother's hat was of the neat variety and her make-up discreet; nor did Mrs. Marlow, having had experience of school functions, show any desire to kiss them.

'And why aren't you taking part in this?' asked their father when the greetings were over.

'We *are*,' said Nicola, reflecting that it wasn't really much good telling people things in letters for they never took anything in. 'At least, we're in the play later. That one,' indicating the blue and grey poster, strategically placed by the entrance to the covered way leading to the theatre.

'Are you going to stay for it?' asked Lawrie gloomily. She had reached the stage of nerves when she hoped fervently that there would be no audience at all and that they could act the play quietly and without fuss and have done with it.

'Of course, darling,' said her mother. 'Is it going to be good?'

'Shouldn't think so,' said Lawrie despondently. 'I expect it'll be pretty putrid, really. I shouldn't bother to stay.'

'Why, what's the matter, darling? Has something gone wrong?'

'Nothing's gone wrong,' said Commander Marlow tranquilly. 'That's just Lawrie. Look here, oughtn't we to be buying things?'

'So long as you keep enough for our thing,' said Nicola. 'Will you go in early, Father, and put down half a crown and say you don't want any change? And then the people behind'll probably do it too.'

Commander Marlow laughed and promised his co-operation.

'And if you should see anything you'd like for a Christmas present,' said Nicola, as they began the tour of the stalls, 'will you say? Because I haven't found a thing for you yet.'

'How long are you staying?' asked Lawrie, following with her mother.

'We thought we'd stay over until Thursday, and then we could drive some of you home after breaking-up. You two, I expect—'

'—so that we don't have to pay another five pounds on to Nicky's fare—'

'—and whichever of the others like to come.'

'Me!' said Ginty, appearing suddenly at her mother's elbow. 'You wouldn't believe the train rules that have happened since Nick fell out. It won't be a bit entertaining any more with staff all over the place watching to see that no one else does. Are you two feeling sick yet?'

'Yes,' said Lawrie.

'No,' said Nicola.

'You *ought* to be,' said Lawrie reproachfully. 'I wish now was Thursday and we were all going home.' And she so far forgot herself as to rub her cheek against her mother's arm.

'Day after tomorrow it will be Thursday and this time then you will be home – nearly,' said Nicola.

'You don't have to worry,' said Ginty. 'People never criticize junior things. They'll say: "Didn't little Lawrie Marlow look *sweeeet* – and weren't the fairies *pretty*?" '

Nicola and Lawrie looked at one another and began to giggle.

' "Little Lawrie Marlow",' said Lawrie happily. 'It sounds just like a child turn in a music hall at the seaside.'

'Come to that, it's about time I changed into my tinsel crown and wings,' chuckled Nicola. 'Come and find your wand, Lawrie dear. We'll see you afterwards, Mummykins, when all the naughty gnomes have been chased away from fairyland.'

They waved and ran off to where Tim was beckoning agitatedly, and disappeared down the covered way to the theatre. Commander Marlow looked faintly puzzled.

'What have fairies to do with it, Ginty?'

'Thirds nearly always have fairies,' said Ginty knowledgeably. 'Their form-mistresses like it like that. Or else someone has a dream and it's all highly magical—'

'You've got it wrong, Gin,' said Karen, joining the group and kissing her mother without self-consciousness. 'First and Second forms have fairies. Thirds lie down to dream and are wafted to islands with talking animals. Unless, of course, Kempe takes a hand and then they go all Anglo-Saxon with Beowulf and Caedmon.'

> 'THIRD REMOVE PRESENTS
> *THE PRINCE AND THE PAUPER*
> Adapted from the novel
> by
> MARK TWAIN
> At 6 p.m. in the theatre'

read Commander Marlow from Nicola's poster. 'Well, unless they've made it into a Christmas Pantomime, I don't see where the fairies come in or the animals either.'

'You may be right,' said Ginty dubiously. 'I never read the book. Anyway, can I sit with you and Mother? 'Cos then I can sit near the front and hear what goes on. No one can ever hear what Thirds say unless they sit on the stage, practically.'

III

The theatre clock showed twenty-five to six. Tim sorted through her records of incidental music once more to make sure they were all to hand, and went along to the dressing-room to see how the rest were getting on. There was a buzz of nervous chatter and a steady sequence of personal crises over lost props, to which no one else paid much attention. Make-up had been a problem, but Tim had been lavish over buying a large private store so that they could all practise beforehand. No one would get any Christmas presents from her this year, but as she looked round at her cast, all making themselves up with a fair show of confidence and efficiency, she felt it had been worth it. Nick and Lawrie were the easiest, of course. They had only to look young and boyish the whole time; the others all had to do a certain amount of whisking on and off and exchanging of robber's grime for courtier's polish. Still, they'd had plenty of practice; so long as no one got carried away and sat down to create a theatrical masterpiece . . . Tim counted heads to make sure that they were all there and missed Lawrie.

'Where is she?' she asked Nicola with would-be casualness.

'Being sick,' said Nicola laconically, buckling on her sword with hands which shook slightly. 'Really being sick, I mean. Not just fussing.'

'Will she be all right?' asked Lois beside her, voicing Tim's alarm. 'I mean, oughtn't we to do something—?'

'She'll be all right,' said Nicola crisply, not looking at Lois. 'She does it before parties. She's all right once they start.'

'Are you *sure*? Because—'

'If anyone knows about Lawrie's inside it's probably me, I

should think,' said Nicola, cutting Lois out of the conversation. It had been decent enough of Lois to help, and Tim and Lawrie had been rapturous with delight and relief, and the rest had all been tremendously admiring and appreciative. But one couldn't, thought Nicola stubbornly, suddenly like people just because everyone else did, or forget that they had been fairly swinish, even if they were doing their best now; and she would be glad when the play was over and she needn't even smile at Lois in corridors. She turned to Tim. 'Are people arriving yet?'

'The first trickles. I say, are you *sure* Lawrie's going to be all right?'

'Yes,' said Nicola curtly. 'Don't fuss, Tim. She's always the same.'

Tim, realizing suddenly that Nicola was probably just as nervous as anyone else, let it pass. Then Marie Dobson turned round from the mirror to ask in an injured voice why there were no names on the programmes?

'Because there are so few of us,' snapped Nicola. 'We don't want them to know in advance that it's always the same people.'

'Oh,' said Marie doubtfully; and Tim, seeing there was nothing practical to be done in the dressing-room, went back to the stage to watch from the side of the curtain the steady stream of people flowing over the red plush. There were very few gaps; and those of the school who, like Ginty, had wangled seats in front with their parents, were beginning to get up with polite expressions and retire to stand at the back with the rest of the school so that another visitor could sit down. Tim, gripping the edge of the curtain, was suddenly overwhelmed by the agitations she had been holding in leash fairly successfully since breakfast. Suppose the play were a ghastly flop from the very start . . . suppose it dragged and people didn't change fast enough and there were terrible gaps while the audience grew politely restive . . . suppose people were horribly kind about it tomorrow and said: 'Of course, it was a very ambitious effort – perhaps if you were to try something just a little simpler next time—' There'll never be a next time, thought Tim wretchedly, watching the clock's minute hand slide towards ten to six; and thought what a relief it would be to leap out in front of the curtain and announce that there would be no performance after all. Instead, she went down to the dressing-room again and asked if everyone wasn't nearly ready by now?

'Are there many people?' asked Lawrie wanly. She was sitting dejectedly on a heap of discarded sacking, looking as though she had passed beyond the reach of any emotion, either good or bad.

'Packed,' said Tim briefly. 'Look here. If you people are ready, I'm going to start the overture. Let's be punctual, whatever else we are. Will you come, Lois? And for goodness' sake, hurry up, the rest of you.' She paused and added: 'Good luck, everyone. Hold thumbs,' and fled back to the stage.

With shaking hands, she switched on the radiogram and put on the record of *Greensleeves* – Miss Keith's known favourite, if not Tim's, thought Miss Keith's niece, glancing swiftly through the gap in the curtain and noting the gently gratified expression which overspread her aunt's face. Headmistresses always sat in the front row with the guest of honour and the staff all round them, though really one would think they ought to let the visitors have those seats, while they went to the back with the school; but they never did, thought Tim, as *Greensleeves* came to an end and Handel's *Water Music* took its place. Dim the house lights now. Lois, looking white and tightly strung, was coming on to the stage.

She looked boyish and handsome, thought Tim, glad that they had not, after all, dressed Lois in the farthingale Tim had vaguely imagined for herself. The black and white robes and square cap Lois had copied from a portrait of Sir Thomas More looked much better; and she liked the great flashing ring they had contrived from stones found in a penny saucer outside a second-hand shop. The audience was quietening now, the allegro movement beginning: time to switch on the floats: wait for the trumpets – wait – Tim nodded to Lois, gave her a quick grin, parted the front curtain slightly to let her through and shut her eyes. They had begun.

'*. . . a boy was born to a poor family of the name of Canty, who did not want him. On the same day another English child was born to a great family of the name of Tudor . . .*'

Lois's voice, clear and steady, settling into its stride; no sound from the auditorium now, only the white blurs of attentive faces turned towards the stage or an occasional dark patch where someone whispered to their neighbour. Tim, who had been bringing the music gradually down to a diminuendo, switched it off and put on the next record – a single trumpet – ready for Nicola's entrance. A group of Third Remove – Tudor citizens – crept up. 'How's it going?' they whispered.

'All right,' whispered Tim briefly. Nicola had just come into the wings on the opposite side: Lawrie, pale and shivering, was standing beside the radiogram. Tim tried not to look at her. If Lawrie were to fail—

But there was no time to think of that. Tim, her eyes on the lighting and music plot, switched on floods and battens ready for the scene outside the Palace; Lois was coming to an end; Tim nodded to the citizens, crossed her fingers hard and eloquently and raised the front curtain . . . Lois reached her chair, the citizens were on: and there had been no confusion. Tim breathed again.

Unexpectedly, the audience applauded – partly for the backcloth, partly for Lois. 'It's going to be all right,' thought Tim suddenly, feeling the audience's liking as though it were something tangible, 'they're going to take it seriously.' And she tried to give Lawrie a reassuring smile. But Lawrie was staring before her with a blank, frightened face, her lips moving silently. Lois was reading again; it was just on Lawrie's entrance; Tim tried to attract her attention. But Lawrie heard her cue clearly enough; without looking at Tim she dodged round the radiogram and made her entrance, mingling with the citizens, who, pleased and excited by the audience's applause, were miming for all they were worth.

Nicola's trumpet. To her infinite horror, Tim saw that Nicola was signalling wildly. Hurriedly she switched on the radiogram again and a moment later Jean and Hazel shouted together offstage: '*Way for His Royal Highness! Way for the Prince of Wales!*' Tim sat down again, her cheeks hot. Luckily she hadn't been very late with it – only a moment or two – it hadn't spoiled anything.

And Lawrie – Tim found that she had been holding her breath and let it out again in a sigh of relief – Lawrie was all right now she was on stage. She was being every bit as good as she had been at rehearsals. No, thought Tim, suddenly recognizing a new quality in Lawrie, better; she was liking the audience. Marie wasn't, though; Marie was acting the guard as though she felt a fool. She looked it too, thought Tim crossly, hating Marie for being such an ass. Still, the scene was nearly over and Nicola was rating her in a fine royal rage, so perhaps if Marie looked abashed it didn't matter too much. And now they were turning to go into the

Throne Room – for a frantic moment Tim tugged uselessly at the wrong rope, fumbled wildly, and watched with relief as the Palace of Westminster rose gently into the flies.

That was all right. Nick and Lawrie were safe enough together. They were playing well and fast, no pauses, snapping up their cues. Tim glanced at the lighting plot to make sure when her next cue came and permitted herself to relax and enjoy it. Tom eating hungrily, watching the Prince with round-eyed hero-worship, answering Edward's questions with artless childish deference . . . the sudden plan to change clothes . . . Nicola dashing off-stage and tossing her apparel to a Lawrie almost hidden behind the throne ('Because if they don't *see* you change, they won't believe it,' Tim had insisted when Nicola had protested that it would be much quicker if they both changed off-stage); Lawrie swaggering down-stage, smoothing her hair, peacocking before a mirror, Nicola coming on a second later, and the sudden burst of applause from the delighted audience . . . Edward's sudden rage over Tom's treatment by the guard, his impetuous exit, checking only to hide the Great Seal – and Lois taking up the story again from her seat at the side of the stage, while Tom strutted and acted the prince, became alarmed as time passed and the true Prince did not return, tried to escape, failed . . .

To Tim, losing her anxieties, it seemed that the play had begun to gather momentum. The long scene of the 'Prince's' apparent madness (and Pomona was *good* as the King; there was no getting away from it), with Tom's gradual progress from stammering terror to defeated acquiescence as he listened helplessly to Lord St. John telling him that although His Royal Highness had unhappily lost his memory, it was the King's command that he should cease instantly to deny his royal parentage, protest against customary ceremonies, or show by any sign that he failed to recognize people he had known from childhood – the whole scene seemed to be over amazingly swiftly. Almost before she was aware, it was time to dim the lights on Tom sitting alone and solitary on the great throne, and, in the momentary darkness, bring down the backcloth for the street scene.

Lawrie came scampering off-stage, found someone's coat, and sat down beside Tim with a pleased expression to watch Nicola's scene. 'It's going well, isn't it?' she whispered as Prince Edward limped tiredly on to the stage to be collared by John Canty and mistaken for Tom; and then with a frown, 'What's the matter with Marie, Tim? Did you notice when she was the guard? She nearly left out half the scene, only Nick prompted her.'

Tim said, under her breath: 'Blast the girl!' and then was silent, digging her thumb-nail into the palm of her hand and watching Marie helplessly. Marie had been tiresome enough at rehearsals, loud-voiced and assured, telling people what to do and where to go and arguing violently with Tim; but Tim would have been relieved to have had some of that assurance back, in place of this miserable, shambling figure, who stumbled over her lines and forgot what came next and cuffed Nicola without conviction. But – thank goodness! – the others were rising to the emergency. Tim, her hands clutched together, listened, painfully attentive, as Nicola snatched up one of Marie's mangled speeches and twisted it adroitly so that she could say it herself. And – Tim and Lawrie smiled broadly at one another in sheer pleased astonishment – Elaine Rees of all people! – that pale idiot rabbit! – was rushing into the breach, making Tom's sister into a harridan, picking up Marie's part, so that Nicola had someone to act with. Tim heaved a sigh of relief as the scene neared its end, calculating how much more Marie had to do in the play. One more short scene as John Canty, and then just odd bits with the gang of beggars and being a lord at the Coronation. Could be worse, thought Tim, while Canty was accused by his neighbours of the priest's murder and began to make hurried preparations for flight; one might, Tim supposed acidly, imagine that Marie had suddenly thought how effective it would be if Canty were struck dumb with horror and thank heavens Elaine and Elizabeth were making plenty of guilty outcry. She listened thankfully to the words which meant that the scene was coming to an end, swallowed up by the entry of the citizens making their way to the Palace of Westminster to see the Prince and Edward's escape as he twisted free from Canty and dodged through the crowd—

'Golly,' said Nicola. 'Wasn't that painful? What did it sound like to you?'

'All right,' said Lawrie reassuringly. 'I don't think people will have noticed it was wrong – only that Marie's a stick. What's the matter with the girl?'

'Dunno,' said Nicola briefly, as the Palace of Westminster settled into place in the momentary darkness and she prepared to go on again. 'She's trembling so that it shakes the stage and when she opens her mouth nothing comes out. S' long.' And Nicola went on again, to force her way through the crowd, insisting that she was His Royal Highness, Edward, Prince of Wales—

'They're jeering well, aren't they?' said Lawrie happily.

Tim nodded abstractedly. It was the end of the scene that she liked best and was most anxious should not be marred. It was coming now, the sudden whisper that the King was dead, stilling the mob, which slowly began to kneel, ignoring the dumbfounded figure of Edward in their midst. She held the moment as long as she dared, before she shouted at the full pitch of her voice: '*The King is dead – long live the King!*'

and watched the mob take it up, shouting and cheering, while Edward stood motionless, unheeded and solitary, facing the great door, and a single bell began to toll, and the curtain descended slowly, slowly, until it rested on the stage.

Tim blinked and flicked the house lights on. Lawrie said: 'Nice work – I'd better go and help Jean change,' and went off while the others crowded round briefly to say: 'Listen to them clap,' and 'Wasn't Marie awful?' and 'I say, did it notice that my shoe came off in the mob-scene?' Then they rushed off to change and become courtiers and Lois got out of her chair to stretch herself. It was a brief, restful interval and the clamour of talk from the auditorium was immensely reassuring. Then Lawrie and Jean came racing back and it was time to go on. Tim jerked the switches, noting crossly that Marie was standing beside her with a defiant, miserable expression as though for two pins she'd say she wasn't going on again if they were all going to be so horrid. She had obviously been crying, Tim thought, suddenly impatient with people who got themselves into messes and then cried because of it. And she kept her eyes on the stage, refusing to look at Marie, conscious that Marie was watching Lawrie with an expression carefully arranged to indicate that anyone could act if they thought it worth while, only sensible people didn't think it worth the trouble.

After a time, however, Tim forgot about Marie. It had come to her, with a queer little pang, as Lois took up the tale after Tom's scene with the whipping-boy, that this was the very last time she would ever see the play; how queer, thought Tim, rather shaken, how queer to have been bounded for so long by the timeless circle of the play, and now to realize suddenly that in half an hour it would be over, a thing to be talked about as one of the things that had happened, happened well, perhaps, but still, sliding away into the past, never to be repeated. Oh dear, thought Tim sadly, staring sorrowfully at the stage, this is the last time I'll ever see Tom ape the King and preen himself when the courtiers flatter; and she ticked off her favourite moments as they slid by: Edward's reception by the gang of beggars; his cudgel fight with Hugo and his crowning as King of the Game Cocks; his arrest and imprisonment for Hugo's theft; and his face – his face as he watched from the prison window the burning of the witches. Nick had always done that bit well, thought Tim, her heart thumping, as she listened to Edward saying, over and over, in a voice gone suddenly lost and dead: '*Would God I had been blind – would God I had been blind—*' but never as well as that. She brought the curtain quietly down and Lois began to read again, of Edward's escape and progress towards London, so that no one was able to clap and break the frightening enchantment of the moment.

Last scene. Tim dropped her lighting plot on to her chair, and dashed on stage to help Nick and Lawrie and any others who weren't changing tear down the Throne Room trappings and disclose the Abbey scene. The Peers and Peeresses were thrust into place and Tim switched on the flood behind the great window so that when Edward stole in amongst the workmen to hide in the tomb there would be only the one pale shaft of light down the centre of the stage.

'All set,' said Lawrie, rushing off to fetch her coronation robe; and the curtain went up on the darkened stage, Lois still reading, while the workmen came on and set the throne under the great window and Edward hid in the Confessor's tomb, and the lights came gently up and the workmen dressed the bare grey scene into magnificence (the best of the trappings they were spreading so lavishly about the stage came from the cherished, traditional store for the Christmas

Play – archangels' robes, mainly; Tim hoped, ostrich-fashion, that no one was going to notice) and Lois read on, telling of Tom's triumphal ride through the City.

It was nearly time now. Tim put on the *Trumpet Voluntary* record; and the procession went slowly up the stage, standing on either side to bow very low as Tom Canty went grandly towards the steps to the throne and Edward stood suddenly before the Coronation Seat and shouted: '*On your knees, usurper! The King stands here!*'

Nearly done now, thought Tim, bringing the lights full on, nearly done; only the identification bit now – I wish it wasn't finished – here we are, here's the Great Seal – '*I used it to crack nuts with' – dear* Lawrie – get on, get on, take off the robe of state – that's it – for heaven's sake someone, fasten it so that it hides the rags – oh, Nick's done it herself – quick, *Trumpet Voluntary* again – I wish this thing kept the sound lower—

Edward accepted the sword from the kneeling Chancellor, kissed the blade, then held it so that the point was towards the floor, and began to speak the Coronation Oath. 'Last time,' thought Tim desolately, 'last time—'

'*. . . never to desire to live or reign longer than my life and reign shall be for your good: to so reign by virtue of your loves that I may account my chiefest strength and safeguard the loyal hearts and good will of my subjects: and to defend the liberties of my people and the shores of this my realm as a true king even unto death. All this I swear.*'

Tim turned the sound knob and let the trumpets come through, shrill and sweet and exultant. And then, since she could delay it no longer, brought down the final curtain.

No curtain calls, Tim had said in a moment of pessimism, forestalling the possibility that none might be required. But she had not been prepared for the sudden roar of applause which came from the body of the theatre; it would be ill-mannered not to answer that. She signalled to them to stay put and raised the curtain again, watching Nicola's face break from its expression of rapt gravity into a sudden curling grin of pleasure. Then she dropped the curtain again and dashed on to the stage to hug anyone within reach; and everyone's pent-up excitement overflowed at once.

'Didn't it go well?'

'Wasn't Nick marvellous?'

'And Lawrie. Did you see Lawrie when—?'

'And I say, wasn't Hazel good? and Elizabeth? Elizabeth, you were super—'

'And Lois's reading – no one *breathed*, did they? – wasn't she marvellous in that bit about—'

'Tim!' said Lois, hurrying round from the prompt side, 'Tim, are you there? Quick, go on in front. They're calling producer – Keith's looking madly agitated – quick – hurry—'

'Me!' said Tim, petrified.

'Yes, quick. Here, comb your hair. That's it – go on—'

Tim swallowed, took a deep breath, and stepped out in front of the curtain. After all, there was nothing to mind. It was just that they were pleased with her. Only, if she'd remembered this might happen, she'd have seen to it that she was a bit tidier for the occasion.

Still, it was no good worrying about that now. Stiffly, carefully, Tim bowed – centre, right, left and centre again; and remembered, what she had till now forgotten, that as soon as she stepped back from this narrow rim of stage between curtains and footlights, she must put on the record of *God Save the King*.

18 Marie Puts Her Foot In It

It was the greatest fun. Third Remove, tumbling back into their best uniforms amongst the welter of discarded costumes, shouting exultantly across the dressing-room to one another, and doubling up with frequent uncontrollable laughter over nothing at all, found it difficult to subdue their faces and voices to the proper expressions of modest unconcern when the time came for them to return to the Assembly Hall, where staff and visitors were having a stand-up supper of coffee and cakes and sandwiches, while school chatted politely with its parents or handed cups and plates in its best manner. Lawrie and Nicola, edging gently through the crowd towards their family, were continually stopped by other people's parents who smiled delightedly and said: 'Surely you're the little ones who – now were you the King or the little poor boy – no, don't tell me—' and sometimes guessed right and sometimes not. It was the queerest feeling, thought Nicola, this mixture of shyness and pride and exultation, which must on no account be allowed to show in your face while you murmured shyly to the grown-ups or, with real bashfulness, to school people whom you knew only by name and sight as they marched out of Prayers or Assembly, and who now seemed to know you very well indeed and to have known all along that this was going to happen.

The Marlows were all standing together under one of the big windows. Nicola and Lawrie joined them and Nicola said distantly: 'Hullo,' and tried sternly to keep her mouth from curling upwards at the corners; but it was all right; they laughed at her and said at once how good they and the play had been and how much they'd enjoyed it; Karen remarking with an air of detachment that one could never tell with Thirds – most of the time they were abysmal, and then, just occasionally, they brought off a quite amazing fluke; and Rowan laughed, offering a plate of sandwiches ('two *only* and no cakes until the visitors leave') and said that they were superb, stupendous, colossal and all in glorious Technicolor; and that she had seen Ann weeping bitterly at the end and what did they know about that?

'At the end?' said Nicola, puzzled. 'I don't see why *then*. Everything was all right then. Edward had been re-in – re-in—'

'Reinstated,' suggested Karen.

'Yes,' said Nicola. 'So why?'

'I know that,' said Ann, flushed and confused and not much liking her family's amused glances. 'I know it was all right for Edward. But what about Tom? All that heavenly time of being King and then having to climb down and give it all up for ever.'

'I don't see that it was *so* bad for him,' protested Nicola, feeling obscurely that she was somehow defending Edward. 'After all, he was made King's Ward and given all sorts of special privileges—'

'Like the Headmistress's Niece,' said Lawrie aside to Nicola, and giggled into her sandwich.

'Oh yes, I *know*,' said Ann rather wildly. 'But if you could have *seen* Tom kneeling at the foot of the steps—'

'—ah ha!' said Lawrie triumphantly.

'—all right, Ann,' said her father, 'that'll do—'

'—no, honestly, Lawrie was marvellous,' insisted Ann, saying something which, Nicola felt, had already been said before they arrived. 'I don't mean for a moment that Nick wasn't good too, but it was a heaps easier part. Lawrie's needed tons of acting – real acting. You don't mind, do you, Nick? But it did.'

Her father made a quick, impatient gesture; her mother looked anxiously at Nicola; Karen, Rowan and Ginty looked at Ann as though such imbecility had to be heard to be believed; and Nicola eyed them all with cold impatience and said: 'I know that. I mean, I know Lawrie's better than me. Tim always said so.'

'Oh,' murmured her family, courteous and relieved. 'Is that so? Did she really?'

'Tim did?' said Lawrie loudly, colouring deeply. 'When? She never did, Nick. Never.'

'She wouldn't say so to you,' retorted Nicola. 'Naturally not.'

'When did she to you, then? What did she say?'

Nicola thought back, frowning and perplexed. 'I don't know,' she admitted. 'P'rhaps she didn't actually say it ever. But she always had that sort of look.'

'What sort?'

'Sort of "Here's-Lawrie-thank-goodness-I-needn't-worry-about-her".'

'Well!' said Lawrie. She dropped her sandwich, trod heavily on it, and lurched wildly against her mother.

'One man stampede,' remarked Karen, dextrously righting the cup of coffee which Mrs. Marlow was holding resignedly away from her skirt. 'Tim's opinion obviously carries weight.'

'Oh, Tim knows,' said Lawrie earnestly. And then seeing the implications of her remark, blushed violently and looked at Nicola for support.

Nicola grinned and said that Tim indeed knew and didn't

Tim know it. And her father asked quickly whether Ginty was right in saying that they'd had no help from the mistresses ('*Staff*,' hissed Ginty) in any way at all?

Lawrie nodded.

'Jennings drew the scenery,' protested Nicola hastily.

'But we painted it all,' said Lawrie.

'But the drawing part's the worst,' said Nicola, shocked by such ignorance of the relative values of the job. 'Anyone can stick in the colours afterwards if the picture's there. That's easy.'

'Takes time,' said Rowan laconically.

'Y-yes,' said Nicola doubtfully. She found she could not describe her admiration for Jennings's professional competence, nor the deep pleasure it had been to watch Forest and Street and Westminster Palace spring from the canvas under the clean, sure strokes of the charcoal stick; putting the paint on afterwards was only a workman's job. But it was easier to feel these things than say them and she let it go.

'And that was all the help you had?' pursued her father. 'What about that older girl – all right, Ginty: senior – who did the reading?'

'You could have knocked me down with a seven-pound weight when I saw Lois Sanger suddenly emerge, looking like death and high water,' said Rowan in unwilling admiration. 'How on earth did you get her to come and play with Third Remove?'

'Tim asked her, because of being producer. Wasn't she *super*?' said Lawrie blushing deeply.

'Lois always reads brilliantly,' said Rowan, saying what must in honesty be said, though as if she didn't much care about it. 'She's always read in Literature lessons all the way from Ballads onwards. Only she can't act. She used to practically die in IIIA if Kempe ever told her to come and be a Banished Man.'

'But I expect she helped you a good deal with the production, didn't she?' suggested their mother.

'Not a bit,' said Lawrie.

'Only the dummies,' said Nicola, a remark which the rest of the family found unintelligible and ignored.

'You mean that this Tim of yours really did produce the whole thing?' said their father patiently. 'Was she the dark untidy child who came on at the end?'

'You'd have been untidy too,' said Lawrie indignantly. 'She had all the lighting and curtains and music to do – and she did comb her hair. Lois lent her one.'

'Don't be rude, darling,' murmured her mother, aside.

'I'm not,' protested Lawrie, also aside. 'At least, I didn't mean it. But honestly: untidy. After all we'd been through.'

'Yes, she did,' said Nicola, answering the first part of her father's question. 'She wrote it, too. At least, she called it "adapting" it. Like they do for films, you know.'

'*Did* she?' said Rowan. 'And what did you do with Cartwright while all this was going on? Lock her in the stationery cupboard?'

'No,' said Nicola vaguely. 'Tim just kept her off. She wasn't any bother.'

Karen and Rowan looked at one another.

'Produced it—' said Rowan.

'Wrote it—' said Karen.

'Press-ganged Lois Sanger—'

'And saw that her form-mistress gave no trouble,' concluded Karen. 'Next term someone had better keep a very special eye on T. Keith.'

'Why?' asked Lawrie.

'Dangerous,' said Karen, grinning at her father. 'Organizing ability highly developed. Too much spare time owing to present position in school. Highly explosive combination unless superfluous energy directed into constructive channels—'

'And what about us?' Lawrie wanted to know.

'What, indeed? We never knew we had two Bernhardts in the family. We'll watch you too.'

'Were we really as good as that?' asked Lawrie blissfully. And then other people's parents began to come up and say over their heads: 'Do tell me which was which. They *are* alike, aren't they? Can you tell them apart at home? My husband and I thought they were both excellent – of course, one can't compare them, really, can one? – two such different rôles – but there was *something* – something quite exceptional about the little beggar one, wasn't there? – but really, the whole play was quite delightful – and everything done by the children themselves, Mary tells me—'

Their father turned to Lawrie and told her to see if she couldn't scrounge some cakes. Lawrie grinned and went off to the long buffet table; and after a few moments Nicola followed her, for school people, particularly Sixth and Upper Fifth, were beginning to stroll up and talk to Karen and Rowan on the outside of the circle, so to speak; and it was absurd even to try to pretend that you had no idea that they were talking about you, even though it would have been interesting to stay and hear what they were saying about Lawrie with that odd mixture of awe and enthusiasm. But Miss Keith and the guest of honour were also making their gracious way over to their group, though constantly impeded by other parents . . . one couldn't possibly, thought Nicola, suddenly and freakishly shy, be here when they came. She turned and dived unobtrusively into the crowd by the buffet and found Lawrie casting a practised eye over the cakes.

'Hullo,' said Lawrie. 'Don't take those. Those are the ones we made yesterday. Remember? Take another lot of these. These are Upper Fifth ones. Rowan said they were doing puff pastry last week.'

'Let's not go back yet, anyway,' said Nicola. 'Keith's on her way.'

'She's arrived,' said Lawrie, glancing over her shoulder. 'Let's don't, then. I say: s'pose you stood in front of me and I ate one of these very quickly, would anyone notice?'

'Yes,' said Nicola. 'People always see things like that.'

'Oh. I say, wasn't Ann *stupid*?'

'How?'

'Saying about us. I was looking at Rowan when she said it and Rowan looked as if she could hit her.'

'I don't see why.'

''Cos I expect she thought you'd mind. So you might have.'

'It's being in the Lower Fifth, I expect,' said Nicola with kindly tolerance. 'They used to come into the studio sometimes when I was there and get all sloppy over that Chinese coat Jennings is so keen on.'

'Well, I like it too.'

'So do I. But we wouldn't go there if there wasn't a lesson and hold hands and sort of sigh over it, would we?'

'Gracious, no,' said Lawrie. 'Do they?'

'Some of them. Not Ann, as a matter of fact. But I expect that sort of thing's catching.'

Lawrie nodded and accepted the somewhat allusive explanation of Ann's behaviour as both probable and intelligible. And remarked that she wished their father and mother would *say* how frightfully good they'd been instead of just looking calm and pleased.

'But they never do,' protested Nicola. 'You know they don't if it's anything proper. Even when Kay got Matric with distinction in practically everything, they just said it wasn't bad at all and she must keep it up. You don't want them to make a special fuss like when we got our Brownie Wings, do you?'

'Yes,' said Lawrie candidly, 'I do. I like being told.'

Nicola looked at her doubtfully.

'Not that it really matters,' added Lawrie with an enchanting smile, 'because everyone else is telling us *lots*. I say, Keith's gone now. Let's saunter back.'

They returned decorously, to all appearance wholly unaware that their names might have been mentioned in their absence; an effect Lawrie promptly spoiled by asking instantly what Miss Keith had said.

'Nothing to your detriment,' said her father repressively, looking at his watch. 'We should be going, I think, Pam. I'll go and bring the car round to the steps. Care to come for the ride, Nicky?'

Nicola thrust the plate of cakes she was holding at Miranda West and went off with him, pleased that he looked, on the whole, taller and cleaner than other people's fathers. He paused at the top of the steps to light his pipe, and Nicola waited, finding the night unexpectedly cold and silent after the heat and chatter of the Hall.

'I suppose you ought to have a coat?' he said doubtfully, as they went down the steps.

'Oh no,' Nicola assured him. 'I was simply boiling in the Hall. It's lovely to feel a bit chilly.'

They paced down the drive between the two rows of gleaming cars.

'Nicky,' he said at length. 'How good does Lawrie think she is?'

'Not a bit,' said Nicola, emphatic and horrified, lest Lawrie were about to be accused of conceit.

'Really not?' her father said in an oddly puzzled tone; as though, thought Nicola, equally puzzled, he had expected her to say that Lawrie thought herself marvellous and wouldn't have been at all annoyed if she had. She temporized.

'Well – how d'you mean, exactly?'

'I mean, how much of her acting is instinctive and how much was she doing what she was told to do?'

'I don't think Tim told her anything,' said Nicola slowly, answering the part of the question she understood. 'Not after about the second rehearsal, anyway. And not nearly as much as she told me. She told me heaps. So did Lawrie.'

'You did them credit,' he said abstractedly, pulling at his pipe. Nicola held her breath. 'You did all right. But what I'm really trying to get at is: does Lawrie *know* she has this special flair for acting?'

Nicola, still tingling from the casual, almost unwitting compliment, endeavoured to pull herself together and answer the question intelligently.

'I think p'rhaps she does,' she said at length. 'At least, she's awfully queer about it. She wanted to do Tom at once, when any sensible person would want of *course* to do Edward, wouldn't they? Even Tim was surprised. And she's awfully sure about it. Once or twice when Tim did tell her to do things a bit differently, she just said it was wrong and didn't.'

'H'm!' said her father and was silent. They reached the car and he opened the door for her so that she could wriggle past the driver's into the passenger's seat. He got in after her and sat sucking at his pipe in the darkness.

'Well,' he said at length, and, so far as Nicola could tell, more to himself than to her, 'I suppose it's early to say yet. One can't tell whether she'll ever pull it off again. So don't,' he added, switching on the dashboard light, 'let her get over-excited and think it's Drury Lane next stop. And if Ann or any of the older girls start being really silly again, just jump on them hard.'

'All right,' said Nicola, knowing the impossibility of convincing a parent that Third Remove did not rebuke Lower Fifth, however foolish. 'But I don't think—'

'What don't you think?'

'I don't think it matters whether she's told how good she is or not. She knows, anyway. She likes being told because it's fun, but it doesn't make any difference.'

'Is that so? And what about you?'

'Oh, I'm all right,' said Nicola flippantly. 'I need telling, but then heaps of people have.'

He laughed, smacked her head, and they trundled up to the steps in a friendly silence. Nicola hopped out, Mrs. Marlow got in, and they drove away.

'Well, I still think they might have said something,' said Lawrie, ceasing to wave as the red rear light disappeared through the gates. 'I don't see at all what harm it would have done.'

Ginty chuckled. 'I suppose Father should have pressed you to him and said in a voice choked with emotion: My little daughter has made me a proud man this night. You are a chump, Lawrie.'

'They said quite a piece while you were changing,' said Karen, giving Lawrie's hair a friendly tug. 'They sounded – well – quite fairly pleased, I think. Wouldn't you say so, Rowan?'

'What sort of things?' demanded Lawrie hopefully.

'You are a little tyke,' remarked Rowan. 'Can't you tell we're all brimming over with admiration and respect?'

'That's more like it,' said Lawrie calmly.

'I hope this is for family consumption only,' remarked Karen.

'Bless me, you don't think I'd prance up to the Sixth and say it, do you?'

'Dunno,' said Rowan. 'I wouldn't put it past you.'

'Well, I wouldn't. And you ought to know it without telling.'

'So ought you the other thing,' countered Rowan swiftly.

'It's all right,' said Nicola to Lawrie. 'They're so overcome with admiration that they just can't find the words. Let's go and see if there's anything left to eat.'

The Marlow family split into its component parts and Nicola and Lawrie went back to the Assembly Hall to find the rest of Third Remove. The last few parents who remained, were, to everyone's politely concealed delight, already shaking hands and saying good-night to Miss Keith; and then, as at all parties, once the last visitor had gone, those who belonged were able to begin to eat what was left, standing in talkative groups, or strolling up to the Third Remove bunch and Lois on the platform steps, to say how tremendously good the play had been and how on earth had they managed this or that particular bit?

'The Sixth are cutting sandwiches madly in the kitchen,' said Rowan, carefully lowering two plates, piled high, on to the platform and giving Lois a stiff little smile which somehow managed to convey congratulation without liking. 'So I thought you people had better have first pick. One lot's spam and the other's sandwich spread, but I've forgotten which is which.'

Third Remove, who had not, even in their most confident moments, supposed they would rise to the heights of being waited on by Rowan Marlow, murmured their thanks and looked overcome. Tim, less sensible of the honour and putting it down, more or less accurately, to a sisterly anxiety that Lawrie and Nicola should not starve, smiled cheerfully at Rowan, helped herself to a sandwich and went on telling Nicola about the flaws Miss Ferguson, the History Mistress, had found in the play.

'She's in a frightful flap,' said Tim serenely, picking the spam out of her sandwich and eating it separately. 'Surely she'd emphasized most carefully in class that Edward VI was never created Prince of Wales; and had I realized that your Coronation Oath (which, you'll be glad to hear, she thinks you delivered with great sense of style) was pinched from two of Elizabeth's proclamations.'

Nicola took a quick look at 'great sense of style' and then put it aside to be gloated over later.

'Well, I didn't know all that. Did you?'

'I didn't know about Edward, actually, but of course I knew about Elizabeth. I couldn't not, could I? And then she got madly excited over Handel and Purcell being out of period; and I said there wasn't any Purcell – *Trumpet Voluntary* was Jeremiah Clarke, so she's rushed off to Lucas to find out if that's true. But she was quite a pet, really; she said she'd enjoyed it immensely and she hoped we'd be allowed to do it again sometime.'

'Oh, Tim, can't we?' pleaded Third Remove, as though Tim held the decision between her hands. And Lawrie, emerging from a golden and beatific haze in which quite senior people came and talked to her and said how good she'd been, and Kempe remarked to Lois that she must remember Lawrie when she began to think about the Summer Play, said trustfully: 'Do let's. Oh, Tim, don't you wish we were a proper theatre and could do it for a week, evenings and matinées?'

'I'd like to do it again tomorrow,' declared Elaine Rees, happily conscious that at one moment she had undoubtedly helped to save the play from collapse. And those members of the other Thirds who were standing round, too impressed by the play to pretend otherwise, said that it would indeed be fun if it could be done again next term.

'And then some of *us* could be in it,' said Miranda West, 'and it would be properly a Third Form thing. Don't you think so, Tim?'

Third Remove eyed Miranda with cold discouragement, serenely conscious that they could leave the verbal scoring to Tim. But at that moment Miss Keith and Miss Cartwright came up to them and the outsiders stood courteously back as Third Remove scrambled to its feet feeling crumby and conspicuous.

Miss Keith, it seemed, was very pleased with them. She was particularly pleased, she said, by the fact that it had evidently been a corporate form effort and not merely the work of one or two enthusiastic people who ran around doing everything while the rest waited hopefully to be told what to do next. It was clear that everyone concerned had worked very hard indeed; and since that was so, and since the play itself had been so successful, she had decided not to tell them what she thought of their examination results. (Third Remove risked a few self-conscious smiles. Miss Keith and Miss Cartwright exchanged glances of rueful benevolence.) Just this once she would overlook the most deplorable set of examination papers which had ever been brought to her notice. But only this once. Next term they must show the same energy over their class work as over the play. (Third Remove murmured virtuously.) And Lois – Miss Keith turned to Lois who was standing a little apart, uncertain whether she belonged in this interview or not – she hoped Third Remove realized what a notable contribution Lois had made to the success of the play.

'Gracious me, yes,' said Tim fervently, being an enthusiastic junior; 'it was going to be me and I was ghastly. We were awfully lucky to get Lois.'

Miss Keith looked faintly taken aback by such vehemence; Lois blushed and laughed; Third Remove looked its admiration.

'So long as you realize your good fortune,' said Miss Keith pleasantly. 'The only other thing I want to say is that the scenery and costumes had better be labelled and put away in a safe place. I haven't *quite* decided yet, but I think I may ask you to do one or two scenes on Speech Day next summer. So bear that in mind and don't forget your parts completely.'

She nodded to them and passed on. Third Remove looked at one another and at Miss Cartwright, overwhelmed almost to silence.

'Speech Day!'

'*Us!*'

'Which scenes, Tim?'

Tim, looking mildly overcome, remarked, with an eye on Miss Cartwright, that probably Miss Keith would decide that.

'Still, think of *us* doing things on Speech Day,' said Hazel. 'It's nearly always the Sixth and Upper Fifth in something got up by Miss Kempe after Matric. and Higher, isn't it, Miss Cartwright? Never the Thirds, I don't think.'

'I hope Miss Keith doesn't put it off later than the summer, though,' observed Lois. 'Because probably I shall leave after Matric.'

'Oh, Lois!'

'Won't you really be in the Sixth?'

'Couldn't you come back for a bit if we had to do it when you'd left?'

'We couldn't do it without you, possibly.'

Nicola, her eyes averted from Lois's pleased, charming face, said nothing. Her eyes fell on Marie Dobson, sitting hunched on the bottom step, against the wall. She looked sullen and miserable and silent, as though she had not spoken to anyone for a long time. It must be a horrible feeling, thought Nicola, to be so very left out, the only one who could not be told at all that she had been frightfully good. Of course, everyone had been very forbearing and tactful about Marie's collapse and taken immense care not to refer to it in front of her; but still – it must feel beastly—

As though she felt Nicola's glance, Marie looked up and smiled, over-effusively. Nicola, her momentary sympathy quenched, smiled briefly and looked quickly away.

'But acktcherly, Miss Cartwright,' Audrey was saying painstakingly below her, 'Miss Keith was all wrong about it being a corporate form effort. Tim wrote it and produced it, and Liz cut out all the costumes and Nick did everything else almost.'

There was a chorus of agreement. Nicola and Elizabeth blushed and looked confused; Tim looked calm. Lawrie said ferociously, not because she minded the other three being lauded, but because she really didn't think it true:

'They *didn't*. We all did heaps. We were always rushing about doing daggers and scenery—'

'*You* weren't,' said Audrey, a child of morbid honesty. '*You* didn't do a thing except your part.'

'She did that very well, anyway,' said Lois, smiling first at Miss Cartwright, then at Lawrie. 'Concentrated effort.'

'I'm not saying anything *against* Lawrie,' persisted Audrey. 'I hardly did anything except my parts myself. Only when Miss Keith talks about a corporate effort, it was Nick who did nearly all the scenery, f'rinstance, 'cos everyone else felt sick.'

'Probably Nick has a strong stomach, coming of a seafaring family,' suggested Lois, smiling at Nicola as she had previously smiled at Lawrie. But unlike Lawrie, Nicola did not respond. She looked away, making as though she had not heard, and listened to the Third Remove chorus asking Cartwright, who was regarding them with a pleased and friendly eye, whether she had noticed this or that special bit and if she didn't think Nick and Lawrie terrific – and did she know before that Tim had actually written it – and hadn't Liz done the costumes marvellously – and had people really liked it – and weren't the other Thirds simply ramping?

'*All* the Thirds have done very well,' said Cartwright repressively to this last. 'The bazaar was a great success, too. Miranda tells me they've sold practically everything they made.'

'But not as exciting as us,' said Third Remove promptly, not in the least deceived by this tribute to the theory that the Thirds might be three divisions, but were only one friendly form. And Tim said impishly: 'But you'd rather be our form-mistress than theirs, wouldn't you? Think of all the reflected glory.'

It was all right for Tim to say things like that, thought Nicola. She could say them without sounding impertinent or conceited or even over-excited. In that kind of way she was awfully like a senior. And Cartwright seemed to recognize this too, for she laughed and agreed and said how honoured she was to be allowed to supervise such brilliant people. Pomona, sitting beside Tim, who, oddly, didn't seem to mind, began to tell Miss Cartwright with considerable animation how her father had said that her face looked *much* better when half of it was covered with beard—

'So it does,' said Tim, amused, but nicely. 'So it does. What did your mother think?'

'She said she didn't know *who* it was till practically the end of Henry,' said Pomona complacently, but at the same time as though she were rather astonished by her prowess. 'And then she did see and she was *horrified.*'

The crowd laughed, but with Pomona, not at her. Everyone, thought Nicola, was behaving a little other than themselves, seeming rather larger than life in the luminous afterglow of the play. She wriggled happily, liking the feel of the evening which was continuing gay and exciting quite spontaneously, without needing a lift every now and then. One of the Lower Fifth had begun to play dance music, and Miss Jennings strolled up while they were bagging partners to say that she thought they could both congratulate themselves on their backcloths, although she hadn't met a single person intelligent enough to have noticed the different tavern signs.

'You didn't think they would,' Nicola reminded her, and Miss Jennings laughed and said No, she supposed not, and that it was probably a pity for English History that Edward wasn't as nice as Nicola had made him. Nicola blushed speechlessly, and Jennings smiled and went off with one of the Upper Fourth who had come up with devoted bashfulness to ask her to dance.

'It is being fun,' thought Nicola contentedly; and with her thought knew that the true, keen edge of pleasure was, if ever so little, dulled and dimmed. She looked round her; Third Remove had sorted itself into partners while she had been talking to Jennings and she was alone on the steps; even the sandwich plates were empty. She felt immensely tired suddenly and as though her face and mouth would never smooth out from their smiling expression; and all at once the lights were too bright, the talk and laughter and music too loud—

'The dressing-room,' thought Nicola with relief. 'I'll go and tidy that for a bit and then come back.'

It was blessedly dark and quiet, walking alone down the passage to the theatre. She had almost reached the door when, tiresomely, feet thudded over the matting behind her.

'I say,' panted Marie Dobson. 'I say. Where are you going?'

'Only to do a spot of tidying,' said Nicola ungraciously. One might be sorry for Marie Dobson in an idiotic kind of way, but one certainly didn't want her along.

'Shall I come too?'

' 'F you like,' said Nicola curtly, something inside her curling away from Marie's too-eager friendliness. 'But I'm not going to do it for long.'

'Oh, well, I'll help you while you do,' said Marie.

The dressing-room door opened on passive confusion. Costumes were tossed down wherever people had stepped out of them or left them lying in the first whirling excitement at the end of the play. Nicola picked up Lawrie's green and silver doublet, shook it out, and folded it carefully.

'I'll put the make-up stuff away, shall I?' said Marie.

' 'F you like,' muttered Nicola. There was no possibility of Marie going until she did; but at least one could shut her up a bit, so that she didn't keep on with her silly yammering. Only one couldn't say too much, because of the play. Nicola, wrestling with the fine distinction of the rudeness permissible to someone you disliked all the time when they had made a bigger fool of themselves than usual, began to shake and fold cloaks and tunics with a great air of preoccupation. There was quite a silence while Marie fitted sticks of grease paint clumsily into the japanned make-up boxes.

'It was a nuisance I forgot my part that time, wasn't it?' said Marie suddenly and loudly, laughing a little.

Nicola felt a squirm of discomfort. She said casually, to the cloak she was holding: 'I don't expect anyone noticed.'

'Oh, it didn't matter,' agreed Marie instantly. 'Only it was a bit of a nuisance. But acting's rather tripe anyway, isn't it? Gosh, I hope we don't do it for Speech Day; I shouldn't think anybody really wants to do it again, do you?'

Quite a number of replies occurred to Nicola as she began to fold an archangel's golden robe. One might say: Don't worry about Speech Day – we can easily get someone better. Or: Acting is tripe the way you do it. Or: We all know you messed up your bit only we're being polite about it. Instead she found herself saying laconically:

'I expect Keith'll have forgotten about it by the summer.'

'I don't suppose *anyone*'ll remember it that long,' laughed Marie. 'Goodness, it wasn't all that marvellous.'

'It's awful when people are obvious,' thought Nicola carefully, spinning out her thought so that she should not whirl on Marie and tell her, savagely and primitively, just what kind of a fool she was. 'It makes them much sillier than the things they've actually done. You ought to be sorry for them, not furious. You just keep quiet and go on folding things and don't listen. You never did like Marie anyway . . . it doesn't matter if she's so obvious about minding . . . not like it would if it were Lawrie . . .'

Footsteps sounded in the passage, coming towards the door. 'She may be in here,' said Lawrie's voice, stiffly polite, just outside. 'Oh, you are here, Nicola. Miss Redmond wants to speak to us.'

Lawrie held the door for Miss Redmond to pass through, raising shoulders and eyebrows to show Nicola that she had no idea what came next. She closed the door and stayed by it.

'Tidying up?' said Miss Redmond, sounding, Nicola thought, almost as over-friendly as Marie had done. 'I should leave that to someone who didn't have so much to do in the play if I were you.'

Privately, Nicola thought that that was nothing to do with Redmond one way or the other; but she said politely: 'I'm not doing very much,' and picked up another robe.

'I shouldn't. Besides, I don't doubt that it can be left till morning.'

Nicola shook the robe she was holding into another fold and laid it on the tidy pile. Then she put her hands behind her back and waited.

'What I really came to tell you,' said Redmond, smiling brilliantly, and glancing over her shoulder to include Lawrie, 'was that Miss Keith heard from Mr. Probyn today about the rick fire.'

Nicola's mind gave a convulsive leap. She said nothing.

'The insurance company have decided, Miss Keith says, that the fire was started by a piece of glass. Some careless person, apparently, threw a bottle over the wall into the rick-yard – a beer bottle, rather fortunately for us; if it had been ginger beer or lemonade – but anyway, the great thing is that neither you nor Lawrie need feel any longer that you might have been responsible.'

'Yes,' said Nicola politely. She would have liked to add that as a matter of fact they never had, but she felt that only Tim could have said it properly.

Miss Redmond smiled again, quickly and uncertainly. 'Well, that was all. I knew you'd both like to know. It makes a good finish to a successful day for you both, doesn't it?'

'Yes,' said Nicola, doing her best. 'Yes, it does. Thank you very much.'

'Well, don't work too hard. I should stop soon, if I were you, and come back and enjoy what's left of the party.'

She smiled again, hesitated a moment as though she

expected one or other to say something more, then nodded brightly and went out. The twins looked at one another.

'Well!' said Lawrie.

'Sh,' said Nicola warningly, listening to the quick steps going back along the passage.

'I don't care if she does hear,' retorted Lawrie. 'Fancy bothering with all that! You'd have thought it was something important the way she got hold of me and said she'd something special to tell us and she wanted to tell us both together – I almost thought she knew a film magnate and wanted to arrange a test. I mean, I didn't, but you'd have thought it was that.'

'I think she meant well,' said Nicola, but not as though she had much patience with such people.

Lawrie kicked the leg of the table crossly and then, unexpectedly, began to giggle. 'She sounded as if she felt such an ass,' she managed between spasms. 'There she was, making us *so* happy, and we didn't say any of the right things – oo! Nick – when you said – you said—'

Laughter throttled her. She lay down on Nicola's tidy pile, burrowing her face into the costumes, and crowed convulsively. Nicola laughed a little too, but more because Lawrie made it difficult not to than because she really thought it funny.

'Do stop, Lawrie,' she protested. 'It can't be as funny as all that.'

'Oh dear,' gulped Lawrie, lifting a scarlet face, 'ow, I hurt – oh, Nick! – oo, my ribs – oh, dear – I can't laugh any more—'

'It was funny, wasn't it?' said Marie.

Lawrie sobered, instantly and completely, as though someone had slapped her. 'Oh. Oh, hullo. I didn't know you were there.'

'Yes, I was here. I was helping Nicky.'

Lawrie rested her hot face in her hands. 'Oh, well. I don't suppose it matters. Oh, dear. Isn't laughing a lot awful afterwards?' She climbed to her feet and began to brush herself. 'I say. I've just thought. Why didn't they ever suspect you? You were in the yard. You could have struck a match. Or you might have walked on one of mine and scraped it on the cobbles—'

'No, I couldn't,' flared Marie, instantly defensive. 'I couldn't possibly. I wasn't over that side.'

There was a moment's silence.

'But you must have been,' said Lawrie slowly. 'You said you saw us and called and waved and all that.'

Marie turned crimson.

'Yes, but I saw you – I didn't – I wasn't over by the other gate anyway.'

'You said,' said Nicola in a small detached voice, 'you said you ran after us and called and we looked round and waved. If you didn't run at least as far as the other gate you couldn't have done all that because the ricks would have been in the way—'

'No, they wouldn't—'

'Yes, they would,' insisted Nicola. 'The only place you could have been for all that to happen was on the cliff path, because I thought it over afterwards.'

'Well, I was,' stammered Marie, 'I was – but I didn't go across the yard at all. There's another gate – a small one – most people don't know—'

'Oh, yes?' said Nicola courteously.

'There is,' insisted Marie, plunging and panic-stricken. 'There's a – a gate at the side—'

'At the side of what?'

'Wh-when you've gone through a little way – you just turn off—'

They stared scornfully and said nothing.

'I didn't mean that really,' gasped Marie. 'About the other gate, I mean. But I did see you – only I didn't – I wasn't over by the other gate—'

There was a silence.

'Don't you like the look of the second little gate any more?' enquired Lawrie.

Marie, closing a make-up box with trembling hands, said nothing.

'I thought at the time it wasn't true,' said Nicola, at length, dispassionately, leaning against the table and watching Marie fumble, 'because I knew we hadn't looked round and waved and all that. But I never thought we'd know for certain.'

'You don't know for certain,' said Marie in a hurried, frightened voice, which jerked and wavered wildly. 'You don't know anything. You only think you do. I did see you, only I wasn't by the gate—'

'Don't be so fatuous.'

'I'm not going to explain anything,' said Marie with tearful hauteur. 'I wouldn't dream of it—'

'You're not being asked to, actually.'

'Mind the make-up,' said Lawrie suddenly and violently, pushing Marie aside. 'You're making the most awful mess.' She picked up the remaining sticks and boxes of powder, thrust them into their compartments and slammed the case closed, not looking at Marie.

Marie, standing useless and dispossessed in the middle of the room, twisted her hands together.

'I tell you I did,' she stammered incoherently; 'it was like I said – I ran across – only not as far as the gate—'

With meticulous care, Lawrie stacked the make-up boxes together and set them neatly on the corner of the table against the wall; tenderly, as though they were made of glass, Nicola began to put daggers and jewelled belts and chains into a boot-box. Neither said a word; they went on with their self-imposed tasks as though there were no one and nothing else important in the world. It frightened Marie. Her heart thumped and the blood drummed in her ears. She wished desperately, her mind banging to and fro like a blue-bottle in a small room, that she could catch back the past few minutes so that she could alter all she had said to a simple agreement that she might indeed have fired the rick and it was lucky no one else had thought of that. It would have been so easy then; there would have been no more to say. Only now she had said such stupid things and there was this thick, crushing silence humming on and on—

'I say,' said Marie hoarsely. 'I'll tell you what did happen if you like. Only don't tell anyone else, will you?'

As though she had not heard, Nicola began to wind a silk cord round and round her hand.

'I wasn't going to be bossed by Lois,' said Marie, trembling, with an air of frightened bravado. 'You don't like her either, do you, Nicky? So I didn't do anything. I just got over the gate and hid.'

There was a pause.

'Did you?' said Nicola indifferently. 'Move, please. You're in the way.'

Marie stepped hurriedly aside.

'I say, Nicky—'

'Oh, go away,' said Nicola.

Marie opened her mouth, closed it, stumbled over one of the dummies, and crashed out of the room.

'She's crying,' said Lawrie impersonally.

'She's disgusting,' said Nicola fiercely.

Lawrie looked at her anxiously. 'Do you mind, Nick?'

'I don't *mind*. She's just so horrible. All wet and clammy like a jelly-fish.'

'We're not going to do anything about it, are we?'

'What? Go to Redmond and say: Please, Captain, Marie says—? I wouldn't think of it. Miserable little worm.'

'That's funny, you know,' said Lawrie, interested. 'She is too beastly to do anything about. She's like those revolting things Mother's so keen on – you know, we gave her some for her birthday – medlars – all brown and depressing inside and no taste at all.'

'Yes,' said Nicola. She contemplated the silk cord in her hand and said: 'Actually, I don't care a hoot what the silly ass did, do you? I'm not even interested any more. Are you?'

'Not tonight,' said Lawrie meditatively. 'I might be tomorrow. She was a fool to tell us, though, wasn't she? Supposing we had minded and gone haring off to Redmond? A nice row there'd have been. I say, I wouldn't like to be Marie when she calms down and remembers she's told us and starts wondering what we're going to do about it, would you? Golly!' said Lawrie, vicariously appalled. 'What an absolutely awful feeling.'

'Beastly, I should think.'

'And even when we don't do anything,' said Lawrie dreamily, 'it won't be very nice for her, will it, to know that we know, all the way up the school till we're all prefects. Think of being prefects with someone who knew what a louse you'd been in Third Remove.'

'You couldn't say anything,' protested Nicola. 'You know what Father said about dry bones. It'd be a stinking corpse by then.'

'It wouldn't, you know,' said Lawrie grinning. 'Stinking corpses come before dry bones. And of course I wouldn't say anything. I'd just *look* at her sometimes.'

'Are you going to look at Lois, too?'

Lawrie blushed.

'It's very lucky for Lois,' said Nicola distantly, 'that we aren't more interested. Even if you are cracked on her, which I don't see how you can be, anyway, you know just what kind of low hound she was over the hike. And if we went bleating to Captain about Marie and they started to think about it again – or p'rhaps Ann'd think she ought to say something – or even Kay – I don't expect Rowan would—'

'It isn't only me who's cracked on her,' said Lawrie defensively. 'Everyone is since she was in the play. All Third Remove except you, I mean. And even when she's friendly you aren't a bit.'

'I should think not,' said Nicola coldly.

'Actually,' said Lawrie placatingly, after a pause, 'we had forgotten about it, hadn't we, till Redmond started? So I expect it isn't really an important thing. It's just I'd like to be a little vengeful about Marie because she's such a worm.'

'If you could get over Lois, you could get over that, I should think,' said Nicola sardonically.

'I expect,' said Lawrie, once more skirting the question of Lois, 'it'll do really, if she – Marie, I mean – knows that we know, all the way up the school till we're all prefects. I'd hate people to know something like that about me. Wouldn't you?'

' 'M,' said Nicola reflectively. 'She's a wet mess, anyway. She was ghastly in the play, wasn't she?'

Lawrie stretched and yawned.

'Awful. Is that stage-fright, d'you think, or just Marie? Anyway, we'll leave her out next time, don't you think? Lots of the other Thirds are absolutely bounding to have parts.'

Again Nicola felt that unwilling, and, to her mind, wholly unnecessary sympathy. She opened her mouth to protest and then remembered that probably, if they ever did it again, Cartwright or Kempe or someone would be in charge, particularly if it were for Speech Day. Lawrie wouldn't be able to pursue her private feuds – and then she remembered the row over Tim's reading and thought it probably wasn't because Marie was Marie at all. Lawrie, perfectly genuinely, didn't want her play spoiled.

'It was fun, wasn't it?' Lawrie was saying. 'The play, I mean. I say. It just occurred to me a while back. We really are good at something now. Quite like other Marlows.'

'So we are,' said Nicola, much struck by this. 'That's very odd. It feels quite natural, somehow, doesn't it?'

'Tim says we've got to study to remain boyish and unspoilt by our phenomenal success and she must too. I don't know exactly what she means,' said Lawrie candidly, 'but she thinks it's frightfully funny and so does Lois. They keep saying it at one another and giggling madly. Do you know?'

'No,' said Nicola. It had been fun. And there was still lots of the evening left. One ought to go back and join in . . .

'Gosh, I'm tired,' said Nicola; and yawned hugely. 'Think anyone'd mind if I went to bed?'

19 Holidays Begin Tomorrow

I

End of term.

Dismally, Lawrie piled yet one more chair on top of another and stumped off downstairs with them. Since half-past nine the Thirds had been collecting chairs from the form rooms, carrying them into the Assembly Hall, and placing them in long straight rows under Miss Craven's direction. On Last Day there were so many lists for Miss Keith to read – examination results, games colours, form trophies – that school was accustomed to sit on chairs for the two hours or so of breaking-up, instead of cross-legged on the floor as on other days. All over school there was a surge and clamour of talk in classrooms, passages and on stairs, much louder and more jubilant than the usual between-lesson noise of ordinary days; and people looked gay and pleased and friendly as though the imminence of breaking-up made them like everyone else very well indeed. Lawrie didn't. Lawrie felt cross and sad – queerly on the verge of tears without wanting to cry at all. Neither the thought that it was the end of term nor that it was Christmas Eve tomorrow could cheer her in the least. She didn't want Christmas Day and presents and parties and coming back to school next term. She wanted it to be the play for always and ever and she couldn't see why no one else except Tim still felt the same. Lawrie set her chairs down with a thump and waited moodily while Miss Craven decided whether or not it was time to start a new row.

'Someone to go round and see whether the ground floor form rooms have been cleared,' said Miss Craven suddenly. 'Lawrence, you're doing nothing but stand on one leg. Hurry up, and let's see whether you still have the use of two.'

The others giggled and Lawrie grinned unwillingly. Anyway, it was a change from chair carrying; and she rather enjoyed bouncing into the seething form rooms, casting a practised eye over the body of the room to see whether any loose chairs still remained and taking a quick look at the bouquet of flowers which lay on each staff desk: carnations in the Second; curled, yellow chrysanthemums in IVB; carnations again in the Lower Fifth. Lawrie frowned, wondering dubiously if Cartwright had been as pleased as she pretended with the Third Remove offering. Tim had been very positive that it would be all right, but then Tim was positive about most things.

The Sixth. Lawrie grinned to herself as she turned the handle. The Sixth Form room was a source of perennial fascination to the juniors, who rarely saw inside, because of the Sixth form habit of coming quickly outside and closing the door if anyone wanted to speak to them, and keeping the curtain drawn across the glass door-panels at all hours of the day. But this time Lawrie was on an official errand; she opened the door and walked in decorously, so that Karen need not see her if she didn't want to.

The Sixth, who seemed to be standing about in groups and talking, much like other people, looked faintly surprised and then smiled at her. Lawrie, recognizing the atmosphere of the play, grinned back, her spirits rising instantly.

'Hullo, young Tom,' said Janice Scott. 'Kay, you're wanted.'

'Hullo, Kay,' said Lawrie cheerfully, pleasurably aware that no one was going to mind if she were a little cheeky, since it was Last Day, and she was a Marlow and people still thought of the play when they saw her. 'I don't really want you, as a matter of fact. It's only for chairs in case we missed any before.'

'I don't think so,' said Karen equably. 'But you can look if you like.'

'I am,' said Lawrie. 'I've always wanted to see inside the Sixth. I say! What absolutely super roses. Are they your thing to Kempe?'

'Glad you approve,' said Margaret Jessop, amused. 'So did she.'

Lawrie gazed respectfully at the long-stemmed yellow roses.

'We couldn't do much about Cartwright because of the play,' she said, apparently to Karen, but including any of the rest of the Sixth who cared to listen. 'We hadn't any money left at all hardly. So she had to make do with a buttonhole. She said she didn't mind a bit, but we aren't sure. Will she feel very out of it in the staff-room when they start showing what they've got?'

The Sixth chuckled, and Margaret Jessop said it was a happy thought, the staff comparing bunches and then going miserably away to weep because their form hadn't done as well as the form of their bosom enemy.

'Probably some of their worst feuds spring from end-of-term bunches,' said Janice Scott, obviously pleased with the idea. 'One can just see it happening. Everyone feeling scratchy and term-weary, standing round comparing their forms' scruffy offerings, all catty and polite, and then Kempe sails in with a dozen and a half choice yellow roses which she tosses casually on to the table—'

'—whereupon they cut her throat,' said a cheerful soul called Olive Randall, joining in the game, 'and dump her body in the swimming bath, where it rots undiscovered till next half-term and all English lessons come to an end.'

'Gosh,' said Lawrie, making an awed expression.

'Still,' argued Karen, 'one can't tell. Everyone gets bunches. Buttonholes are something new. Suppose Cartwright goes into the staff-room flaunting her – what did you give her?'

'An orchid,' said Lawrie. 'It was one of those or about four roses, which looked mad. Tim said one orchid would be better.'

The Sixth gazed at her.

'You know,' said Janice to no one in particular, 'I can foresee the most frightful things happening when that Tim child is head girl. Nothing will ever go wrong, exactly, but everything will be hideously unexpected. Ices instead of bread-and-butter and buns for match teas and a box of cigarettes on Keith's table in Hall instead of our decorous little vase of flowers. The staff will have a ghastly time.'

Lawrie, who had learned not to protest that they had settled long ago that Nicola was to be head girl and herself games captain and that Tim did not come into the matter, smiled politely and said nothing.

'But it's such a neat idea,' said Karen. 'Think of the rest of the staff staggering about under their great bunches which I'm sure they loathe, and Cartwright strolling round looking cool and chic with one carefully chosen orchid. If the idea isn't copyright to Third Remove, I think we might try it on Kempe next term.'

'I don't expect Tim would mind,' said Lawrie seriously, and wondered patiently, after the fashion of juniors confronted by seniors, why they laughed.

'It's been the oddest Third Remove I ever remember,' said Cathy Wilson, sitting on the edge of the long refectory table, which the Sixth used instead of the desks common to the rest of the school. 'Usually one never hears of them except when they come bottom of this or that; but this lot's managed to make quite a name for itself.'

'Probably set a fashion for Third Removes full of brilliant eccentrics.'

'Single orchids for their form-mistresses are what I can't get over.'

'And that play the other night.'

'And one of them stopped a train its very first day. It's not a bad record as records go.'

'And we've all failed our exams,' offered Lawrie, who was enjoying herself. 'Or nearly all of us, anyway. Cartwright says they're absolutely the worst results that any form's had ever.'

'That isn't so clever,' said Karen firmly, catching Val Longstreet's eye and realizing that Val, a humourless character, disapproved of the whole conversation as detrimental to Sixth Form dignity. 'Oughtn't you to be running along now, Lawrie? The bell will be going any minute.'

Lawrie grinned, snatched up the chair Val Longstreet had hoped to keep hidden until after Assembly so that she need not be reduced to perching on the edge of the table with the rest, and went away. The bell rang and school began to lead in to Hall, most people carrying pencil and paper so that they could write down their examination results, even though, as the staff pointed out, term after term, they were only putting down information which appeared all over again in their reports.

By custom, form-mistresses sat with their form between the two form prefects. Jean and Hazel had been uncertain whether Tim would allow this, but Tim's only desire, apparently, was to sit between Lawrie and Nicola and behind someone tall.

'Then I can sleep through the lists,' she explained. 'I think it's barbarous, making us listen to everyone else's tatty marks. Who cares what anyone else has got? I don't care all that much about my own. Or else I'll play a quiet game of gun-boats with Nick. You'd like to be Admiral of the Blue, wouldn't you, Nicky dear?'

Nicola grinned and nodded, liking the end of term feeling, which seemed to be compounded of the clamour of conversation and the shining silver cups and clean white envelopes of Colours on Miss Keith's table. Then Karen, who was standing by the swing doors, jingled the school bell once, the voices stopped dead, and school stood as Miss Keith, her black gown billowing, walked up the steps and on to the platform. She sat down in the tall carved chair behind her table and motioned the school to sit also. Breaking-up had begun.

II

'And what,' said Tim, nudging with her foot the whiteframed copy of Van Gogh's painting of a chair, 'are we supposed to do with this?'

'Hang it on the wall,' said Nicola calmly, routing round her desk to make certain she was leaving nothing at school that she might conceivably want at home.

'*Must* we?' said Tim, being perverse. 'Couldn't we hide it away and pretend it was all a mistake? After all, we don't want to remind people that we've won a prize for Form Tidiness. It'll be bad enough if they remember on their own.'

'Why?' demanded Jean and Hazel belligerently. As form prefects they had been the two to go up for the Tidiness Picture and they had greatly enjoyed their moment; and they didn't want Tim to spoil it for them as they knew very well that in a few quick phrases she could. 'Why?' said Jean and Hazel, defensively.

'Tidiness,' said Tim in a voice of ineffable scorn. 'Such a thing to win. We're not that kind of form at all. We're—'

'We're brilliant eccentrics,' said Lawrie, depressed, for the temporary exhilaration of her interview with the Sixth had long since worn off, and she felt, as she looked, hunched and sorrowful. 'That's what the Sixth said, anyway.'

'There you are,' said Tim, pleased. 'Brilliant eccentrics is exactly right. And brilliant eccentrics don't win Tidiness Pictures.'

'But they have,' said Nicola.

'It's all your fault,' said Tim, grinning at her. 'It's *entirely* due to you. And how are you going to like it next term when all the staff mooch in and say: What's that piece of paper doing on the floor? I thought Third Remove won the Tidiness Picture last term?'

'I shan't be Tidiness Monitress,' said Nicola, unmoved. 'So I shan't care.'

'P'rhaps we could lose it,' said Tim meditatively, eyeing first the picture and then the balcony as though she thought one might well be dropped from the other. 'I don't see why we shouldn't have an accident – just a little one—'

'No, Tim, don't,' said Hazel in urgent alarm, for she still took Tim seriously. 'You mustn't, honestly. Cartwright's rather pleased about it. And that's just as well, 'cos she doesn't like our exam results a bit, really. She kept looking at me and Jean all the time they were being read out.'

' "One in honours – Nicola Marlow – 76: no passes and eleven failures",' quoted Tim serenely.

'Wasn't it *awful*?' said Daphne Morris with a horrified giggle. 'Did you fail *everything*, Tim?'

'Everything. Even lower than Lawrie. But then so did

practically everyone fail everything, except Nick. She kept up the family tradition nicely.'

'No,' said Nicola coolly. 'The family tradition gets *all* honours and *all* in the eighties. Not some measly seventies and a couple of scruffy passes.'

'Still, it'll make your report look more like the others,' said Lawrie morosely. 'Not that I care. Oh, dear, why can't we do the play again before we go home?'

'Why not, indeed?' said Tim. They gazed at one another sadly.

'There wouldn't be time,' said Hazel, too obviously. 'And besides, we *are* going to do it again in the summer.'

'Scenes from,' said Tim savagely. 'For Speech Day. With Kempe pushing in to give us a final polish. It won't be a bit the same as it was on Tuesday.' She slammed her desk lid furiously. The others looked at her doubtfully. If she had been Lawrie and not Tim they would have thought she might be going to cry.

'Was that what Miss Keith was talking to you about in the passage?' said Marie Dobson, coming clumsily forward in order to stand in the group with the others. 'She was talking to you for simply ages, wasn't she?'

'What a noticing girl you are,' said Tim, her voice steady again. 'The things you see.'

Marie blushed. Her eye met Nicola's involuntarily and she looked away at once, standing uncomfortably in the group, but miserably aware that she was not of it.

'What was she saying to you?' said Pomona stolidly. 'Was it about the play?'

'Of course,' said Tim. 'What else could we have to talk about?'

'What did she say?' demanded Third Remove.

'Well—' said Tim considering. Then she grinned. 'Well,

she wanted to make perfectly certain that I didn't think I was personally responsible for the play in any way. After all, it couldn't have been done without the full co-operation of each and every one of us, and the important thing was that we'd all worked so well together, if you know what I mean.'

'No, I don't,' said Pomona.

'Oh, yes, you do, Pippin. You know Aunt Edith's thing – the individual effort is only important in so far as it contributes to the success of the whole. So we *all* wrote it and we *all* produced it and we *all* did the scenery and we *all* acted Tom marvellously—' Tim clasped her hands modestly behind her, '—and I looked all serious and respectful and said: "Yes, Aunt Edith. Yes, of course, Aunt Edith. Yes, I know, Aunt Edith, they were all simply wonderful." '

'Didn't she say anything properly about it?' said Third Remove, disappointed.

Tim hoisted herself on to the lid of her desk, and smiled, gently reminiscent.

'Bless her heart, she did try so hard to remember that she mustn't on any account give me the impression that she thought I'd been really rather clever. But she did say' – suddenly, to her own immense surprise, Tim stammered and blushed furiously – 'she did say that though she'd had many qualms since she first gave me permission, last night had amply justified her faith in me.'

'Coo!' said Third Remove. 'Anything else?'

'Anything *else*?' said Tim, recovering a modicum of flippancy. 'She nearly frightened herself into a fit saying that when she thought of all the awful things it might do to my character.'

'It's odd about families,' agreed Lawrie. 'Ours didn't want to tell me, either. You should just have seen them trying to shut Ann up every time she said how good I was.'

'*Lawrie*,' said Nicola, scandalized.

'Well,' said Lawrie, 'so they did. I'm tired of being modest.'

'Aunt Edith had an easier time. She only had to shut herself up.'

'P'rhaps,' said Lawrie, eyeing Tim gloomily, 'the Sixth are right. P'rhaps you will be head girl.'

Tim gasped, but recovered herself quickly.

'I shouldn't think Aunt Edith'd go as far as that. I expect it'll be Pippin. You'd like to be head girl, wouldn't you, Pippin?'

'Yes,' said Pomona stolidly, 'I would. And when I am, you'll have to call me Pomona *always*.'

They grinned at that, and Nicola said:

'I don't suppose by then we'll be able to. You'll have been Pippin far too long. But I don't see why you need mind it. It's quite a liking sort of name.'

Pomona looked pink and pleased and speechless. Marie Dobson said something aloud, to which no one paid any attention, about getting on with tying up her books, and went back to her desk, sheltering behind the upraised lid. Nicola and Lawrie glanced briefly at one another, relieved. It was awfully difficult to be anywhere near Marie and behave naturally. As Lawrie had remarked the previous day, it was a wonder no one had noticed the little bristles of embarrassment which rose all over them.

'And what are you people doing, still in here?' asked Miss Cartwright, coming in and scattering the group on her way to the staff desk. 'No packing to do? No homes to go to?'

'We were just talking,' said Hazel meekly.

'And we thought you might want a few words with us,' suggested Tim gently.

'Not one,' said Miss Cartwright briskly. 'If your exam

results haven't chastened you, no words of mine will. Nicola, you'd better hang the Tidiness Picture at once. It's Third Remove's one claim to respectability at the moment.'

'We could shift Anne of Cleves,' suggested Nicola obediently, avoiding Tim's eye lest they both giggled, 'and put the Peter Scott where she was and then the Tidiness thing can go over the mantelpiece. Would that be all right?'

'And what about Anne of Cleves?'

Nicola eyed the copy of Holbein's masterpiece without enthusiasm.

'Let's give her to IIIA,' said Tim instantly. 'She'd make a nice consolation present to them for coming second.'

Miss Cartwright looked at her. 'Do you realize that if this form's work had been even a decent pass standard we might have won the Form Shield too?'

Tim looked politely non-committal. It was the only alternative to saying outright that she didn't care a scrap.

'The All-Round Shield?' protested Jean. 'Oh, we wouldn't have, Miss Cartwright. Miss Cromwell's form *always* wins it.'

Miss Cartwright's lips twitched and she suddenly became friendly. 'Well, never mind. See what you can do next term. And don't climb on to the mantelpiece, Nicola. Take my chair to stand on instead. And now get along, all of you. Good-bye. Happy holidays. Come *along* Marie. You must have finished those books by now.'

III

As a rule, only those few who had very long journeys left before lunch on Last Day. The majority stayed to race round school collecting addresses and saying goodbye to the staff, or watch the Upper Fifth and Sixth line up to say goodbye to Miss Keith one by one, and speculate as to what could possibly be said to people so old in goodness and wisdom. At some point during this time, people also packed their over-night suitcases, and Rowan, striding round school to collect her dormitory, insisted that they should all do it at the same time.

'I'm sure it's inconvenient,' she retorted to Ginty's protests, 'but it's infinitely easier for me. Once it's done it's done, and after that if you miss your train or keep Father waiting, no one can blame me.'

There was reason in this, and Ginty galloped upstairs with only a few further conventional mutterings. Once in the dormitory, however, she seemed in no great hurry to proceed, and lay down flat on her stripped bed, her hands behind her head, apparently engrossed by the patterns formed by the long fine lines – too thin to be called cracks – in the ceiling above her head, while the others pulled their suitcases from under their beds and the uproar of voices and slamming of doors continued around, above and below.

'You know,' said Ginty at length, emerging from her trance and interrupting a desultory and slightly acrimonious conversation concerning borrowed handkerchiefs and lost stockings, 'it's a great pity we aren't allowed to be in for the Dorm. Cup. I think we'd have beaten Margaret Jessop's lot.'

'Would we?' said Lawrie, sprawling across her bed, while Ann packed her small suitcase for her. 'How much would we have won by?'

'Quite a bit, I think.' Ginty sat up and hunted for a piece of paper and a pencil. 'Chuck me that note-book on the floor beside you, Nick – thanks. I'll put it down properly: there's colours for me and Rowan – and Ann's All-round Cords – do Guide things count as much as school? – oh, well, I'll make it the same as colours. It's not like a Book-lover's Badge . . .'

Nicola, who was sitting on the floor, carefully unfastening the flat parcel addressed to her which had come by the mid-morning post, suddenly crowed with pleasure.

'Giles's ship! His new one! Golly! Just *look* at her!'

Rowan looked and remarked: 'One destroyer always looks very much like another to me. But I suppose a trained eye can detect the difference.'

'Oh, Rowan,' protested Nicola. 'Of course they're different. They're completely different classes—' and then realized that Rowan's mouth was carefully serious as if it held in a laugh, grinned good-temperedly, and sat back on her heels to gloat in silence. There was no message except for the 'Affec – G.A.M.' neatly written in one corner on the reverse, but it was good to know he wasn't still furious. No one would send a picture of their ship to someone they were livid with. She would write and thank him and tell him about the play and not mention Port Wade at all.

'. . . How many honours did you get, Nick?'

Nicola blinked and considered. 'Six.'

'That's twelve. And Lawrie's failures are minus one – that's eight. I can't think how you managed to fail *everything*, Lawrie.'

'Tim did too,' said Lawrie flatly. 'It was the play. Keith quite understands.'

'How much would you get for the play?' mused Ginty. 'Fifteen each for initiative, I should think. And the Tidiness thing would count five each and IVA's Shield another five for me—'

'Do you have to take off any for Nick and me being thrown out of Guides?'

'Oh, bother. Yes, I suppose so.' Ginty frowned, calculating.

'Captain said she'd told you about the rick,' said Ann, colouring, and folding Lawrie's dressing-gown with scrupulous care. 'Did she say anything about your coming back?'

'No,' said Lawrie briefly. She watched Ann put her bedroom slippers into her suitcase and hoped Ann wasn't going to be what Nicola called 'Lower Fifth' again and ask whether they didn't want to come back and shouldn't she speak to Captain for them.

'How much do we win by?' said Nicola rather hurriedly, getting up and crossing to Ginty, as though she too felt that question hanging in the air, and, equally anxious to avoid answering it, was trying to thrust the conversation out of the danger zone. 'The train I stopped wouldn't count, would it?'

'Don't think so,' said Ginty. 'Keith said at the time she didn't want to call it a school thing. I think I've got everything in. Let's see – twenty-eight from a hundred and twenty-three—'

'Ninety-five,' said Nicola.

'Then we do win it. We beat Margaret's lot by five.'

'I shouldn't count on it,' said Rowan, looking in all the drawers to make sure nothing was being left behind. 'You can't be sure you're counting it as Keith would.'

'I'm pretty sure,' said Ginty instantly. 'Because it's the same markings as for the Form Shield and Ironsides told us at the beginning of term exactly how that went.'

'Then we're absolutely magnificent in every way,' said Rowan, tossing a roll of stockings on to Ginty's bed, 'and a credit to our dear parents. Only don't tell anyone, will you? They mightn't like it.'

'I'd like to tell Monica,' said Ginty. 'because she's so cocky about being in Margaret's lot. But,' catching Rowan's eye, 'I won't *say* anything. I'll just think it inside.'

'I shouldn't even think it too hard,' retorted Rowan. 'Oh, look, Gin. Here's a whole small drawer full of your stuff. What on earth are you going to do with it?'

'Pack it,' said Ginty, swinging her legs off the bed and diving for her suitcase. 'It's all right, Rowan. I haven't started yet. Don't flap at me. I say. Monica says she heard something about starting swimming next half-term instead of only in the summer. Is it true?'

'How things do get round,' said Rowan with an air of perennial wonder. 'They haven't decided yet, actually. It depends on the weather. And of course it'll be in the Baths. Not the sea.'

'It's diving I'm thinking of,' said Ginty candidly. 'It's lucky you're senior and I'm middle school still, isn't it, Rowan dear?'

'Lois is just as likely to win it as I am,' said Rowan, strolling over to the window. 'More, really, if she doesn't lose her nerve.'

'But she always does,' said Ginty.

'She didn't in the play,' cried Lawrie.

'The play! That was a freak effort all round.'

Ann closed Lawrie's suitcase. Lawrie, released by this even from the responsibility of looking on, crossed over to the window and hoisted herself on to the inner sill.

'Are Third Remove allowed to dive?'

'Far's I know. Never heard they weren't.'

'*Well*. Couldn't you two teach me and Nick? And then we could go in for the junior diving cup and p'rhaps we'd win one each – junior, middle and senior.'

Rowan groaned softly.

'There she goes again. Hasn't experience taught you anything, my child? Aren't you a sadder and wiser girl in *any* way?'

Lawrie looked depressed.

'Well – I'm only planning a very little bit. I've got to do something next term, haven't I? And there won't be any sort of play – and Speech Day isn't till the summer – and nor's the School Play—'

'I shouldn't count too much on that,' said Rowan. 'You and Nick'll probably turn out to be Cobweb and Peasblossom – or Moth and Mustardseed. I don't think Kempe's done *The Dream* for quite a time.'

Lawrie screwed her face in disgust.

'One of them might be the Egg in *Macbeth*,' suggested Ann. 'You know – the "young fry of treachery" – Macduff's son.'

Lawrie and Nicola looked at one another.

'What about the one who wasn't being the Egg?' asked Lawrie.

'I don't know. She'd have to be understudy, I suppose. I don't expect, you know, you'll ever be able to be in the same play again. I mean, you couldn't have twins on the stage unless they were actually being twins in the play, could you? You'll have to take it in turns.'

'No, we won't,' said Lawrie instantly. 'One of us'll wear a wig. Black and curly. Bags me always.'

Nicola grinned and went on with her packing, carefully making her clothes into a bed, a padding and a cover for Nelson and Giles's ship. It did not matter at all in what condition her clothes arrived so long as the pictures came out undamaged. Above her concentration she could hear Lawrie lamenting the inevitable dullness of next term, and how it would be necessary to alleviate this by learning to dive, perhaps also by becoming really good at work and getting moved up into IIIA at half-term, so that they could stake their claim to the junior netball team – and the others were joining in, Ann looking ahead to the Guide camp at

Easter, Ginty speculating aloud about the Form Hockey Cup, Rowan wondering aloud whether she was doing enough work for Matriculation or whether the people who stewed in the library before breakfast had more sense than she—

'Kay doesn't,' argued Ginty. 'And Kay's got her Oxford Schol. exam next term.'

'Kay's no argument. Exams are what Kay likes. Oh, well, I suppose it's better to be placid about these things. I can't really see myself rushing about school with a strained expression and a Latin dictionary. And what are your plans for next term, young Nicola? Are you going to dive? Or would you rather have the Gym Medal?'

Nicola, stuffing her pyjama tops into a last gap, considered the matter. She went on thinking it over while she laid her dressing-gown across the top, folding it into three thicknesses, guaranteed to cushion any shocks which might, despite all precautions, shake Nelson. Plans for next term. But you couldn't really plan ahead. She and Lawrie had made the most careful detailed programme for this term, and not one thing had happened as they had intended. They couldn't even have begun to think, three months ago, that they would act in a play and be really awfully good in it. It was probably better to let things happen as they wanted to, instead of trying to arrange them, without knowing all the circumstances . . . much more interesting . . . much less disappointing . . .

'I don't think,' began Nicola, closing the suitcase and clicking the locks shut with an air of firmness and finality; and then found that she had been thinking for so long that Rowan's question was past and forgotten. She scrambled to her feet. 'Come on,' she said to Lawrie. 'Let's go and find Tim. There's ages before dinner and we haven't got her address yet.'

FABER CHILDREN'S CLASSICS

The Children of Green Knowe
by Lucy Boston

The River at Green Knowe
by Lucy Boston

The Big Bazoohley
by Peter Carey

Autumn Term
by Antonia Forest

The Mouse and His Child
by Russell Hoban

Charlie Lewis Plays for Time
by Gene Kemp

Meet Mary Kate and Other Stories
by Helen Morgan and Shirley Hughes

Frances Fairweather – Demon Striker!
by Derek Smith

Marianne Dreams
by Catherine Storr

The Mirror Image Ghost
by Catherine Storr

The Sam Pig Storybook
by Alison Uttley

Make Lemonade
by Virginia Euwer Wolff